The Black Diamond Trilogy

The Black Diamond Trilogy

Brittani Williams

www.urbanbooks.net

Urban Books, LLC
300 Farmingdale Road, NY-Route 109
Farmingdale, NY 11735

ISBN 13: 978-1-62286-623-6
ISBN 10: 1-62286-623-1

First Trade Paperback Printing January 2018
Printed in the United States of America

10 9 8 7 6 5 4 3 2 1

Distributed by Kensington Publishing Corp.
Submit Orders to:
Customer Service
400 Hahn Road
Westminster, MD 21157-4627
Phone: 1-800-733-3000
Fax: 1-800-659-2436

The Black Diamond Trilogy

by

Brittani Williams

Black Diamond

Chapter One

Diamond: Who's Betraying Who?

I heard the moaning loudly through the halls and had I not been standing here myself I would have never believed it. Two people that I trusted, the two people that I would have taken a bullet for, were right there in my home betraying me. Sorry would never be enough to ease my pain, and at that point there was no turning back. My footsteps couldn't be heard over their loud lovemaking, and not even the door opening interrupted them. I stood there in the dark hallway watching. Hell, I figured I might as well let them finish before I let my presence be known. At least then it would all be worth it. As Kemp laid flat on his back, his arms tightly gripped Mica's waist. She grinded into him and let out moans each time the strokes hit her spot. The flickering of the candlelight bounced off of her body, making it radiant. Even the beads of sweat that formed on her back were evident. Though I was furious, I can admit that watching the two of them in action was slightly turning me on. Under different circumstances I would have gladly joined in, but I had to focus on the action at hand. She continued to ride him jockey style and soon he was yelling her name and palming her ass until he had expelled every drop of his love inside of her.

She slowed her pace and after stopping I knew that it was my cue. I raised my gun and aimed in their direction. I released the safety, which quickly gained their attention. Mica jumped off of him and began backing up to the top of the bed, covering her naked body with the sheets. Kemp sat up in shock and spoke immediately, trying to calm me down.

"Baby, it's not what you think," he spat, the same bullshit line that every man speaks when they get caught. What the fuck did he think—I was blind? I clearly walked into this room and saw him fucking my best friend and all his stupid ass could say was that it's not what I think.

"What kind of asshole do you think that I am?" I screamed, trying not to lose my cool. "Did you actually think you could get away with this?"

"I'm so sorry you had to see this. I never wanted you to find out this way!" Mica cried, as tears began pouring out of her eyes. "I didn't want to hurt you."

"You didn't want to hurt me? That's bullshit! Fucking my man is definitely not the way to avoid it. I trusted you and this is what I get?" I pointed the gun again.

"Please, Diamond. Don't do this. This is not the way to handle this," Kemp continued to try his hand.

"Fuck you! You don't have the right to tell me what to do and what not to do. I'm running this shit! Do you see this gun—remember this sight cause this is the last thing that you are going to see. I hope the pussy was worth it!" I cocked the gun and began shooting, releasing five shots. The blood spraying all of the room was something that I would never forget, somewhat like a bad dream that seemed too real not to believe. I would take this to the grave.

I never wanted to resort to murder. Hell, I wasn't a criminal. Well, not a convicted one anyway. I worked hard to get to the point where I was today and I didn't plan on letting anyone take me down. You never really know the things that lie ahead for you but all of the choices you make ultimately have an effect on the way things turn out. Looking back on the way I grew up, most would say that they wouldn't have expected anything different from me. I, on the other hand, expected much more.

I was adopted at the age of two and it wasn't until I was ten that my mother decided to reveal the truth. I knew I didn't fit the mold of the family from the beginning but I never had any concrete proof. After my mother and father divorced we moved in with my grandmother to a small row house in North Philly. In total, there were about five houses on the block occupied by humans. The rest were boarded up and infested with rodents, most of which the crackheads used as shelter to get high. My mother always said that eventually we would move on to bigger and better things, but *eventually* never happened.

My grandmom had lived there all of her life and refused to move. Shit, she still had the old sofas with the plastic on them, so you know she wasn't going anywhere. We weren't the only ones in the family that had run to Grandmom's for shelter. There was my aunt Cicely who swore her shit didn't stink. She was on welfare and worked under the table at the hair salon as a shampoo girl. She was the reason the working class hated paying taxes, since she was more than capable of getting a full-time job but she'd rather collect money from the government to go clubbing every weekend. She barely saw her children since they were stuck in the house with my grand-mom most of the time. Her idea of quality time was stopping in and giving them a few new toys. It was bullshit to me; I fig-ured that anyone who wasn't capable of being a good parent should never have kids.

It was rough in the neighborhood. Resisting temptation was the hardest. With all of the drugs and things around, how could I not get involved? I know that sounds like bull, but try living in the world of sin and see if you'll come out of it a saint. I didn't have a lot of friends in the neighborhood because girls weren't my choice of companionship. I was into boys early, which only got me into trouble.

I met Mica through her brother Johnny. Johnny and I met after we both were caught stealing from the supermarket. There was a room in the back of the store where they would hold you until your parents arrived. I sat there quietly waiting for my mom to come and watched as Johnny cried buckets of tears. He must have been scared of an ass whooping or some-thing because he was definitely a little extra with his reaction.

"Are you okay?" I asked, trying to get him to stop crying, be-cause he was annoying the hell out of me.

"Yeah, I'm fine!" he replied, turning his face in the opposite direction.

"What's got you so upset? I mean, damn, is the beating go-ing to be that bad?" I asked, still not done probing him for information.

"Why do you care? You don't even know me," he replied.

"I know that, but I'm tired of hearing you cry like a little girl, so I'm trying to make small talk to get you to shut up!"

"What?" he replied, turning to look at me.

"You heard me! Stop crying like a little girl!" I yelled.

He jumped up out of his chair and ran over to where I was sitting. Soon, we were rolling around on the floor fighting like two cartoon characters. It was probably comical seeing us trying to hold the other one's hands down.

He wasn't really that much stronger than me, but I didn't really feel like fighting. I simply wanted him to shut up.

"Get your hands off of me," I yelled, struggling to get my hands loose. "I knew you were a little girl, boys don't fight girls!"

"They do when girls don't know how to keep quiet," he yelled, not releasing his grip on my wrists.

"You know you like it, you like a girl that's slick with the tongue," I said, trying to make him lose his concentration.

"What?" He loosed his grip for a second, and that was all that I needed to get the upper hand. I flipped him over and was now sitting on top of him holding his hands down.

"Now, why don't you just give up? I got you now," I said, looking him in the eyes as he tried to get loose.

Just then the door opened and his father and sister came in with the security guard from the store.

"What is going on here? Get off of him!" his father yelled.

I quickly got up and moved over to the chair that I had been sitting in before our fight started.

"Nothing, Dad. We were just playing," he lied.

"Just playing my ass, you know how much trouble you're in right now?"

"Yes Dad," he answered after getting up from the floor. "Let's go, don't worry, he'll never steal anything from your store again," his dad said to the security guard as they headed out of the room.

I felt sorry for him because I could tell that he was afraid of his father. It was a few weeks before I ran into his sister. I was walking to the corner store to buy a loaf of bread for my grandmom when I saw Mica. She looked at me strangely before coming over to talk to me. I thought for sure that she was going to want to fight since she walked in on me and her brother, but I was surprised by what she had to say.

"You're the girl that was in that security room with my brother, right?"

"Yeah, that's me. Why?" I asked, preparing for a throwdown.

"Girl, what's your name? My brother hasn't stopped talking about you since that day. I think he's in love," she said, laughing.

I stood there for a second in shock. In love? *After the way I talked to him, he must be crazy,* I thought. Then I replied, "My name is Diamond. What did he say about me?"

"He just said that he liked your style and you were sly with your mouth but he could deal with that."

"That's crazy, he really said that?" I asked. Now I was blushing because though I thought he was a little punk, he was cute. He wouldn't be able to protect me but he was good to look at, as long as he wasn't crying.

"Yeah, he did. My name is Mica and his name is Johnny. We live right over there on Dover Street. Why don't you come hang out with us sometime? We're always outside."

"I might just do that. Thanks, Mica, I'll be seeing you around soon," I said before turning to head into the store. Soon Mica and I were best friends and Johnny was my first love. I found out that their father was really abusive and Johnny got it the worst. He was afraid of his father and that was why he cried that day in the supermarket. Johnny was really calm, not like all of the other boys I had dealt with. Most of them already had a sample of sex so they didn't really care about quality time and conversation. Johnny, on the other hand, did. We would talk on the phone for hours every night about anything you could think of.

During this time Mica and I hung out a lot too. We got really close but grew closer before Johnny got locked up for murder. After years of abuse he was finally fed up and in a rage he shot and killed their father. I was shocked when Mica called and told me the news. I was even more shocked that she blamed part of it on me. She said that it was me that pushed him to do it. I knew I had nothing to do with it. Johnny was fed up;

all I did was encourage him. I never wanted him to be afraid of anyone. I hated that he was being abused. Shit, if anything she should have thanked me. It saved her from being beaten too.

A few months later Mica and her mother moved out of the neighborhood to somewhere in Delaware County. It would be years before I would see Mica again, and now that I think of it, it may have been better if I'd never seen her at all. Then I wouldn't be in my home covered with her blood. Damn, what happened to the good old days?

Chapter Two

Mica: Dreams

I hated the long ride up to the Camp Hill Prison, but I had to show my brother love. Besides the fact that we didn't have much family, most of the family we had didn't want to see him. I knew my brother too well and had it not been for him falling too deep in love he would have never been in prison in the first place. Though it had been five years since the day he murdered my father it still felt like yesterday.

I was only fifteen the day they hauled him off to prison. At the time I didn't get a true sense of what was happening, but it didn't take long for me to figure it out. As time passed I realized that both my father and brother were gone. Johnny wasn't dead but he was gone from the life that I'd been used to. That gunshot, to me, killed two birds with one stone. Most of my family completely erased him from their life. I loved him too much to treat him the way that they had. Where others couldn't forgive him, I did. The person I couldn't forgive was the bitch who pushed him to do it. I mean, I've been in love—don't get me wrong—but if there is a love that can make you kill your own parent, then I don't want it.

After I arrived and checked in to see my brother I had to sit and wait until they brought him down to the visiting area. I was anxious to get this visit over with because I had a date with a fine-ass hustler that I couldn't miss. I know that sounds inconsiderate, but shit, a girl's gotta do what a girl's gotta do. He might be the key that would finally get me out of the fucked-up neighborhood we called home.

As my brother entered the room, I smiled. I missed my Johnny so much and even the letters weren't enough to make me feel the closeness that we once had. He had gotten so big in prison and had turned into a man. It saddened me that he had to grow up this way.

"Hey, baby sis!" he said, smiling and looking me up and down as if he hadn't just seen me last week. I made it my business to get up there every week no matter what else I had to do. In my book, family came first. Everything else was secondary.

"What's up?" I said, reaching out to give him a quick hug. Hugging wasn't really allowed but the guards were cool and would allow it for a second. "Did you get the money I sent last week after I left?"

"Yeah, I got it. I told you not to do that. You are supposed to be saving that money for school," he replied, sitting down on the opposite side of the table.

"Johnny, when are you going to give up? I'm not going to school. I told you that I'm going to be all right without that. Shit, Mom can barely make ends meet so the little bit of money I make working at the mall I give to her. I can't see you in here without, so I do what I have to do. You know me, always looking out for the family."

"Yeah, I know, but sometimes you got to look out for yourself."

"I will soon, trust me; I have something in the works."

"Like what? I hope it's not illegal. I don't want to see you behind bars too. One of us is enough."

"No, it's not illegal. You know I'm not into shit like that," I responded, twisting my lip because I wasn't hardly trying to do anything that would land me in jail. I wasn't that damn crazy.

"Just checking but hey, have you seen or heard from Diamond yet? Or checked on her old address? I still haven't gotten a response from her. I must have sent her hundreds of letters since I been here."

"Hell no, I haven't seen her and that's the way I want to keep it. You know how I feel about her," I replied, annoyed that he would even say her name to me. Just the mention of her made my skin crawl.

"I wish you would stop blaming her for what I did. I made my own decision, Mica; she didn't have anything to do with what I did. I don't have any family that keeps in contact with me but you. I asked you to find out where she was so that I can have some contact with the outside world. That's all I've ever asked you to do for me."

"You can say what you want, but the bottom line is that you wouldn't be here if it wasn't for her and you know that I'm telling the truth."

"Neither of us knows if that's true. Who knows what I would have done if I was pushed hard enough?"

"Look, Johnny, I came a long way and I damn sure don't want to waste our visiting time talking about her."

"Well, I'll drop it for now but you're still going to have to find a way to let the past go and move on. You can't be bitter all your life. Shit, I'm the one in jail."

I wasn't bitter but I didn't want to keep the debate going. I could care less about Diamond and if I saw her on the street it would probably be as if I never knew her. I know you are supposed to forgive, but I couldn't find it in me. How could I forgive the person that ruined my family? It was definitely easier said than done and yes, he was the one in jail but for years I felt like I was there with him. Things weren't all peachy on the outside either. My mother struggled with depression and had been on medication for it since my father died. Some people thought that Johnny did all of us a favor, but neither she nor I saw it that way. Yes, he was abusive and yes he was an undercover drug addict, but he kept us afloat. Now, if it weren't for my little part-time job we probably wouldn't even have food to eat. I hated that he was gone. I didn't miss getting my ass whooped but I missed being a kid. I had to grow up quickly in order to make it. I had to learn how to take care of myself when my mother was too depressed to get out of bed. She hadn't been there to talk about sex or anything for that matter. She was like a shell with no life, and nothing I did was bringing her back.

I finished chatting with my brother for the remainder of his visiting time and headed back out to the bus that drove back to Philly. Since moving from North Philly we lived in a two-bedroom apartment in Germantown. I mean, if there was a hood in Philly worse than North Philly it was Germantown. The craziest part about the chicks up there was that you couldn't tell them they weren't hot shit even when their doors on their houses were practically hanging off the hinge. I got into more fights the two years I went to Germantown High than I had in my whole life. I had never been afraid to speak my mind so whenever they had something to say I came back with the truth. Obviously, the truth hurt and they would wait for me after school each time. I always came out prepared for a fight since most days I got into some sort of altercation during school hours.

I hated the school just as much as I hated my life, and there had been plenty of times when I thought about swallowing a bottle of pills to end it all. But then I thought about my mother and how devastating that would have been to her, especially since my brother was locked up. I realized that keeping her as sane as I could was more important and that thinking of taking my own life was just me being selfish.

On the ride home all I could think about was the date that I was about to go on. I felt that I was finally going to get a slice of the pie. Living the fabulous life was something that I dreamed of. The difference with me was that I wanted the man with money but the money wasn't the most important. I wanted a man to be happy, which was something that I hadn't had in a long time.

Soon, we were pulling up in the bus station and I was smiling from ear to ear. I couldn't wait to get home to get dressed and head out for my date. It took me another hour on buses to get home and once I made it I hurried to my room to rummage through my clothes. I hadn't bought anything new in a while, so I had to mix and match to try and make the perfect outfit. Finally, I settled on a black pencil skirt that was fitted and reached my knee with a black-and-white shirt that showed just the right amount of cleavage. You know, enough to make his mouth water but not too much that he'd think I was a slut. My mother must have heard all of the commotion going on in my room. You would have thought I had company the way I was dancing around and giggling like a kid.

"What the hell is all the noise in here about?" she asked, opening my door and looking in to see that I was alone.

"I'm just happy, Mom. That's all."

"Happy? What the hell are you so happy about?"

"I have a date tonight and this guy might make a difference in both of our lives."

"Don't you go letting some nigga sell you a dream. Most times they are lying anyway."

"Mom, stop being so negative all the time. Can't you at least be happy for me?"

Without saying a word she turned and walked away. I knew that she didn't want me to get hurt. Hell, that definitely wasn't my intention, but shit happens and if it wasn't meant to be I'm sure that I would find out soon enough. Tonight, I wasn't going to focus on her negative energy but on seeing the man that I knew in my heart was going to make all of my dreams come true. I know that sounds corny but it was true. Tyson was supposed to pick me up at nine and I made sure that I was ready. I had borrowed some of my mom's Miracle perfume and put on just enough accessories to accentuate the outfit that I had put together. On my way out my mom told me to be careful, but she still didn't crack a smile. Damn, I hated depression!

Nine-oh-five, Tyson was beeping the horn and I couldn't have gotten out to his car fast enough. I'd had so many disappointments so I prayed that today wouldn't be one of those times. Tyson sat in the driver's seat, speaking on the phone and unlocked the doors once I got close. I thought he could have at least opened the door for me, but maybe being a gentleman wasn't in his character. That didn't mean he was a bad guy, though, because all of the other nuts I dated opened the door but once they got some, all of that shit was gone. At least he wasn't trying to impress me by being extra, and that was definitely a plus in my book. Who the hell opens the door for you nowadays anyway?

He turned briefly and looked at my ass as I sat down — a typical guy, but I loved it. He continued his conversation as I buckled my seat belt and he drove off. I didn't even know where the hell he was taking me, but at that point it didn't even matter. I was just happy to be around him.

"I don't give a fuck what he said, I know he better have that man money right!" he yelled, frowning. "Well, where is he?"

He continued his ranting as I sat quietly, trying not to look in his direction though I was trying to hear what the person was saying on the opposite end. "Well hit me up, I got some shit to take care of right now. Make sure you get all the money! One!" He hung up and immediately turned his attention to me. "What's up, sexy? Sorry about that; niggas always call me at the worst time with dumb shit."

"I know the feeling," I lied. I didn't know anything about what he was talking about, but I thought it would sound cute if I said I did.

"I see you got all dressed up, I'm feeling the outfit," he said, smiling, showing his softer side. You wouldn't have known he had one by the conversation he just had on the phone, but I guess business was business.

"Yeah, I tried to look sexy for you tonight."

"Well, you did a damn good job, sweetie."

"So where are we going?"

"Over to my spot. I had a caterer hook up a crazy spread. I got some Moët and all that shit over there too."

I smiled but inside I was a little uneasy. Over to his spot? I could see where this was going to lead. I wasn't trying to have sex with him tonight; I wanted to get to know him. Most times when you have sex with someone so fast you never learn anything about them because the relationship stays sexual. Well, I guess I had to hope for the best because I wasn't going to turn back now.

"Cool," I said, after a few seconds of thinking.

He bobbed his head to the sounds of his Jay-Z CD. I loved his swagger. I felt like he could protect me, and that was also something that I yearned for. He had on a baseball cap tilted to the side with jeans and black button-up shirt. His diamond Cartier watch continued to sparkle even in the night. His chain had diamonds bigger that any I had ever seen and his earring was just as big as those in his chain. The jewelry that he donned probably cost more that my entire wardrobe. His mustache and beard were jet-black and shaped up perfectly, not a hair out of place. His skin was golden brown like a glazed doughnut and his cologne filled the air with an irresistible scent. He kept peeking over at me from time to time during the drive. He even reached over and grabbed my hand when he wasn't on the phone cussing someone out about money. Witnessing that showed me that money didn't erase all of your problems. It only brought new ones.

Tyson was a drug dealer who did pretty well. I didn't know who he worked for, but whoever he was Tyson made sure he stayed loyal and everyone that worked under him did as well. I didn't know firsthand how hard that must be, feeling the weight of all of your men. Since, if one of them messed up Tyson would be the one to pay for their mistakes.

I met Tyson while hanging out in the area where he did most of his business. One of his workers was actually going to rob me, but Tyson stopped them and told me how dangerous it was to hang in that part of town. I didn't really take heed to that. Shit, I figured that since Tyson stopped them once they wouldn't try me again. I was wrong, and it took me almost getting raped before I did. Tyson stepped in again and drove me home. We talked that night and he took my number before I got out of the car. It took him a few days to call but once he did we set up the date that we were on now. I guess I was in the right place at the right time because I probably would have never met him otherwise.

Once we pulled up in front of his house my stomach started doing flips. I was nervous about going in because I wanted to keep him around. I didn't want to go in and have sex with him and he'd forget me by tomorrow. I mean, I had been told I was good in bed, but a man like him probably had women coming from left and right. There were probably some much more experienced than me who could get his attention at any given moment.

We got out and entered his house, which was so clean it looked like no one even lived there. I knew he must have had a maid or never stayed there because it was too perfect. Out of nowhere a huge black pit bull ran into the living room and jumped into his arms. I stood still, stiff as a board. I was so afraid of dogs, especially pit bulls, and it didn't matter how many times someone told me their dog didn't bite. Hell, they had teeth, which to me meant that they could bite whenever they wanted to.

"What, you scared? He ain't gonna hurt you," he laughed, noticing how petrified I was of the huge dog that weighed probably just as much as me.

"Yes, I'm afraid of dogs."

"Cool, I'll put him out back."

"Thanks," I said, still not budging and watching his every move.

I relaxed once I heard the back door open and close. He re-appeared, still laughing. He walked into the dining room and gestured for me to follow behind him. I took a seat at the table that had plates laid out as if it were a restaurant. There was a bucket for champagne sitting in the center. He grabbed it off the table and returned it with ice and a bottle of Moët inside. He took the plates off of the table and brought them back a few minutes later filled with soul food—chicken, macaroni and cheese, and collard greens. I laughed at how I thought it would be something different. He had everything set up so classy I would have thought he would have a spread of food that I didn't even eat. I was cool with the food, though, and his money wouldn't go to waste.

We ate the food and drank so much Moët that I could barely stand. I was laughing at everything he said even when it wasn't funny. I was so relaxed. I had kicked off my shoes and got comfortable on the sofa as he put in a movie, *South Central*, a classic hood movie that I hadn't seen in a while. We sat and watched the movie as he massaged my feet. Soon, we were both asleep on the sofa. It was about one-thirty AM when he woke me up to take me up to the bedroom. I stumbled most of the way but made it and plopped down on his bed like a load of bricks. He helped me get undressed and put one of his T-shirts on me. I thought for sure he would make a move. Surprisingly, he didn't; he crawled into bed with me and fell asleep.

Chapter Three

Diamond: King of the World

As women, why do we settle for less? I had asked myself this question a million times and could never seem to come up with an acceptable answer. I had been through a lot in the five years after losing Johnny, my first love. After the day he went to jail I had never been able to find a man to treat me the way that he did. I know that we were just teenagers at the time, but shit, love is love no matter how you slice it.

Now, there I was, twenty-one, drop-dead gorgeous with a college degree but still I settled for a man who didn't even care enough about me to protect himself when he went out and cheated. As I sat in the waiting area of CVS Pharmacy, waiting on my prescription, I was about to explode. I was so angry that I could barely contain myself. I had just left my GYN for my recent test results and found out that I had chlamydia. I knew that I was faithful to Davey, my boyfriend of four years, so there was no other way that I could have contracted the disease. I had never been so embarrassed and once I left I planned on going straight to his house to give him a piece of my mind.

After I left the pharmacy I was on my way to his apartment. I called his cell phone a few times and when I didn't get an answer my instincts told me that he was up to no good. I couldn't hear anything else but the words that the doctor spoke before I left the office. It was like a broken record playing over and over again. Once I got to the door of Davey's apartment I began knocking. I waited a few minutes before knocking again. I knew he was home because his car was parked outside. I continued to knock and yell his name.

"I know you're in there. Open this fucking door!" I continued to scream, waiting for him to acknowledge the fact that I was standing outside acting like a damn fool. Soon I heard him unlocking the door and I already had my fists balled up, ready to swing.

"What the hell is wrong with you, Diamond?" he asked, still trying to fix his clothing.

I pushed him out of the way and entered the apartment. I didn't make it very far before he grabbed ahold of me. "Get the fuck off of me, you dirty bastard!" I screamed, trying to get my arm free from his grip.

"What is going on?" he asked, still holding on tightly.

"I have chlamydia, you dirty motherfucker! That's what's going on!" I continued to yell. He still wouldn't let me go. I was sure that he had someone in there, and I was trying to get back to the bedroom to see exactly who it was.

"What? How did you get that?" he asked with a dumb expression on his face. He knew damn well how I had gotten it. I had never cheated on him and he knew that.

"Don't play dumb, Davey. You know damn well how I got it. I haven't fucked anyone else but you. I'm positive that you can't say the same!" He finally let go of my arm but blocked the hall that led to his bedroom. "Move out of the way. I want to see what nasty ho you have back there. I know you were in here fucking around!" I screamed, trying to push him out of the way. He was much stronger than me, so I knew that he would never let me get past. I wasn't about to give up trying, though.

"It ain't nobody back there, Diamond. Stop tripping. What did the doctor say?"

"Oh, now you're concerned? Fuck you! You don't give a damn about me, you can't even wrap your dick up when you go screw around." I began to break down. My anger was now tuning into pain. As many times as I had caught him cheating on me I still hung around. If someone were to ask me why I loved him, I wouldn't be able to answer them. Honestly, I wasn't even sure if I really loved him; it could be that I was just used to the things he provided. I didn't know of any other way to live but broke in a brokedown neighborhood, and I wasn't ready to go back there. I wanted the old Davey back. The Davey I met four years ago. I could remember that day as if it had just happened, and just the thought of it warmed my heart.

I had just left school and was headed to the bus stop with a group of friends. I wasn't feeling too good and was anxious to get home and lay down. I stood there on the corner not really paying attention to my surroundings but more so to the pain in my stomach. A black BMW pulled up on the side where I was standing and parked. The windows had full tint so I couldn't see who was inside. Soon the windows began to reveal the driver behind the wheel of the luxury car. His eyes were pointed in my direction, but I tried to act as if I didn't notice him. I didn't want him to think I was money hungry, though I was always down to be treated to something nice. He motioned with his fingers, telling me to come over. I pointed at myself just to make certain that he really wanted me. I mean, I was pretty and had a nice figure, but I wasn't dressed all that spectacular and my hair was plainly pulled back in a ponytail. I would have never expected a man of his stature to want me.

He nodded his head yes and I slowly headed over to his car to find out what the mystery man had to say. He smiled as I got closer. He had skin the color of a Hershey's kiss and jet-black hair that was perfectly trimmed. His smile was accentuated with two dimples that made you smile just looking at him. Everything about his face looked perfect as if it were a painted picture. Not even a hair in his mustache was out of place. I wondered what the hell he wanted with a plain Jane like me.

"I won't bite. Come closer," he spoke in a deep tone that sent chills through my body.

I gave a little girlish giggle before moving closer. Was it that obvious that I was nervous? I smiled and waited for him to speak again.

"What's your name?" he asked, still holding his position inside the car.

"Diamond," I replied, trying to put on the sexiest voice that I could muster up.

"Diamond. I like that name. It fits. Where are you headed?"

"I'm going home; I don't feel too good," I replied.

"Well, why don't you let me drop you off and once you're feeling better we can hang out?"

"I don't even know your name."

"My name is Davey. I'm sorry, sweetie. That was rude of me."

I didn't want to agree, even though it was rather rude. I was hesitant about getting in his car but the sooner I got home the better. I agreed to get in, saying a silent prayer that I would make it home safely. The inside had the new-car scent, and you could tell by looking around that it was recently purchased. I was impressed; I had never been in a luxury car and it was definitely something I could get used to. My body was so comfortable in the plush leather seats that I almost forgot I was sick. Funny how a man can do that to you.

"So how old are you, Diamond?" he asked, trying to make small talk as we headed toward my neighborhood. I smiled as I noticed all of the neighborhood chicks trying to peer through the tinted windows to see who was inside. "I'm seventeen. I graduate high school next month," I replied.

"That's what's up. I'm glad to hear that because I would have had to back away if you were any younger." He laughed.

Within a few minutes we were pulling up to my house. I wanted to stay, but I knew I had to go. I didn't want to seem desperate, so I thanked him for the ride and told him I would be seeing him around. I was surprised he went through the trouble to bring me home and allowed me to dismiss him without even giving him my phone number.

A few hours later I was still lying down, trying to rest, hoping that my run of sickness would go away by the end of the night. The doorbell rang and I hurried down the stairs, unsure of who it was. My grandmom and I were the only ones home, and I wasn't expecting any visitors.

"Who is it?" I yelled, because in this neighborhood you could never be too sure.

"I have a delivery for a Ms. Diamond," the voice responded.

I slowly opened the door to a huge bouquet of pink roses with a pink and white teddy bear tied to the vase. I signed for the delivery and quickly shut the door to see who the hell sent this to me. I was sure that there had to be some mistake because no one would send me flowers. Or would they?

The card read:

To my Diamond in the rough,

Get better so I can show the world my new girl.

Love, Davey

Okay, he has to be crazy, I thought. His new girl? I didn't even know him. The gesture was definitely appreciated since no one had ever done something so nice for me, but who the hell did he think he was? King of the world? I put the flowers and teddy bear in my room and soon after that I fell asleep.

He wouldn't give up, and it was that determination that turned me on. He managed to always keep me hanging on, hoping that the sweet guy I met that day would come back. I was fooled because the scene we were at right now had been repeated so many times. I guess love will do that to you.

I sat down on his sofa because I refused to leave the apartment until I knew who he was in here with. He came over and sat down beside me. I didn't even want him to touch me. I felt disgusting and the pain I felt at this point was probably worse than any other time before.

"What are you doing?" he asked, probably wondering why I had sat down.

"I'm not leaving until I see who's in here! I mean that shit, so you might as well bring the bitch out here," I responded as I eased back and crossed my legs. I know that I had been a fool in the past, but I'd be damned it he was going to get away with this one.

"Babe, I told you there is nobody back there. You need to stop being so fucking suspicious!"

"Suspicious? I just told you I have an STD. If that's not a reason to distrust you then I don't know what the hell is. You need to stop being so fucking trifling and wrap your dick up!"

I retorted. I still hadn't budged from the sofa, though I wanted to jump up and hit his ass.

"Oh, so now I'm trifling? Well, why are you with me then, Diamond? Am I trifling when you're out spending my money?"

"That doesn't have anything to do with this, Davey. Don't try and turn the heat on me. I haven't done anything wrong," I was well aware of his strategy to try and change the subject, but it wasn't going to work this time.

"I'm tired of arguing with you, Diamond. If you're gonna step, then step!" he yelled while motioning his hands at the door.

"What?" I yelled. I was furious. Here, he was the one who messed around and he was telling me to step. I looked around for something to throw. My eyes landed on a basketball trophy he had sitting on his end table. Without thinking twice, I picked it up off the table and threw it at him. He didn't have enough time to duck so it hit him on the side of his head. Next thing I knew I was back on the couch with his hands around my throat.

"What the fuck is wrong with you? Don't you ever throw something at me again! I will kill you, Diamond." He released his grip when he noticed he was hurting me.

I rubbed my neck that was now sore from his strength. I knew I was wrong for hitting him, but I was hurt. I was embarrassed and then I was pissed that he told me to step. I cried and he went into the bathroom to look at his head in the mirror, which had a small gash on it. I thought this was my cue to see if I could get into the bedroom. I eased off the couch and headed to the door. I tried to turn the knob but it was locked. I kicked it and immediately began screaming obscenities.

"Open the door, bitch! I know you're in there, you need to take your nasty ass to the clinic."

"Diamond, get the hell out." Davey came up behind me and pushed me from in front of the bedroom door. I could see the anger in his eyes. I had pissed him off, but he deserved it.

I decided not to fight anymore. I knew I would never see who was behind that door. I knew he would run to me later and tell me how sorry he was, but it didn't matter. He wasn't sorry now or any other time he'd said it. He probably didn't even know the meaning of the word. How could he? When you're truly sorry, you don't do it again. *Am I finally tired of his shit?* I asked myself. I didn't know the answer to that question and I probably never would.

I looked at him with tears still flowing freely from my eyes. I wanted to believe that there wasn't anyone in that room. I wanted to believe that today was just a nightmare and I would wake up in his arms. I wanted that old thing back. Instead we were here, fighting because he couldn't love me the way that I wanted him to.

I turned my back on him and headed to the living room. Exhausted, I grabbed my purse off the floor and headed out the door. I didn't even close it behind me. I got in the car and started it up. Looking up, I saw him standing there looking at me. *How did we get here?* I wondered. I'm sure he wondered the same thing. I backed out of the driveway and drove off. I wasn't in the mood to go home so I decided to go over to my girl Kiki's house.

Kiki had been my friend since the demise of my friendship with Mica. Kiki was older than me and had been through a lot. I could always go to her for a few words of wisdom. I sat in the car and tried to get myself together before going in. She hated to see me upset, so I didn't want her to know that I had been crying. She opened the door and immediately knew something was wrong.

"What the hell happened to your neck?"

"You wouldn't believe it, girl." Damn, I had forgotten about that. I couldn't even lie now if I wanted to. It was obvious I was choked since I had handprints around my neck. I stepped into her living room and headed for the sofa.

"Try me," she replied.

"I'm too embarrassed to even tell you." That was the honest truth. I didn't want anyone to know that I had an STD. I felt disgusting.

"Girl, you're like my baby sister. You can tell me anything."

I reluctantly gave up the tapes. "I had a doctor's appointment today and I found out that I have chlamydia."

"What? That dirty motherfucker. I told you to leave his ass alone."

"I went to his apartment and I know he had some bitch in there because he wouldn't let me get to the room. I wasn't leaving and then he had the nerve to tell me that if I wanted to step, then step. I lost it. I picked up one of his old basketball trophies and hit him right upside his damn head."

"He deserved that shit. I can't believe that he said that to you after all of the shit you've done for him."

"Then he fucking choked me. That's how I got these marks on my neck. He didn't hold on long. I can't even be mad that he choked me, though, because his head was bleeding on the side and shit." I laughed a little, trying to hide my pain. Because deep inside I wanted to cry and run back to him telling him I was sorry. Sorry for not being the woman that he wanted me to be. Sorry for not keeping him from straying away. I mean, some of it had to be blamed on me, right? If I was doing everything possible to keep him satisfied, he wouldn't be out fucking other people.

"I don't care if you hit his ass or not, he shouldn't have choked you. He's the one in the wrong here. Sometimes you have to hit a nigga upside the head so they can understand."

"Well, I don't think it made him understand anything. Shit, he still told me to get out after I tried to kick that damn bedroom door in."

"Fuck him, girl. You can't sit around and stress about a nigga like that. Yeah, he has money and I know that he spoils you, but what is that shit really worth? There are too many men like Davey out here."

"But I don't want another man. I want him to get his shit together," I said.

"Girl, you'll learn. You can't make a man be who you want them to be. If they aren't ready to settle down then there isn't anything you can do to change that. It's not your fault that he's a dog."

"So what should I do, just leave him alone?"

"Do what your heart says, baby girl. I can't tell you what to do but I will say this: Don't sit around being sad about the shit. Come out to the club tonight, have a good time, and let him come begging you. Not the other way around. If he really cares, he'll be back."

I sat there and took in what she said. I decided to take her advice and not call, begging him. I agreed to hang out at the club with her that night and in a way, I was excited. I hadn't been out in a while without Davey by my side. I wanted to try and have fun without worrying about chicks being all in his face. Though I had gotten used to it, it didn't make it any easier to deal with.

"So are you coming or what?" she asked, waving her hands in front of my face to break my daydream.

"Yes, I'm coming."

"Good, now take your ass to the store and get something for your neck. You can't come out to the club looking like someone gave you the death grip." She laughed.

I laughed, too though I didn't really find it all that funny. My relationship was in ruins and my man was with someone else. I left her house feeling a little better than I had before I got there. I went to the nearest Rite Aid to grab some cocoa butter for my neck and headed home to try and relax for a few hours before it was time to get ready for the club.

I got dressed that night in my little black dress, the kind that makes a man's mouth water. It hugged each of my God-given curves and was just tight enough at the butt to give me a Buffie the Body effect. My hair was down in a wrap with a Chinese bang. I had recently learned how to apply my make-up like a professional so I would definitely look like I was ready for a photo shoot. Davey was the last thing on my mind when I walked into the club called Solo, right on Columbus Boulevard—or if you're from Philly, you would call it Delaware Avenue. Kiki was a barmaid at the club so she always asked me to come down. Most times I would be with Davey but today I was rolling alone and it didn't bother me one bit.

As I headed inside I got tons of looks from both men and women. They probably wondered why the hell I was there alone. I could see the whispers and funny looks from the women. I tried my best to ignore them as I headed to the bar to find Kiki. Once I spotted her I headed over and waited until she got finished serving her customer.

"Hey girl, I'm glad you came out." She reached over the bar to give me a hug.

"Me too. I feel a little weird now that I'm getting a bunch of stares."

"Fuck them, girl. Enjoy yourself. What you drinking tonight?"

"Give me Hypnotiq and pineapple juice," I replied as I took a seat on the bar stool. It was still early so the club wasn't packed yet. After I got my drink I sat there and sipped it while scoping out the club. I was enjoying the music and feeling a buzz from the liquor. Soon, I was up out of my seat, dancing to the music. I didn't care that I was alone and my confidence must have been showing because the men were all over me.

After a couple hours of dancing I headed up to the bathroom. I hadn't even drunk that much, but I felt like my bladder was about to explode. As I was fixing my clothes, two girls walked in and as one went into a free stall, the other one stood on the outside and talked to her.

"Girl, I know you were cracking up inside that room," the one inside the stall said.

"That bitch was determined to get in there. I only stayed in there because Davey told me to."

Instantly I stood still. Was this the trifling bitch that gave him chlamydia? I became enraged.

"Davey is crazy. I'm glad he kicked her ass out of there. He knows you two belong together."

I couldn't take it anymore. I finished fixing my clothing and without a second thought burst out of the bathroom stall. She stood back when the door flew open, shocked. I didn't waste any time jumping on her. She fell to the floor from my weight and adrenaline combination. I began punching her, not giving her a chance to fight back. I grabbed hands full of her hair and began banging her head against the tile floor. Soon, there was blood coming from it. Her friend came from the stall, trying to jump on my back, but the bathroom attendant had already gotten security, who had come in just in time to pull her away. They grabbed me and as they pulled me away I gave her a couple of kicks. I continued to scream obscenities as they dragged me out of the club. Kiki noticed the commotion and ran from behind the bar.

"What the hell happened?"

"The bitch from the apartment was in there. I couldn't let that shit slide, Kiki. I just couldn't," I admitted.

The security guards held on to me until the cops arrived and handcuffed me. *What the hell did I get myself into now?* Now I wasn't using my head. The cops took me down to the 26th police district and put me in a holding cell. After all that I had been through that day the only person I could think to call was Davey. When I was allowed to make a call, I dialed his number. I was nervous as I waited for him to pick up.

"Hello," his deep tone boomed through the receiver. "Davey?"

"Diamond?"

"Yeah, I'm locked up. I need you to come and get me." "Locked up?"

"Yeah, I saw that girl, Davey, and I couldn't help it. I wasn't thinking."

"That's why she's been blowing my phone up. Diamond, I can't believe you."

"Could you just please come and get me? I don't have anybody else to come."

"All right, I'll be there."

I knew he would be upset about my actions, but I also knew he loved me and wouldn't just hang me out to dry over a fling. Out of all the other incidents we'd had where another woman was involved, I never felt threatened until now. I always knew that they were just temporary and he'd drop them soon enough. This time was different, and it wasn't until now that I realized what my feelings for him truly meant. If I'd lost him, I wouldn't know what to do. I still felt bad about being there. I wasn't a criminal; I didn't belong there. I was simply a woman, crazy in love. Davey was mine and I wasn't going down without a fight.

I sat in the cell determined to make things better between the two of us. I knew that there were just some things that I was going to have to deal with. Today was the first time that he'd ever told me to leave, and I wanted it to be the last. I didn't want to lose him and whatever I had to do to keep him around, I planned on doing it.

Chapter Four

Mica: Role-Play

I lay stretched out across the bed trying to get some sleep. The day had been pretty long and I wanted to clear my head. I didn't know where the hell Tyson was but I never knew where he was. His business was always kept separate from me and I actually liked it that way. I knew that there would be things that I didn't like about it so I felt it was best that I knew nothing. We had been going strong for the past three months and I could admit that I never even wondered what he did when he wasn't around. The bottom line was that he always took care of me; he even kept my mom's bills paid, so I couldn't complain.

After a few minutes of tossing and turning I was asleep. Soon, I was awakened by a whisper in my ear. "Don't move," the male tone spoke lowly.

I didn't move as he removed the sheets, exposing my naked body underneath. I wanted to turn around to make sure that this was Tyson, but I knew if I did it would ruin the fun. The object of the game was to make the scene seem as real as possible, even though we both knew that it wasn't.

I loved changing roles; it kept our relationship spicy. The way I figured it is that most women lose their men when they are afraid to step out of the box and try something different. I wouldn't say I was freak, but I did enjoy freaky things. I was pretty much down for anything and if giving him the feeling of being with someone different every night was what I had to do, I would do it. Don't get me wrong, I needed to be satisfied, and my man would do whatever he had to for me as well.

We didn't care what other people thought. Our rules were our rules and whatever happened outside stayed outside. I

kept my eyes closed and my mouth shut as I had been directed to. I had butterflies in my stomach that were going crazy
as his soft hands began to examine my body. He slowly massaged my back and caressed my ass as if I were a steak being
prepped for a flavor rub. His tongue was wet and warm in
the small of my back. The tickle of it sliding in between my
cheeks was sending me wild. I tucked my head deep into the
pillow trying not to make too much noise. I didn't want him to
stop and I knew he would if he thought I was enjoying it too
much. It was my duty to stay in character to make it enjoyable.
So there I was, naked with my ass facing him. He continued
to plant wet kisses all over my back before turning me over.
The room was darker than it was when I fell asleep. I hadn't
looked at the clock so I didn't have an idea of what time it was.
I really didn't care about the time anyway. I wanted to make
this last as long as possible.

Next, he took my hands and tied them to the headboard
of the bed. I pretended to struggle a little. He was wearing a
mask so I still couldn't see his face.

"Please, let me go," I begged, continuing to play the woman
in distress.

"Shut up if you want to make it out of this alive."

I obeyed and didn't say another word. He stood up, staring
at me for what felt like an hour before he began to fondle my
breasts. My nipples hardened as he licked his fingers and
rubbed them one by one.

"I'm gonna fuck the shit out of your fine ass."

I loved the sound of those words mixed with his deep voice.
I wanted to be fucked. Hell, I needed it. I wanted to feel good
tonight. With force he turned me over, tied my hands to the
bedposts, and spread my legs almost to the limit. His fingers
were tickling my legs—up and down he went as I squirmed,
trying to free my hands from the top of the bed. I wasn't
blindfolded but the room was dark and my eyes were closed.
I would peek every now and then to see what he was doing. I
could hear the zipper on his pants going down, which excited
me. I was anticipating feeling him deep inside of me. He used
two of his thick fingers to massage my wet clit. I almost came
all over his fingers but he moved them just in time.

The next thing I felt was the head of his dick rubbing up and down my wet mound. He would slide the head and then pull it back out to continue massaging me. After awhile I started rocking my hips to make more friction on the spot that I wanted him to hit.

He still was quiet but I found it extremely hard to hold in my moans. I was on my way to ecstasy and I didn't want to make any pit stops along the way. Soon he had my legs resting on his strong shoulders. His dick was moving in and out of me for what seemed like an eternity. He was going like the Energizer bunny and I was enjoying every minute of it. I could hear him panting as if he was leading up to an orgasm. I rocked my hips harder to make sure that I came first.

My legs began to shiver as I erupted all over him. The load moans that escaped my mouth sent him into his release. He was shaking as I wrapped my legs tighter around his neck. He didn't waste time getting up and releasing my hands. Before I knew it he was out of the room like a bandit and I was on my way back to sleep.

He never came home that night, but I wasn't mad since he had hit me off earlier. It wasn't as if he came home every night so I was never surprised when he didn't. The next morning I got up and showered. I had to meet my mom to take her out for lunch. Once a week I made it my business to spend time with her. I got to her house around eleven AM and we headed down City Line Avenue to go to Tequila's, the best Mexican restaurant in the city. I had a thing for Mexican food and I didn't know why. It wasn't like I'd hung around Mexicans or anything.

After we were seated I took the opportunity to break the ice. I always had to break the ice when talking to my mom because she was the type that wouldn't say anything unless you said something to her first.

"So Mom, have you been out on any dates lately?"

"Dates? Girl, I'm forty-five years old. What the hell would I look like on a date?"

"What does your age have to do with anything? Nobody needs to be lonely." I stared at her, trying to figure out what the logic was in that. I don't give a damn if you're seventy, you're still entitled to have fun.

"A lot. Grown women don't date casually like young ones do. By the time you get my age you are supposed to be married with kids in college and settled down."

"Well, Mom, things didn't work out like that for you, so it's time to try something else. When was the last time you had sex?"

"Excuse me, I don't believe that's any of your business," she replied, annoyed by my line of questioning.

"Why not? I am your daughter so I believe that I have the right to be concerned. Maybe if you had a man you'd be happier."

"Who said that I wasn't happy? Having a man is definitely not the answer to all of your problems. If you ask me, they tend to make things worse."

"That's possible, but not all men are evil. Take Tyson, for instance, he's a good man. He even breaks his back to make sure that your bills are taken care of. It takes a special kind of man to do that."

"Well, maybe he's an exception to the rule, Mica. It doesn't mean that I should jump on the first thing smoking hoping things will be better. I can do bad all by myself."

It was like talking to a brick wall when it came to my mom. Sometimes I felt like I was the mom and she was the daughter. Why was I trying to give a forty-five-year-old advice on how to get a man? Shit, by the time you're that age you should be a professional. I knew my dad was all she knew for years, but he'd been dead long enough for her to move on. It didn't make any sense to me. I got tired of trying to convince her that there was so much more out there for her to do. I decided not to continue the conversation and instead glanced at the menu to decide what I wanted to order before the waitress came back.

My mother sat across from me trying to avoid making eye contact. I definitely wasn't trying to upset her. I was merely trying to open her eyes.

"Are you mad?" I asked, trying to break the ice.

"Mad about what, Mica? Most of you young women think that you know it all. It's easier to imagine a perfect world than to live with reality. I've heard it all, seen it all, and been through it all. It's nothing that you're doing that I haven't done in the past. You may think that everything is gravy now because you're living the luxurious lifestyle, but my suggestion is that you hold onto some of that money so that when he's gone you'll be able to make it on your own."

"Tyson ain't going nowhere, Mom. Me and him got something different and ain't nobody gonna break us apart."

"Well, it doesn't have to be a person."

I give up. I wasn't going to sit there and keep trying to convince her. As soon as I saw the waitress I flagged her down. I was ready to get my food, hurry up and eat, and then take my black ass home. I would remind myself never to bring up men around her again.

The food came pretty quick and we were out of the restaurant in record time. I couldn't wait to get far away from her. I know most would say that I was a fool for not listening to what my mother was saying, but I was happy with my life and my man. I know you are supposed to get wiser with age, but things had been too perfect for me to believe anything different. There had to be something said for a man who could make me smile just by the thought of his name. I had never loved anyone in the capacity that I loved him. I wanted the title, and he gave it to me, so my job was to keep playing the role that I longed to keep.

Chapter Five

Diamond: Him, Me, and She

"Babe, hurry up, we're going to be late!" Davey screamed through the apartment. I didn't understand what all the rush was about; he acted like we were late for something important.

"You act like this is so important, Davey. We're only going to have sex," I replied. As much as I hated to say it, it was the truth. Davey had bugged me for months to have a threesome. I wasn't interested in it, but I knew that I had to do whatever he wanted to keep him around. I figured that this was his way to cheat without me flipping out.

"It is important to me, and if making me happy is what you want to do, then it should be just as important to you as it is to me."

I still wasn't convinced and I really hoped he would change his mind and not make me go through it. "You know that I want to make you happy, I just don't understand why I have to do this."

"You always wondering why I cheat, that's why. You don't ever want to try new things and then you're pissed when I go get it from somewhere else."

"Davey, that doesn't have shit to do with it. You get it from somewhere else because that's what dogs do. Stop trying to blame all your fuckups on me."

"Babe, can we just go? This is turning into an argument for no reason. I just want to try something different with you and you told me that you were going to do it for me." I reluctantly agreed to go because I didn't feel like arguing anymore. What was the point? He would do whatever he wanted to whether I went through with it or not. The entire car ride I was quiet. I didn't even know what to say. I just hoped that once this was over I would never have to do this again. I was nervous once we exited the car and headed to her apartment door. *What the hell was I doing?* I thought. I had never been interested in women, now here I was about to have sex with one all for the love of a cheating man. There was a time when I really believed that he loved me, but now I felt like he just used me to show off. He made sure that wherever we went everyone knew that I belonged to him. Shit, I couldn't even remember the last time that he told me that he loved me. I longed for that and for some strange reason I thought that the longer I kept doing what he needed me to do, he'd care about me the way he used to.

So, there we were sitting in her living room drinking whatever the hell she'd concocted. The more liquor I consumed the more comfortable I was with the surroundings. Nyssa was her name, and by the way the two of them conversed I knew that they had known each other for a while. She was a beautiful woman and just like me she'd probably been dragged into this by him. I wondered if she thought I was just a jump-off or if she really knew our history. I wasn't going to ruin the night by asking too many questions. Besides, I was feeling a buzz from the alcohol I had consumed.

I stared at her and registered everything about her in my mind. She had her hair wrapped with a Chinese bang sort of like mine. I didn't know if it was a weave or not because if it was, they did a damn good job putting in. Her eyes were slanted a little, which made the hairstyle look even cuter. Her lips were perfectly covered with M•A•C lipglass. The neutral pink in the lip gloss was accentuated by the pink and black bustier she wore with the panties to match. When she opened the door with just her underwear on I was shocked at first and I don't why, since I was well aware of what we came here to do.

"So, how are you feeling, Diamond?" she asked, with her legs crossed and her shoe hanging off of her foot.

"I'm feeling good. I don't know what you put in these drinks but they have me on cloud nine," I admitted.

"That's good." She set her glass down on the table and stood up from the sofa. "So, that means you're ready to get busy?" she asked.

"Yes," I agreed because at that point I had made up my mind—I was going to enjoy everything that they were going to give me tonight. Hell, if I was going to go through with it, I might as well get some satisfaction out of it. The worst thing I figured that could happen was that I'd enjoy it too much.

Soon, Davey was all over me as Nyssa instructed his every move. I thought it was strange that she was taking control of the situation but obviously it was her nature. I just tried to keep myself relaxed and go with the flow.

"Kiss her neck, she'll love that!" she spoke as she began to strip off her clothes. He softly kissed my neck as I became moist downtown. He took my ear into his mouth and sucked it, slowly letting it slip. He hadn't even touched my pussy yet and I was about to explode. The smell of his cologne was flowing up my nose and loosening me up even more. I was now even more relaxed and ready for whatever was approaching next.

He continued to kiss my neck as Nyssa sat in the chair on the opposite side of the room, watching. I was definitely turned on and wished that I had thought about having a ménage à trois a long time ago. His hands slowly found their way under my dress and as he pulled my panties to the side I released a loud sigh. I opened my eyes long enough to glance at Nyssa, who was smiling from ear to ear. She was obviously enjoying the show. I quickly shut my eyes again after he began to slowly massage my clit. With his free hand placed gently around my neck he removed his finger from my wetness and instructed me to taste it. I stuck out my tongue to lick my juices from his finger.

"Do you like that?" Nyssa asked.

"Yes!" I replied, trying to stay focused on Davey, who was now sliding his finger inside of my juicy tunnel. *Damn*, I thought to myself, *if this is only the beginning I can't imagine what the rest will be like*. His thick fingers continued to move in and out of me as I practically begged for more.

Nyssa stood up from the chair and made her way over to the sofa and began to unzip his pants to release his stiff rod. At that point I was like, *Okay, she's about to suck my man's dick.*

Is this the point where I stop it or is this the part when things get heated? I didn't stop it. Instead, I closed my eyes again and continued to enjoy the pleasure and attention Davey was giving me. She slowly licked the head of his dick, taking in the pre-cum on the top. Within seconds she was deep-throating his stick and the sounds of it were exciting me even more.

"Do you want to taste this dick?" she asked as she glanced up at me. I quickly responded, "Yes!" since I was eager to wrap my lips around the beautiful masterpiece. He stood up to remove his pants completely before sitting back down, and I got in position on my knees in front of him. Nyssa climbed up on top of the sofa so that her pussy was staring him in the face. I was soon sucking his dick like an icecold Popsicle and loving every second of it. Nyssa held her position up top, grinding her pussy into his face and moaning loudly. Soon his dick began to throb and the taste of his release was satisfying my taste buds and trickling down my throat. Nyssa got down off the sofa and instructed me to stop.

"Climb up top so he can suck that pussy, baby!" Before I moved forward she grabbed me to plant a sensual kiss on my lips. *Okay, before tonight that would have definitely made me uncomfortable.* She smacked me on the ass before nudging me to move forward. I climbed up on the couch and got in the same position that she had just been in. As soon as his tongue made contact with my clit I exploded and my juices poured out and ran down his chin. I tried to move away because the orgasm was causing me to tremble, but he quickly grabbed hold of my ass and pulled me back down. Soon I was riding his face like a trained jockey and he was sucking me like a lollipop.

Nyssa continued to suck his manhood while reaching up to insert one finger in my ass. As I moved back and forth on his face her finger moved in and out of my ass, which was more enjoyable than I could have ever imagined. As I neared another orgasm I bent over to grab hold of the back of the sofa and as I began to shake uncontrollably, I squeezed the plush leather.

"Come down and sit on this hard dick!" Davey spoke aloud. I was already exhausted but definitely anticipating feeling him inside of me. This was by far the best sex that I'd ever had. He pulled me close to him to kiss me. This was the most attention that he'd paid to me in months. His lips were soft and instantly put me at ease. He instructed me to get on my knees in front on the sofa while Nyssa sat down and opened her legs wide so that I could kiss her wetness. *Okay, what was I supposed to do now?* Eating pussy was definitely not something I knew how to do. I had seen it done in porno movies but had never stared a pussy in the face.

Davey slowly and deliberately entered me from behind as she palmed the back of my head to force my face deeper into her burrow. His dick filled me up completely and hit my G-spot continuously. Davey held on to my hips like a set of handlebars and picked up the speed. I forcefully sucked Nyssa's clit until she erupted, screaming loudly with delight. With the expression on her face, I figured that I had done the job right. Davey continued pounding me until we both came in sync. We were all exhausted as we relaxed. After I went to the bathroom and cleaned myself up, I waited patiently on the sofa for Davey.

"You ready to go?" he asked, as he headed back out to the living room, now fully dressed.

"Yeah, I'm ready," I replied, as I got up from the sofa and headed to the door. Nyssa walked over and opened the door for us.

"I'll talk to you later," Davey told her before giving her a hug.

"Thanks for coming, Diamond. I enjoyed myself. I hoped that you did too." She reached over and gave me a hug as well. With that, we left her apartment and walked to the car. Again, I sat quietly in the car. I still didn't know what to say. I didn't really want to talk about how I just saw another woman suck his dick or him eating her pussy or me eating her pussy, for that matter. I just wanted to get home and go to bed. I hoped that this was enough for him to see that I was there for him and I was the woman that he needed to be with. I guess that he knew that I didn't want to talk about it, because he didn't say anything. He just kept his eye on the road and glanced over at me every so often. He softly held on to my hand with his right hand and drove with his left. *Was this a sign that we would grow closer again?* At least, I prayed that it was. I needed to be happy.

That night Davey lay next to me, snuggled up closely, and told me how much he loved me. I had my man back and I was planning on holding on to him.

Chapter Six

Mica: Three-Letter Word

I always wondered how a word so short could cause so much havoc. Just when you think things are going your way, *sex* comes into play and ruins it all. I wasn't an expert at how to handle relationship issues or infidelity, but I was soon about to learn. I knew that Tyson probably fooled around on me. I mean, what drug dealer doesn't have many women to choose from? What I didn't expect was to have to see it with my own eyes and figure out how to deal with it. No one really thinks about what they'll do if placed in certain situations, but we always hope that we will come out of them okay.

Tyson picked me up from the salon and told me that he had to make a stop before dropping me off at home. I hoped that it had nothing to do with drugs since he knew how I felt about that. I wanted to be as far away from that side of him as I possibly could.

Anyway, he pulled in front of a house off a small street and told me to wait in the car. He left the car running and told me that he'd only be a minute. Of course, I believed him and though I wasn't comfortable about being out there in the car alone, I agreed. I was becoming more annoyed as the seconds passed. I had been out there for at least a half hour, and he'd left his phone in the car so I couldn't even call him. I wondered what the hell was taking so long. After another ten minutes I was pissed.

I grabbed the gun he kept in the armrest of his car and put it inside my bag. After all, I didn't know what the hell I would run into once I got out. It was getting dark outside and I wasn't familiar with anyone or anything around there. The block was pretty much empty besides a few corner hustlers hanging in the Chinese restaurant at the end of the block. I was nervous as I exited but put on the persona that I wasn't. I knocked on the door a few times and waited, tapping my foot on the ground, hoping they would hurry up and open the door. A few seconds later a tall, thin-framed woman opened the door, tying her robe, which barely covered her naked body underneath. She was hazelnut in color and her hair was short and spiked. Her round breasts were practically hanging out of the robe. On looks alone I'd give her about a seven out of ten. Now, I considered myself a ten, so she was creeping up on me and that alone made me nervous.

"Can I help you?" she asked, stuffing her breasts into the robe, making sure they were covered.

"Yes you can. You can tell my man to get out here because I'm ready to go," I said, annoyed and wondering what the hell was going on inside the house.

"Well, he's a little busy right now, sweetie, so you're gonna have to go wait in the car until he gets finished." She looked me up and down as if I was two feet tall.

Sweetie? I wanted to slap her for trying to play me. I didn't think I looked that stupid.

"No, what you're going to do is go get him and tell him to come now," I raised my voice. I was getting angrier by the second.

"What I am going to do is close my door and finish what I was doing. I suggest you head back to the car like a good girl and wait for him to come out." She pointed her finger in my face almost close enough to touch me.

What the fuck was going on in there that would make her talk to me as if I were some groupie? I was fed up with talking to her. I quickly pushed her, making her stumble a little and pushed the door open. She began charging toward me but stopped when I took the gun out of my bag and pointed it at her.

"Back the fuck up, bitch! Now, where the fuck is my man?" I yelled.

She was backing away now and all of the mouth she had before disappeared. "What, are you going to shoot me?"

"Don't tempt me." I heard footsteps coming toward the steps. I hoped it was Tyson so we could just leave. I wasn't trying to go to jail, but if this bitch said one more word I was definitely going to shoot.

"Mica, what the fuck are you doing?" Tyson now stood at the bottom of the steps a few inches away from where Miss Smart-ass was standing.

"What the fuck are *you* doing? You had me sitting out in the car while you're in here fucking this bitch?"

"Mica, come on now. Why the fuck would I do some shit like that? Do you think I'm that crazy?"

"I think you're disrespectful, leaving me in that damn car and coming in here with her."

"She's such a fucking crybaby, Tyson. Why don't you get her the fuck out of my house?" she yelled, trying to hide behind him.

"You're still talking?" I asked, turning the gun in her direction.

"Mica, let's just leave and I'll explain everything to you in the car," he pleaded. I really wasn't trying to hear much of what he was saying.

I was standing there looking at them both, wondering how the hell my feelings for a man could make me go crazy enough to pull out a gun. I didn't want to believe that it was just him, but instead that it was the disrespect that the female standing across from me showed. I didn't take to that sort of thing kindly.

"I'm going to leave, but you can stay here with this bitch. I'll call a cab." I tossed his gun to him and turned my back to head out of the door.

"Mica, I'm not letting you leave me. This house is where they bag up the drugs, okay? I'm not here fucking anybody. If you don't believe me I'll show you."

I turned back around and looked at him, and then I glanced at her while she stood there with a smirk on her face. I wanted to smack the shit out of her. Even if he was telling the truth I didn't like her nor did I like the way she talked to me when I came to the door. In my mind I was thinking that I didn't really want to see what was upstairs, but in my heart I had to know if he was lying.

"Yeah, I need to see it," I said, walking toward him.

He walked up the steps and told me to follow him. I was nervous as I headed up behind him. I wanted to just say stop. I mean, if he had gone this far it had to be true. I didn't want to see anything that would put me in a difficult situation had he ever gotten caught. I couldn't tell anything that I didn't know, but knowing and keeping it a secret would probably tear me apart.

"Tyson, I don't need to go any farther. I believe you, okay?"

"Are you sure? I don't want to hear about this later when I have to stop by here again."

"I'm sure. Let's just go, okay?" I said as he turned around on the stairs and began to walk back down. We left the house and got into the car. I was glad that I didn't go any farther but I was pissed that I acted the way that I had. I felt embarrassed. I never wanted anyone to see me in such a vulnerable position. I was almost ready to go to jail rather than lose him to someone else. It was almost as if another person was taking over my body because in the past I would have never let a man get the best of me.

Once we reached his house I felt like a load had been lifted off of me. Not because of the argument, but because he was telling the truth. I still didn't believe that he never cheated on me, but at least he didn't that night. Most women would say that I was a fool, and in some instances I would probably agree. Though I may be a fool in love, I was well taken care of for all of the drama I had to deal with. I loved Tyson more that anyone else that had come my way and for good reason. I had never met a man that could walk into a room and command everyone's attention without saying a word. He was the type everyone fell in love with. He kept you smiling and he never acted like he was better than anyone else or as if his shit didn't stink. He was smart and actually had a college degree. Now how many hustlers can say that? I was proud of my man and happy to be his woman.

Once we entered his house he headed straight to the living room and turned on CNN. He loved to be up on the news. He knew what was going on in every state from shootings to the weekly weather. This was the time that he didn't like to be bothered and most of the time I would respect that, but tonight I wanted to give him an apology that he could feel. I couldn't deal with the silent treatment and knew that I had to do something to get back on his good side.

I headed upstairs and took a shower. After my shower I lotioned up with my favorite Bath & Body Works scent. I put on the matching body splash and slipped on a bra and thong with a garter belt and stiletto heels. I put my hair in a little bun and took a deep breath. I hoped that he wouldn't turn me away—I mean, he had never done it before, but tonight I had acted out of the ordinary so there was a possibility that he would too.

I slowly walked down the steps and due to the plush carpet you couldn't hear the sounds of the shoes. I crept into the living room hoping that he wouldn't turn around before I got close enough to him. I wanted to surprise him.

I decided that I would get close to him and sing into his ear. I need it to be freaky and with the voice that I had been blessed with I knew he wouldn't be able to turn me away. I settled on "Nasty Grind" by Adina Howard. I loved the sex-filled songs and I had always wanted to perform for him.

I walked toward the back of the sofa and slowly put my hands on his shoulders. He didn't budge but he didn't push my hands away either, which was a plus and my cue to keep going. I bent down so that I could get close to his ear. I started the song and hoped that he would receive it the way that I wanted him to.

By now I was standing in front of him dancing to the words that I was singing. He had used the remote to turn off the TV, which excited me because now I had his full attention. I continued singing and watching his expressions. I wanted to jump right on him, but I continued the performance to make it sensual.

I moved closer to the sofa and placed one leg at a time onto the seat so that he could remove my shoes. Next, I took off my bra, letting my perfect double D's loose. I slowly bent over so that my breasts were in his face. He didn't waste any time grabbing hold of them and caressing my hardened nipples. I moaned as I got more excited. I wanted to feel his lips all over my body and let him know when he missed a spot. I straddled him as he held his position on the sofa. I met his lips with a deep kiss and massaged his tongue with mine. I can hardly explain how good I felt at that moment. I felt like I was intoxicated with love and he was the designated driver. My insides were going wild as he used one hand to massage my clit through my black lace panties.

"You want this pussy?" I moaned in the sexiest tone. He didn't respond so I pulled back enough to release my nipple from his mouth and asked again, "Do you want this pussy?"

"More than you know," he responded in his sexy baritone voice.

I rose up and began to unbuckle his pants to release his hard dick. I was as anxious to wrap my lips around it as I would be to eat my last meal. I looked up at him just so that our eyes could meet one last time before I went to work. He gave me a slight smile and then he gently put his head back, anticipating what I was about to give him.

Even after a year of us being together we managed to still turn each other on as if it were something new. That was definitely something special, because not many couples can achieve that.

His dick was hard as brick as I took one lick of the head and used my finger to wipe the pre-cum across my lips. He loved when I did the freaky shit and I loved turning him on. I wrapped my lips around the head and slowly sucked from top to bottom. I made sure that his shaft was soaking wet so that the slurping sounds would keep him excited. I had gotten really good at giving head; so much so that I didn't even have to think about it. I would go straight to work on it.

After ten minutes or so of foreplay I was ready to feel him inside of me. I stood up, releasing my grip on his dick, watching it stand on its own at attention. I slid my thong off and let it hit the floor. I straddled him with my back facing him and began going up and down, filling my wet pussy with his huge dick. I was moaning and rubbing my breasts. He was moaning with me, almost in sync. My ass was slapping so hard against him you could have heard it upstairs. I wanted to cum but I wanted us to do it together so I held onto it. I continued to rock my hips and swirl them as if I were trying not to drop a hula hoop. He reached his hands around and played with my clit, which made it extremely hard to hold onto my eruption.

Tyson held onto me and stood up, making sure that his dick didn't slip out of me. I placed my hands on the arm of the sofa as he began to pound me from behind. I was throwing my ass back hard, trying to show him that this pussy was his. I felt my orgasm building and I couldn't stop it because that shit felt way too good.

"Oh shit, I'm about to cum," I moaned.

He grabbed hold of my hips and began pumping faster. He was moaning loudly, letting me know that he was about to cum as well. My legs began to shake and soon my juices were splashing all over him. Within seconds of my release his fluid was pouring out inside of me.

I felt relaxed and I was glad that we had been able to get past the events that took place earlier in the evening. No woman should be able to take me out of my square or threaten to ruin my relationship. I was paying close attention now, and I knew exactly what I had to do to keep from losing my cool again. The three-letter word, *sex*, was no longer a factor. I wasn't going to assume anymore. I had to believe that he wouldn't disrespect me and he'd keep the sideline hocs in check.

Chapter Seven

Diamond: As Seen on TV

Things had been going great for Davey and me in the months to follow. I had even moved back in with him into his apartment. Summer was coming and I was getting anxious because we had planned on taking a much-needed vacation. The episode with Nyssa was behind us and he hadn't mentioned it since the night that it went down. I never told anyone about it and I planned on keeping it a secret until the end of time. I didn't want anyone to think any less of me. I had managed to keep the fire lit between Davey and me but some things are too good to be true and some people are never satisfied.

Kiki called me one afternoon while I was doing some much needed cleaning around the apartment. I had been focusing on my relationship so much lately that I hadn't paid anything else much attention. Had I known what I was about to hear I would have sat down before she spoke, but I didn't and damn near hit the floor in shock.

"Diamond, I got some shit to tell you, girl!"

"About what? You know I'm always up for hearing some gossip," I admitted.

"It's about you and that trifling-ass nigga you're with."

"What have you heard now? People always trying to throw salt in the game when they see we're doing fine."

"Girl, I didn't hear it, I saw it for myself. You know that nigga is going around selling a sex tape of you and him having a threesome!"

"What?" I asked, because I wanted to make sure that I heard it right. Would he really do that to me? I couldn't believe my ears.

"Yes, girl. I didn't know you went both ways, girl. That shit looked like a professional production." She laughed.

I didn't find anything funny about it. There I was doing what I needed to do to satisfy my man and he secretly taped the scene and made money from it. I knew she wasn't lying about seeing it. How else would she have known that I'd had the threesome and actually had sex with a female?

"I don't go both ways and I did that shit for him and this is how he repays me?" I couldn't hold back the tears. I was so embarrassed that something I was so uncomfortable about doing was being spread around like government cheese. The whole world was seeing me in that vulnerable position.

"Girl, I don't know why you are still with his ass. When are you going to wake up and smell the coffee?"

"I'm going to have to talk to you later, Kiki. I have to finish cleaning." I quickly cut her off and ended the conversation. I was furious. With Davey, there was always something. I thought that we had made it past the bullshit and here was another slap in the face. I couldn't answer her question because I didn't know. I didn't know when I would wake up and smell the coffee. I didn't know when I was going to realize that he wasn't shit. I didn't know how many times I had to be hurt by him before I decided to walk away.

I sat there crying for hours. I still had the broom in my hand when he came in. I was sitting on the sofa, still in disbelief. He immediately knew that something was wrong and before he got a chance to speak, I interrupted him.

"Just when I think that you've changed I get a slap in the face. I can't believe that you would sell a fucking sex tape of me that I didn't even agree to!" I yelled.

"What are you talking about?"

"You know what the fuck I'm talking about! I got a call today from someone today telling me that you're out on the streets selling a sex tape of the threesome we had."

"I never sold a tape; I didn't even know that there *was* a tape!"

"You expect me to believe that shit, Davey! I can't fucking believe you would do this to me." I still sat there crying. I was just seconds away from jumping up, but I knew that hitting him wasn't going to solve anything. It surely wasn't going to get him to admit that he would degrade me this way.

"Diamond, Nyssa must be the one selling the tape. I didn't know anything about it, believe me."

"So, if I go to that bitch's house and kick her ass you'll still tell me that?"

"Diamond, you can't do that," he said, still holding his position near the front door.

"What the fuck do you mean I can't? You don't make the fucking rules! Why are you trying to protect her and I'm supposed to be your woman?"

"Diamond, my son will be there. You can't do that!"

"Your son? Since when did you have a son?" I had to ask that question because he never told me anything about having a child before. This was definitely a shock to me. Then I thought about it even deeper. So Nyssa was his baby's mother? What the fuck? I damn sure didn't sign up for this shit.

"He's three years old," he replied in a low tone, almost as if he was afraid to say it any louder.

"You mean to tell me you have a three-year-old son? So you fucking cheated on me and had a baby? And then had me fuck your baby's mother?" That was it; I couldn't sit still any longer. I got up from the chair and began hitting him with the broom. He tried to get ahold of it, but the wooden stick broke over his arm. Once it broke I moved closer and began punching him. After a few seconds he got ahold of my arms and held them. I tried kicking him once I couldn't get my hands free.

"You're lucky I don't have a gun because I'd shoot your ass! Get the fuck off of my hands," I yelled, trying to get my hands free so that I could leave. I wasn't going to stay in this apartment any longer. I couldn't believe the twisted shit that he had gotten me involved in. He'd had a child and never told me. That hurt my heart because at one point I was pregnant by him and he forced me to get an abortion. I went along with it because I wasn't trying to raise a baby alone if he backed out on me. So, to hear this was like a stab in the heart. Then I thought back to the tape. *How many people have seen it?* I guess he felt like a fucking king having me and his baby's mom fucking him on tape.

"Get the fuck off of me," I continued to yell. Tears were pouring out of my eyes and I was like a raging bull trying to get loose. I bit and kicked him until he finally let me go.

"Diamond, I'm sorry that I didn't tell you, but I didn't want to hurt you."

"How the fuck did you think I would never know? I guess you didn't plan on being with me very long, huh? You can keep your apology because it's bullshit, just like this fucking relationship. I never meant shit to you. There is no way that you could love me and do the shit that you continue to do to me. I'm leaving, Davey, and don't bother calling me because you won't get an answer."

I turned and walked toward the bedroom to gather up a few things. Kiki told me that if I ever needed a place to crash that I could come stay with her. I was going to take her up on that because at that point this thing I thought was a relationship was officially over.

"Diamond, please, let's talk about this. Don't walk out on me like this."

"Fuck you. You are never going to do right by me and I'm not going to keep being your fool."

"We can fix this. I know I fucked up, but give me another chance to make it right."

"How many times have I heard that line? I'm done Davey," I replied as I grabbed my bag and headed back toward the door. I couldn't stand the sight of him. I felt sick to my stomach the longer the thoughts weighed on my mind. I would have never believed that he would stoop this low. I mean, how could you not tell me about a child? Three fucking years? I'd been a fool for way too long.

My heart felt like it had been shattered and my body was extremely weak. I could barely stop shaking long enough to control the steering wheel in the car. I made it over to Kiki's house safely, though I almost got in two accidents, being an emotional wreck. I was almost too embarrassed to knock on the door. I hadn't called and gave her a heads-up, but she probably already expected that I would be coming after she told me about the tape. I knocked softly since I couldn't exert enough energy to use any force.

"Girl, I knew you were coming. I hope you're leaving his sorry ass for good!" She reached out and grabbed my shoulder to pull me inside. "You know you can stay here as long as you need to."

I was glad I had a friend like Kiki. I had some relatives, but since I found out I was adopted I never really felt like I belonged. I hadn't even seen my mother in months. I called from time to time to check on her, but I never made it down to the place that I once called home to actually see her. I had heard through the grapevine that she'd been using drugs. I knew I couldn't believe everything I heard, but once she and my dad broke up, she lost it. She gave up on herself, and living in North Philly surrounded by a bunch of drug dealers didn't help, either.

Once I got with Davey things changed. My family grew jealous of the things that he did for me. I strayed away from them and hadn't been back since. So, there I was clinging on to the only person who had been my friend since leaving my grandmom's house a few years back. I met Kiki while hanging out at the club with Davey. He was pretty well known and when he said that he wanted to show me to the world, that was exactly what he did. He didn't waste time showing his trophy off. Kiki, though cordial with him, never really cared for his type. She always told me that men like him aren't to be trusted. She warned me about falling in love, but by that time I had already fallen hard. I had smacked the ground hard and couldn't peel myself away from it.

Surprisingly, he allowed me to hang out with Kiki when he was working or when he wanted to get loose in the club. The women would be all over him and there were plenty of times that I almost came to blows with chicks for the blatant disrespect. Kiki always had my back but at the same time tried to diffuse any altercation. I respected her for that the more I learned that men will be men. She had been there for me every time I had a blow with Davey. Whether it was an ear to listen, a shoulder to lean on, or a place to lay my head until I decided to take him back, she was always there. For that I was grateful and I planned to repay her one of these days.

I took a long shower that night, damn near using all of her hot water. I let the water hit my face, hoping that it would drown my pain. The more I tried to think about him the harder it was. I pulled myself together and after the shower I went to bed in her extra bedroom. I closed my eyes and soon I was off in la-la land, praying that tomorrow would be a better day.

Chapter Eight

Mica: Family Matters

In my attempt to get close to Tyson I'd moved in with him. At first I wasn't all too keen on the idea, since I knew it would take time for him to get used to me being around all the time. I didn't want to impose on his daily routine, but I wanted to get closer to him.

A little over a month had passed since the day I burst in the stash house making a fool of myself and I had managed to stay on his good side ever since. Things were good but there's always drama and I knew there was someone waiting in the wings to throw salt in the game.

"Hello, is Tyson there?" a female voice boomed through the receiver.

I had to sit for a second before responding. I couldn't believe that a bitch would have the audacity to call here for him. I didn't know what to say so I said the first thing that came to mind.

"Excuse me?"

"I *said*, is Tyson home," the female replied, annoyed.

"Who is this?"

"None of your business. I just need to know where Tyson is."

"That's not an attitude that gets answers."

"Well, if you must know, this is Deanna, his son's mother."

"Well, Deanna, Tyson isn't here and I suggest the next time you speak with him you get his cell number."

"First of all, Little Miss Prissy, I was around long before you and I'm still going to be here when you're gone so you can talk that shit if you want, but you're going to end up with the broken heart."

"I'm not going anywhere, so if someone is going to end up with a broken heart it's going to be you."

"Why would I have a broken heart? If you don't know, I know Tyson like the back of my hand and he changes women like he changes his drawers. I'm the one who's got the baby and the title. Have you forgotten he married me, or did he not tell you that? He's got to divorce me to get rid of me, and even then I got his kid so he's bound to me for life."

"Is that why you called here? Does that make you feel better? Because honestly, I don't give a fuck about that. The bottom line is he's my man and I ain't going nowhere."

"Don't be so sure about that. Tyson doesn't give a fuck about you. You'll see. Now when he comes home, tell him I called and you make sure you have a good day."

Click.

I heard the sound of the dial tone before I could say another word. Tyson always told me how crazy his ex was, but one thing she didn't know was how crazy I could get. I tried to keep my cool but the bottom line is there wasn't but so much that I could take before I was fed up. I couldn't wait to talk to him to let him know about the conversation. It was about six o'clock when he walked in the door and I instantly began my case.

"You know that bitch called here disrespecting me? When are you going to put her in her place?" I yelled, walking toward the door, where he was still standing in the vestibule.

"What bitch? Who are you talking about, Mica?"

"Deanna. I wish you would put her in her place!"

"And where is that? She's a grown-ass woman. I can't tell her what to do."

"What the fuck do you mean you can't tell her what to do? So what you're saying is that it is okay for her to disrespect me?"

"That's not what I am saying, I'm saying that I can't do shit about her ways. That's just how she is, that's why we aren't together now."

"You might as well be with her, you won't divorce her." I was pissed. It was bad enough they were still married but he wouldn't even stand up for me. It wasn't rocket science. All he had to do was tell her that she had to stop calling here.

"You know what, Mica? The attitude ain't gonna make shit change. She knows that I'm with you and that's all that matters. I don't know what the fuck else you expect me to do."

"I don't want to hear shit when I have to fuck her up! Ain't nobody going to keep disrespecting me."

"It's not that deep. You're turning it into something else."

"How do you figure it's not that deep?"

"Look, would you just drop it? I'll talk to her, Okay? I got enough shit to deal with for y'all to keep arguing all the time. Satisfied now?"

"I'll be satisfied when she stops calling," I snapped before leaving the room.

I knew he probably wouldn't talk to her. I was tired of her feeling like she was in control. When things got serious with me and Tyson, he told me that she would never be an issue. It didn't take very long before I found out that was so far from the truth you couldn't reach it. I thought I could handle it but the longer it went on the more I realized I couldn't.

I headed upstairs to get my purse so I could leave. I needed some fresh air to calm me down. I started thinking of where I could go, and my thoughts about cousin Deidra, from my father's side of the family, popped up in my mind. I hadn't seen her in six months, and the last time I saw her it was so brief that I hadn't been able to find out what she'd been up to. I missed her. Deidra and I were pretty close growing up, but once my father passed we kind of strayed apart. My mother never really cared too much for my dad's family, but dealt with them because of him. After he was killed his family didn't want anything to do with us. They blamed my mother for his death. I never understood why they blamed her. I mean, Johnny was *his* child too.

I was tired of being cooped up in the house. I wanted to take a drive, which was something that I didn't usually do. I rarely drove anywhere, especially long distances. That was why I always caught the bus to see Johnny. I dialed Diedra's number from my cell phone but the number was disconnected. Since I didn't have any other number to reach her at I decided to just drive to her house and surprise her with a visit. I got on I-95 North toward Aramingo Avenue. I sat in the car bobbing my head to the sounds of Mary J. Blige. I loved her music. No matter what you were going through you could always find a song of hers that matched your situation. I found a parking spot and walked toward the entrance of the building. I noticed a guy named Money, who I hadn't seen in a while, standing on the corner.

"Money? Is that you?"

"Mica? What's up? What the hell you doing in this hood?" he asked before hugging me.

I had the biggest crush on Money while I was growing up. I was always the shy one in the bunch, so I never had the opportunity of telling him. By the time I gathered up the courage to tell him, he had already gotten with Deidra. I never told either one of them that I had the crush, so I couldn't blame anyone but myself.

"I came by to see Deidra. I haven't seen her in a while."

"A lot has probably changed since the last time you saw her."

"What do you mean by that?"

"I'm not going to throw no salt on her but she ain't the same ol' Deidra no more."

I didn't know what the hell he was talking about. I mean, how much could she have changed in six months? She looked perfectly fine to me before.

"I still don't get it, Money. What happened to her?"

"You'll see for yourself, but it's good seeing you, though. I see life's treating you good."

"Yeah, I'm doing good, found me a good man finally," I said, laughing.

"That's what's up, you deserve it. I'm not gonna hold you, though. Go see how you cousin is. I'll see you around."

"Okay, good seeing you," I replied, before heading toward her apartment. I climbed the two flights to get to her door. I knew I needed to exercise more because I was exhausted after that. Anyway, I knocked a few times before I heard the locks being turned. I was nervous to see who was behind it. The comment Money made was replaying in my mind like a skipping CD. Still, I stood there hoping that he was just exaggerating.

"Who the hell are you here for?" a thin-framed woman asked through a crack in the door, showing only her body. I couldn't see her face so I knew that she couldn't possibly see mine.

"I'm here to see Deidra."

"Who are you? What do you want with her?"

"I'm her cousin, Mica. I just want to see how she's—"

"Mica? Hey girl, where have you been?" The thin frame was that of Deidra. I didn't know what to say as she reached her arms out to hug me. I had never seen her so thin, and I wasn't sure if I even wanted to know what was going on with her. Instantly two things popped in my head: either she was on drugs, or she had HIV. The last time I saw her she looked perfectly healthy. It wasn't as if she had been a big woman, but her frame looked healthier than the emaciated look it had now.

"Come in, girl. I missed you," she said, motioning for me to come inside the apartment.

"You were on my mind so I tried to call you. The number was disconnected so I just stopped by." The apartment was a mess. Clothes and food containers were everywhere. I didn't even want to sit down for fear I would carry some unwanted rodents home with me.

"Yeah, I couldn't afford it, girl, so I had to let it get cut off. I see you dressed all fly. Life must be good for you."

"Yeah, it is. What's going on with you? I have never seen you this thin."

"I know, girl. To be honest, I got messed up on some shit. Hanging with the wrong people getting high, the drugs kept calling my name. I couldn't stop."

I was shocked that she just blurted that out. I'd never seen a drug addict who could be honest about their habits. "Deidra, how did that happen? You were doing so good the last time I saw you."

"I know, I'm embarrassed for you to even see me like this. Truthfully, the last time you saw me I was already hooked. I couldn't tell you that. You always looked up to me but now what do you have to look up to? I look like shit and I know it. The problem is that I don't know another way—this is all I know now." She couldn't even look me in the eye as she talked.

What the hell happened to the strong woman I knew? She had the best of everything, clothes, money, and a man that most women would fight tooth and nail for.

"What happened to G? Last time I saw you y'all were on the way down the aisle."

"Girl, he left me for some skinny bitch that he knocked up. I was depressed for a long time, but the drugs helped ease my pain."

I still sat there as if the whole scene wasn't really happening. I hoped it was just a cruel joke and things were really okay. I couldn't believe what my eyes were seeing, and even if someone were to pinch me and say wake up, this is real, I still would doubt it.

"Is there any way that I can help you? I hate seeing you like this." I was almost in tears. It hurt my heart to see her in such a vulnerable state.

"If you can lend me a few dollars that would help me a lot." She still hadn't looked me in the eye yet.

I grabbed her by the chin to lift her head. "You know I can't do that, D. You won't use it for what you should. I want to help you out of this. If I find a rehab program for you, will you go?"

"Rehab? Hell no, I'm not going to no rehab."

"What's wrong with rehab? Is this the way you want to live? The woman I know would never turn down help,"

"I'm not the woman you used to know, baby girl, a lot of shit has changed. I'm not happy like this, but who's to say that I'll be happy when I'm clean? Ain't shit out here for me."

"Yes there is D, you just don't want to see it."

"I don't have nobody, no man, no family. Without love in my heart I might as well be dead. Nobody gives a fuck about me."

"I do," I replied as a tear fell from my eye. "Let me help you, please, I can't see you like this; it's hurting me, D."

"I'm sorry Mica, but I can't, okay? I appreciate the offer, I really do, but it's just not for me."

I grabbed my purse and took out a business card and fifty dollars. I didn't know what else to do. I gave her the card and told her to call me if she changed her mind or needed me for anything. I prayed that she would use the money wisely, but I knew that it would never happen. I didn't know many drug addicts, but I did know that they would lie, cheat, and steal to get high. I felt that at least she was honest and told me about her addiction. I gave her a hug and told her how much I loved her. I really did care about her and at that point, probably more than she cared about herself. I left her apartment saddened. I kind of wished that I had never stopped by. I know things happen for a reason, and maybe it was meant for me to see her to help her out. I wasn't going to give up on her that easily, but I wanted to give her some time to think. If there was one thing that mattered to me it was family and I was coming back for her whether she wanted me to or not.

That night I had the hardest time sleeping. I tossed and turned so much Tyson woke up and asked what was wrong. I broke down and told him about Deidra.

"When I left earlier I went to see my cousin Deidra, who I haven't seen in a while. I wasn't prepared for what I saw and it's eating me up inside."

"What do you mean, what you saw? What's wrong with her?"

"She's strung out—I mean she's so thin. This is a person I used to look up to. Back in the day she was the shit, she had the looks, the money, and the man. I was so jealous of her. She needs help and I feel like an asshole for walking out of there."

"Babe, you can't blame yourself for what's happening to her."

"I don't, but I shouldn't have left, I should have stayed. I'm all that she has." I began to cry. I honestly believed that I should have stayed even though she turned me down.

"Come here babe, you can't save everybody. I know that's your family and you love her, but if she's not ready to be helped nothing you say will change that. Hopefully she'll come around before it's too late." He wrapped his arms around me and wiped the tears from my face. I knew that what he said was true even though I didn't want to believe it. I wanted to believe that I could just walk in there and drag her to a rehab to get help. Unfortunately, that wasn't a reality. When she was ready I was sure she'd let me know. The best thing I could do now was let her know I was there for her and I loved her.

At least if she had that to fall back on she would fight to get herself on track. I soon fell to sleep in Tyson's arms, forgetting about the brief argument we'd had earlier in the day. He'd always been good at consoling me, and right then I needed him more than ever.

Chapter Nine

Diamond: Running His Game

"If it isn't little Miss Diamond Diva. What the hell brings you to this part of town? I thought you were allergic to North Philly," Cicely said, standing back, looking me up and down. "Mom, you'll never believe what the wind blew in."

"Hey, Aunt Cicely, it's nice to see you too," I replied sarcastically. I wasn't really happy to see her. On the real, I never really liked her ass anyway. I only dealt with her because she was my mom's sister. I didn't know what made me stop by there, but once I saw her face I wanted to turn back around and leave. I made sure to press the alarm pad on my key ring again to make sure my car was locked before going inside. You could never be too careful in that neighborhood. I'd be pissed if I came out and my car was missing.

"Where's my mom at?" I asked, trying to get straight to the point. I didn't want to stay there longer than I had to.

"Your mom? Who the hell knows where she is? Maybe you should try the local crack houses or speakeasies," Cicely replied, being the bitch that she normally was.

My grandmom stepped in. "Cut it out, Cicely. All of that isn't necessary."

I was about two seconds away from punching Cicely in the face, and my grandmom could probably sense that. There had been many times that she and I had come close to blows. I never knew if her anger came from jealousy or if she just hated me so much that she had to continuously push my buttons. I remember the day we moved in, she had to rub it in my mother's face how she knew she'd be back. My mother had been the only one of my grandmother's children who was successful, and Cicely, being the oldest, hated it.

"Why? It's the truth. She needs to know that her perfect mother ain't so perfect after all," she said, before leaving the room and heading toward the kitchen.

My grandmom came over to try and calm me down. "Don't let her rile you up, you know how she gets."

I was still pissed and it would take a lot more than a few words to put out the steam. "I don't know why she always has to be so negative. She acts like I did something to her."

"That's just her attitude. She's always mad at the world, but you can't let that stop you from doing what you came here to do."

"What's that?" I asked, confused. I only stopped by to see my mother, and since she wasn't there I was planning to be on my way. I didn't have anything else on the agenda but maybe she knew something that I didn't know.

"To save your mom. She really needs you. She's been so depressed and she uses those drugs to break away from reality. I tried everything that I could think of, but God has a strange way of working sometimes. Everything happens for a reason and it was meant for you to come here today whether you believe it or not."

I sat there listening to all she said and I was definitely a firm believer of things happening for a reason. Some things I just didn't know the answer to, and I guessed I would know when I was supposed to.

Just as Grandmom was wrapping up all that she had to say, the front door opened and my mother walked in. I hadn't seen her in months, and I almost didn't recognize her. Her hair was all over the place and her clothes were so big they were barely staying up on her small frame. She had lost so much weight and looked far different from the woman who raised me. What the hell happened? I mean, when I left her the last time she was doing well with a new job. She was excited that she was going to finally be able to make it on her own. I could barely stand to look at her. She glanced over at me but appeared to be so high that she didn't even know who I was.

"Mom, it's me, Diamond," I said, standing up from the chair that I had been sitting in and heading in her direction.

"Diamond? Girl, what brings you around here?" she asked before sitting down on the sofa on the opposite side of the large living room.

"I came to see you, to find out how you were doing. I wanted to see if you needed anything."

Her eyes lit up like the sun when I said that. I didn't know if that was good or bad. "Actually baby, if you could help me out with a few dollars, I can go out and look for a job."

"What happened to the job you had?"

"I got fired, baby. I couldn't make it to work on time. It was so far away."

I knew she was lying, but I couldn't prove it so there wasn't any sense in arguing about it. "How much money do you need?" I asked, reaching into my bag to get my wallet.

"Just about fifty dollars. I can get me a TransPass and get my hair done up nice."

I knew she was lying but I wasn't going to tell her no. She had done far too much for me, and I couldn't stand to see her the way she was. My grandmom saw that I was about to give her money and looked at her with disgust as she headed out of the room. I pulled out one hundred dollars and gave it to her. She smiled and gave me a hug.

"Are you really going to look for a job, Mom?"

"I am, baby. I promise."

"I'm going to come back and check on you. I want you to get better, Mom, so things can be like they used to be."

"I know you do, and things will get better."

I took her word since I hoped that she would get better. I didn't know what else to do. I thought about moving her out of the neighborhood, but that wouldn't stop her from coming back if she wanted to. I even thought about offering to put her in a rehab, but one thing about a drug addict was that they wouldn't take the help if they weren't ready for it. I prayed that she would get better before if was too late.

After saying my good-byes I left feeling a little better that I had gotten to see my mom. There was nothing worse than hearing through the grapevine that your mother was on drugs, especially when you bailed out on her. I did believe that if I'd stayed around she may have never been steered the wrong way. Once I left I figured that she felt like she had no one to live for. Somehow I had to make her believe again, since I knew that I was the key to her getting better and I understood what my grandmom meant. I had to meet Davey at five and I was running late. I hated being late because when I was in a rush everyone in the city was driving Miss Daisy. Davey claimed that there was something important I had to do for him. I didn't have a clue what it was, but I damn sure hoped that it wasn't another threesome. After the sex-tape incident I knew that I should have just up and left, but it was something about him that made me stay. It took the last four months to shake the visions of that night. I definitely wasn't trying to go there again.

So what made me love him? I couldn't pinpoint it, and even if I could no one would understand it anyway. There are a lot of relationships that don't make sense to us from the outside looking in. I was on the inside and I couldn't see my life any other way. So again I ask, was I a fool? Probably so, but I was happy that I had someone to love me. Yes, I believed that he loved me. Even though he'd done a lot of things to almost break my heart into a million pieces he was damn good at patching things up. He bought me everything I could think of following that night. He'd even come home before the sun came up. Getting him in before four AM was definitely unusual but I was getting used to it. He'd also managed to keep Ms. Nyssa out of our lives. He brought his son around and I began to enjoy playing the stepmom role. We were becoming a family made for TV and I felt that things could only go up from that point.

I didn't want to upset him so I quickly maneuvered through traffic. The last thing I needed was an argument.. As hard as I tried I still made it home about fifteen minutes late. I knew that he'd be pissed but hell, I had to fight through traffic to get there.

"Damn Diamond, what took you so long? I said five o'clock," he yelled, as he walked toward me.

"I tried, traffic was crazy."

"Where were you at anyway?"

"I stopped by to see my mom."

"Your mom? How the hell did you find her?"

"She was at my grandmom's."

"I'm surprised she wasn't at a crack house!" he laughed.

I really didn't find anything funny.

"What is it that you need me to do?" I asked, changing the subject.

"I have this car I need you to drive to south Jersey for me."

"What?"

"Yeah, I need you to take this car over to Jersey. I'm going to give you the directions. Someone is going to take the car, give you another car and you drive it back home."

"That doesn't make any sense, Davey. What the hell is in the car?"

"Nothing, I just need you to drop off the car. Simple as that."

"How come you can't do it?"

"Because I'm on probation. You know I can't drive out of state!"

"So there isn't anyone else that can do it for you?"

"What's the problem, Diamond? It's not rocket science. As much shit as I do for you, I just need you to do this one favor. Besides, everyone else is working, that's why I asked you."

"I hope this shit isn't illegal, Davey, you promised that I wouldn't have to be involved in any bullshit."

"Look, are you going to do it or not? I can find another bitch to take your place if you want!"

"Why do you always have to say that, Davey? I know you can find somebody else; I don't need you to keep threatening me with that shit. Just give me the damn directions and the car keys so I can go." I turned so that I wouldn't have to see his face. I hated when he did that and he knew that I would do anything to keep him around. He came up behind me to give me a hug. I still stood there, annoyed by his last comment. He put the keys in my hand as I loosened up a little bit. I didn't want to go but I felt like I had to. He gave me the directions before I headed out to the car, a black Toyota Camry. I still didn't know all of the details of this transaction, but deep down I knew that it was better that way.

I got in and began my drive to south Jersey. There wasn't much traffic as I took the Benjamin Franklin Bridge.

I was pretty happy about it because I knew that I would get back pretty fast. I had Lloyd playing on the radio and I bobbed my head and sang along like it was karaoke. It had to be a funny sight seeing me act as if I had a microphone and everything. I was feeling the music but at the same time trying to block out the fact that I was being a mule for Davey. I was so into the music that time went by extremely fast. I was almost to the exit before I knew it and glad that I was almost done and on my way home.

After getting off the exit and taking the small streets to the address that he provided, I parked and hurried out of the car. The neighborhood was pretty quiet. There weren't many people outside except what looked like a few hustlers and some children running around in the street. I knocked on the door and waited for someone to open it. I had to knock a few more times before anyone came.

"Can I help you?" a tall, thin-framed woman asked as she opened the door and looked me up and down.

"Is Benny here?"

"Who the hell are you?" she responded. I figured that this was his woman by the attitude she gave when I asked about him.

"I'm here to drop off a car. Tell him Davey sent me."

"He don't know nobody named Davey."

"What do you mean? Davey sent me here from Philly to drop off a car." I was getting annoyed. I didn't know what the hell type of game they were playing, but I wanted to get this over with so I could leave.

"I just said he don't know nobody named Davey."

"Look, here is the note he gave me with the directions and this address. I'm pretty sure that I came to the right place."

"I don't give a fuck about what you have on that paper. You might as well turn back around and head home 'cause Benny don't know him," she yelled, as she began to close the door shut.

I put my hand on the door to stop her from closing it in my face. "Excuse me, don't shut the door in my face. All you have to do is tell Benny I'm here."

"Unless you want to end up a chalk outline on the ground you better back the fuck up off of my door and take your little prissy ass home!"

I could feel the heat rising in my body. I wanted to push the door open and slap her. I decided against it and turned around to walk back to the car and call Davey. He had a lot of explaining to do. I wasted a big part of my day driving here and to be talked to the way I just had been was definitely not in the plans.

I followed the path back to the car. As I was walking, I noticed how the neighborhood was even quieter than it was when I came. I had a strange feeling but I couldn't put my hands on it. I used the keypad to open the car doors and as soon I attempted to open the door cops swarmed around me. I didn't know what the hell was going on.

"Put your hands on the hood of the car," one officer yelled.

"What did I do?" I asked, as I began to cry. I knew I should have listened to my heart and stayed home.

"You have the right to remain silent, anything you say can and will be held against you in a court of law. . . ."

I couldn't even hear him anymore. I was so detached from the situation you could have pinched me and I wouldn't have budged. *Is he reading me my rights? Am I going to jail?* I didn't understand what happened. After I was frisked they put me in handcuffs and put me in the back of a police car. They proceeded to search the car; I noticed them pointing to something in the trunk. *What the hell was it?* I thought.

I didn't find out what it was until I was being questioned in an interrogation room. There was a small amount of cocaine in the trunk. I went numb. Now I realized why the female was acting like she didn't know what I was talking about. It was a setup, and I couldn't believe Davey put me in the middle of it.

Worst of all, it didn't matter how many times I told them the drugs didn't belong to me, they still treated me like a criminal. I told them over and over again that I didn't know who the drugs belonged to. I was simply supposed to drop off a car. The cops didn't believe me. They had even gone so far as laughing as if I told a joke. I knew there wasn't anything I could say to get me out it so I decided to keep quiet and pray for a miracle.

I was placed in a holding cell and after being arraigned the following day I was carted off to a detention center in Philadelphia. I knew at that point it was the end of me and Davey. There was no way I could go back to him after this. He promised that I would never be in the line of fire and that's exactly where I ended up. This was definitely going to ruin my life. It was now that I realized this life isn't so glamorous after all. I couldn't be with a man that didn't care about me the way I cared about him. Davey didn't care and I should have realized that after the cheating and the STD. Me, being a fool in love, I couldn't stop going back. At one point I felt like I needed him. I didn't know any other way to have the best of things without being with him. After this, I would have plenty of time to get my mind right and figure out what I would do once I got out of there. Whatever I decided, running his game was out of the question.

Chapter Ten

Mica: The Glamorous Life

Things with Tyson couldn't have been better. I was enjoying the life that he had blessed me with and I surely wasn't trying to give it up anytime soon. For the most part, we hadn't had many arguments lately. Hell, even his crazy-ass ex Deanna hadn't been calling. I could admit that even though things were rocky between us at times we always managed to put the bad times behind us and move on. I hated arguing. Growing up, yelling was all I heard at home, so I wasn't trying to subject myself to anything that even closely resembled what I grew up around. With all that had been going on, I still hadn't been able to visit my brother, which bothered me more and more each day. I'd sent letters and made numerous attempts to visit and had still been turned away. What the hell had I done that was so bad? My mom tried to get him to talk to me but I assumed he wasn't too interested since he had yet to reach out to me. I believed that he might have been a little jealous of Tyson. I hadn't been one that the men would fight over growing up, so maybe it was just the fact that he was always used to getting all of my attention. Unfortunately, I was a woman now and he would just have to get over it. I just hoped that he would see that no one could replace him in my life and regardless of any relationship that I pursued he'd always be my big brother and I'd always love him the same. The sad part about it all was that I wasn't able to tell him about it since I was getting the silent treatment.

Tyson had set up a special date for us and I was excited because we didn't usually get to go out much. He was always so busy so I appreciated all of the time that he gave me. I had taken all day to make sure that I had the right outfit, hairstyle, and perfume. I hoped that I wasn't overdressed. He said that our destination was a surprise so I didn't have a clue where we were going. I enjoyed surprises, so honestly it didn't even matter. What mattered was that I was going to be able to spend some much needed alone time with him. I was dressed and ready at nine PM like he wanted me to be. I wished that his ass knew the meaning of punctual because I sat there for another hour and I still hadn't heard from him.

I dialed his cell phone so many times that I lost count. He probably hadn't answered it because he knew that I was going to flip out. I was sure going to have an earful for him. If there was one thing that I hated it was wasting time. I always felt like I could be doing something else and sitting in the house in a little black dress and four-inch stilettos was definitely a great example of that. I mean, unless it was a costume for a sexual fantasy there wasn't any reason to be shitty sharp with nowhere to go.

I was getting sleepy the longer I sat there and angrier by the second. Around 10:45 he came strolling in, drunk as hell. I could smell the liquor from the door. My face was twisted in a knot. I couldn't even stand to look at him I was so furious and to make matters even worse he was carrying an opened Heineken beer in his hand. His clothes were even falling off of him. I stood up from the sofa and gave him an evil stare. If this were TV this would be the part where the steam would begin to shoot from my ears.

"What the hell you all dressed up for?" he asked, still unsteady on his feet.

"What the fuck do you mean, what am I dressed up for? We were supposed to have a special date tonight," I yelled, walking closer to him with my finger pointed. I couldn't believe that he'd forgotten and then had the audacity to come in here pissy drunk.

"What date? Who said we were going on a date?"

"So now you don't remember? I can't believe you, Tyson, every time I think that things are going good for us you go and fuck it up!"

"Fuck it up? You want to talk about who's fucking up, huh? Maybe if you'd stop fussing all the time and fuck me like you're supposed to things would be better."

"Are you kidding me, Tyson? Where the hell did that come from? You weren't saying that shit last night when you were fucking me and sucking me!"

"Of course not, what nigga is going to say something to fuck up some pussy!"

"Pussy? So is that what I am?"

"That's not what I said. Look, I've been drinking and this shit is blowing my high!"

"Fuck you, Tyson. When your ass is sober remember the shit you just said to me because I sure as hell will," I yelled before grabbing my bag and going to the door. I couldn't believe the shit that just happened. Earlier in the day he called and told me he had something special planned and now he was drunk and had forgotten all about it and me for that matter. To make matters even worse he belittled me. I couldn't even wrap my mind around the things that he said to me. I was hurting and I didn't even care about the fact that it was now pouring outside and I didn't even have a damn umbrella over my head. I just wanted to get away from there, far enough away that he couldn't see or hear me cry.

The only place that I could think of going was my mom's. I hated for her to see me upset since instead of being there to console me she'd probably try and figure out a way for me to get back in good with Tyson. I'm not saying that my mom was selfish or that she didn't care about my being hurt or upset, but she did care about her bills being paid and since they wouldn't be without him, I'm positive she wouldn't be too happy about us fighting. I almost hated to tell her when we were at odds because her reaction was never one that you'd expect from a mother.

I was soaking wet when I got in the car. I sat there for a few seconds to see if he'd come running out of the house after me. Instead, I was still sitting there for ten minutes looking like a fool. He still hadn't come out and no matter how silly it may sound I was still hoping that he would. I was ready to go back in but that would have made me appear weak. I wasn't weak, but I did love my man. I just hated when he got drunk and no matter how many times I'd been in this same situation I hadn't learned that he wouldn't change.

I'd bet money that most women have been in my shoes rather a little bigger or a little smaller but we've all loved a man a little more than we should have. I had been a victim of love but I didn't want to give it up. I wanted him to love me just as much as I loved him. Was it possible? I don't know, but what I did know was that he cared about me even if it wasn't as much as I cared for him.

I slowly pulled out of the parking spot and began to drive to my mom's house. I was about five minutes into the drive when my cell phone began to ring. I fumbled through my purse while trying to drive at the same time and managed to get it before it stopped.

"Hello?" I said, without even looking at the caller ID. "Babe, where are you?"

"Babe? So now I'm your babe again?"

"Look, I said I was drunk. Now come back home. It's late," he slurred.

"I'm not coming home to be talked to that way again."

"I apologize, okay, just come home so we can go to bed."

"I'll see you tomorrow, Tyson. Go to bed and get sober."

Click.

I hung up, which was one of the hardest things I'd done since I met him. I wanted to go home but I knew that it wouldn't make me feel any better after the argument we'd had. I looked down at the phone and watched him call over and over again. I turned off the phone to avoid the temptation of answering it and being talked into coming home. I continued the drive over to my mom's house and got soaked again trying to run down the block to her door. I used my key to open up the door. The lights were off and the house was quiet. Good, I thought, since I could sneak up to my old room and go to sleep without her even knowing that I was here. I knew that I couldn't avoid talking to her about what happened but at least I could put it off until the morning.

I walked up the steps and almost into the room when I heard her bedroom door opening. Damn, I thought I was going to make it in.

"What are you doing here?" she asked, standing in her robe, wiping her eyes.

"I need to stay here tonight, Mom. I'll leave in the morning."

"Where's Tyson?"

"He's home, Mom, I just need some rest. Can we talk about this in the morning?"

"No, we can talk about it now. What the hell happened?"

"He came in drunk and said some hurtful things, okay? Things that I don't want to repeat."

"Why not?"

"Why the third degree? All I want to do is lay down, rest my brain, and forget about it. Why do I have to go back and forth with you on this?"

"Because it's after eleven at night and you're in here soaking wet in a little-ass dress like you just left the club. That's why," she yelled. She always made things harder than they actually had to be. I didn't understand why I just couldn't come in there and not be questioned. I mean, damn, can I want to visit? I guess not, since she was interrogating me right now.

"I didn't leave the club, I came from home. Can I at least take off these wet clothes first?"

"Go ahead before your ass catch pneumonia. I don't know why you young girls come out in the worst weather with those little-ass clothes on anyway!" she blurted, before turning around and going back into her room. She left the door open, which told me that she wasn't planning on going to sleep without talking to me. I took my time taking off the dress and putting on a T-shirt. I went into her room, where she was sitting up on the bed waiting.

"So, what happened?"

"It was just an argument. We were supposed to go out but he forgot. I sat in the house dressed and waiting on him until he came in drunk with an attitude. It caused an argument and I decided to leave rather than stay there and keep arguing. He needs to get sober and then we can talk."

"If it's one thing that I learned is that you don't walk away for something so silly. If it was just an argument you could have worked it out. I don't know why the first thing you think to do is run. You're going to lose your man like that."

"No, he's going to lose me like that."

"And then what? What are you going to do without him? You don't have the money or the skills to keep up that lifestyle without him," she yelled.

She was only doing what I expected her to do. One thing about my mother was that she was always the same. You pretty much always knew what she was going to say before she said it. I wished that I had somewhere else to go but I didn't. She was right, I didn't have anything without him but shit, neither did she. I remembered the struggle and how I had to work to help her pay the damn bills in here. I didn't want to admit it but I had to go home. I wasn't trying to go back to where I'd been before him.

This life was something that I had become accustomed to. I wasn't going home tonight but tomorrow I would find him and try to get things back in place. I'd be damned if another woman was going to come and take my place. The glamorous life had its downside: you had to fight to keep your place. I had to stop sweating the small stuff and learn how to turn things back around.

Chapter Eleven

Diamond: A Place Called Home

Prison, a place that I'd never thought I would be forced to live. How can a person get comfortable being here?

From the moment I walked through the door and had to strip down ass naked to wash and be searched, I knew glamour was no longer a part of my vocabulary. The jumpsuits were huge and smelled like they'd been washed in the cheapest detergent you could use. I was itching from head to toe just thinking about the fact that someone else had worn it before me and I didn't care how many times it had been washed, I still felt my skin crawl.

The first week was the hardest for me. I cried silently every night, wondering how I could have been so foolish. It took everything in me not to tie knots in the sheets and hang myself. Here I was the pretty girl that once had it all donning an orange jumpsuit and sneakers without shoelaces.

It was embarrassing and I could just see all the bitches in the hood laughing and chanting. Miss Diamond the diva had gotten what was coming to her after all. Was that really the case? Was this what I deserved? I couldn't allow myself to believe that, since I'd probably be worse off if I did.

My cell mate, a woman named Tiny, was eventually my savior. At one of my lowest points she was there to help me get the pep back in my step. I didn't believe that I would ever meet a person who was as foolish as me when it came to men, but she was also locked away because she'd do anything for her man.

It had been a long day and I was exhausted. You never really realize how stress can make you even more tired than you actually are. I lay in bed staring at the ceiling thinking about the time I had left there. Soon tears began to flow, and as quiet as I tried to be I guess that it wasn't quite enough because Tiny heard me even in her sleep.

"Crying isn't going to make your time shorter in here," she said as she sat on the side of her bed.

"Excuse me?" I asked, offended by the comment. Of course I knew that crying wouldn't make my time any shorter, but being there didn't stop me from having feelings either. Shit, I still had feelings.

"I said, crying won't make your time shorter. Nobody cares about your pain in here. All they care about is making you suffer for the crime that you committed."

"Obviously, I realize that or I wouldn't be here," I snapped. I was annoyed. I never asked her for her damn advice.

"Listen little mama, there's no need to get all antsy with me. I'm trying to help you out. Sitting in here depressed is only going to make it worse. You gotta suck it up and deal with it. Shit, this is going to be your home for a while so you may as well make the best of it."

"Make the best of it?" Was she serious? I didn't believe that it was even possible to make the best of a situation like this. I wanted to go home and I'd be damned if I'd get comfortable here.

"Yes, make the best of it. I was just like you when I came in here. I thought that it was the end of the world. Then I realized that I was too young to just give up. Yeah, I made some foolish choices, but I'm smarter than that. I just got caught up with some nigga."

"A nigga, huh. Sounds a lot like me," I replied, surprised that she was even being so honest. She didn't know me from a can of paint. As much as I didn't want to I was getting more relaxed talking to her.

"Shit, that's half of the women in this damn place. None of us saw it coming," she said, lying back down in her bed. "So sleep on it and trust me, in the morning you'll wake up with a new attitude. Do your time, get out, and don't make the same mistake again."

I didn't respond. Instead, I lay there quietly taking it all in. She was right, I couldn't give up. That would prove that he'd won and gotten the best of me after all. There was a time when I would do anything that he wanted me to do. I knew now that I had to be all about me and as selfish as that may sound, there damn sure wasn't anyone else that was going to do it for me.

I woke up the next morning with a new confidence and not even the sloppy-ass food trays we were served could break me down. Before long Tiny and me were the best of friends and I learned a lot from her each day. I think that I clung to her because she'd been there. Though she voluntarily transported drugs for her man, she still could relate to what I'd been through. Her man of five years hadn't stepped up when she got caught, and now she'd have to serve a one-year sentence, leaving her daughter with the man that snitched on her. When I thought that I had it bad, the fact that she had a child made my situation not look as grim. I always wondered how she could be as calm with a child out there to worry about but she was a firm believer in things happening for a reason, and if she wasn't supposed to be here she wouldn't be.

I felt sorry for her and I knew that once I left I would miss our talks. I did promise that we'd keep in touch. I needed a friend like her, someone that would have my back. How did I know this? What's prison without someone trying to test you? I found this out firsthand. After leaving the area where we'd sit and eat we were headed over to the library area. Tiny had been researching her case since the day that she'd been locked away and since I didn't have anything else to do, I helped her out.

Walking down the hall, I didn't notice the stares, but Tiny must have. Soon, I felt something under my feet and I hit the floor. I didn't get a chance to react because Tiny was already all over the girl that had tripped me. The guards came and separated them before hauling them both off to solitary confinement. I later found out that the girl who'd tripped me had been eyeing me since day one. I thought that it had to have been mistaken identity or something because I had never seen her prior to being locked up. Through the grapevine I heard that she and Tiny were once really close and she was pissed that I'd come and taken her place. It was never my intention. I never had any intentions coming in here, not even to survive it.

Either way, this run-in would land Tiny in the hole for two weeks. When they let her out, she looked tired. Tiny was beautiful for a woman with so much fight in her. She stood about five feet eight and appeared to be about a size eight in clothing. She had long hair, which she kept pulled back in a ponytail, showing her round face. Even stripped of glamour you could tell that she was a looker. She hugged me when she entered the cell. I was glad to see her. It was a lonely two weeks.

"Girl, I'm glad to see you. What the hell was that all about, anyway?"

"Doesn't matter, girl, it's over now."

"Well, thanks for having my back."

"No problem, I know you'd do the same for me."

Would I? I guess it was at that moment when I realized that I would. Anyone that would stick their neck out for me would definitely get the same from me. I realized that she would be here long after I'd left but she'd definitely be my friend either way. It took this situation to know where home really was and I was comfortable laying my head down each night knowing she was by my side.

Chapter Twelve

Mica: The Battle Within

"Come on, Deidra, stay with me. I can't lose you now." Tears were pouring out of my eyes as the ambulance driver sped through traffic with his siren on. The paramedic continued to administer CPR but she still wasn't responding. I couldn't lose her. I didn't have a lot of family and she and I had grown close in the past months.

What the hell had happened? I didn't understand how things had gone so wrong. We had planned to hit the town for the night to celebrate D's birthday. She'd promised me that she wouldn't get high that night and instead have a drug-free good time. All I remember is her opening the door and barely standing up straight. She walked away from the door after letting me in and soon fell to the floor. I ran over to her and once I noticed that she was foaming at the mouth I grabbed the phone and dialed 911.

I prayed that this wouldn't be the end. To die on your birthday, how ironic is that? She had been through so much growing up and even as an adult; to just simply die this way didn't seem right. I was losing it, sitting here on this bench clinging to her hand. It was stiff but warm, which gave me hope that she was still holding on.

Though it only took about ten minutes to reach the hospital, it seemed like forever. It was as if everything was moving in slow motion and I was on the outside looking in. She was rushed to the trauma room and I was told to wait in the waiting room. I paced back and forth. I couldn't even think. I hadn't even called Tyson to let him know what was going on. What was I going to say? He didn't like me around her anyway, since he assumed that her bad habits would rub off on me.

I would go up to the window every ten minutes or so to ask about her and each time I was pointed back in the direction of the waiting area. The woman at the counter was obviously annoyed since after a while she stopped speaking and just pointed her fingers instead. I didn't give a fuck about her attitude. That was my cousin dying in there. She was lucky to have the thick bulletproof glass in front of her because I was ready to break that damn finger off. The longer I waited I felt that the prognosis wouldn't be good. Damn, had I just come earlier that day I probably could have swayed her away from using in the first place. After I'd waited for about an hour, someone finally came out and escorted me to the back of the ER. I was nervous as I followed the female doctor in all green scrubs. She was pretty quiet and wouldn't say a word as we walked what seemed like a mile. She took me into a small conference room and shut the door.

"Have a seat," she said, pointing to the green cushioned chairs that matched the ones that I'd been sitting in for the past hour. Once this day was over, I never wanted to see a green chair again in my life. "Deidra is doing much better than when she was brought in so you can relax."

I let out a sigh of relief. I though for sure I would hear the worst. "So what happened?"

"She had a seizure, which was caused by a drug withdrawal. A drug addict's system gets used to the drug and eventually depends on it like our body depends on food and water. When they try to go cold turkey without any help it sometimes has bad effects. The extreme could be what you witnessed today or even worse, death. Luckily, she made it here on time or else she might not have made it."

Was I really hearing her right? Withdrawal? So, D was actually trying to quit? What the hell would make her do that? I knew that my talks with her made a lot of sense to me, but, damn, I hadn't gotten through any other time so there had to be something other than that to make her change so drastically. Either way, I was glad that she made it out okay.

"So what does that mean?"

"She should probably be checked into an inpatient rehab. It's great that she wants to quit but she has to do it the right way. I can give you a list of treatment centers and you could go over them with her and maybe she'll make the right decision."

"When can I see her?"

"You can actually see her right now, she's awake but a little groggy. I'll take you in the back where you can see her."

She led me out to the room where they'd taken D. She smiled when she saw me, I smiled as well. I had never been happier to see her.

"Baby girl, I scared the hell out of you, huh?"

"Scared isn't the word. What the hell were you thinking?"

"I was trying to quit. I know that I'm pretty much all that you have out here in this world, and prior to you showing up on my door that day, I didn't give a damn about life. Now, I care. I care about you a lot. More than you may believe." She grabbed hold of my hand as I sat on the edge of the bed.

I never dreamed that someone would care about me that much. I know some people would think it was bull for a lifelong drug addict to want to change because they love someone, but honestly, I believe it was a combination of loving and being loved at the same time. Her family shut her out and when I came around and showed her how much I cared it helped her see things in a totally different light.

We sat and talked for what seemed like hours. I didn't want to leave but eventually I had to. Once I left I headed home. I was ready for a blowout with Tyson since it was now three AM and I hadn't called him to let him know where I was. As soon as I walked in the living room he began ranting. I damn sure was in no mood for his temper tantrums.

"Where the hell were you?"

"Tyson, please don't start. I've had a very long night and I don't feel like arguing with you."

"Who's arguing? I just asked a damn question. It'll only turn into an argument if you don't answer me."

"Listen, D got sick and I had to call an ambulance to take her to the hospital."

"She got sick? A drug addict? They can handle anything, you expect me to believe that?"

"Yes, I do, because it's the truth. She damn near died, Tyson. If I would have showed up just a few minutes later she might have been gone for good."

"You're real smart, Mica. You deserve a damn Oscar. I'm going out, call me when you're ready to tell me the truth about where you really were all fucking night!"

I didn't respond. I knew that he wouldn't believe me. Most men that are out doing dirt believe that you are doing the same shit, so they never think you're telling the truth. I wasn't out doing dirt—shit, I hadn't did anything wrong since dating him. I cared about him too much to cheat but that shit didn't matter. He was stuck in his own world and it didn't matter what I told him, he still would assume that I was lying. I headed up to bed and after saying a prayer climbed in and got comfortable.

I visited Deidra the next day and told her how foolish Tyson had acted when I came home. She assured me that things would get better. He was probably guilty about something and it would either come to light or pass by. I didn't spend too much time on that topic since I wanted to forget it and focus on her recovery. She decided to go to an inpatient rehab for three weeks and continue the treatment as an outpatient after that. I was happy with that and I felt like things could only go up from that point. She had a three-day hospital stay and checked into the rehab with confidence. It would take a lot of determination to win the battle within, but I planned on helping her every step of the way.

Chapter Thirteen

Diamond: Free to Roam

After my nine-month stay in the Philadelphia Federal Detention Center, I knew that I had to change my life for the better. Looking back, I couldn't figure out how I ended up where I was. I had no family to run to, I had no man or money. I definitely had to get my strategy together to figure out how I was going to get back to the top. I had no access to money and luckily I could stay at Kiki's until I got back on my feet. I had a degree in accounting but had never actually worked anywhere. Davey had always supplied me with more than enough money, so I felt that a job wasn't necessary. I wished now that I had used my brain because now I was in a position that I had never been very fond of. It reminded me of the hard times living at my grandmom's. There were plenty of times that our only source of nourishment was from Oodles of Noodles and Hug juices. Now, you couldn't pay me to eat any of that shit. I'd rather starve than eat anything less than what I felt I deserved. I know that may sound conceited and in my current position some would probably say I should eat whatever the hell I could get my hands on, but that wasn't me.

Kiki loaned me a few dollars to get my hair and nails done. If I was going to go out looking for a new man I had to at least look the part. I headed to the salon that I used to go to on a regular basis before I got locked up and found out just how much things had changed in such a short time. When I walked in everyone instantly got quiet except Gea, my hairdresser, who damn near knocked me down running over to give me a hug.

"Girl, I am so happy to see you. You look good, girl!" she said, looking me up and down.

"What was I supposed to look like?" I said, playfully putting one hand on my hip. I guess people thought that I would come out looking a wreck. I guess I proved them wrong when I walked up in there still clad in designer gear from head to toe. Kiki had managed to gather some of my things from Davey's house when I got locked up and held onto them for me. "I'm glad to be here, girl. I can't wait to get back on my job!" I said, laughing. My job meaning scooping me up a nigga with cash.

All of the girls in the neighborhood had dreams of catching dudes with money like Davey. The problem with most of them was that they appeared too desperate for the money. Niggas weren't going to just give their cash away so if it was too obvious that your main goal was to tap their bank, you would get played in the end. I had mastered the trick of getting their attention and keeping it, but this time around I had to make sure that I didn't fall victim and end up like I had done the last time.

Soon, I was in Gea's chair getting my hair pressed and curled. By then, the crowd in the shop had loosened up and I was getting caught up on all of the gossip.

"Girl, you know Kemp Lo is a free agent now," one girl, said turning her lip up on one side.

"What? He finally let Deja go? I can't believe that. You know the bitches are going to be flocking to him like pigeons all that damn money he got!" another female said, slapping the other one high five and laughing.

My ears instantly became glued to the conversation. Kemp Lo? That was a name that I had never heard, but I was sure interested in hearing it again. I loved a nigga with money and the way they talked about him he seemed like he was just my type. I wanted to ask more about him but I knew that it would seem too obvious if I did. I decided to wait and do some research. I had to know who he was, especially since he was single, which was every reason for me to place myself in his view.

After I left the salon and headed back to Kiki's, I couldn't ask her fast enough if she knew who Kemp was.

"Kemp Lo, yeah, I know him. Why?" she asked, washing dishes and glancing at the television.

"I heard them talking about him in the salon today and I wanted to know who he was."

"Girl, when are you going to learn, these hustlers don't mean you no good. Wasn't nine months in jail bad enough?"

"What the hell else am I going to do? I have a record now, so getting a good job is out of the question. I need to get back on top, Kiki, and that's the only way that I know how," I replied. That was the only way I knew how to be on top. I knew how to be on the bottom too, and I wasn't trying to stay there for too much longer.

She looked at me for a few seconds before speaking, probably wondering how a girl as smart as me could be so stupid. She turned off the faucet and took a seat at the kitchen table and lit a cigarette. Taking a puff of her Newport, she began revealing the information that I was desperate to hear.

"Kemp Lo is a major hustler, I mean *major*. Not a lot of females even get him to look their way. He used to deal with a girl named Deja, last I heard. They have a child together too that he spoils to death. It's a rumor that Kemp has millions in a safe buried somewhere. People only speculate where it is but no one's ever found it. He's fine as hell for sure and he commands everyone's attention when he walks into a room. Now, I've also heard that he's abusive, so I wouldn't run to jump in his bed if I were you. I mean, you've been through enough ups and downs with that other asshole. I know that I can't stop you from dealing with him if that's what you want to do, but don't ever say I didn't warn you. You are my girl and I want to see you happy. I never want to see you in a situation like the one you just got out of."

"I know, Kiki, and believe me, I don't want to be in another fucked-up relationship either. I was real naive with Davey, but this time I'm on my game. This isn't about finding love, it's about finding money. I need to get me enough money so I can make it on my own. It's just a stepping stone, Kiki. I promise you I won't end up like I did the last time," I said, grabbing hold of her hand. I appreciated her warnings, and trust me, I took heed to them. I knew what I needed to do, and I was so focused on it. I didn't plan on falling in love. For me, that wasn't an option.

"I believe you, girl, but I need you to be careful, okay? Don't get yourself hurt."

"I won't, girl. I promise."

I needed to find him just to see what all the fuss was about. I planned on following him around until I figured out a way to get close to him. I was beautiful, but there were a lot of beautiful women out there, so the key was to get his attention and make him believe that I was the one he needed to be with. I didn't think it was going to be too hard, but I was soon going to find out.

I followed him for weeks. It didn't matter where he went, I made sure I was watching from a distance. Some would probably think that I was crazy, but I had to do my research before I stepped into any situation. I wasn't about to go into it blind like I had done before. I wasn't going to get fooled. Kiki thought I was nuts for what I was doing, but since she was usually the voice of reason, what she said went in one ear and out the other. I wasn't in the state of mind for reasoning since I had my eye on the prize. I just had to keep my eyes wide open and not fall in love like I'd done in the past.

I had done it without being noticed until one day I headed into the barbershop where he got his hair cut. I was bold this particular day because I wanted him to see. I was sure that he'd seen me around on other occasions, but I wanted him to at least get a close-up. I found a local promoter who had an event coming up and needed some help with promotion. I was eager to help since passing out his flyers and posters would make it less obvious that I was everywhere that Kemp was. Dressing up and hitting the streets was a guaranteed way to get in a hustler's view. Most girls used this method, but the difference between them and me was that I was going to get more than a fuck. Most guys felt like the women who tried too hard to get their attention were only good for sex anyway. Philly was party central, and if you wanted to meet a baller you had to get out into the nightlife. It just took a little skill to snag the right one without seeming too obvious. Me, I wouldn't make it obvious, and once I got his attention it would be all over.

I put on the shortest pair of shorts that I owned and a tight tank top with some heels. Yes, heels. I wasn't really going to be walking around in them all day but just long enough to catch his eye. I walked in to Big D's barbershop with a stack of flyers and a few posters in my hand. As soon as I walked in of course every eye was on me, including Kemp's. I went over to D's chair and asked if it was okay for me to leave the flyers and put a couple of posters in the window. Once he agreed I put on my model strut to place the flyers on the counter. I even walked up to every man in there and put one in their hands. I stood in front of Kemp just a few seconds longer so he could get a whiff of the perfume that I was wearing. He slowly lifted his hand to take the flyer from me.

"Are you going to be here at this party? If so, I'll make sure I'm there!" He laughed, looking down at the flyer.

"Most likely I will be."

He smiled. "Good, hope to see you there."

"Count on it," I said, returning a smile and heading toward the door.

Damn, I thought for sure that he would have tried to put a move on me, but I guess since he was in front of all these guys he had to keep it basic. I didn't care; I knew I would get him eventually. It was just going to take a little longer than I thought.

The week went fast and it was party time. I felt so good going out. The nine months that I spent locked away felt like an eternity. Now that I was free to roam I was going to party like there was no tomorrow. I had to enjoy myself. Shit, I deserved it after all I'd been through.

The party was at a club called ICE, and Kiki was able to hang out with me. I was excited about going with the hopes that I would run into Kemp there. The party was packed and the line outside was damn near curving around the corner. Luckily, we knew the bouncer and were able to skip it. I might have contemplated leaving if I'd had to wait in that long-ass line. We squeezed through the crowd and made our way to the bar. It was like pulling teeth to get the bartenders' attention. Niggas were so rude, damn near pushing us out of the way to get their drinks. I was getting annoyed, and if I didn't get a drink soon to mellow me out I would probably be on my way back out of the door.

I felt an arm reaching over my shoulder and I was ready to lose it. I turned around and had a shocked look on my face when I saw that it was Kemp. I hoped the look wasn't too obvious, but figured it probably was since he started laughing.

"Damn, did you see a ghost or something?" He continued to laugh.

"No, it's just too crowded in here and I'm getting annoyed because the bartenders are acting like we are invisible," I yelled in his ear over the loud music.

"I feel you, but if y'all want to come over in VIP we're popping bottles over there."

A tall, thin-framed guy came up behind him and tapped him. He turned around and the guy told him something that quickly made him walk away without even turning back around to me. I was pissed. Damn, I hadn't even gotten a chance to tell him my name. I grabbed Kiki and tried to make it over to the VIP area, and when we peeked in we noticed that Kemp and his friends were all gone.

"Damn, where did they go?"

"Girl, I don't know. You said someone came and told him something. Something must have gone wrong if they all just picked up and left."

I pouted and Kiki laughed. I didn't find it funny. I knew now that I had to get more creative if I wanted to make it happen. Just being in his eyesight wasn't enough.

"Stop looking like a sad puppy." She continued to laugh.

"I'm upset, girl. I thought that this was going to be my chance."

"You'll get your chance, D. Things happen when they are supposed to."

I knew that what she said was true but I wasn't a true believer in that saying. I always believed that the go-getters were the ones that had it all. You weren't going to get shit if you just sat back all the time and waited for things to happen because "they happen when they are supposed to." I felt like things happened when you took the initiative to make them happen. Either way, I knew that I had gotten his attention, even if only for a few seconds.

Kiki and I stayed at the club until it closed. I was so drunk but I had fun, which was something else that I hadn't done in a long time. We went back to her house and as soon as my head hit the pillow I could feel myself drifting off into la-la land. Tomorrow was going to be a better day and I went to sleep satisfied with that.

Chapter Fourteen

Mica: That Old Thing

"Babe, come on, if we don't get down there early enough we won't get a good seat," I yelled loud enough so that Tyson could hear me.

"I'm coming," he yelled, before coming down the steps. We were headed down to South Street to the Laugh House, a comedy club that had stand-up Thursdays. I loved to get a seat early because I'd be damned if I was going to walk into a comedy show late so they could talk about me. Comedians were good for that. I wasn't trying to be the butt of anyone's jokes. I was excited about hanging out with Tyson. Since our last fight things had gotten back on track and we were closer than ever. He said that he wanted to do something special because it was our one-year anniversary. It seemed like yesterday that I met him and fell in love with him.

We got down to the show just before it started and made it in without incident. I felt relieved. The comedians kept me laughing all night. I was practically rolling on the floor at their jokes. I needed to laugh—they say laughter is good for the soul.

I remembered growing up and not having a lot to laugh about. Since my dad was always drunk, cussing and fussing all the time we never really got the chance to be a close family.

I can admit that I was damaged. It wasn't something I was proud of, but I knew it was the reason that I wasn't confident enough to do things on my own. I felt like I needed a man, and I didn't really know why. It could have been the fact that my mother went crazy after my father was gone. Was it the loss of my father that sent her into depression or was it simply the fact that she didn't have a man to take care of her anymore? I never wanted people to think that I couldn't do for myself, but it was reality.

Since things were going good between Tyson and me I wasn't going to jinx it and think that something bad was going to happen. I wanted to look at the future and be confident that things could only go up from here.

The show was over around ten o'clock and we went back home. Tyson told me to wait five minutes before coming in the house. I laughed because he was actually trying to be romantic. Romance wasn't his department, but if he could pull this off it would impress me.

"Five minutes, I'm trying not to stay out here alone," I said, trying to hurry it up.

"Babe, I'm trying to do something special here. You always say that I'm not romantic. Five minutes won't kill you." He smiled.

His smile warmed my heart, so much so that I agreed. I wasn't really trying to stay outside alone, but he was right, five minutes to get to ecstasy wasn't going to kill me. I watched him walk inside and instantly began watching the seconds on my watch like a hawk. Five short minutes seemed like an eternity but once the time was up I ran up to the door like it was the half-off sale at David's Bridal.

As I walked up to the door I could hear the music playing along with the flickering of candlelight shining through the window. As I slowly opened the door, the lavender aroma tickled my nose, immediately sending chills up and down my spine. I took off my shoes at the door so I could feel the plush carpet underneath my tired feet. A pink piece of paper caught my attention and I made my way over to the table to retrieve it. The note simple read: *Take off your clothes*. I didn't waste any time obeying and after I was naked I wondered what to do next. I didn't see any more notes posted so I slowly wandered through the house trying to find the next clue. Once I noticed the trail of rose petals leading to the bathroom I knew exactly where to go. The lights were dim and as I entered the room there was another note sitting on the table next to the sink that read: *Get in*. I smiled as I set the note back down next to the plate of chocolate-covered strawberries and two champagne flutes filled to the brim on a sliver serving tray. I thought, *Damn, he's really trying to show off.* He hadn't done anything this nice since we'd been together. I was enjoying it tremendously and I hadn't even seen him yet. I eased into the tub full of hot water that soothed my body. I hoped that I wouldn't fall asleep and ruin his plans since the water felt so good against my skin. I sat in the water and before closing my eyes Tyson appeared with a towel around his waist.

"Baby, this is—" I tried to speak but he quickly bent down to kiss me. His lips were soft as silk and I was eager to feel them on the sensitive parts of my body. He grabbed a sponge and after lathering it up with soap he made slow circles on my back. Though he'd washed my back for me many times, it had never felt so good.

I didn't say a word but instead let him lead. After washing my entire body he grabbed me by the hand and as I stepped out of the tub the excess water trickled down my body. He stood back and licked his lips as he watched the glow my wet figure had. I could sense how bad he wanted to taste me and I couldn't wait until he was able to get his wish. He grabbed a towel from the cabinet and started to dry me off after I stepped out of the tub. My nipples stood at attention as he brushed past them. We walked into the bedroom where the bed was also covered with rose petals. He grabbed a strawberry off of the serving tray that he had carried from the bathroom and after I lay across the bed he kissed my lips with it. The chocolate melted instantly from the heat of my body. He moved close to me and licked the few drops off of my lips.

He began to suck on my erect nipples, causing my body to shiver. His tongue continued to caress them as his fingers found their way to my clit. He made circles on it, quickly causing my already juicy mound to explode. He used his thick tongue to move in and out of my tunnel. He pushed my legs up in the air so that my ass lifted off of the bed just enough to create a wider opening. He ate my pussy for what seemed like an eternity, giving me so much pleasure. After my body shook uncontrollably he knew his mission was complete. He sat up, and as I watched him lick my juices from his lips I prepared myself to satisfy him the same as he'd done me.

He removed the towel that he had around his waist, revealing his hard dick. I couldn't wait to taste it. I motioned for him to lie down on the bed. I looked into his eyes as I moistened the head of his dick. Both of us were in heaven, and I enjoyed the taste of his pre-cum running down my throat. I used my fingertips to massage his balls as I licked his shaft and watched his body begin to tremble. I contracted my cheek muscles and moved up and down his thick member. As the head met my tonsils, I used my deep-throating skills to satisfy him the best way that I knew how. While my throat muscles massaged the head, my hands massaged his balls. Soon I could feel the hot cum shooting down my throat, and I swallowed it with ease. I continued to suck wildly as his knees trembled. I refused to let go, and within minutes his once semi-soft member was hard as a rock and ready to meet my hot, juicy tunnel.

I quickly straddled him, slowly easing him into my tight pussy, and a moan escaped him. I moved back and forth with my hands on his muscular chest. The excitement had me sweating, which got me moving faster. I was riding him like a winning racehorse. My prize would be an electrifying orgasm, and as I felt his dick begin to pulsate I decreased my speed to tap my clit with each stroke. Soon I grabbed ahold of his hands as we exploded together.

We had gotten that old thing back that I missed and I wanted to pause this moment, hoping that things wouldn't ever change.

Chapter Fifteen

Diamond: Fly like Me

Boom.

I held my breath, hoping this would go the way that I had planned. I had run Kiki's car into the back of Kemp's brand-new Mercedes-Benz GL-Class truck. I only tapped it enough to cause him to stop. I didn't really want to do any damage. Kemp's door flew open and I saw the anger in his face. I was almost afraid to get out of the car, but sitting there wouldn't get me any closer to him.

"What the fuck, your brakes don't work?" he yelled, walking toward the back of his car to see what damage had been done.

I nervously got out of the car, adjusted my mini-skirt, and began walking toward him. "I am so sorry; I almost dropped a hot cup of coffee on my leg. I tried to stop, I'm really sorry." I batted my eyelashes as I bent down to look at the back of his truck, which only had a tiny scratch on it. I made sure to reveal as much leg as possible while he stood in back of me.

He changed his tone. "It's cool, ma. You only scratched it a little." I knew that I had him right where I wanted him. "What's your name?"

"Diamond," I replied, standing up and focusing all of my attention on him.

"If you were anybody else, I would have snapped. I didn't expect a beautiful woman like you to be behind the wheel. My name is Kemp. It's nice to meet you, Diamond," he spoke, reaching his hand out to shake mine. His hands were smooth as a baby's butt and his nails were perfectly manicured. I smiled, waiting for what he would say next. "You hang out with that girl Kiki, right?"

"Yeah, that's like my big sister."

"I know, I've been seeing you a lot lately. Are you new to the hood?"

"No, I was away for a little while. I just came back."

"Well look, do you have a number I can reach you at? I'd love to finish up this conversation but I have some business to take care of."

"Yeah, I do," I said, grabbing his cell phone out of his hand to put my number in. He looked at me with a grin that could make you melt. I was getting moist just thinking about spending time with him. "I hope to hear from you soon," I said, as I gave the phone back to him.

"Trust me, you will. Keep looking sexy like that and you won't be able to get rid of me." He licked his lips and smiled, heading toward his car.

I turned to walk away and put on a switch as I did to make sure he would really make that call. Shit, if he didn't I would have to find another way to get his attention. I was determined to be the next woman on his arm and the more I was warned about him the more that I wanted to get next to him. I knew that most people would think I was crazy, especially looking at the situation that I had just gotten out of. I wasn't crazy; I was just a girl with a goal, a goal to be on top and not let anyone take me under.

I headed back to Kiki's to tell her my good news. I knew she wouldn't be all that amused, but hell, I was ecstatic. I was so close to that success that I could taste it. Once I got to her place I found her cleaning up the kitchen while singing to a music video on BET. You couldn't tell her anything when it came to singing. Kiki thought she was Mary J. Blige, Faith Evans, and Beyoncé all wrapped up in one. Quiet as it's kept, she couldn't sing a lick, but I refused to break her spirit.

"Hey girl, I got some good news, bad news, and some more good news to make up for the bad news," I said, turning down the volume on the television so that she could give me her undivided attention.

"This better be good since you're interrupting my jam," she said, laughing.

"Okay, first I ran into Kemp Lo today and I think that I've caught his eye."

"Who says that's good news?" she replied, sarcastically.

"Me, of course, but I ran into the back of his car today and—"

"With my car?" She turned, looking at me in shock without letting me finish up the sentence that I had started.

"Yes, but it only has a few scratches. The other good news is that he has my number and he's going to call me. So once he gets a whiff of this girl, he'll be like putty in my hand and if the money is like everyone claims, I'll be able to buy you a new car!"

"Really, what makes you think that he won't treat you just like everyone else?" she asked, not impressed with my hopes.

"Because I'm Diamond and he's never had a bitch like me," I laughed, as I took a seat on the stool. "He won't be able to do nothing but treat me like a queen once he gets a taste. I stand by that shit, one hundred percent."

"Well, I hope that it works out for you, because I could use a new car." She joined in my laughter, while slapping me a high five.

I knew that she wanted me to be happy and probably deep down hoped that things would go my way. I promised myself that I would never be hurt again so going into this I was at a different place mentally then I had ever been with relationships.

I hadn't heard from Kemp following the accident. Three weeks had passed and I was beginning to get nervous that he might have found someone else. I had to find out where he would be so that I could get in his eye view again. I wasn't trying to be a stalker or anything; I simply called it keeping my eye on the prize.

So, once again I was on the hunt and again it paid off. I found out that he was going to a Sixers game on Wednesday of that week. Of course he had box seats so I had to see how the hell I could get some to even get up to the area where the doors were. Kiki was able to talk to a friend of hers that worked down at the Wachovia Center to get me a pass to go down to the box-seat level. What the hell was I doing? Was I going overboard? No, I snapped back to reality. I wasn't going overboard, I was doing what I had to do and I didn't really care what anybody thought.

Once I gained access to the level of the boxes I had to look for the one that was his. The Wachovia Center was pretty big so I had to damn near walk around the entire circle before I found it.

As I slowly walked past the door that led to his box I prayed that someone would walk out. Unfortunately, no one did. There was a guy standing outside of the door who I assumed was a guard. I headed over to him and took a chance; the worst thing that could happen was that he would turn me away. I could hear the chants from inside the box the closer that I got to the door. I prayed that Kemp didn't have a female with him inside because that would completely crush my plans.

"Excuse me, but is this Kemp's box?" I asked, batting my eyelashes and trying to look as irresistible as possible.

"Yeah, why?" he responded with a dry tone.

"I'm here in a box down the way and I just wanted to say hi to him if that's possible."

"Well, he doesn't like being interrupted while watching the game."

"I'm sure if you tell him that it's me he won't mind," I responded, hoping that what I just said was true. "My name is Diamond, could you just tell him that I'm out here?"

He looked me up and down for a few seconds before responding, "Wait right here." He opened up the door and quickly closed it behind him.

I stood patiently and waited for him to emerge. To my surprise Kemp appeared instead of the guard. I smiled when I saw his face.

"What's up, sexy? How did you know I was here?" he said, reaching out to give me a hug.

I gladly accepted the hug and held onto him as long as I could. "Everybody knows you're here. I just wanted to stop by and say hi. You never did make that phone call that you promised."

"I know, I've been busy as hell but I will. You want to come hang out inside?"

"I wish I could but I'm here with some friends. I just wanted to say hi and see your face again."

"See my face, huh? You sure that's all you wanted to do?"

"Well, that's all I want to do at the moment," I said, putting my head down, trying to avoid eye contact. He was turning me on but I couldn't let it be too obvious.

"You don't have to be shy with me, tell me what you really want," he said, moving so close to me I could feel his breath on my forehead.

"What I really want is to see what you have that drives all the women wild."

"You sure about that?" he asked, as he gently touched my chin to raise my head.

"I'm positive." I looked him in the eye. *What the hell was I getting myself into?* I thought as we stood so close I could feel the heat from his body. Without saying another word he grabbed me by the hand and walked toward the door. He looked back at me before opening it. I still didn't know what he planned to do but I went along with it. The room was full of guys. I was nervous once they all turned to look in our direction. After only a few seconds of staring they all turned their attention on the game. He led me toward the small bathroom in the corner of the room and closed the door behind us. I still was silent. I was wearing a knee-length dress and shirt that generously showed my cleavage. Kemp picked me up and sat me on the sink where he moved close, tilted my head to the side, and began to kiss my neck. How he knew that was my spot, I'll never know but I did know that I instantly became wet when he made contact. My nipples were as hard as a rock peering through my shirt. Just the feeling of him rubbing against them made me tingle all over as I tried not to make enough noise to be heard through the door. His hands made their way down to my underwear that he quickly removed and got back in position, paying close attention to my neck. His thick fingers were now massaging my wet pussy down below.

"Damn, this pussy is wet," he said, as he slid two fingers inside of me. I was about to explode but I didn't want to waste it all over his fingers. I'd rather cum all over his tongue or his dick for that matter. I held onto it as he fingerfucked me and continued licking my neck at the same time. I tried to rub his dick through his jeans but he wouldn't let me. I loved a man to take control. In one motion he dropped his pants and put on a condom. I didn't even know where the hell he got it from, he was so quick. Before I could even think about it his dick was filling my walls from end to end. He grabbed me lightly around my neck and fucked me with force. I loved the rough shit from time to time so this definitely excited me. I grabbed ahold of his ass to force him all the way inside of me, making sure to hit my G-spot. My legs were wrapped around him, not wanting to let go.

"You like this shit?"

"Yes," I moaned. I more than liked it, I fucking loved it. His dick was perfect, the right length, girth, and curve. Who could ask for anything more? I was in heaven as he continued to move in and out of me. I was trying to keep my ass from falling into the sink and keep his dick tightly nestled in my pussy where it belonged.

He continued to fuck me like there was no tomorrow, and I was in a trance, enjoying the strokes that he delivered. My hands were cuffed around his neck. I could feel the muscles flexing as he continued to move in and out of me. It wasn't long before his body was shaking and we were both having orgasms in sync.

"So where do we go from here?" he asked.

I was surprised by that question. I didn't know what to say. I knew what I wanted to happen at this point, but I wasn't sure what he wanted. As I got up off the sink and began to fix my clothes, I looked up at him and replied, "Depends on you. You like to fly coach or first class?"

He looked at me and smiled. "A nigga like me only goes first class."

"Well, in that case, we can work something out 'cause I'm a fly bitch. You ain't gonna find another chick like me." He laughed. I was dead serious. I was dressed by then and looked in the mirror to make sure my hair was straight. I couldn't go out of the door looking crazy because they'd know for sure what we had been doing in there. He said he would call later on that night. I was smiling from ear to ear as we headed out of the bathroom and toward the door of the box. The guys inside just looked and smiled; they knew what was up. I walked out of there with confidence because I knew that after that sample he just had, he'd definitely call. Who could turn down a girl like me?

That night I did get the phone call that he promised and after that day we spent all of his free time together. I never thought that he would be the type that cared or showed his feelings, but he surprised me everyday. The more I tried not to care about him the more I did. He was hard to resist and I was losing sight of the reason I sought out after him in the first place. I learned a lot about him but the most important thing I learned was how much he was really worth and where he kept his money. I guess he felt comfortable telling me all of this. Why, because I made him love me. I did everything perfect. He sometimes thought that I was too perfect but I knew better.

I moved in with him about three months after we were together and I was happy to have a permanent place to stay. Things hadn't gone so good for me since getting out of jail, so he was making my life enjoyable. Besides the occasional hood rat calling and yelling obscenities we didn't really have too many problems. Things were good for us and I felt like I was finally where I belonged.

Chapter Sixteen

Mica: Risky Business

I had just gotten four brand-new tires on my car because they were slashed. I was pissed when I walked outside to find them all slashed again. *Who the fuck is doing this?* I knew that it was probably one of Tyson's groupies trying to make a point. I wasn't afraid, but I was pissed and whoever it was better hope that I didn't find them because it was definitely going to be a confrontation.

I had shit to do and this was an inconvenience. I went back into the house to call Tyson and tell him I needed his car for the day. His cell phone kept ringing and going to voice mail. Soon the phone started ringing but it was a blocked number. I started not to answer it but I did just in case it was Tyson calling me back.

"Hello!" I yelled into the receiver

"Guess you can't go anywhere without wheels, huh?" the female on the other end burst into laughter.

"Who the fuck is this?"

"Ask your man, he just got through licking my pussy too so you may not want to kiss him unless you like eating pussy too!" She continued to laugh.

"Listen bitch, you can keep flattening the tires; it won't make him leave me. You have to come a little harder than that."

"Harder is not a problem, bitch, and don't be so sure about him staying there. He said that you can't fuck anyway!"

"Whatever, you need to grow up whoever the fuck you are. Just know, bitch, you are just another number. He has tons of groupies but I'm the first lady. Have a nice day, bitch!" I said before hanging up.

The phone rang over and over again until I picked it up again, and this time it was Tyson so I was ready to give him an earful.

"Babe, what's going on?"

"What's going on? You have a groupie out here that thinks it's funny to keep flattening my fucking tires."

"What?"

"Yeah, the bitch just called, I just changed the fucking tires last week. If you're gonna cheat, Tyson, keep these bitches in their place!"

"Mica, I don't know who the hell that was."

"I don't know, she didn't say her name and she called from a blocked number. I need you to come home and bring me your car. I have things to do."

"So do I, Mica. I can't come home right now."

"Well, what am I supposed to do? You need to figure something out, it's your fault that this is happening. If you stop lying to these bitches and tell them you have a girl maybe they wouldn't expect more from you."

"Come on now, don't nobody be lying to these bitches. I can't stop them from doing crazy shit. I don't even know who it is."

"You're fucking that many people that you can't narrow it down to one?"

"You're taking this in a whole different direction."

"Well, how about I help you narrow it down, she said that you just got through licking her pussy so unless you eat pussy for a living now, I'm sure you know who it is. How about you get me a fucking car and take care of that bitch!" *Click.*

I hung up and screamed. I was so pissed. I was even more pissed that he tried to act like he didn't know what the fuck I was talking about. He knew good and goddamn well who he'd fucked. I stood in the living room pacing back and forth. I was close to calling him back but I knew that he probably wouldn't answer the phone anyway. I swear if he had been standing there at that very moment I would've smacked his ass. To me having a relationship should follow the same rules as drug dealing. No female should ever be able to infiltrate the home structure. If it's possible, then the structure is weak.

I had gotten used to the fact that he cheated. Shit, all men did. What I wasn't going to stand for was more disrespect. I couldn't stand when a female on the outside had so much control over what we had.

After about an hour he came home. I was sitting on the sofa staring at the TV. He looked at me without speaking and threw his car keys on the table.

"Happy now?"

"Happy? What the hell is wrong with you? I don't understand how you can have an attitude. I didn't do anything to you."

"I don't have an attitude, I just don't feel like arguing. I brought you the keys and the car so you can go do whatever the hell you had to do that is so important. Tim is towing the car and they'll put the tires on today. I'll bring the car back when they're done."

"You do have an attitude," I replied, knowing full well he was upset. "It shouldn't be directed at me; it should be on that bitch that flattened the tires."

"I took care of that already so you don't have to keep fussing about it. You'll get the car back later." He turned to head back out the door.

"That is not what this is about, Tyson. I don't understand why you don't feel like I deserve respect."

"I never said that and I already said I took care of it. This conversation is over, I'm out," he responded before leaving and slamming the door.

How was it that each time we fought he always tried to turn the focus on me like I did something wrong? I was never the one to blame, but he tried his best to make it appear that way. I've never cheated—or even thought about it, for that matter— but he had done it so many times that I lost count. Why is it that when a man gets caught doing wrong they can't just fess up to it and apologize or try to make it better? I believed that Tyson's method of covering up his wrongdoings wasn't to lie but merely to make you forget what the hell you were angry about.

I can't say that I blamed him, but I just wished that things with us would run a little smoother. I didn't want to fight, I didn't want the women calling my phone, and I didn't want us to break up. I wanted things to get better, but our ups and downs were like the tracks on a roller coaster. With us, everything happened so fast, things got good really fast and went bad even faster. So, there I was at the same place that I had been so many times before. Angry that I let myself get so upset about something that I expected to happen anyway. Was I a fool for that? I guess so.

I went out to the driveway and got into his car. I had to go check up on Deidra to make sure that things were still on the up-and-up. I hadn't been over to see her in a week or so and it was about time for a visit. I never wanted too much time to pass for fear that she'd fall back off the wagon. I noticed Money hanging out on the same corner that he always hung out on. He really needed to get a life. I mean, even the small-time hustlers didn't hang on the corner all day anymore. Things had gotten more sophisticated than they were back in the day. So, I didn't understand why he still stood out here all day. I laughed as he looked over at me when I got out of the car. I thought it was hilarious.

"What's so funny?" he asked, stepping away from his post. If I didn't know any better I'd think he was a permanent fixture for the Puerto Rican store.

"You, you're always on that corner. I know your legs get tired," I said, laughing again.

"You got jokes, huh? Girl, I'm a hustler. I gotta watch my block. A lot of these young niggas will test you. I can't have my shit go up in smoke."

"Really, so you're not just trying to look cute?" I joked.

"Cute? Shit, I ain't gotta try to look cute. That shit comes naturally like that fat ass you got."

I continued to laugh at his charm. I must admit, he was pretty good-looking. For some reason it brought back memories of my crush as I was growing up. Was it because I was mad at Tyson? Hell, I didn't know what it was, but I wished that I would have sooner because he was definitely someone I wouldn't mind taking a look at every day. I laughed at myself. A girl can think some crazy things sometimes.

"Well, then I guess we are two of the lucky ones, huh?"

"I guess so, but we'd be even luckier if we hook up on some real shit."

"If I wasn't already attached to someone I would probably take you up on that offer."

"What your man don't know won't hurt him. I'm a nigga that knows how to play the background."

"Really?" I asked. I didn't believe that he could play the background. I didn't believe that any man could. Men talk the game but as soon as they get some and start feeling you they lose control.

"Really. What, you don't believe me?"

"I didn't say that, but that's a little risky for me."

"Why, are you scared of your man or something?"

"No, I'm not scared of him, but I'm happy," I lied. I wasn't happy at the moment, that was for sure.

"It's cool, ma, I'm not trying to pressure you but if you ever change your mind you know where to find me."

He walked away and waved. Of course I knew where to find him. It wasn't like I had to go really far. I laughed again, just thinking about my earlier jokes. I would definitely keep him in mind if things didn't work out with me and Tyson. Even though I planned on staying with him, you can never really be too sure about the future. I headed to Deidra's door and knocked a few times. She peeked out of the door before taking off the chain lock and opening it.

"Girl, why don't you ever call me when you're on your way over?"

"Why? Then I wouldn't be able to catch you in the act."

"The act of what?"

"I'm just playing. What's up, though, how's the program going?"

"It's going, you know the only reason I'm going is because of you."

"I know, and I appreciate it. I just want you to get better. I need the old Deidra back," I said, laughing.

"I know, girl; don't worry, you will. I'm positive you're going to make sure of that."

I stayed over her house for about an hour before I decided to head back home. I gave Money one more wave before I got into the car. I almost thought about taking his number but I decided not to. I couldn't let temptation screw things up. It was a well-known fact that when in a relationship and things go bad we quickly migrate to someone else that can make you feel good in that time of need. I didn't want to fall victim to the risky business of having an affair. It would take too much energy. More energy than I was interested in using. Especially for a guy who lived the same lifestyle as the man I was with. He would probably do exactly the same things Tyson did. Either way, I'd probably end up unhappy and fighting to keep things stable. Was it even really worth it?

Chapter Seventeen

Diamond: Down the Aisle

I couldn't believe what I was getting myself into. Here I was about to do something that I promised myself I wouldn't do. I was on my way down to city hall to marry Kemp. Why? Shit, I'd be a millionaire if I could answer that question. We had only been together for six months, but he felt that the only way to keep this relationship together was to jump the broom. It didn't take a lot of convincing, since I wanted to keep the life that I had with him. I couldn't tell him no and risk losing him. So, the night that he crawled into bed, wrapped his arms around me, and whispered in my ear "marry me" all I could say was okay. Yeah, I might be a little crazy and even though I wasn't trying to be tied down to anyone I felt that I had to. How would I say no and convince him to stay with me? With so many women on his heels I was positive that he could pick up and leave when he got ready. I felt like the only way to keep him tied to me at this point was to marry him.

We took Kiki and his friend Black with us as witnesses. I decided not to dress up in white since to me there wasn't anything traditional about this courtship. I had always dreamed that the day I got married I would walk down the aisle with a twelve-foot train, the kind you only see on TV, and have my father standing by my side. My father, yeah, this made me think of him. I know that he wasn't my biological father but he was the only father that I knew. I could remember the day that I found out that I was adopted. I could never forget that day. I had just come home after school, starving. I had decided to play at recess a little while longer and skip lunch. As it neared the end of the day I knew that it was a mistake. I felt like my stomach was barking at my back. I ran in the house hoping that I could find a sandwich or something. I didn't even notice my mother sitting on the sofa but once I settled down I heard sobs. I looked into the living room where she was sitting with a letter in one hand and tissue in the other.

"Mom, what's wrong? Were you and Daddy fighting again?" I asked, kneeling down next to her. Fighting was something that I was used to. There had been many nights I couldn't sleep listening to them argue.

"I have something that I need to talk to you about, baby. Come over here and sit down for a minute."

"Mom, what's going on?" I didn't like the sound of what she said. I was preparing myself for the worst. Even at ten years old I knew that it didn't sound good.

"You are so special to me and I don't ever want you to think any different." She put her hand under my chin so that I could look her in the eye.

"I know that, Mom," I said, smiling. I was still trying to figure out what the hell was going on.

"Baby, I'm not your biological mother. You were adopted."

"Adopted?" I had to say the word out loud to hear it again myself. I knew what the word meant but it couldn't possibly pertain to me. How could she not be my real mom? I looked just like her or at least I had psyched myself up to believe that I did. To me, this seemed like the end. Was I being shipped away or something? Why would she be telling me this now? And what were the tears for? My mind was going a hundred miles a minute. I didn't know what to say.

"Yes, baby, you're adopted, but that doesn't mean that I don't care about you and love you like I gave birth to you."

"So what are you saying, you're giving me away or something?" A tear escaped the well of my eye. I was nervous. I thought for sure that this was the end of life the way that I knew it. Well, actually it was. It didn't matter what her answer was, my life was a lie.

"No baby, I'm not giving you away. You are my daughter."

"So why now, why did you have to tell me now?"

"Your father is filing for divorce."

"What? Divorce?" I knew the definition of this word too but I had to repeat it. I just wanted to eat. I never expected to come home to this. Just that morning my dad kissed me good-bye and gave me a long hug. Then I thought about it; the hug was longer than usual. It was as if I would never see him again. Was that the case? Was he telling me good-bye for good and not until he got off work? I got up off the floor and ran to my parents' room. I opened the drawers and found all of his empty. I looked in the closet and only saw my mother's things hanging. Did I miss something? Just the night before we had sat at the table and eaten dinner together, and today all of his things were gone and he was filing for divorce.

My mother came in the room and wrapped her arms around me from behind. I couldn't hold in the tears any longer. I wanted to leave the house, go back to school, and try this again. This couldn't be true.

"I'm so sorry, Diamond, but he's gone. He's not coming back."

"He has to, Mom, he just has to." I still didn't want to believe that what she was saying was true. I felt like I was losing it. I couldn't imagine my life without my dad. Who would fight off the boys? Who would be there to watch football with me on Sundays? That's not a mother's job. Besides, my mother wasn't strong enough to do both jobs. I cried the rest of the night and fell to sleep hoping that I would wake up the next morning and he'd be waiting for me at the breakfast table. Knowing that I was adopted wasn't as bad to swallow, since that meant that they really wanted me if they would take the responsibility of someone else's child. I didn't care who my real parents were; it didn't matter. I wanted my daddy back. Unfortunately, my wishes would fall on deaf ears because that morning was the last time that I had seen my father. I didn't even know where to look for him. I wanted to find him and tell him that he had to come back. Sadly, I never got that opportunity.

So there I was, standing in front of this judge, Kiki, and Black, about to marry a man I didn't even know too much about. Was I afraid of losing him like I'd lost my dad years ago? Deep down did I blame myself for my father's departure? I guess I did. I had to hold on to what was mine.

The ceremony was short and sweet and we walked out of there husband and wife. We didn't even have any of our relatives there. I had never even met his mother and shit, I couldn't find mine to introduce him since she was too busy getting high. Even though I wasn't really in love, I was happy. Happy that I had a man that would marry me to keep me and one that was more than capable of taking care of me. I left city hall with a huge smile on my face and butterflies in my stomach.

We all left and Kemp took us over to Mélange, a black-owned Italian and Southern restaurant in Cherry Hill, New Jersey. The space was small and you had to bring your own bottle. Kemp had two bottle of Rosé that they put in the ice buckets for us. We talked and laughed, and I never had so much fun doing something as basic as eating. We stayed all of about two hours. The restaurant was damn near closing when we left. Black offered to drop Kiki off so that we could head home. Kemp was happy about that. I knew that he was sure to tear this up once we got home and I was ready for whatever he had coming next.

The ride home we were quite both probably thinking about what we wanted to do to each other. I was getting wet just thinking about it. We couldn't get to the house fast enough. I took it upon myself to reach over and rub his dick through his pants. It was getting hard just from the touch. I was horny and I wanted to suck his dick right at the moment. Fuck it, I thought, why not? He was my husband now.

I loosened his belt and unzipped his pants, releasing his dick from captivity. He looked at me shocked like he didn't believe that I would do something so daring. I didn't care, shit, even if someone saw me, I was going to lick his dick like a Tootsie Roll Pop. The pre-cum was right on top waiting for me. I loved the taste of it and I got every drop off before going down the shaft. He was trying to watch the road and me at the same time. He always said that watching me suck his dick turned him on. Shit, just thinking about his dick turned me on. If I could hop on him and fuck him while he was driving I would have.

My thick lips were wetting his dick from top to bottom. I felt his hand on the back of my head guiding me into a deep-throat routine. I loved to feel it on my tonsils and feel it beating as he moaned out loud. I was excited, which made me do a little extra, of course. I was moving to the beat of the song that played in the background.

"Damn, babe, this shit feel so good," he said in a low tone.

I was shoving every inch of him in my mouth. I didn't want to stop; it was tasting so good. Was I crazy? Did dick really taste good? Well, his did, and I couldn't wait to get home. Soon I felt the car pulling over but I knew that we hadn't reached home yet. We were still on the expressway. Kemp pushed the seat down and told me to take off my panties. I hurried up and pulled them off. I climbed over the seat and got on top of him. My pussy was already wet so his dick slid right in. I almost came as soon as it got in since it was building up the entire time I was giving him head.

"You love this pussy, don't you?"

"Damn right, I love it, it's my pussy, right?"

"Yes, it's your pussy."

"I can't hear you. I said, is this my pussy?"

"This is your pussy!" I came all over his dick. Adrenaline ran through my body and I picked up speed. You could hear my ass slapping up against his legs even over the loud music. He was holding onto to my ass cheeks tight. I knew he was about to cum. I wanted to see his face. I pulled his face close to me.

"Look at me when you bust in this pussy."

With that, he let go and his eyes rolled in the back of his head. Damn, that shit was good. I moved in to kiss him. It was a sensual kiss, probably one of the best that I'd ever had. He loved me and I felt bad knowing that I didn't feel the same way, but I was damn good at playing it off.

He started the car back up after I hopped back in the passenger seat. We headed home and once inside we had a race to the shower like two kids. He won so, I got in with him and got a little bit more before we went to bed. Well, before I went to bed, anyway. He had to go back out and work as usual. Now, what man goes out to work on his wedding night? A true hustler is what I'd call him. I didn't care about him leaving out because more work meant more money. I did want to be ready to head to the lawyer in the morning, though. Yes, the lawyer's office. I wasn't playing any games or wasting any time. I wanted to get everything signed. Shit, I had an insurance agent coming out to the house as well. I wasn't about to be married without any insurance. I might sound like a true gold digger but I simply called myself smart.

I knew what I had to do, so that the day I went through with my plan I would be able to reign over his assets the way that I imagined. I could see it now, for a change something I wished coming true. I had been unlucky most of my life with men starting with my father. I missed him and I always thought for sure one day he would come back and tell me how sorry he was for leaving me and how much he loved me. It never happened and it most likely never would. My relationships were doomed from that day. Just look at them. Johnny was in jail because I pushed him to stand up for himself. For that I was blamed. I landed in jail because of Davey and I would probably never trust another man because of the way he did me. I could partly blame myself since I let my father's leaving mold the way I reacted to men. I never wanted another man to leave me so I jumped through hoops for Davey, hoping that it would keep him with me. I wasn't about to be a fool with Kemp. I walked down that aisle confident about not turning back or ending up in the same situations that I had been in in the past.

Chapter Eighteen

Mica: Held Hostage

Where the hell was Tyson? I had been calling him for hours and he still hadn't answered. I was getting angrier by the second. He should have been here by now. I heard some footsteps near the door. I thought, *Good, he's home*. But each time the footsteps kept walking by. I picked up the phone again and it went to his voice mail.

"Tyson, where the hell are you? I've been sitting here waiting and now I'm getting worried. I know you better not be out with some bitch! Call me as soon as you get this." *Click*.

I could just scream. I hated when he promised me to go somewhere and he didn't show up. I was almost ready to get in the car and drive around until I found his ass, but I didn't want to look like a damn fool. I always thought that women were fools when they did stuff like that and here I was about to do the same damn thing.

I heard a few more footsteps then a couple of knocks. What the hell, did he lose his key? I got up from the sofa and walked over to the door. I couldn't see anything out of the peephole so I opened it. The door flew open, damn near knocking me to the floor. Instead, it slammed me up against the wall. Three guys wearing black ski masks ran in. One guy came and covered my mouth with his hand. I didn't scream because I was too afraid to. I didn't know what the hell was going on and I wished that Tyson would have been here with me.

"Where's your man at?" the tallest guy asked in a deep tone.

"I don't know," I replied. Hell, I wanted to ask him the same damn question.

"He owes me a lot of money and I need to find him. If you know where he is I suggest you tell me before you become a casualty for him." He put his gun under my chin.

"I really don't know. I have been trying to find him for hours and he hasn't answered me." I figured if I told them the truth that they would let me go. Next thing I knew he hit me over the head with the gun and I fell to the floor. I couldn't even open my eyes to see what was going on. . . .

Chapter Nineteen

Diamond: We Meet Again

"Diamond!" Kemp screamed my name through the house.

"What?" I yelled.

"I need you to do something for me, come here."

I headed down to the living room to see what the hell he wanted. I was trying to get a nap since he was out working, but I guess that was out of the question. "What's up?"

"Look, get dressed. I have somebody at the warehouse that I need you to keep an eye on. I got some shit to handle."

"Keep an eye on someone, what the hell is going on, Kemp? You know how I feel about getting involved in your mess." After my experience with Davey he knew I wasn't trying to do anything that would land me back in jail. Since the wedding three months ago, all I did was run errands. I wasn't a damn errand girl and I was getting pretty annoyed.

"Diamond, I just need you to watch someone. That's it."

"Why me, where are all of you workers?"

"They have to go with me. Come on, babe. I need your help."

"This shit better not land me in no bullshit, I mean it!" I pointed my finger at him. I reluctantly agreed to go. I wasn't trying to hear any bullshit from him. Besides, I didn't need anything standing in the way of me getting to his fortune. I wanted him to think that I would do anything for him. I needed him to believe that to get me one step closer to where I needed to be. I had already gotten him to confide in me, so believing that he had a down-ass chick was next. I put on some clothes and got in the car with him to head over to his warehouse. I didn't know what the hell was going on, but I was soon about to find out. Once we entered the building, I noticed a female tied up in a chair with her back facing the door.

"What the fuck is this, Kemp?" I asked. I was instantly pissed off that he would put me in this position.

"I said I needed you to watch someone for me. That's all I need you to do."

"Your not going to hurt anybody, are you?"

"Look, someone has stolen from me and she's my bait, okay. Just sit in here and watch her until I can free up another guy to do it for me. Babe, please do this for me," he said before pulling me close and kissing me on the forehead.

"Don't have me here too long. I don't want to be mixed up in this."

"Okay, I'll be back soon. Thanks, babe." He left with the guy that he had sitting here before we came. I didn't know what to do or what to say. I just stood there, stiff. Why the hell was she here? I didn't really want to know. I thought about trying to make small talk, but I didn't want her to know who I was. I didn't want her to see my face in case anything bad happened and she could ID me. I grabbed a chair and sat down, still sitting in an area where her back was facing me.

"Who's there?" she asked, trying to turn her head to see me.

The voice sounded so familiar to me. I still sat quiet. "Please, who's there? Let me go, please," she continued to plead for her freedom.

I definitely wasn't in any position to let her go. Hell, I didn't even know why she was there. I did know that I wished that I had never agreed to sit there. Her voice continued to stick out to me like a thorn. I knew that I'd heard it before, but I couldn't put a finger on it. The longer I sat there the more anxious I got. It had already been an hour and after listening to her sob and beg for an hour I thought that I should talk to her to calm her down. The whining was definitely getting on my last nerve.

"What's your name?" I asked as I still sat in the chair. I figured that I could make small talk without her seeing my face.

"My name is Mica."

"Mica?" I said, shocked. That was a name I hadn't heard in years. I knew the voice sounded familiar. How the hell did she know Kemp? Now I knew I had to reveal myself, especially if I wanted to get more information out of her. I got up out of the chair and began to head over to where she was sitting. She was squirming in the chair, probably unsure of what was going to happen next. I walked around in front of her. She looked up at me and before speaking she gave me a look of death. I knew that she'd hated me ever since her brother had been locked away. What was I to say to her? I hadn't seen her since she moved out of the neighborhood.

"Diamond? You little bitch, are you the reason that I am here?" Her eyes pierced me like a knife.

"I still see things haven't changed. I didn't even know that it was you here, so how the hell would it be because of me?"

"I've never trusted you. You've caused nothing but trouble in my life."

"Trouble? How have I been trouble?"

"Everything you touch turns to shit! My brother, me; shit, your own family gave you up!"

"First of all, my family didn't give me up and you should do your research before you speak. You don't know what the fuck you're talking about and you aren't in any position to be throwing jabs." I was pissed. Me being adopted had always been a sore spot for me and she knew that.

"Whatever, Diamond, you know that what I'm saying is true and the truth hurts, doesn't it?"

"It's not the truth so it doesn't affect me. Good try, though." I tried to blow her off, hoping that she would just end the conversation or change the subject. I hated that I had been adopted and I tried my hardest to act as if it weren't true.

"You can try and fake it but you can't hide your true feelings."

"I'm not hiding anything and since you're Miss-Know-It-All, I want to see you get yourself out of the bind that you're in!" I walked away angry. I was going to try and help her out because deep down inside I did feel bad about the way things turned out with her brother. I knew that I couldn't change any of it and I wasn't sorry for anything that I'd done. I had moved on with my life and I stayed as far away from her as I possibly could to allow her to do the same. I could see now that she still held a grudge and she probably would never shake it if she hadn't by now.

We both sat silent for a while. I pulled out my cell phone to play a game of solitaire since there wasn't anything else to do in here. I was counting every minute waiting for Kemp to come back so that I could go the hell home.

"Diamond," she called out, in a low tone. I hesitated before answering because I wasn't in the mood for anymore of her ranting.

"What?"

"Look, I'm sorry for what I said. I was just pissed off."

She sounded sincere but the way I looked at it, she could be faking just to get me to let her go. I wasn't about to do that since Kemp would have my head on a platter. If there was one thing that Kemp didn't play with it was money and since she was obviously here because of that I couldn't go there.

"And what's your point?" I rudely responded.

"Look, Diamond, we were friends at one point. We are grown women now and the way I see it we can put the past behind us and let bygones be bygones."

"What made you change your tune? Because you were definitely singing a different song a few minutes ago," I asked, confused. Was this chick bipolar or something? I didn't know what the hell to think about her attempt at reconciliation, especially since she was just putting me down a few minutes earlier. But I also had to acknowledge the fact that she'd probably say any damn thing to get out of here alive.

"I know, and that was just me being selfish. I thought that you were the one that put me here. I know that you didn't have anything to do with it now and I'm sorry."

"What makes you so sure that I didn't have anything to do with it?"

"Because I know you, and I know that you wouldn't do anything like that to a friend."

"Friend? Are you fucking kidding me?" I laughed.

"Yes, Diamond."

"We stopped being friends the moment that you blamed me for your father's murder," I said. I hated the fact that she blamed me for it. I could have never predicted what Johnny would do.

"I know that I blamed you but I'm over it. I was young and I didn't understand what was going on. I didn't want to lose my brother and I thought that it was your fault. I recently visited him and he told me how much he misses you. I didn't even know that he still thought about you."

"He misses me, he really said that?" I began to move back over to the chair where she was sitting.

"Yeah, he did. He said that he writes you all the time but you never respond."

"I never got any letters from him."

"He sends them to your grandmom's house. That's the only address he knows. You should probably ask them."

On the outside my expression was pretty stiff, but inside I was smiling all over. I actually thought he'd written me off like everyone else. It felt good to know that my very first love still loved me.

"So, where have you been all of these years? I never thought we'd meet again, especially not like this." I asked. I was warming up to her by now.

"Out Germantown, I wasn't that far. I guess we just hung out in different places."

"So, why are you here? Did your man steal from Kemp?"

"I don't believe that he would do that. I mean, he was loyal to him. He made sure that things were always on point. I warned him about his crew, though. They were too sloppy and if anybody stole from him it was one of them."

"When is the last time you seen him?"

"I haven't seen him in a week. I've been worried as hell calling him all day but his phone goes straight to voice mail. I don't know what the hell is going on."

Now I felt bad for her. I was well aware of the shit that you go through for a man. I'd had many ups and downs but I knew how to keep it moving. It's a shame that we put so much trust in a man and then they leave us out to dry. Kemp was crazy as hell and I could see him blowing her away for something that she couldn't control.

"Look, I'll tell you straight up, Kemp is crazy and if he doesn't find your man I can see him hurting you."

"But I don't know where he is," she cried, probably realizing the severity of the situation.

"No man is worth dying over, so I would try every avenue I could to find his ass."

"How will I do that if he doesn't let me go?"

"I can try to talk to him about letting you go just as bait to find your man. Then you can let them square it out."

"I can't do that, Diamond. I love Tyson."

"Well, Tyson obviously doesn't love you. He knows how Kemp is and he left you out to dry," I replied, honestly. She needed to see the truth one way or another.

"I don't believe that."

"Well, if you want to die, then so be it. I tried to help you."

"I can't make it without him, Diamond. He's all that I have. I don't have any life or money without him."

"You do have a life, I learned that a long time ago when I thought the same thing. Get your mind right, Mica. You're going to die because he doesn't give a fuck! Girl, I care about Kemp, don't get me wrong, but I'm in this shit to win it. He's filthy rich and I'm trying to have it all. Fuck a man, you can do it on your own, you feel me? Me and you, we can take this shit together. All you gotta do is find Tyson for Kemp and he'll let you go. Then we can work on the master plan together." I had just thought a few minutes earlier how I could use her in my plan. Two heads were definitely better than one.

"Are you serious, Diamond? How the hell are you going to take his money? You just said how crazy he was."

"I know, but I know him like the back of my hand. I know his weak spots. We can make this shit work," I continued to pitch my plan to her, hoping she would go along with it.

She sat silent as if she was contemplating what she would do. Shit, I thought it was pretty simple. There was no way in hell I would die for a nigga. A long time ago I probably would have felt the way she did but I had grown up so much so that I knew when a man wasn't shit. Her man hadn't been anywhere to be found for a week. He'd probably taken the money and went into hiding. If he cared about her the way she thought that he did he would have taken her with him. I mean, that's what a real nigga would do but he seemed like a nut anyway.

We heard the door opening without warning. I could see the fear in her eyes. I turned toward the door as Kemp came in and headed in our direction.

"What the fuck are you talking to her for?" he yelled, probably pissed that he still hadn't found Tyson.

"Excuse me, Kemp; don't talk to me like that, okay? I did you a fucking favor!"

"Babe, you don't need to be talking to her. I asked you to watch her, that's all."

"Look, we need to talk. Can we go in the back?"

"Not right now, I need to holla at her."

"No, we need to talk. Now," I raised my tone to get his attention. He looked at me and then looked at her. He hesitated before moving.

"Come on," he said, turning away from her and headin toward the back of the warehouse. "What is it that's so important, Diamond? I have shit to do."

"Stop acting like I'm the fucking problem, okay. I had shit to do before you dragged me over here."

"Okay, Diamond, what is it?"

"Look, I talked to her, okay? She doesn't know where he is, but if you let her go she agreed to act as bait to find him," I lied.

"Why the hell would she do that?"

"Because I told her that he ain't worth dying for."

"So she just gonna take your word and set up her man? Get the fuck out of here, Diamond, I don't believe that shit."

"Well, go ask her yourself," I instructed.

He gave me a strange look and then walked away heading back to where she was sitting. If she didn't go through with it then I could at least say that I tried. Hell, at this point the choice of life or death was hers.

"So my girl tells me you told her you'll help me find your man?" He stood in front of her. I stood in the back, waiting to hear her answer. I hoped for her sake she wouldn't be stupid.

After a few seconds, she replied, "Yes, I did say that."

"Well, I think that takes balls, sweetie, and I'm gonna let you go, but know this right here: If you try to bullshit me, I'll blow your fucking brains out."

"I won't," she said in a low tone.

I kept my silence but inside I was happy that I was another step closer to what I was trying to accomplish. I didn't think it would be that easy to get Kemp to let her go but I guess I underestimated myself. Kemp definitely trusted me and I needed to keep it that way if this was going to work.

Chapter Twenty

Mica: Seal the Deal

"Where the hell are you, Tyson? I've been worried sick." I left out the part about me being kidnapped and beaten, how they held me while they searched for his ass.

"Mica, I'm sorry. I got into some shit, okay, and some dangerous people are looking for me. I couldn't stay there; I had to go."

"Why couldn't you take me with you? You just left me, Tyson."

"I couldn't do that, Mica. I'll be back soon, though, as soon as the smoke clears."

"How do you know it will clear? What the fuck did you do?"

"I took a shitload of money from my boss. I had to; I was tired of working for pennies while this nigga made fortunes from my work."

"You really stole from him?" I asked. At that moment, I believed what Diamond said. He didn't give a damn about me. He knew that he took money from a dangerous man and he just left me in the line of fire. I couldn't believe that I had been so stupid. "Tyson, I miss you, I really need to see you."

"Maybe I can meet you somewhere, but you have to give me a chance to think of somewhere safe. I will call you back in a couple of days."

"You promise?"

"Yes, I promise. Make sure your phone stays on."

"Okay."

Days turned into weeks and I was nervous wondering when Kemp would come banging on my door. I prayed that Tyson would call me soon so I could get this over with. I wanted to move on with my life and there was no way Kemp was going to allow me to do that if he didn't find out where his money was. I barely left the house in the two weeks that had passed. Shit, even when I did leave I was looking around like I was a damn fugitive running from the police.

What the hell had I gotten myself into? I mean, when I met Tyson I thought that he was perfect in every sense of the word. He took control just the way that I liked it. He helped me and my mother out of our financial rut and kept me wearing all of the flyest clothing. Now, I could see that his greed meant more to him than I ever did and I had to make him just as important to me as I was to him, which wasn't much at all.

My funds were running low and I wasn't about to look for a job. I had to figure out a game plan to get back on top. Besides the fact that I had grown accustomed to it, so had my mother and I didn't want to let her down. I was beginning to get depressed and I damn sure didn't want to mirror the look my mother had when my father died.

It was Friday and I had to hurry up and make the bus to go see my brother. I was determined to patch things up with him and I'd prayed before boarding that he wouldn't refuse my visit as he'd done in the past. On the long ride to the prison I continued to think about the turn that my life had taken and it was strange that I still didn't regret any of my decisions. Even though the happiness was coming to an abrupt end it was happiness that I probably wouldn't have had otherwise.

After checking in and being searched I was sent to the waiting room to be called. I was getting annoyed the longer I sat. I couldn't figure out what the hell was taking so long for them to bring him down to the visiting area.

After sitting for another hour I walked up to the window and waited in the long-ass line. Once I got up front the woman looked at me as if I was diseased or something. I didn't know what the hell her problem was but if I'd seen her on the street and she gave me the same look her ass would be hitting the floor.

"Hi, I've been sitting here for over an hour and my name hasn't been called yet. I was trying to see if there was anything going on with my brother."

"What's the name?" she asked, twisting her lip.

"Jonathan Brooks."

She looked over at the book that was on the side of her desk and looked back up at me. "What's your name?"

"Mica Brooks."

"Okay, it says here that he refused your visit."

"Refused?"

"Yes."

"Why wasn't my name called, then?"

"I don't know, I just got here."

"Does it have a reason for him refusing?"

"No, we don't ask. If they don't want to see a visitor we leave it at that."

"Are you sure that's what it says? I'm his sister; he doesn't even have any other visitors besides me."

"That's what the paper says; now could you step aside? There is a long line behind you."

I couldn't believe what I had just heard but I knew that there wasn't anything that I could do at the moment. Why the hell would he refuse my visit? What had I done? I was going through so much and now was the time that I needed him the most. I wanted to cry but I held it in because I didn't want everyone in this crowded room to see how upset I was. So many thoughts were running through my head. Was he pissed that I hadn't been up to see him? Or was he upset that I hadn't responded to any of his letters? I would have to write him now since he didn't know any of my phone numbers to call me. I felt bad that I had been so distracted that I'd forgotten about him. I mean, I did have a life and I was trying to get things straight for me and Mom. I guess that doesn't matter to you when you're locked behind bars and no one seems to care about you. Most would say that it's the time when you find out about who really cares. I did care about him—hell, I probably loved him more than myself—but I still had to live and I hoped that he could understand that.

I had to wait another hour for the bus to get back to Philly and I couldn't have been more upset. I had come all the way up there just to be turned away. I thought back to the times when we were younger and how close we were.

My father was the most abusive man that I'd ever known. I could remember covering my head with the pillow trying to block out the sounds of the lashes my brother received. My father would use anything that was in arm's reach, from a shoe to a chair. Anything that he could grab he would use to hit Johnny with. Now, my abuse was a little bit different. Instead of using random objects he strictly stuck to the belt-over-the-behind method with me. I guess he didn't want to leave welts and bruises all over my body for fear that someone would see them. My brother always vowed that he would get us out of there as soon as he could make enough money to take care of me. Unfortunately, the murder of our father came first. I always wished that I could turn back the hands of time beyond that day so that I could talk him out of it. Who knows if it would really work but at least it would be more than I can say that I did now. I kind of blamed myself for hooking him up with Diamond in the first place. Johnny was pretty shy and would never talk to a girl on his own. Had I not been so quick to tell her that he had a crush on her they would have never been an item.

Once I was back in Philly I caught a cab from Center City to get back home. I wasn't in the mood to catch another bus, so I would just pay whatever the cost was to bypass the aggravation of the bus riders. My phone rang just as I was a few blocks away from my apartment so I fumbled through my purse until I found it. The number was private and I usually don't answer private calls but something told me to pick it up.

"Hello?"

"Mica, it's Tyson."

"Where the hell have you been? You were supposed to call me weeks ago." I was angry because I could have been killed, thanks to him.

"I know, I'm sorry. I got caught up in some shit, but where are you now?"

"I'm in a cab about to go home."

"Look, tell the driver to drop you off down Hilltop at the store."

"Okay," I agreed. I knew exactly what store he meant and I guess he said that just in case anybody was listening. I told the cabbie to head down Lansdowne and then I did the unthinkable. Actually, I did what I had to do. I called Kemp and told him where I was meeting Tyson and he told me I better be telling the truth or he'd kill me. I was scared shitless praying that Tyson would be where he told me he would be. I couldn't imagine what Kemp would do if he got there and Tyson was nowhere to be found.

I paid the cabdriver the forty dollars it cost me for the detour and got out of the car. It was getting dark outside—it was about 7:15. The street was pretty empty besides the men who held the corners down. I hated corner hustlers—to me they would never make enough money to do anything else. I looked around nervously as the cab sped away. I held my pocketbook close to my body hoping that no one would try to rob me. I entered the store and asked the guy at the counter if Tyson was there. He looked me up and down for a second before picking up his phone and calling him. Tyson came out the back of the store and smiled when he saw me.

I smiled too. I was happy to see him though I knew that I had set him up for his downfall. I didn't say a word. I just wrapped my arms around him for what would probably be the last time I'd ever see him.

"I missed you so much," he whispered.

The sound of his voice so close to me sent chills up my spine. What the hell was I doing? How could I feed him to the dogs? This was once a man that I admired and now he was going to be out of my life. I stared into his eyes as if I was trying to read his mind. I didn't want him to let me go but I knew what was coming next.

"I missed you too," I replied, after a few seconds delay. "Why did you do what you did, Tyson? I don't understand."

"Baby girl, you'll probably never understand it. Things are so different when you're hustling for a fucking crook. Kemp was trying to break me off with shit and I always went above and beyond. I tried to keep things basic but the longer I stayed the more I say that he didn't give a fuck about me. Kemp doesn't care about anybody, not even that fucking trophy bitch Diamond he carries on his arm."

"Baby, there had to be another way. I mean, what are you going to do? You can't be on the run forever."

"I know, but I don't plan to be. I just want to let things die down a little bit."

I didn't get a chance to respond before I heard the bell of the store's door opening. We both turned to look, though both of us had different reasons for it. I saw Kemp' face and I quickly moved to the side. Tyson looked like he had seen a ghost as he looked at Kemp and then back at me.

"Thought you could rob me and run away, huh? Guess you're not as smart as you think you are."

"What the fuck do you want, Kemp? I broke my fucking back for you and you never gave me what was due to me."

"Nigga, I made sure your pockets stayed fat. What the fuck are you talking about?"

"You know exactly what I am talking about," he yelled, as he stood his ground.

I was practically shaking in my boots. I didn't know what was about to go down but whatever it was I prayed that I came out of it alive. They stared each other down as I tried to get as close to the wall as I could. Without warning, Kemp pulled his gun out and shot Tyson five times, not wasting one bullet. Blood sprayed all over me, the counter, and the potato chip rack that was close to where Tyson had stood. As if five shots weren't enough, Kemp moved closer to him and pumped two more shots in his head.

"No one steals from me! I mean that shit," he yelled, before spitting on him. He looked at me standing in the corner crying. I couldn't believe the man that I had loved was gone.

"Let's go!" he yelled, grabbing me by the arm. I didn't say a word. I just did as I was told. I thought for sure that I was next. We got inside of a black Yukon where there were two other men inside. I had blood all over my leather jacket, face, and hair. Kemp got in the driver's seat and drove off. "You all right, baby girl?" he asked as he sped up the expressway.

I didn't respond. I couldn't respond. What the hell was I supposed to say? I just saw him blow away the love of my life. He was my everything and now I was going to be forced to fend for myself. I mean, I was glad to be alive but I wasn't glad that things had to be this way. I had hoped that there would have been a way that they could have worked through their differences so that I could have my life back, but I guess Kemp did what he had to do.

Kemp continued the drive to the unknown destination since I had been too afraid to ask where he was taking me. Soon, we pulled up in front of an apartment building. I was still staring out of the window thinking about what I had just witnessed. The sight played over and over in my mind. All I could see was Tyson's body falling to the floor. "Get out," the slim thug sitting next to me spoke while nudging me.

I did as I was told and slid out of the car. Kemp got out of the driver's seat and grabbed me by the arm, leading me to the apartment entrance. He unlocked the door with a key, swung it open, and pushed me inside.

"Look, you can stay here as long as you need to. I know you probably won't be able to pay the bills at your man's place alone. I'm going to send somebody over with some clothes so you can change. You're gonna have to lay low for a little while. That asshole said my name so I'm sure the cops will be looking for me."

I still didn't speak. I sat down on the sofa and listened to what he had to say. What else could I do? I was stuck here whether I wanted to be or not. Kemp wasn't the kind of guy that you wanted to test.

"If you try to turn me in you'll end up like your man, so I'd suggest you go along with what I say. I'll be back later on tonight, in about an hour or so someone will bring you the clothes, so open the door."

"Okay," was all I could say. I still had tears running down my face. He glanced back at me before walking out of the door. I broke down once he was gone. I know Tyson wasn't the perfect man but he was all that I had. I was sorry now, but it was too late to make a difference. I know that I had no other choice since I would have been dead. Kemp proved that he would kill so I wouldn't have stood a chance. Tyson's murder had sealed the deal, and now I had to figure out what I was going to do next.

Chapter Twenty-one

Diamond: Together Again

"I need you to take these clothes over to the apartment on Wayne Avenue," Kemp said, passing me a stack of women's clothing.

"What bitch you got over there that I'm dropping clothes to?" I replied, putting my hands on my hips.

"The chick I had you watch before. Her clothes are all bloody so I need you to take these to her."

"Bloody? What the hell did you do, Kemp?"

"I handled my business, that's all you need to know."

"Did you kill somebody?" I asked, as I began to tremble.

I was afraid to hear the answer to the question.

"You don't need to know all of that, Diamond. Stop with all the questions and just drop the damn clothes off."

"Excuse me, I'm your wife, I'm entitled to know what the hell you've done."

"No, you don't. I'm not going to argue about this shit, Diamond. I got other shit to do."

"I'm going to take them but this conversation isn't over."

"Whatever," he responded, heading up the steps, leaving me standing there with the pile of clothing and a question mark above my head. By his reaction I knew that he killed someone and since Mica was who I had to drop the clothes off to I figured that it was her man. I had to come up with what I was going to say to her. I could definitely use her if I was going to get the money I was trying to get. I didn't feel bad about it since she had shut me out of her life years ago and blamed me for something that I had no control over. For me she was just an added bonus and another part of my plot. She was someone to cause a distraction for Kemp and at this point he still didn't know that I knew her. For now, that's the way I wanted to keep it.

I got in the car to head over to the apartment where he had stashed her. She probably was all bent out of shape and needed a shoulder to cry on. I wasn't really into all the emotional shit but I would have to fake it to get her to trust me. I had built up a wall after being hurt so many times that it was hard to break. Nowadays you had to be that way 'cause a weak heart is only going to get stepped on. The one thing that I cherished was my sanity and I wasn't going to let anyone take that away from me. It took me all of fifteen minutes to get there. I took a deep breath and got ready for my performance before using the key to enter the apartment.

When I opened the door she jumped out with a knife. She got pretty close, almost stabbing me. I moved out of the way just in time for her to fly right past me.

"What the hell are you doing?" I asked, grabbing hold of her arm so she could drop the knife.

"I'm trying to protect myself. I thought for sure he was sending someone here to kill me," she cried, as the tears flowed and she dropped the knife on the floor.

"Trust me, if he wanted to kill you, you'd already be dead. Here, he told me to give you these clothes."

"I don't understand. He killed him right in front of me and he's going to just let me go?"

"Obviously, you're still here."

She sat down on the sofa and buried her face in her hands. She cried out loud, probably wishing she were dead. Her life was going to be different now whether she wanted it to be or not. I sat down next to her and placed my hand on her back. Appearing to be supportive was the first step to gaining her trust.

"I'm sorry, I hate people to see me cry. I've never been this scared before in my life. I don't know what to do."

"All you have to do is listen, I'm going to get you out of this."

"How are you doing to do that?"

"I told you that day at the warehouse I had a way that you can have your own money and your own shit without a man. I meant what I said and I'll guarantee that things work out for you."

She didn't respond. I wondered what was going on in her mind. She probably still didn't trust me, but I knew that I could work my way up to that. After about a minute of silence she got up and headed to the bathroom. I sat still on the sofa. I heard the shower running so I took that time to call Kemp and let him know what was going on.

"Did you get there yet?" he asked in an annoyed tone.

"Yeah, I did, what the hell is wrong with you?"

"Nothing you need to worry about. What is she doing in there?"

"She's taking a shower. She's just upset but I'm trying to get her together."

"All right, well hurry up and get back on this side, it's getting late and you know I don't trust these niggas."

"I'm leaving in a few minutes."

"All right, I'll see you later."

"All right," I said, before ending the call. I sat on the couch and flipped through the TV channels waiting for her to get out of the shower. She came out of the bathroom dressed in the clothes that I had brought over. I wondered where the hell Kemp got the clothes from in the first place. They damn sure weren't mine. I didn't even wear sweat suits. He probably got them from one these tricks he deals with on the side. I didn't ask any questions because I didn't feel like arguing.

"I didn't think you would still be here."

"Where did you think I'd be?"

"I don't know. I don't know anything right now, I feel like I'm flying on autopilot."

"Look, I didn't leave because I wanted to make sure you didn't need anything before I left. I gotta get back home because it's getting late. I'll be back in the morning to check on you. Get some rest, all right?"

"I'll try. Am I really safe here?"

"Of course, I wouldn't leave you if you weren't." I continued to lay it on thick. I had her right where I wanted to be.

"I really appreciate this. I know I don't deserve it for the way that I treated you and some of the things I've said."

"It's okay, we can talk about this tomorrow. You've had a traumatizing day so go to sleep and I'll see you in the AM."

"Okay," she said, while reaching out her arms for a hug. I instantly felt uncomfortable. I wanted to play it off but I didn't want to be so affectionate. I loosened up once I quickly thought about how good things would be for me once this was all over with. I leaned into the hug and headed toward the door. After making sure that she locked up I got in the car and headed back home. I wasn't surprised that Kemp wasn't home. He was rarely home; he normally got in around three in the morning. I never really worried about where he was because the bottom line was that if anything happened to him, I was going to have everything. Shit, they would be saving me time and effort if they got to him first.

Besides the steady drug business that Kemp ran, he owned property from North Philly to Cheltenham. He owned a barbershop, a small-car dealership, and two restaurants. Being his wife had its perks, and I sucked every ounce of it up. I stood to inherit it all, plus the money that he had stashed away in a safe. He told me everything and that's the reason why I married him. There wasn't any way I was going to mess up. See, some people talk too much and that was his problem. A little bit of pillow talk goes a long way. He trusted me more than he should and that was going to be his downfall.

After getting home and changing I jumped into bed. I probably was asleep as soon as my head hit the pillow.

I woke up when he climbed into bed at two-thirty but easily went back to sleep. I woke up around nine the next morning and he was gone. I hadn't even felt him get up. I did wonder why the hell he was so damn early. He never got in the bed until the afternoon. I dialed his cell phone but he didn't answer. Forget it, I had plans for the day anyway and I wasn't going to let him ruin them. I took a quick shower and got dressed. Within an hour I was on my way back over to check on Mica. Isn't that what friends are for? I cracked myself up.

Once I got there I noticed Kemp's car in the lot. What the hell was he doing there? I hope I didn't have to go in here and act a fool. It was too soon for this, I didn't need her to get his attention this quick. I needed more time. I used the key to open the door. Kemp was talking on the phone but I didn't see Mica in the living room.

"What the hell are you here for?"

"I was about to ask you the same thing," he replied, ending his call.

"I came here to check on her, I told her that I would. Now what's your excuse?"

"Same, I had to check on her to make sure she ain't try to run out on me."

I didn't believe him but it didn't matter, what you don't see won't hurt you, right? Well, at least that's what I was brought up to believe. I looked around the apartment to see if things were out of place. Everything pretty much looked the way that they did when I left last night.

"Where is she at anyway?"

"She's in the room 'sleep. I was on my way out I had to make a phone call first. Good looking out, though, maybe you can keep her occupied so she don't do nothing stupid," he said, before getting up out of the chair and heading over to where I was standing. He grabbed me and hugged me. I returned the affection but it was hardly genuine. I knew he wasn't telling me the absolute truth but I couldn't really feed into it if I wanted things to go right. I could have played the wife role and come in there having a fit but what would that have accomplished? Kemp and I would have argued and Mica probably would have never trusted rekindling our friendship. I had learned not to be too nonchalant but I had also learned not to take things overboard. He kissed me on the cheek before he headed out of the apartment.

I set my bag down on the table and walked into the bedroom where Mica was still sleeping. I stood there and stared at her. I know that it was a really weird thing to do, but it gave me a little time to think. First, I thought about the fact that I planned to willingly use her to entice my husband. Now, that could go either way. Kemp was extremely good-looking and with all of the money he had, most girls would wait in a line ten city blocks long just to get next to him. She could end up falling for him and letting him know what I had planned. That would probably land me six feet under, a place that I wasn't trying to visit any time soon. Next, I had to think about the possibility of him finding out that both of us was trying to set him up and he'd end up killing both of us. Last, I had to evaluate the fact that he could end up surviving, leaving us both in the danger zone. Was it all worth it? I asked myself a million times, but then I remembered my grandmom's house and the way that I used to live. There was absolutely no way that I was going back there. I mean, I knew people who lived in worse situations. I could have been living in one of those abandoned houses, I could have been living with a pedophile, and I could have been in so many situations that I've known others to be in but I wasn't. Yes, my mother was on drugs now, and that was something that I was going to fight tooth and nail to change, but it still wasn't as bad as it could have been.

Regardless of all of that, I wasn't going back to North Philly. I wasn't going to school and I damn sure wasn't going to get a job. So, what other choice did I have? Was I supposed to stay married to him, as controlling as he was? Was I supposed to keep doing his dirty work and end up in jail again? Was I supposed to really fall in love and make a bunch of babies? Hell no! None of the above was going to happen. I came up with the plan and I was sticking to it.

I had just turned around and was on my way back out to the living room when she woke up.

"Hey, you made it back over, I'm glad you came," she said as she sat up in the bed and began rubbing her eyes.

"I told you I was coming, and I'm a woman of my word."

"So, what do you have planned for today?"

"Well, I was going to suggest that we go out to the mall or something."

"I don't know if that's a good idea since Kemp told me I need to lay low for a while."

"Girl, he doesn't make the rules for me. What's the point of keeping you locked up in this apartment? That makes you look suspicious, if you ask me. You need to live your life as you normally would."

"I'm just afraid."

"Listen, trust me. He's my husband so I know him like the back of my hand. He'll probably be a little pissed but he'll get over it."

"Okay, but I don't have any other clothes but these."

"We'll take care of that, now hurry up and clean up so we can go. It's nice outside too, girl. I'm gonna let the top down on the convertible. I'll be waiting for you outside."

I left the apartment to go out to the car. I felt like I was on my way to the top. There wasn't anything in the world that would give me the ultimate satisfaction. I was smiling from ear to ear as my hair blew in the spring air. It was a beautiful day and I was dressed to kill in a little black dress and wedges. Everything was perfect and I was a firm believer that everything happens when it's supposed to. I was meant to be a boss and I had no doubt that I was going to succeed. Mica and I were back together again as friends and this time it was going to be worth my while.

Chapter Twenty-two

Mica: New Horizons

I was relieved that I was still breathing. I had never been so thankful for something in my life. I thought that I would never be able to be happy if I wasn't with Tyson but now I saw things a little different. Yeah, I was silly and a fool in love but how many of us aren't at one time in our lives? Since he gave me a life that I wasn't accustomed to I thought that staying with him was the only way to keep it. I wasn't stupid by a long shot—I was just stuck in that mind-set. Though I hadn't been close to Diamond in years, at one point in time she was my best friend. Honestly, I knew that she wasn't responsible for my father's death but I had to blame someone in order to come to grips with the fact that he was gone. I could never blame my brother because he was the only person in this world that I loved more than myself.

I had to live my life and I wasn't going to sit around depressed about the past. I'd be damned if I was going to end up like my mother. So, I had a new outlook on life and thanks to Diamond I was about to find out how to make it in this world alone. I would never have to depend on a man again. I thought my brother would be proud of me. I knew that he would be happy that I was going to be friends with Diamond again. He never stopped loving her, even after not having contact with her for years. There had to be something special about that.

I hurried and got dressed, excited about our outing. I was ready to show everyone the new me. Though Kemp was a ruthless murderer, he did have a heart and I got a taste of his heart this morning when he came over. He sat down and talked to me and apologized for tearing my life apart. I never expected him to be so nice. I thought for sure that he didn't have a heart. I knew that what happened had nothing to do with me but I also knew that he had to handle his business. He still didn't want me to leave the apartment just yet and he still warned that if I told anyone what happened he would have no choice but to get rid of me as well. I promised that I wouldn't and we shook hands on it. I fell back to sleep and by the time I woke up he was gone and Diamond was there.

I opened the door to the bright sunlight. It was nice, Diamond definitely hadn't exaggerated. She was sitting in her car blasting the Jay-Z *American Gangster* CD. I was a huge fan of Jay-Z so I was surely going to enjoy the tunes mixed with the spring air.

"So, what mall are we going to?" I asked, as I stood outside of the passenger side of the car. She hadn't even heard me walk up, she was so into the song that was playing.

"You'll see, hop in so we can get out of here!"

She continued to sing along with the music as we headed through the street to the expressway. By the look of the roads she was taking it appeared that we were going to the King of Prussia Mall. I could go crazy shopping in any mall, but that mall was definitely my weakness. With so many stores, I could shop for hours and not miss a beat. I was ready to run through the mall like a kid in a toy store. I sat quietly on the ride just enjoying the moment. Before long, we were pulling into a parking spot and she was closing the top of the car.

"Don't worry about any money, girl, I got you covered. You can grab whatever you want."

"Thanks, Diamond, you don't know how much I appreciate this," I replied. I really did appreciate it because I couldn't go back to Tyson's place and I didn't have any clothes or enough money to start over.

We hit almost every store you could think of. I tried on clothes while she sat in the waiting area and vice versa. She promised me a night out on the town to have some fun, so I was desperate to look my best. I grabbed shoes and bags. I got makeup from M•A•C and lingerie from Victoria's Secret. I was set from top to bottom with clothes. The only thing left was to get my hair and nails done and I would be set. She spent more money on me than I probably would have spent on myself.

I had to evaluate a few things, though. Was all of this kindness genuine? Or was she just using me as a pawn in her little game? I would hate to think that but I didn't have a choice. For some reason, the longer we hung around each other at the mall the more I started to believe that it was all a facade. I mean, she seemed to be overly nice, which made it a little difficult to be optimistic. Either way, I was going to go with the flow for now. If she were up to something, it would come to light sooner or later anyway. In the meantime, I was going to enjoy myself because I deserved it. After shopping we decided to get something to eat at Friday's. I hadn't eaten all day and it was almost four o'clock before I realized it. I'm surprised that my stomach wasn't growling. There wasn't a wait so we were seated immediately. I was a picky eater so there wasn't much on the menu that I would order. I decided to keep it basic and get some chicken fingers. I figured that you couldn't go wrong with that. I hadn't had a drink in a while either so I ordered an ultimate margarita. I didn't drink often because me and alcohol don't mix well at all. I'd done some crazy things when I was drunk and would wake up the next day and not know where the hell I'd been or what the hell I'd done. I didn't know how to stop when I'd reach the point of no return. So, my method was to psych myself out, thinking that I drunk a lot when I really hadn't. It may sound silly but it worked for me.

"So, how is your mom doing? I haven't seen her in so long," I asked, trying to make conversation.

"My mom is strung out, girl; you probably wouldn't know her if you saw her."

"Are you serious? Damn, I'm sorry to hear that. Do you remember my cousin Deidra?"

"Deidra . . . Yeah, I remember her. What's up with her?"

"She was messed up on drugs too but I finally got her into a rehab and she's doing so much better now. Have you tried to get your mom into a program?"

"She's hard to find and when you do find her she doesn't stay long and she will tell you she's not going to a rehab. I don't know what else to do so I see her when I see her and I give her a few dollars and keep it moving. I got my own problems. I can't be chasing her around. Shit, she's a grown-ass woman," she spat, as she dug into her salad.

Damn, I thought, that was cold. I knew how hard it was to get a drug addict to a rehab but that's what you do for your family. How could you just give up on your mom like that? I decided to change the subject since I could feel myself saying something that would most likely cause an argument.

"Is that all you're going to eat?" I asked, looking at her soup and salad. She had a perfect figure so it wasn't like she needed a diet or anything.

"Yeah, this is pretty much all I eat, girl. How you think I stay this size?"

I laughed, since I knew she would say that. It's always the small chicks that swear they need to lose some weight. I was happy with my size-eight frame.

"So what's up with your mom, last time I saw her y'all were packing up a U-Haul truck," she asked.

"She's doing okay now, but she was depressed for years. Shit, I had to get a job to help her with the bills because she couldn't handle them alone. I feel like I never got a chance to be a kid. I don't regret helping keep us afloat, but I wished that my father would have been alive to take care of us. That's why I fell in love with Tyson, because he kept my mom straight." I got sad just saying his name. I was definitely going to miss him.

"I know you miss him, girl, but you'll be okay. Women are born to survive tragedy. Just like you took ahold of the situation when your dad died you'll do it again. Don't ever feel defeated, because it's not becoming. You'll never get anywhere in life like that. Believe me when I tell you I've been through some things but I never let any of it get me down. I kept it moving and I won't stop until I get enough. You feel me?"

"Yeah, I know exactly where you're coming from." Okay, now I had a newfound respect for her. What she said was so true and I believe that I once felt defeated. I had actually felt that way on more than one occasion. From the time I sat and begged my brother not to shoot and watched him pull the trigger. Or the time that I was forced to lose my virginity and I kept it to myself. Or when I focused so much of my attention on a no-good man that I forgot about my family. I had lived a lie for these last few years of my life. Tyson couldn't love me the way that I loved him and it wasn't until that very second that I realized it.

"I learned a lot from my last relationship, girl. I had to sit in jail for nine months for some shit that he got me into. After that shit, I promised myself that I would never ever love a nigga more than I love myself. It's not feasible for me, fuck getting a nigga with money. I'm about getting a nigga but I need my own money!"

"I know that's right!" I agreed. Everything that she said made perfect sense. You had to be a fool not to understand it. "I can't believe that you went to jail, that shit is crazy, girl. What happened?"

"I really even hate to talk about it but in a nutshell, he sent me over to Jersey with drugs to drop off and the nigga I was supposed to meet up with set me up. I was sick, girl, I thought I was gonna lose my fucking mind. When I got out, I saw him and he tried to apologize. It wasn't that much apologizing in the world. I never wanted to get wrapped up in his world. I loved him too much and I would do anything for him. Each time he talked me into doing something it was worse than the time before. I don't know if he was testing me to see how far I would go or what. The bottom line was that I had to walk away or end up in jail for murder because I was surely ready to blow his ass away!" She laughed, trying to bring humor to a serious situation. I didn't know what I would do in jail—she was definitely stronger than I would ever be.

"You're strong, girl, I couldn't have survived!"

"A girl's gotta do what a girl's gotta do!"

I smiled at that comment. She had grown so much mentally to a level that I wanted to reach. I guess you have to experience something devastating to learn and to overcome it. I had learned a valuable lesson today and I was going to hold onto it for life. After we finished eating we got back on the road. All the food I ate along with the one drink had me ready to take a nap. Before I knew it I was snoring. I woke up just as we were parking at a day spa.

"Hey sleeping beauty, let's go get our nails done."

"Okay," I agreed, trying to focus. That nap was much needed. I hadn't slept that good in weeks. We were treated like queens in the salon. The Asian culture was definitely serious when it came to business. They treated you so good you almost never wanted to leave. I enjoyed every minute of my foot massage, pedicure, and manicure. I hadn't been that relaxed in a while. We were in there all of an hour and change before we left to head to out final destination, the Dominican hair salon.

I came out of there looking like a new woman. I damn near didn't recognize myself. On the way back to the apartment Kemp called her cell phone. I was surprised that he hadn't called all day.

"What? . . . She's right here . . . I took her shopping, Kemp, she couldn't stay in there with no clothes . . . Who are you yelling at? . . . I hear you . . . I just said I hear you, Kemp . . . I'll see you when you get there then . . . Goodbye!" *Click*.

"What did he say?" I asked nervously. I knew he wouldn't be happy about me coming out of the apartment.

"He's only talking shit, he's mad, but trust me, he'll get over it," she replied nonchalantly. She wasn't afraid but I sure as hell was.

"What is he going to do to me?"

"Nothing, don't worry about him. All you need to worry about is getting ready to hang out and party tonight. I'll take care of him, trust me," she reassured me.

"Is he coming to the apartment?"

"No, he's going home."

We pulled into the lot of the apartment building within a few minutes of her ending the call. She walked me into the apartment because I was afraid that he would have someone waiting in there for me. She was cracking up the whole time. I didn't think anything was funny. I had witnessed firsthand how he handled business. After opening the door she checked the rooms.

"Okay, there is no one here. Satisfied?"

"A little. What time are you coming back?"

"Be ready by ten."

"Okay, I'll be ready."

"Come behind me and lock up."

I followed her and put every lock on the door. I didn't want him to catch me off guard. I should have told her to call me and let me know what he said. Hell, she couldn't call me—she didn't even know my cell number. I did a quick search of the apartment myself. I looked under the beds, in the closets, I even checked the shower. I couldn't get comfortable till I was absolutely positive that he wasn't there. I had just got on his good side so I hoped her game was as good as she said it was. If not, I would have to hope for a miracle, praying that he would forgive me for going out when he told me not to.

My view of a new horizon was slowly getting dim. I needed conformation that it wasn't a big deal. I decided to take a bath to calm my nerves but first I had to pin-curl my hair since I'd just got it done. The steam from the hot tub would ruin it. I put on some smooth R&B, dropped some bath salt in the water, got in, and relaxed. It was just what I needed. I planned on being ready at ten, and I was going to turn heads tonight. I had a new attitude and tonight was the premiere.

Chapter Twenty-three

Diamond: Hook, Line and Sinker

I couldn't wait to get home. I was doing damn near sixty MPH on neighborhood streets. If there was one thing that I couldn't deal with it was a man thinking he ruled me. I was a grown-ass woman, and it was about time he realized it. He was not my superior, he was my husband and that didn't mean he could disrespect me. I got out of the car and walked fast toward the door. I opened it and Kemp was in the living room with his best friend, Black. I didn't have a thing for dark-skinned dudes but I swear he was the finest dark-skinned man I'd ever seen in my life. He had bright white teeth and some juicy-ass lips. He looked like he could do some things in the bed. Anyway, back to the problem at hand. I walked straight in and interrupted their conversation.

"I need to talk to you, now!" I pointed toward the kitchen so Kemp would follow me. I was on fire and ready to explode. He got up from the chair, gave Black a devilish grin, and followed me out of the room.

"Yo, what the fuck is your problem?" he asked as soon as he stepped over the threshold of the kitchen.

"No, what the fuck is your problem? How dare you call me out of my name? I am not now nor have I ever been so degraded. I am your wife, not some trick you're fucking on the side. Don't you ever do that shit to me again."

"Are you finished?"

"No, I'm not finished. I'm upset. I can't believe that you did that."

"Babe, I was mad because you know I told her to stay in. I'm not saying I was right for disrespecting you, but she can fuck shit up for me."

"First of all, keeping her in hiding is gonna seem suspicious. What the hell is she on the run for? If the cops want to talk to her, so what, she ain't gonna tell them nothing, Kemp. She's too fucking scared. She had me checking the closets and shit to make sure you didn't send nobody there to kill her."

"Word?"

"Yes. You can't leave her stuck up in that apartment. What's wrong with her hanging out with me?"

"You know I don't trust people and I don't want to have to murk her, but I will if I have to."

"Listen, she's not going to mess up."

"Look, I'm sorry for what I said, okay?"

"You should be."

"Do you forgive me?"

I didn't answer. I was still mad but I admit I had a weak spot for a man begging me for another chance. He moved in to hug me but I didn't budge.

"Stop being so damn stubborn and give me a hug," he said, grabbing ahold of my arm and pulling me close to him. "I'm sorry, okay, for real, I won't do it again."

I hugged him back. "I'm taking her out to the club tonight. She needs to get out and have some fun."

"All right, what club? I'm coming out too."

"Solo. What, you trying to spy on me or something?"

"Come on now, you know better than that. I just want to go out, buy a couple bottles, and have some fun. Is there anything wrong with that?"

"Naw, it's cool. Make sure you have those bottles poppin'!"

"Most definitely." He slapped me on my ass as I was walking out of the kitchen.

"Watch that, you gonna get yourself in trouble." I laughed.

"Trouble? Yeah, whatever!" He joined in the laughter.

Black looked at us and shook his head. He was probably thinking we were crazy as hell. We weren't crazy, we were married and all married couples have their ups and downs. I had figured out how to stand my ground when it came to men. Kemp was a ruthless killer but when it came to me I could always get him to back down. I was still mad about what he'd said but I let it go once I thought about all the money and power I'd have once he was gone. I smiled at Black before going upstairs. He smiled back at me but played it off with a laugh when Kemp noticed him looking at me.

I knew that dealing with Black was out of the question— for now, anyway. Hell, once Kemp was out of the way I could deal with whomever I chose to. Yeah, I had my eye on him but isn't that how men work? Was it wrong to be attracted to him? I didn't think so. It was harmless.

I got dressed in record time. Kemp and Black were still sitting downstairs playing *Madden* on the PlayStation. I had on a tight-fitting sateen black dress with spaghetti straps. The top of the dress was shaped like a corset so my breasts were popping out of the top of it. My ass looked perfectly round and my shoes were animal-print wedges with a gold buckle on top. I didn't expect them to still be here but, hey, and least I could get a man's opinion on my outfit before going out.

"So, how do I look?" I said, turning around so they could get a 360-degree view. Kemp barely looked but said I looked good. He was too busy in the damn game to pay me any attention. Black, on the other hand, had his eyes glued to me like a magnet. He didn't say anything, at least not verbally; his expression said it all for him. Satisfied, I kissed Kemp and left the house.

Mica was ready once I got there. I was glad that I didn't have to sit and wait. I hated to be dressed for hours waiting on someone and they are fresh to death when we get in the club because they just got dressed. Kiki was good for that. Oh, shit, Kiki. I had gotten so tied up with Mica that I hadn't talked to her all week. I didn't know if she was working tonight or not. I felt bad; Kiki and I normally talked every day. She was probably worried about me and here I was trying to swindle Mica.

Once we got to the club, the line was ridiculous. I was glad that I never had to wait in lines. I knew pretty much every security guard at the clubs so they always let me skip the line. The music was on point and it was full of players and wannabe video chicks. I scoped the club trying to see who was there. I didn't see Kiki, so she must have been off or hadn't gotten here yet.

About an hour after I got there, Kemp and his crew made their grand entrance. I saw all the hoes running up to give him a hug. It didn't bother me until one of them was hanging on him a little too long. I grabbed Mica by the hand and walked over to where he was standing to make my presence known. I wasn't trying to go to jail again but I would whoop someone's ass for messing with my money. "Hey babe," I said, hugging him and making sure I flashed my four-karat wedding-ring set. The girl turned her nose up and waved goodbye. I returned the gesture, adding a middle-finger move.

"You're crazy, you know that? That's why I fucking love you," he laughed. "Now let's go to the VIP and get these bottles poppin'."

The VIP was crazy packed. There were some local celebrities in there along with some basketball players. We were drinking Moët like it was water. We were dancing and having tons of fun. I stepped out for a minute to go check my makeup in the ladies' room. I ran into Black on the way.

"You're looking extra sexy in that dress tonight. I had to let you know since your husband didn't," he said, looking me up and down, licking his lips like he wanted to eat me. Shit, I wouldn't mind getting my salad tossed by his fine ass. Too bad he was Kemp's best friend, because I would have given him a piece.

"Thanks," I said, keeping it simple.

"Don't get too drunk you might end up in somebody else's bed," he laughed.

"Oh, I won't, trust me."

"Just warning you," he said, smiling, and walked away.

What was that about? He might as well just have come out and said he wanted some. I wouldn't have said yes, but damn, we're both grown and he could have kept it funky with me. I went into the bathroom and fixed my makeup while getting strange looks. I tipped the lady who gives you the paper towel and grabbed some gum out of her basket. I went back out and pushed through the crowd to get to the VIP room in the back. I was getting pulled in too many directions by different men but I managed to get my arms free each time. I still hadn't made it through yet, but felt a grip too strong for me to get loose.

I turned to find out who it was because I was just a few seconds away from snapping and smacking the shit out of somebody. Could these men be that ignorant that the only way to get a girl's attention was to grab her? What has happened to the days of the mack or smooth operators? Once I realized that it was Black, a little bit of steam wore off. He didn't say anything—he just pulled me close with my back facing him and made me dance with him. Was he crazy? Kemp was just a few feet away and here he was grinding on my ass. I was drunk as hell so of course I moved to the beat of the song. After the song was over, he turned me loose. I went back into the VIP section as if nothing happened. Realistically, nothing did happen but you never know how other people would react.

Kemp was drunk as hell, he was even dancing and that was extremely unusual. I joined in the fun. I noticed Black coming back in, standing off to the side making sure I was in full view. I was putting on a show, dancing all around Kemp like he was a stripper's pole. I continued to make eye contact with Black and for some reason I was getting turned on. Kemp was going to be in for a treat when we got home. I just hoped that he wouldn't get too drunk and fall asleep on me. When I was drunk I was always horny. Half of the time, Kemp wasn't even home so I had to play with my toys or just go to sleep and forget about it. A girl needs that hunger to be fed sometimes. I was always too afraid to go out and get me a piece on the side. Kemp knew pretty much everyone in the city, so any little slipup could screw up all of my plans.

Mica was enjoying herself too, dancing and rubbing up on one of Kemp's friends, JB. I was glad to see her loosening up because being depressed wasn't attractive. I couldn't stand a woman laying up worrying about a man. Even though he was dead and hadn't just stepped off, the way he was acting he probably would have left her ass eventually anyway. Mica was the kind of girl that was cute but she was the only one that didn't realize it. She always had low self-esteem and though she may not have realized it, it was true. If a guy paid any attention to her she always wondered why. I mean, how hard is it to look in the mirror? There were a lot of women who wished they had her looks. I thought it was pathetic, but it was something that I could definitely use to my advantage.

Soon, the lights were coming on and people began to disperse into the streets. For some reason I didn't feel right. I guess you could call it women's intuition but I knew that something was about to go down. I heard arguing from a distance. It was a mixture of men and women's voices. I grabbed Mica's hand to pull her down the street toward the parking lot. She was busy trying to look back and see what was going on. Being the wife of a drug dealer I learned to keep it moving. I was not interested in a fight—hell, niggas don't fight anymore, they shoot first and ask questions last.

"Mica, come on girl, let's go!" I yelled, continuing to tug on her arm.

"Girl, I'm trying to see what's going on."

"Unless you want to get shot you better come on."

The more I tugged the more she moved away, and I was ready to leave her ass. If she wanted to be stupid it would be her funeral, not mine. I started to walk a little faster and within a few seconds I heard her heels as she ran to catch up with me. We hadn't even made it to the car before gunshots erupted. I got down on the ground and pulled Mica down with me. I knew that some shit was about to go down and I was glad that I didn't stick around close to the door. I heard people screaming and scattering all over Delaware Avenue. After a few minutes the shooting stopped and seconds later the crying started. I peeked around the side of the car to see who was hit. I saw someone that resembled Black lying on the ground. Oh shit! I thought, where the hell was Kemp? I got up off the ground and began to run over to where he was. Kemp came flying around the corner with his gun still in his hand.

"Kemp, what the fuck happened?"

"Diamond, go home," he yelled. Even though I had ulterior motives for being with him I was glad that he hadn't gotten shot. I mean, I hadn't found out everything that I needed to know. It was too soon and losing him right now would just ruin everything. Kemp and his friend JB bent down and picked Black up off the ground. He was still alive but blood was pouring out of him like a faucet. I didn't know what the hell had happened but I prayed that Black would make it through okay. They ran toward Kemp's truck and placed him in the backseat. It was like a scene from a movie and as many times as Kemp hollered at me to go home I didn't budge. I was stiff. I thought about Black's family and his children. What if he didn't make it through this? Kemp walked over to me as JB got in the driver's seat of Kemp's truck.

"Diamond, get in the car and drive the fuck home! I mean that shit." He pushed me toward Mica.

Tears began to fall from my eyes. I was scared. I didn't know what happened and I knew that I should have listened but I couldn't. I was almost frozen in that spot. Mica came behind me and grabbed me by the arm. Kemp stared at me as he backed up to get in the car. Once he got in the car JB pulled off. I watched them drive away and hurried to the car. The cops swarmed the area. There were two dead bodies in the street around the corner on Spring Garden Street. The cops gathered any witnesses and questioned them. I told them that I hadn't seen anything, which I really hadn't. I was given a card with a number to call if I remembered anything. We left the scene and I drove home quietly. Mica agreed to drive home with me and stay until I heard from Kemp.

Once we got in the house we sat on the sofa. I turned on the TV and laid my head back to rest it on the back of the sofa. I dozed off without even realizing how fast the time had passed. It was almost seven o'clock in the morning when I realized it. Mica was on the other end of the sofa asleep. I got up and dialed Kemp's number. I knew he hadn't come home and I didn't have any missed calls so I knew he hadn't called. It took a few rings for him to answer it.

"Babe, what's going on? Why didn't you call me?"

"I'm still at the hospital, Diamond, I'm sorry. Black is still in surgery. They said he should make it out okay."

"That's good to hear." I felt a little relieved that he was going to be okay. I knew that Kemp wouldn't tell me anything more especially over the phone so I didn't pry for any more information. I knew that he wouldn't be home anytime soon so I went back to sleep on the couch. In my mind I knew that whatever beef they had wouldn't be over but I was satisfied that Black was alive. All I could remember is seeing his body lying on the ground, still. I could imagine a chalk outline on the ground tracing the spot where his body had been laid out. The good thing was that it was only in my imagination.

Chapter Twenty-four

Mica: Sucka for Love

I woke up with a pain in my neck. I wasn't used to sleeping sitting up on a sofa so I was suffering for it. Last night's excitement was a little more than I'd expected. In all the years that I had dealt with Tyson I'd never witnessed anyone being gunned down. Besides my father, I didn't even know anyone who had been shot. Was this the life that I wanted to continue with? I didn't really know the answer to that question and I knew that it didn't really matter since I didn't have a choice. Diamond was still sleeping on the other end of the sofa. I couldn't imagine being in her position. I mean, I would love the money, the jewels, and the power but all of the other shit that came with it was for the birds. I wasn't really trying to have to duck from bullets each time I went out for a night of fun. I got up and headed upstairs to use the bathroom.

For the first time, I got a chance to look around their house. It was definitely like something in a magazine. I walked toward the end of the hall and pushed open the door that led to their bedroom. The bed was huge with posts on each end that almost reached the high ceilings.

The linens were beige and cream, which matched the wood of the bed and hardwood floors. There was a huge area rug with the same colors in it. I moved close to the bed that was perfectly made. I could tell Diamond's side of the bed from Kemp's by the items neatly placed on their end tables. I bent down and placed my nose close to the sheets and could smell cologne. I wasn't crazy but I needed to at least imagine that it was my place. Even though it hadn't been that long since I was with a man, it was long enough for me to feel lonely.

I peeked in the drawers to find everything folded perfectly. Who the hell had time to organize things like this? I mean, both of them were pretty busy so unless they never touched any of these things they had to have a maid. After awhile, I felt like I was intruding too much and I would have been too embarrassed if she walked in here and caught me snooping around. I left out of the room and just as I was walking into the bathroom Diamond was coming up the stairs.

"Hey girl, you were knocked out down there. I was looking for a washcloth so I could wash my face and stuff," I lied, because I was almost caught coming out of her room.

"Oh, they are right in the bathroom closet behind the door."

"Okay, thanks, how are you feeling?"

"I'm okay, girl, just stiff as hell," she laughed, as she rubbed the back of her neck.

"Did you hear anything about Black?"

"Yeah, I talked to Kemp he said he was still in surgery but was expected to make it out of it okay."

"That's good. Well, could you drive me back to the apartment today?"

"I thought we were going to hang out for the day. I'm stressed, girl, I need some company."

"Okay, we can hang out, what did you have planned?"

"I wanted to go shopping but I also wanted to stop by and see my mom. It'll be good for her since she hasn't seen you in years. I know she'd be happy to see you."

"That's cool, I'm gonna freshen up and if you drive me by the apartment I can change and we can hit the road."

"You can wear something of mine. You're not too much bigger than I am and I got tons of shit I haven't even worn yet. When you're done in there just look in my closet and grab whatever you want."

I was glad that we were getting back on track. I hadn't really had a lot of friends that I could hang out with. I missed it and I felt like things were going to happen for the better. I thought about last night, before the shoot-out and how much fun we had. JB seemed like someone I could get used to. He wasn't as fine as Tyson was but he was definitely more attractive with the money he had. I know it sounds like something a gold digger would say, but I wasn't a gold digger by a long shot. I was just used to a certain kind of lifestyle and the only men that I was attracted to were men that could help me keep it up. I had my eye on him and I was going to try and get any information on him that I could.

After freshening up in the bathroom, I went back into Diamond's room where she was now in the master bathroom taking a shower. I opened up the double doors that led to her huge walk-in closet. There was so much to choose from, I didn't know where to start. I'd never seen so much designer shit in one place in my life. I had been treated well by Tyson but he'd never spoiled me like this. I took down different articles of clothing and put them close to my body, modeling in the mirror. I felt like a kid in a candy store. If there was one thing that I loved, it was to dress up. Normally, I didn't feel like I was pretty or desirable. I always needed someone to tell me that I looked pretty and even then I still didn't believe it. Putting on one of her outfits would definitely boost my confidence and a little boost was just what I needed. I settled on a black Betsey Johnson dress. It was a casual dress and would work perfectly in the spring air. I put it on and it fit perfectly. How Diamond and me ended up the same size, I'll never know. I was always a little thicker than her especially in the thigh and booty area but over the years she'd filled out in the areas where she was once lacking.

She came into the room and looked at me with a smile.

I stood there waiting for her approval.

"Good choice, I love that dress. It looks good on you," she said.

I was relieved. For some strange reason I felt like I needed to hear her say those words to me. I was desperate for attention and I was going to try my best to be as perfect as possible. I knew that was what I had to do if I wanted to snag a hustler. Diamond quickly got dressed and put on her makeup. She looked as if she was ready to go walk a runway, definitely not like she was going to pay her mom a visit.

Once we got into her two-door convertible Mercedes-Benz, she let the top down. She turned on the radio and instantly began singing along with the popular Beyoncé tune

"Get Me Bodied." I did like the song, so I started singing and dancing along with her, quickly forgetting about the wind and my hair.

Driving through the old neighborhood brought back so many memories. Even though it wasn't the best neighborhood it was what I called home. I didn't know anything better existed until I met Tyson. All I knew were abandoned houses, drug dealers and fiends. The streets were filthy but we skipped and ran all around them as if they were invisible. I smiled inside, thinking of being a kid again. Having my brother to watch my back and keep me safe. Though my dad was abusive, I missed him. What girl wants to grow up without a father? There were a lot of things that I didn't get a chance to learn from him. I was forced to fend for myself when my mother's depression turned her into a shell.

Soon I turned my attention off of the sad things and focused on the good. At least I made it through okay because there were plenty of people that had fallen victim to the same society that I grew up in. We parked in front of her grandmother's house. I laughed because everything looked exactly the same. Even after the years passed she still had the same lawn chair on her porch and a bunch of flowerpots hanging around the awning. Diamond looked at me, probably wondering what the hell I was laughing at but I straightened up when she turned back around. She walked up to the door and began to knock. It took a few seconds for someone to open the door.

"Diamond?" her aunt asked, as if she wasn't sure who she was. I knew that she didn't come down here very often, but damn, how could you forget your niece. I soon realized that she did know who she was but was just startled by her visit.

"Why are you acting like you don't know me?" Diamond asked, turning her face into a frown. She was clearly annoyed.

"I'm not, Diamond. I'm just surprised to see you, that's all," Cicely replied, still holding her spot blocking the door.

"Well, the good thing is that I didn't come to see you or else I would've been crushed by the warm welcome," Diamond replied sarcastically. "Where is my mom?"

"Your mom?" Cicely asked, still playing dumb. I didn't know what the hell was going on here but I could tell that there wasn't going to be a happy ending to it.

"What's up with you today? I don't think I'm speaking in another language."

Cicely stood there silent as if there was something that she wanted to say but just couldn't muster up the courage to say it. What the hell was going on? Now I was curious. Diamond was becoming more agitated and soon she pushed her way past Cicely and went into the house. She stood there staring at me as if she wanted me to do something. What was I supposed to do? I didn't even want to move from the step that my feet were planted on. I heard Diamond in the house calling her mother's name over and over again, then I heard her grandmom call out her name from a distance. I assumed that she was upstairs because I heard the sound of Diamond's shoes on the hard wood. It was so strange because I was still standing on the steps and Cicely was still standing at the door with a blank look on her face as if we were stuck in time or something.

Within a few minutes Diamond came flying out of the house, pushing Cicely out of the way and heading toward the car. She had tears streaming down her face. I didn't know what to say.

"Diamond," I called out to her. She didn't turn around to face me.

"Let's go!" she yelled in response.

I ran to the car and got inside. I could barely close the door all the way before she was speeding off down the street. She was crying hysterically, wiping her eyes to make sure that she could see the road.

"Diamond," I called out her name again. "What?"

"What happened?"

"If I had a gun I would shoot that bitch! I mean, I knew that she hated me but she took this shit to another level."

I sat there quiet, still confused. I didn't know who or what she was talking about.

"My mother is dead," she cried.

"Dead?" I asked, confused.

"They buried my fucking mother and didn't even tell me. How could they do that shit?"

"They did what?" I had to ask again to make sure that I was hearing her correctly. Who would do that? I mean, you would have to be a real fucked-up individual to neglect to tell someone their mother died.

"She died, Mica, she fucking died and they didn't bother to tell me." She stopped at the light and put her head down on the steering wheel. I put my hand on her back and tried to quietly let her know that I was here for her. I knew how it felt to lose a parent and it was something no one wanted to experience. She probably felt bad since her relationship wasn't as close as she would have liked it to be. The reality of that is once they're gone you can never get the chance to make up for the time that was lost.

The light turned green and the cars behind us started to beep their horns. She wasn't in any condition to drive so I told her to pull over so I could take over from there. She did and I was glad that I didn't have to argue with her to do so. People rarely make the best decisions when they're upset and I wasn't trying to be a casualty of something that I didn't have any part in causing. She got out and walked around to the passenger side, glancing at me before getting inside. I didn't know what to say so I stayed quiet. What could you say at a time like this? Nothing that I said would make her feel better or come close to bringing her mother back.

I figured that we would just go back to her house and get in contact with Kemp to let him know what had just happened. She continued to sob as I made it down the expressway toward their home. I made sure to glance at her every few minutes to make sure she wasn't having a nervous breakdown or anything like that. Shit, that was the last thing that I needed to happen right now.

We pulled up to the house about a half hour after leaving her grandmom's house and the driveway was empty, which meant that Kemp wasn't home. Damn, where was your man when you needed him? She got of the car once I parked and walked like a zombie up to the front door. I followed behind her.

She went upstairs and within a few minutes I heard the bathroom door close and the water began to run. I wanted to ask her Kemp's number so that I could call him but I'd leave that decision up to her. If she wanted to call him I figured that she would have called him herself. Since she didn't, I would mind my business and relax downstairs until she came back down. A few minutes later the phone rang and startled me. I let it ring a few times before I answered it. It was strange that I felt comfortable enough to answer her phone, but deep inside I was hoping that it was Kemp so that I could tell him what happened.

"Hello," I said in a low tone. I didn't want Diamond to hear me.

"Who is this?"

"Mica. Is this Kemp?"

"Yeah, where's Diamond?"

"Something bad's happened, she needs you right now."

"Bad? Like what?"

"I'll let her tell you when you get here but she really needs you right now."

"All right, I'll be there."

Damn, that was easy, I guess he really did care about her. I didn't expect him to just drop everything and come right home. Men like Kemp usually cared more about their work and money more than anything. I'm not saying that they're heartless but their priorities are just different than normal people. The shower was still running, I thought that it was pretty long for her to be in there but I figured that she was using it to drown away tears. I had done it myself in the past and though it wouldn't make everything go away, it eased the pain temporarily.

About twenty minutes later Kemp came in the front door. He looked at me, probably waiting for an answer, but I sat quiet.

"Where is she at?"

"In the shower, she's been in there a long time, though." He ran up the steps skipping two at a time. I heard him banging on the bathroom door and calling her name. I began to get worried so I hurried up the steps and stood at their bedroom door. She wasn't answering and his knocks got louder and louder. After a few more seconds of no response he used his shoulder to knock the door open. I ran to the bathroom to follow him. Diamond was sitting on the floor of the shower with the water running over her. She was awake but had a blank stare on her face. This is what I was afraid of. Kemp shook her a little bit and called her name. She still didn't respond. Kemp picked her up and brought her out of the bathroom. I grabbed some towels and put them on top of her.

"Babe, what's going on?" Kemp asked, as she began to come out of whatever trance she was in. "Talk to me, Diamond."

"I'm okay, I was just a little tired."

"No, that was something else. What the hell is going on?"

"Her mom died and they didn't tell her," I blurted out. She gave me an evil stare, but shit, he needed to know. She was acting crazy. I didn't know what the big deal was. Why wouldn't you want your husband to know what happened?

"What? They didn't tell you?"

"No, they didn't. I was a little upset but I'm okay now. Honestly, I just want to be left alone so I can go to sleep."

"You sure?" Kemp asked, while rubbing her hand. This was the sensitive side of him and strangely it was turning me on. I mean, Kemp was fine as hell and not to mention super-rich. What woman wouldn't be turned on by him?

I stepped out of the room to give them some time. It wasn't long before Kemp came downstairs and joined me on the sofa.

"Is she okay?" I asked.

"I guess so. That's fucked-up, what her family did."

"I know, I couldn't believe it, I just stood there trying to figure out what the hell was going on."

"Well, she's the type that likes to hold shit in until she explodes, so if she doesn't want to talk she won't."

"I'm glad that you came though because I was almost on my way out the door." I lied. I just wanted to make him believe that his presence was appreciated. Shit, his wife damn sure wasn't.

"It's cool, ma, I'm so used to her; it don't even bother me anymore."

"Well, it should. I mean, she is your wife." I sat still, wondering what his response would be.

He turned and looked at me puzzled, probably wondering where the hell that came from. I mean, he didn't know our history so he couldn't possibly think that we were friends.

I was glad that she'd been helping me out but I still didn't trust her and at this point she shouldn't trust me, either. Her man had caught my eye, and if she wasn't willing to do what she had to do to keep him I was going to let him know that he could find what he needed in me. Hell, I was a sucka for love and any way that I could get it I was planning to.

Chapter Twenty-five

Diamond: Stick to the Script

Though I was still angry, I realized that I didn't have a choice but to get over it if I wanted to move on with my plans. I didn't trust Mica as far as I could throw her and I almost doubted her importance. I mean, did I really need her? I didn't doubt that I could handle it on my own, but now that she knew a little bit of what I had planned she could potentially ruin it all. I wasn't about to let that happen. I felt like she was trying to backstab me anyway. I didn't ask her to call Kemp nor did I ask her to tell him what happened so I knew that she had an angle. I just had to figure out what the hell it was.

I tried to steer clear of her for a few days just to get my plan in order. I decided to let Kiki in on what I'd been up to. I hadn't spent much time with her lately and I know that she would probably think I was crazy, but I was far from crazy. I was more determined, if anything. I lightly knocked on Kiki's door, hoping that she wouldn't peek out the door, see it was me, and leave me standing there like a fool. I stood out there for a minute or two and had turned around and began to head back down the steps. I heard the lock on the inside turning and smiled as I turned back around.

"Still impatient, I see." She laughed, while putting her hand on her hip and shaking her finger at me like I was a student that had been bad in class. She was right, I was impatient and I'd probably always possess that character trait.

"I know, girl. I missed you, I thought you would be pissed at me."

"I am pissed but it doesn't mean I'm not happy to see you," she said, reaching out to give me a hug.

"Where the hell have you been?"

"Long story, girl," I said as I walked into her living room.

"I'm listening. Shit, I want to know what had my best friend so tied up she couldn't even call and see how a bitch was doing."

"Kemp got me wrapped up in some crap." I conveniently left out the fact that my mother had died. I didn't want her to feel sorry for me so I figured the only way to do that was simply not to tell her about it.

"Don't tell me you're going down that road again, you promised me you wouldn't do that to yourself again."

"Hell no, girl. I'm not a damn fool. I know better than to get wrapped up in that again. You remember that girl Mica I told you I used to hang with back in the day?"

"I think so, but what does she have to do with anything?"

"Well, Kemp kidnapped her because her man stole some of Kemp's money. To make a long story short we started catching up on time lost and I felt like I could use her in my plan."

"Plan? What the hell are you talking about, Diamond? I don't know if I like the way that sounds."

"Well, you know that when I met Kemp my goal was to get enough money to make it on my own. I wasn't trying to get caught up like I did with Davey's trifling ass. I only made it official and married his ass because I could get so much more from it. I'm about to get what's mine. Shit, I've been through too much pain not to."

"I'm still clueless."

"I'm going to take over Kemp's empire."

"What?" she asked, before bursting into laughter.

"What's so funny about that?" I was a little annoyed—laughter definitely wasn't the reaction that I was expecting. I expected her to be upset and try to talk me out of it. That was the Kiki I knew. Even though what she said usually went in one ear and out of the other I still liked to hear it from time to time. At least that made me think that someone cared about the choices I made, because the reality is most times I didn't. I know that may sound like the dumbest things you've ever heard, but it was just the way that things were. I've made a lot of decisions that were careless, but I usually came out on top.

"It's not really funny. I just can't believe you're serious, but if you are I want to know how I can get a slice of the pie."

Now I was really confused. What the hell had happened to her in the past month?

"Kiki, are you serious?"

"Yeah, girl, shit, if you're going to hit it big why can't I join you? I am your best friend, unless Ms. Mica has come and taken my place."

"First of all, I don't even trust her so there is no way in hell that she could take your place."

"So then tell me about the plan and stop beating around the bush."

"Okay, I have to get rid of him in order to inherit all of his businesses and money."

"What? What the hell do you mean, you want to kill him?"

"That's the only way." She probably really thought I was crazy now.

"You are really serious. What's gonna happen if you get caught?"

"I'm not going to get caught; I'm way too smart for that."

"Being smart ain't got shit to do with it, the smartest people get locked up. I just hope that you know what you're doing because I don't want to see you in the penitentiary."

"That's not even an option."

"Well, you know I got your back and anything that you need me to do I got you"

She reached out to hug me. I was confident that she had my back no matter what. I wanted her help but I knew that there was a possibility that I would get caught. I didn't want to drag her into my mess. I was afraid of going to jail again, especially for murder, but I had to go through with it. Was I crazy? Maybe a little, but who wouldn't want to inherit all that I stood to gain? There wasn't anything that I wanted more than the power of running his empire.

"I love you, girl, even though you're crazy as hell!" She laughed.

"I know." I joined in the laughter.

After leaving I stopped at the Hallmark card store to pick out a get-well-soon card for Black. He had left the hospital and was in rehab. I hadn't gotten to see him since the night of the shooting. I called Kemp to see where he was, since I didn't really want him to know that I was visiting Black. Was there a reason for me to leave that information out? Definitely, since no man wants competition and I'm sure that if he had any competition in the world Black was the strongest contender. It took me all of a half an hour to find the perfect card. I wanted to make sure it said all I wanted it to say. I was just on my way out of the store when my cell phone rang. I took it out and glanced at the caller ID. It was Mica. I really didn't want to talk to her, but I knew that if she knew that I was angry it would screw things up.

"Hello?"

"Hey, girl, what's going on? Feeling any better?"

"Yeah, I'm okay."

"What are you doing? I want to go to the mall."

"I have to make a run, but if I get done early enough I'll call you."

"I can make the run with you if you stop by and scoop me up."

"No, I'll see you when I'm done. This is something I have to do alone." I was getting annoyed. I barely wanted to talk to her ass, let alone hang out with her at the damn mall.

"Okay, then, just call me. I'm bored to death over here."

"All right," I quickly responded before I hung up. I was trying to hurry her off the phone before I made it to the rehab. I didn't want her to hear anything in the background that would give her a clue about where I was. I still didn't trust her and I still hadn't figured out what trick she had up her sleeve.

Once I reached Black's room I was almost too nervous to go inside. I didn't know if I should have been there or not. I definitely couldn't risk Kemp finding out about the visit so I was planning to make it quick. I knocked on the door even though it was open and smiled when he turned around to look my way.

"Diamond, what's up? I'm surprised to see you here."

"I know. Glad to see you're up moving around," I said before passing him the card and bending down to give him a hug. The hug felt so good that I almost didn't want to let go.

He obviously didn't want to let go because each time I tried to pull away he pulled me closer. It was weird but it was something that I wanted. Shit, I wanted more but I knew that now wasn't the time to pursue it.

"This feels too good, I don't want to let go," he whispered into my ear. The whisper sent chills up and down my spine.

"Well, I can't stay here forever so I guess that means you have to."

"I guess so," he laughed. "So what brings you here? I'm surprised Kemp let you come up here unsupervised."

"I didn't tell him that I was coming."

"Why not, you plan on doing something wrong?"

"I don't plan on it but shit happens."

"Shit happens, huh? That's your excuse for wanting me?"

"What excuse? And who said that I wanted you?"

"Come on now, Diamond, we're both grown. You don't have to bullshit me. I'm a real nigga and I know when someone wants the kid."

"I'm happy with Kemp so I'm really not trying to screw that up."

"You're not happy and we both know that. You need a nigga like me in your life. Kemp has the money and power but you'll never be much more than a trophy to him."

"What?" I was a little annoyed by that comment, but honestly it was probably the truth. Was I nothing more to him but a prize to put on display? The fact that I was using him should have meant that I didn't care, but it didn't. Who wanted to feel used? I definitely didn't take that kind of thing lightly. "I doubt that I'm his trophy. I am his wife. Why would he have married me in the first place?"

"Because that's what he does. You're not his first wife, Diamond. Kemp likes control and by marrying you he can keep you closer. You fell right in line like the other ones just because of the dollar signs."

"He's been married before?" I asked. I couldn't believe that he hadn't told me that. I should have known by the way he rushed me to get married. Damn, I hoped that didn't mean I would have competition when it was time to collect the money. I wished that I had known about this from the beginning.

"There are a lot of things about Kemp that you don't know. He's pretty good at keeping secrets. I've known him all my life so I know more about him than anyone."

"So why are you telling me this?"

"Because I like you and I feel like you deserve better."

"But if Kemp found out you know that he would be furious. Why would you risk that?"

"Kemp doesn't scare me and when I've got my eye on the prize I fight to win it."

I had to really sit back and think about what he was saying. Was he really serious? How the hell would he expect to be with me with Kemp still alive? I couldn't let him know what I planned to do, but it was weird that he would come at me as if he already knew. I know that I was smarter than most women and definitely smarter than the other wives he had. I knew this because I was his wife now. I'd be dammed if I was going to let him walk away from me and leave me with nothing.

I was tempted to let the inevitable happen. Black knew that I was attracted to him and it was just a matter of time before I let myself fall for him. But then my plan came back to mind. I couldn't mess it up—I had to stick to the script for things to go my way.

Chapter Twenty-six

Mica: Make Me Love You

If she even had the slightest clue that we were sneaking around behind her back, I'm positive I'd have a fight on my hands. I couldn't resist. Following the night that her mother died I was there for him when she wasn't. We had formed a bond and he promised me that soon I would be able to take her place. Besides the fact that I didn't trust her, I knew for a fact that she was using him and he was a good man, for the most part. He had his flaws as did everyone else, but I'd rather have the man and the money and not the money without the man. What was I supposed to do? Turn down a man that could make all of my dreams come true? I was a sucka when I fell for Tyson but Kemp was different. He was a man of his word. I knew for a fact that whatever he said he would do—would be done.

I thought about my brother a lot lately. I still hadn't been able to see him and even letters telling him that I was friends with Diamond again didn't get me a visit. I didn't know what else I could possibly do to make him want to see me, but I wasn't about to give up on him, either. I decided to try one last time to visit him. If he turned me away this time I wasn't going to force myself to try it again. I took the long ride up to the prison and was searched and put into the waiting area. After waiting for a half hour my name was called. I smiled. He hadn't turned me away. I rushed toward the door that led to the visiting area. He sat there at the table with his head down. Either he was tired or not happy to see me. I didn't care, at least this time he accepted my visit.

When I reached the table he looked up but didn't speak. Almost as if he didn't have anything to say or was waiting to see what I would say first. I had a lot to say, so much that I didn't know where to start. He looked different as if he'd aged five years since the last time I'd seen him. He stood up, silent, and reached his arms out to give me a hug. He was thin, not the muscular body that I was used to.

"I'm glad to see you," he said in a low tone before sitting back down in the seat.

"What happened to you? Are you sick or something?"

"Damn, it's that obvious?"

"What's wrong, Johnny?" I began to get nervous. I could tell by looking at him that something was wrong but I wasn't sure if I was really ready to hear his answer.

"I'm sick, baby girl, real sick," he said without looking me in the eye.

"Well, what is it? What's going on, Johnny?" I could feel the tears building up and I knew as soon as he told me they would begin to fall.

"I have cancer and I don't have much longer to live."

"Cancer?" I asked to make sure that I heard him right.

"Yeah, I have cancer and I want to apologize for not accepting your visits. I was being selfish because I didn't want you to see me like this."

I couldn't speak. The words were sinking in. I was going to lose my brother and there wasn't anything that I could do about it. After the shock came the anger. I was upset that he had denied me the time. His time was limited and he hadn't even thought about how this would affect me, especially since I hadn't been able to see him in months. I wanted to tell him the things that had been happening, but after hearing what he just said I felt like it wasn't even important. Besides, I didn't want to upset him. I was still crying. He reached across the table and held my hand.

"I'm sorry, Mica," was all that he could say to me. There wasn't anything that would make me feel better. I wanted to hear that this was all a big joke or a bad dream. I wished I could turn back the hands of time and he wouldn't have been here in the first place.

"I can't believe this, Johnny. Does Mom know?"

"Yeah, she knows, but I told her that I wanted to tell you myself."

"So she knew all this time and didn't tell me?" I was furious. That was just like my mother to withhold information. I didn't care if he'd told her not to tell me, how could she think it was okay not to tell me that my only brother was dying?

"I'm sorry, Mica."

"Stop saying you're sorry, it's not your fault that you're sick. I just wish you would have told me sooner. Here I was thinking that you just didn't want to see me. I knew that I hadn't done anything wrong but that's how I felt. Horrible."

"I was trying to protect you."

"Protect me from what? I was going to have to know eventually." I didn't care what the reason was. It didn't matter if I found out now or six months ago, I would still be just as upset as I was.

"So, enough about me, let's talk about you. What's happening in your life?"

"Nothing that I want to talk about." I was still stuck thinking about what he'd just told me.

"Listen, Mica, you can't let this get you down. You're a soldier. I'm gonna be all right and think about it this way. At least I won't be locked up anymore. Anywhere's got to be better than here."

He was right, any place would be better than prison but that idea still wouldn't make me feel better about the fact that he would be gone soon. Eventually, I opened up and was able to tell him a little bit of what was on with me before the visiting time was over. I told him that I had a new love in my life but conveniently left out the fact that he was a married man. I also left out all details concerning Diamond. I didn't want to risk anything upsetting him. I had a lot to think about on the way back. I was glad that I'd finally got to see him and know that there wasn't anything that I had done to make him upset with me, but I was still upset about losing him.

I decided to go to Diamond's to see if she felt like shopping. I called a cab, which arrived about a half hour later. If I'd had a choice I wouldn't go with her but I didn't have any friends. I know that's pathetic but it was the truth. I was never able to form any close friendships especially after I fell out with

Diamond. I got to the house and didn't notice her car in the driveway. I still decided to knock just in case she had put it in the garage. I stood there for five minutes or so before I heard footsteps.

"What's up?" Kemp asked, standing shirtless. I almost melted right into their welcome mat. He smiled, probably noticing the trance that he'd put me in.

"Is Diamond here?"

"No, but you can come in; she won't be here for a while."

"Are you sure, Kemp? I don't want her to walk in here and catch me here with you."

"She's not coming anytime soon, trust me."

I hesitated but decided to take the chance and go for it. Hell, I couldn't resist him when he was fully clothed, so looking at him half naked was like a magnet. He closed the door as I walked toward the living room. Before I knew it he was hugging me from behind. I could smell his cologne as it tickled my nose. He must've taken a bath in it for his skin to smell as good as it did.

"Kemp, what are you doing?"

"What do you mean? You know what I'm doing." His hands were steadily caressing me. I still tried to push him away. I was nervous. I had already had a bad day and I didn't want to risk her coming in here flipping out. Each time we'd met it was at the apartment. I had never been so bold to come in their house to meet up with him. Kemp didn't care one way or another since he was looking for a reason to leave her. I, on the other hand, wasn't in a rush to get into a confrontation. The way I was feeling, I couldn't stop him from making me feel good. I wanted it, I needed it, and I was sure that it was going to be worth it. He hadn't let me down yet. Besides his money and looks, I knew firsthand why all the women fell for him and he did too.

He used his instrument to his advantage and that advantage was to make you love him.

He moved me toward the stairs as he continued to caress me and kiss my neck. I didn't fight it, instead I let him guide me up the stairs to the bedroom. *The bedroom.* I thought I was finally going to get the chance to lie in the bed that I'd imagined. I remembered the first time I came in the room and wished that it were mine. I was closer to that dream than ever and nothing could make me see it any other way now.

His lips were making a path down my back and sending chills all through my body. My panties were soaking wet, anticipating feeling him inside of me. I wanted to be with him, I wanted to love him. He moved me closer to the bed and bent me over before palming my ass. I held the position, ready for what he'd do next. He raised my dress and pulled my panties down. I assisted by stepping out of them and getting back in the doggy-style position. I didn't even hear him dropping his pants, but I knew that he had once his dick was rubbing up and down my wet pussy. I almost came early but I held it in. He pushed me down on the bed and pulled my ass up a little then entered me from behind. His dick was thick and filled me up. I was moaning loudly; this was even better than I had imagined. Diamond didn't deserve all of this. She wasn't in love with him. I wanted to prove that she couldn't love him like I could.

Once he turned me over I took the initiative to push him on his back. A man loved when a woman took control, became aggressive. I straddled him and looked him in the eyes. I moved up and down then into slow circles, grinding my hips so that his dick could go deeper. He was moaning with me. At this point, I couldn't hold in my eruption any longer. My juices began to run down the shaft of his dick, making it extremely wet. I was sweating, he was sweating, and I was going wild trying to reach another orgasm before he reached his.

"Oh shit, oh shit, damn, I'm cumming, oh this pussy is so good!" he moaned.

I felt myself reaching another orgasm; again, I came all over him. I was exhausted but satisfied. I stopped and looked at him. He smiled. I hoped that this wouldn't be the last time we were together. I wanted this to last for a very long time. The problem with that was, it wasn't up to me. God had his own plan. I head a *click* as if it were a gun pointed in my direction. I jumped off of Kemp and found Diamond standing at the door with the face of evil. I didn't know what to say, how could I explain this?

I almost went numb as Kemp tried to reason with her and calm her down. It didn't matter, she had her mind made up. Now, instead of me being able to share in the wealth, she was going to kill me too. I had betrayed her, she trusted me. I should have thought about it more before I jumped into their bed. I should have planned this better. Maybe had I told him what she planned to do I wouldn't be sitting here facing a gun. I couldn't even move, I wanted to just close my eyes and imagine that it was all a dream.

It wasn't a dream and the two bullets that hit me confirmed that. All I felt was burning, then wetness, and then I felt dizzy. I couldn't move, I felt my eyelids getting heavy and I couldn't hold them open. I felt pain and then nothing . . .

Chapter Twenty-seven

Diamond: HBIC

Two months had passed since the night that I'd killed Mica and Kemp. For at least two weeks I couldn't close my eyes without replaying the scene. I could still see the blood splattered all over the room. I was sick for days and even the help of Kiki and Black couldn't get me through the funeral. If you'd been there you would have thought I deserved an Oscar, but honestly it wasn't a performance. I couldn't bear to see Kemp laid up in a casket. Not because I loved him and was sorry for what I'd done, but because I couldn't get the scene of the murder out of my head. As for Mica, I didn't go to her memorial because I felt that there wasn't any need to act as if I cared. It may sound cold, but that was just the way it was.

I had inherited all of Kemp's assets, including the two-million-dollar insurance policy that I had on him. His stores, his cars, his homes—everything he had was all mine and there wasn't anyone who could take it from me. His drug empire—well, that was mine too and I know some would wonder how a woman could do a man's job, especially a man with as much respect and power as Kemp. It was pretty simple—since they respected Kemp, they respected me. That may sound foolish because Kemp was dead, but it didn't matter and just as they worked for him they now worked for me. Maintaining order was the easiest part, keeping my feelings for his best friend a secret was the hardest.

Yes, I admit it, I've loved Black since the moment I saw him. I always believed that if this had been another lifetime, I would have been with him a long time ago. I didn't really know how his workers would take to me starting a relationship with Kemp's right-hand man, so I held off as long as I could. It didn't take long before I couldn't resist and his advances didn't make it any easier.

Black had stepped up, helping me run things. I would have never expected him to do that for me. Especially after I found out that he knew about the fact that I killed Kemp. Yeah, I was shocked when I found out too. I wondered how the hell he would know and I was also nervous because I believed that if he knew then that meant there could possibly be someone else that knew too.

Going back to that night, I thought that I had covered everything but obviously I hadn't. The night that he told me, I sat across from him still as a statue wondering how I could have been so stupid.

"I saw you when you left the house with the trash bag in hand. You had on a sweat suit and I've known you long enough to know that you wouldn't be caught dead in that get-up. Plus your face looked strange, like you were upset. I was going to say something but I watched instead. Once you left, I went inside and saw the scene, then I knew what happened. I threw some stuff around to make it look like a robbery gone wrong and I bounced."

I continued to sit still. I thought for sure he would have reported me to the police. I mean, Kemp was his best friend.

"Don't think I'm going to turn you in because I've already incriminated myself. Shit, they'd lock my ass up with you. I don't know what happened in that room and at this point, I don't even want to know."

"So you put your freedom in jeopardy for me?"

"Actually, I did it for us. I see opportunity here. What would you going to jail prove? That I'm a snitch? Naw, I'm far from being a snitch, I'm a businessman. I wanted you for a long time and what better time than now, to make that happen?"

"Are you serious? What the hell would the workers say? They'd think we set the whole thing up."

"No they won't, this makes perfect sense. Why go out searching for a good nigga when you have one right here in front of you?"

Okay, I guess he was serious. What he said made sense. I probably wouldn't find a man that could deal with my newfound wealth nor one that could hold it down for me.

What was I supposed to do? I needed some help. Fuck it, I was going for it. I got up out of the chair and kissed him. He kissed me back. I was ready to tear his clothes off and fuck him right on top of the desk. It had been a few months since I'd had some. Our lips unlocked; he stared at me as if he was thinking what I was. I was about to walk to the door and lock it when I heard a knock. The door opened.

"Girl, what's up?" Kiki said, holding a bouquet of flowers. "These were outside on the step."

"Outside?" I asked. Black looked at me, just as confused as I was. Who the hell would leave flowers on my step? There was a card with a note. I smiled, thinking that I had a secret admirer. I took out the card, smelled the flowers, and laid them on the desk.

"Read the card, girl!" Kiki yelled.

"Okay!" I replied.

I took the card out of the envelope and opened it. Once I did, I wished that I hadn't. Tears began to form in my eyes. Kiki and Black were both looking at me, wondering what the hell was wrong. I put my hand over my mouth and began to cry. How could this have happened?

"What's wrong, what does it say?" Black asked, moving close to me.

"It says, 'I hope you enjoyed the last two months—get ready for a war. You should have checked my pulse to see if I was dead.' " The note was handwritten and resembled Kemp's handwriting. I just knew this had to be a cruel joke.

"What?" Kiki looked at me, shocked.

Black snatched the note out of my hands and read it. He looked at me. I couldn't believe it. This had to be a cruel joke. There was no way that Kemp was alive. My body began to shake. I had to sit down before I fell to the ground. I sat in the chair sobbing. What was I going to do now? If Kemp was alive I was as good as dead. Then I thought about Black. He had gone in the house after me. Shit! That meant Kemp saw him. Now, not only would he be after me, but Black as well. I dragged him into this. I was numb, I couldn't think. Damn, why hadn't I checked his pulse? Why was I so sure that he'd died? Kiki looked as scared as me. Black was pacing the floor as if he was trying to come up with a plan. I hoped that he could. After a few minutes of pacing, he stopped in front of me.

"Don't worry, I'll take care of it."

I looked up at him. I hoped that he could so that we could get on with our lives. I wanted things to go as planned. I wanted to continue being the head bitch in charge. I worked too hard for the title too lose it all.

I instantly flashed back to that night and tried to figure out what I'd missed. Black went inside after me so he should have noticed. Did he see what I saw? I never really wanted to talk about it after that night but I just couldn't understand how I'd been so careless. Yes, I was emotional, but this could be the end for me; this could be the end for both Black and me.

"Don't worry, you'll take care of it?" I yelled.

"That's what I said, don't worry about it."

"How the hell do you expect me to do that? There's no way I can act like I didn't just read that fucking note. How the hell could this happen, Black? What the hell are we going to do?"

Kiki stood still as a statue; she couldn't believe it either. She warned me about this, telling me that I needed to be careful and now look what happened. I wanted her to say something. I wanted someone to say anything that made sense at this point, because saying *don't worry* just wasn't going to get it. It just wasn't possible at a time like this.

"Didn't you see him, Black? What did you see when you went inside the house?"

"Diamond, I just told you what happened."

"Well, I need you to tell me again. Please tell me anything that would make this seem like a joke. This has to be a joke."

"I was sitting in the car when I saw you come out—I didn't see anyone else around. No cars or anything. I was sitting there waiting for Kemp to call me—we were supposed to go make a drop. I didn't know what the fuck was going on but I knew that something wasn't right. I waited until you pulled off and used the spare key Kemp gave me to go inside. I called his name and when I didn't get a response, I went upstairs and saw him lay out on the floor near the bed. I noticed that you tried to throw some things around but it looked staged so I hurried and ransacked the place a little more and then I left."

"He was on the floor?" I asked. From what I remembered he was on the bed, so how the hell did he get on the floor?

"Yeah, he was on the floor. Why does that matter?"

"Because when I shot him he was on the bed. How the hell could he have gotten on the floor unless he wasn't dead?"

Black stood there with a puzzled look on his face. I was still trying to figure this out, there had to be something that we were missing. Kiki still stood in the same spot, silent.

"He has to be dead, Diamond, it just doesn't make any sense."

"I know that it doesn't make sense but I know that someone knows something if they're sending shit like this."

"There was no one else there, though, I sat outside and didn't see anyone else."

"The note clearly says something different." I was frustrated. This was something that I didn't need to deal with—I couldn't deal with it.

"D, I'm kind of thinking Black's right. I mean, if he went in and saw him dead then it can't be him," Kiki finally chimed in, though she wasn't saying anything that I wanted to hear.

This situation had me questioning everyone and everything. I wanted this to be over, I wanted to believe that everything was going to be okay but it didn't appear that way. I took the note from Black's hand and read it again—I still couldn't believe my eyes. I grabbed my bag off of the chair and headed toward the door without saying a word. I heard footsteps behind me but I didn't turn to look.

"Diamond, wait," Black yelled.

"What, Black? I need to get home right now so talk to me when you get there."

"Why are you angry at me? I'm not the one that's doing anything. Shit, you shot him—I just tried to help you cover it up."

I turned around and gave him the stare of death. "I didn't ask for your fucking help, I didn't ask you for anything."

"I didn't mean it like that, Diamond. I'm just trying to figure out why you're mad at me."

"I'm not mad at you, I'm mad at myself. I fucked up and now I could be killed. Look, I have to go. I'll talk to you at home."

"I'm going to follow you, so just wait a minute. I don't feel comfortable with you traveling alone."

I didn't respond. I got in the car and drove off, leaving him standing there. I didn't want to be followed. I didn't want to feel like a damn criminal or a child. I wanted shit to be normal. I looked in the rearview mirror and didn't see him. I needed some time alone. There wasn't anything that he could say to make me feel better. The only thing that would make me feel better was knowing Kemp's body was six feet under where I watched them lower it.

Chapter Twenty-eight

Diamond

Tricks of the Trade, November 2007

I had to see for myself. If I had the strength to dig six feet under I would have brought a shovel out here to this cemetery. It was cold and dark. Most people would think I was crazy for coming out here alone at 12 A.M. but for once in my life I could honestly admit that I was afraid. I had done too much to turn back or to even apologize, for that matter. How could you say I'm sorry for shooting you? The fact of the matter was that I wasn't sorry for shooting him, I was sorry that he hadn't died. I was confused—I could remember that day as if it were yesterday. I stood there at the foot of the bed as both Kemp and Mica's blood poured out onto the sheets and soaked into the bed. Someone was trying to scare me and it was definitely working. He couldn't be alive. I didn't stay around to check his pulse but I knew it had to be him buried there. I put on an Oscar-worthy performance at the funeral, even kissed his cold cheek. I was sure that I had gotten away with murder. What was I supposed to do now? I got down on my knees and put my hand on the headstone that read his name. So many things were running through my mind at this point. I wanted to pray but then I'd feel guilty for what I'd done to get me in this position in the first place. In my mind, things like this only happened in the movies, people who were assumed dead would return to cause a ruckus, but not in the real world. I was losing my mind—I had to know one way or another who the hell was screwing with me. Someone else must've been there that night—that was the only explanation that I could come up with. I heard leaves breaking as if someone were stepping on them and breaking them into pieces. I quickly turned my head and looked around. I didn't see anyone. *What the hell was going on?* I thought.

"Who's there?" I spoke loudly enough to be heard, but not too loud to wake up the neighborhood. I wasn't trying to bring more attention to myself. The cemetery on Lehigh Avenue was directly across from residential homes so I knew if I got too loud they could hear me. Then I thought, maybe that was a good thing, in case someone was trying to attack me. "Who's there?" I spoke again but still no answer. I focused my attention back on the headstone but at the same time I reached in my purse and held onto my gun to be safe.

"I know that I buried you. I just don't get it. Who's down there?" I heard the leaves again. I was getting annoyed. I stood up from the ground and looked around again. "Who the hell is out here?" Still no one answered.

Maybe I was just being paranoid. It was mid-November and pretty windy out so it could have just been the wind blowing the leaves around. I looked at the headstone one last time before walking toward my car. I kept looking around the cemetery but with so many trees you could easily hide and not be seen. I still gripped onto my gun tightly, walking so fast I was practically running. The sound of the leaves breaking got louder the faster I walked. My cell phone rang just as I pressed the keypad to unlock the car doors and damn near gave me a heart attack.

"Hello," I said as I hurried inside of the car and locked the doors.

"Babe, where the hell are you?" Black yelled. I could tell that he was angry. With all of the stuff going on, he definitely didn't want me out of his sight. I ditched his security to come here. I couldn't stand to be followed.

"I'm on my way home. I'm just leaving the cemetery."

"The cemetery? What the hell would make you go to the cemetery at midnight? You need to get back here now."

"I just said I was on my way home." I knew he was worried but I wasn't a child. Hell, without me, he wouldn't have half of what he had now. He'd still be Kemp's understudy waiting for a chance to take the lead.

"Just hurry up!" he yelled into the receiver before hanging up. I didn't get a chance to respond but I was ready to curse him from A to Z. Shit, he should have learned from Kemp, no man was going to tell me what to do. Those days were long over. I started the car and tried to pull off but the car wouldn't move.

"What the hell?" I yelled. I got out and walked around to the back of the car and noticed both back tires were completely flat. Someone was definitely out here and the feeling of fear that came over my body damn near buckled my knees. I hurried back inside the car and dialed Black again.

"Come get me, somebody is out here trying to get me."

"What?"

"Black, just hurry up! Both of my back tires are flat and I heard someone following me. Please hurry up."

"I'm coming now."

I pulled my gun from my bag as I nervously sat and waited. I should have never been out there in the first place. Each time I saw movement I put my fingers in place to shoot. I laughed—when it would end up being a tree branch or a plastic bag flying in the air. Was I tripping? Or was there really someone out there? I kept asking myself over and over again until something came crashing through my back window. Glass went everywhere and I heard footsteps going in the opposite direction. Once I could clearly see, I yelled, "I have a gun and trust me, I'll shoot!" I was scared shitless and I prayed that Black would pull up at any minute. My prayers were answered when I saw the headlights of his BMW. I got out of the car and ran over, almost knocking him over.

"Someone is trying to kill me, they threw something through my back window. I'm so glad you came." I hugged him and held on tight. The river of tears began to flow once I knew I was safe. He walked me over to the passenger seat of his car and put me inside. He walked over to my car and looked at the tires and windows before making a phone call. I wasn't sure who he called and honestly, I didn't care. I wanted him to get inside of the car and take me the hell home. I'd had enough excitement for one night. He was still on the phone when he climbed into the driver's seat and drove off.

"All right, get with me and let me know what's up. I need Merk to tow that car early. I don't need that shit getting any extra attention . . . call me after he's done . . . I'm staying with her tonight and we'll link up tomorrow . . . all right one!" He turned and looked at me. I was still crying and shivering in my seat. He didn't say a word—he just reached over and put his hand on top of mine. I couldn't speak. I didn't know what to say. They say what goes around comes around and maybe it was my time to get what was coming for me. I walked into the house like a zombie. Black still didn't speak, which was probably a good thing because I didn't know what to say. I sat down on the couch and soon he sat down next to me.

"I'm glad you're okay," he finally broke the silence but I didn't respond. I looked over at him and kissed him. Shit, I was more than glad that I was okay. I should have never been so foolish in the first place. I couldn't figure out what the hell possessed me to go out to a damn cemetery at night anyhow. Though he was a man and he wouldn't be one if he didn't do or say the stupid shit that men do, he was the one that I loved. I mean, none of the other men in my past truly cared about me the way that Black did. With training, Kemp probably could have but Black didn't need any of that. He did it on his own. It was then that I appreciated him even more. He could have went out to work, which is what kept us living the lavish life but he chose to stay with me. We continued to kiss each other as if it were the last kiss we'd ever have. His hands were soon all over my body and my clothes had since hit the floor. His smooth skin next to mine felt like silk rubbing across my naked body. His movements were slow and deliberate and each touch hit spots that I didn't even realize could send chills up and down my spine. His body was sculpted to perfection and every muscle looked like chocolate greatness like it could melt in your mouth. I tried to relax and not exemplify how anxious I was but it was becoming more difficult to hold back with each second. His Sean John cologne was tickling my nose. I was in heaven waiting for him to reach my wet pussy and massage it as he'd done my nipples a few seconds earlier, but he chose to take his time. His hands slowly moved down my stomach and soon reached my throbbing clit, which was just about to erupt. My body began to shake on contact. The orgasm had been building up and just the slightest touch made me explode. Hell, he could have probably blown on it and gotten the same result.

I moved my hips to grind against his fingers as he continued to kiss me sensually. At that point, I wished that I hadn't waited so long to get with him. I mean, when I met Kemp, Black was hanging in his shadow. I was looking for a leader so naturally Kemp caught my attention. Since money was my main objective, being with Black back then wasn't an option. All I could see were dollar signs. I married Kemp just for the money but being with Black was totally different; it was for love. Kemp had never been a slacker in the lovemaking department but it was just something about Black that I couldn't explain. I had never been with a man who could look at me and cause my lips to quiver. He was perfect in every sense of the word and when I felt his thick fingers slide inside of me I began to fuck them. I moaned loudly but was soon silenced as his lips touched mine and his tongue quickly followed behind. He stared me in the eyes as if there was something that he wanted to say but couldn't find the words to speak. I wanted to know what was on his mind but I was enjoying the feeling of his fingers in my pussy too much to say a word.

"I love you," he whispered gently, almost like sweet poetry.

With just the sound of those two words my body began to shake and my juices were running down his fingers and forming a puddle in the palm of his hand. I wanted to return the favor but he didn't allow me to. He got on his knees and slowly pushed his dick inside of me. He wasn't fucking me like he had any other time. He was making love to me and I was making love to him. I could lie in that position forever, with him inside of me.

"I love you more," I finally whispered back after a few minutes of his slow lovemaking. With a slow lick of his ear and the tightening of my pussy walls he erupted inside of me. His sweat was dripping all over my face and I didn't even budge to wipe it off. I let it dry into my skin. I wanted all of him, even the perspiration from our lovemaking. After lying next to each other quietly for a few minutes the thoughts of my earlier encounter crossed my mind. I didn't want to fuck up the mood but I had to know what was on his mind and what his plan was. Shit, I could have been killed so I had every reason to be nervous.

"What are we going to do, Black? I mean, if he's really alive we're as good as dead." I was still lying next to him with my head nestled in his chest. I could hear his heart beating and surprisingly it hadn't skipped a beat.

"I told you I would take care of it. Kemp doesn't scare me—he never has—but it can't be him, we both know that he's dead. I'm just focused on who the hell else knows what happened."

In a way I believed that what Black said was true, but hell, everyone was afraid of Kemp—or at least I thought that they were. Black was strong and it was one of the things that I loved most about him. I mean, who wanted to be with a wimp? Every woman wanted a man that could protect her. I wasn't crazy and I wanted to know who the culprit was just as much if not even more than Black.

"I know you told me Black, but we aren't together twenty-four hours a day. How can you protect me when you're not around? You saw what just happened."

"I know we're not together all the time but I have eyes everywhere. You have to trust me. I won't let anything happen to you. I've got you now and I'm not letting you go. You just can't put yourself out there like that again, babe. You have to work with me until I figure out what the hell is going on here."

Listen to him getting all sentimental, I thought. I smiled inside because for once I believed that it was true. I'd finally found a man that told me he loved me and meant it. Some would say that Kemp was in love with me and there were even some crazy people that would say Davey was too. I knew the truth and the fact of the matter is neither one of them really loved me. I was just something they could show off and be proud of. They could say they made me and yes, I admit it, they did make me. I didn't have shit before I met Davey and after my stint in prison I didn't have shit when I met Kemp either, so it wasn't a lie that I still wouldn't have shit if it weren't for them.

Black got off the sofa and I knew that it was time for work. Damn, I wanted to enjoy this moment. Being the head of an empire had its downfalls too. You never really get too much quality time. He walked upstairs to the bathroom as I lay there watering at the mouth. His body was a masterpiece. The muscles in his back were sculpted to perfection. His skin was smooth as melted chocolate and the sweat from our love-making gave his body just the right amount of shine. His ass was perfect too. I'd never seen an ass like his on a man. I just wanted to lie next to it all day long. Within a few seconds I heard the shower running and following that I smelled his Sean John body wash filling the air. I inhaled and got chills. I wanted to go meet him in the shower for round two but I knew he had to go to work. I rolled over and closed my eyes. I wasn't sleepy but my mind was exhausted. I knew that I would drive myself crazy trying to figure out how the hell I had gotten myself into this mess. I was so careful—well, at least I thought that I was. Black emerged from the bathroom about fifteen minutes later with a towel wrapped around his waist. By then I was sitting on the edge of the bed in the bedroom.

"Are you gonna be okay? If not, I'll get JB to send someone over here. Matter fact, I will have him do that anyway. I don't want to leave you here alone."

Though I wasn't really comfortable having the workers in my house, it was the best thing to do. I knew that I wouldn't have been able to rest anyway, wondering if someone would creep in here while I was asleep and kill me. It may sound silly, but it was the truth—I was scared shitless.

"That's fine, I'd feel better with someone here anyway," I agreed. Black walked toward the closet and began to get dressed. I just sat there admiring him. I wondered how I'd gotten so lucky and found a man like him. I wished that I had found him a long time ago. Maybe then I wouldn't be sitting here fearing for my life. After he'd finished getting dressed he walked over to my side of the bed and kissed me good-bye.

I fell asleep and woke up around seven A.M. to a ringing cell phone. *Who the hell was calling me so early?* I fumbled through my bag lying on the bedside table to find it.

"Hello," I said in a low tone. I hadn't even fully opened my eyes yet. There were specks of light peeping in through the blinds, which nearly gave me a headache—probably from my lack of sleep.

"Babe, you won't believe this shit!" Black's loud voice woke me up instantly.

"What? What happened?" I was nervous. I didn't really want to hear the answer as I sat up in bed and fought with the sun to fully open my eyes.

"The fucking store on Hunting Park is burning down! I need to know what muthafucker had something to do with this. When I find his ass it's going to be a war for real."

"The store is burning down?" I couldn't believe it. I mean, it wasn't as if it was a big money spot but, shit, it did make money. What the hell were they trying to prove? This is definitely not what I wanted to wake up to. I knew things could only get worse from that point on. I was second-guessing myself again. Who else but Kemp would have something to gain by terrorizing us? That night flashed in front of me like a film on television.

As I made my way down the hall I could see the flickering of a candle and could hear the faint sounds of moaning. I walked slowly to avoid being heard. I almost burst when I saw her straddled on top of him. I instantly wanted to speak, yell, scream or do something other than what I was doing. I was standing there like a statue. My body was doing something totally different than my mind. In my mind I was moving in on them, letting my presence be known but my feet weren't budging. Instead, I stuck my hand into my bag and pulled out my handgun—a handgun that I carried for protection. This protective tool was now a weapon and before I knew it, blood was spraying all over the bed, walls, and pretty much every surface in the room. I didn't know what to do next. My first thought was to throw things around and make the house appear to have been robbed. I didn't bother to check and make sure they were both dead, all I could think about was getting out of the house without being seen. I hurried out of the house and returned just in enough time to find the police and ambulance scattered all around the driveway and lawn. I put on the performance of the grieving wife and was picked up by Kiki, who took me over to her apartment for the night. By the note and the recent incidents, I was sure someone knew what I'd done—but whom? But then, I was so disoriented I didn't even notice Black in his car watching me run into the car in a sweat suit carting a handful of trash bags. I could have missed someone else—hell, he could have missed someone else.

I was becoming angrier by the minute and the conversation with Black wasn't going that great either. I wanted to know what the hell was going on as I snapped back to reality.

"Yeah, I'll talk to you about it when I get home. I'm trying to wrap shit up with the cops now."

"Black—"

"I'll talk to you when I get home, I have to go."

Click!

I sat there and stared at the phone. I was tempted to call him back. I wanted to know what the hell was going on with my store. It just didn't make sense to me and Black's attitude wasn't making things any better. Yes, he ran the businesses but shit, I owned everything, so technically he worked for me. So the fact that he was being so brief was really pissing me off. I got up out of bed and rummaged through my closet for something to wear. I had to go down to the store and see it for myself. Black would be pissed but hell, I was pissed right now so he'd just have to deal with me being there. I put on a Juicy Couture sweat suit and headed out of the door. I still had to look the part since there'd probably be cameras and shit at the scene. I couldn't be caught slipping, not even on a bad day. I sped down to the store in the Mercedes-Benz Black bought me last month, which was a good thing since my Jaguar was sitting on two flats. I immediately noticed the yellow tape and police officers blocking off the scene. I could only get within a two-block radius. I parked and got out to walk over. Black smoke filled the air and you could see the three fire trucks pouring water onto the building. People were crowding around, trying to get a glimpse of the building. I heard a few old ladies talking as I walked by.

"There she goes, right there. I'm glad that fucking store is burning."

"Yes, keep the drugs off of our block!"

I didn't respond. I didn't even turn around to see who said what. It didn't matter. I knew how they felt—I felt that way once. I lived in a neighborhood full of drug dealers and crackheads, and I hated it. So I'm sure people would wonder how I could grow up and fall into the same line of work. Well, the answer is pretty simple: money. Money was my motivation and after all that I'd been through there wasn't any other job out there for me. I saw Black, JB, and a few other workers in a huddle near the corner. I walked over.

"What are you doing here?" he yelled.

"I had to see the store for myself."

"You don't need to be here." He grabbed me by the arm so we could walk away from the workers.

"Yes, I do, Black, it's my store."

"Okay, now that you've seen it, you can go home."

"I'm not going anywhere."

"Why do you have to be so stubborn? Just go home and I'll take care of it."

I stood there silent. I wanted to believe that he could but I wasn't so sure looking at the building burning to the ground. Whoever it was definitely wasn't going to stop until we were both out of the picture. I wasn't going to stand out there in front of everyone and argue with him so I agreed to leave and quietly headed toward my car. I was angry. Not at Kemp or Black but at myself for letting this happen. I got in the car and looked around to see if I saw anyone suspicious. Who the hell was I looking for? For some reason, I still hoped I'd see Kemp. At least that way we'd know who to look for. I didn't really think they'd be stupid enough to hang around the scene but shit, that could be cockiness too. If it were Kemp, he knew we'd never turn him into the cops after what I'd done to him and Mica and if it wasn't him we wouldn't know where to start pointing the finger anyway. I was paranoid. I started the car to drive home. I had to clear my head. I couldn't live the rest of my life looking over my shoulders wondering when someone was going to kill me. I had to focus on something else so that I could move on with my life. Black wouldn't let anything happen to me. He promised me that and I had to believe him.

I had to obtain that thug mentality that men have, the one that sheds all of the fear. I had to learn the tricks of the trade if I wanted to make it in this business.

Chapter twenty-nine

Black

Mind over Matter

"So what's the next move?" JB stared at me, waiting to hear something. I didn't know what the next move was. How can I know what to do to a nigga that's supposed to be dead? And then, what if it wasn't him after all? I'd be wasting time looking for him and someone else could catch me off guard. I wasn't trying to get caught slipping. I had to figure this shit out.

"Let's go to the house, I don't want to stand out here and talk," I replied before turning to walk toward the car. I honestly wanted some time to think. Being alone on the drive would hopefully help me decide what I was supposed to do next.

"Cool, meet you there in twenty minutes."

I got in my car and headed toward the safe house. I didn't even turn the music on. I was too deep in thought. I had to either figure out what their next move was or wait for them to slip up and reveal their identity. I knew Kemp like the back of my hand and with enough thought I knew I could figure him out. But an unknown assailant wouldn't be that easy. Shit was just going as planned. I had snagged the woman I wanted. Diamond was the perfect woman with the business and respect to go along with it. I was turning into the king that I worked hard to become. I'd be damned if I was going to let a muthafucker come in and snatch it away from me. The ride seemed longer than normal since my mind was completely occupied. Everything was moving in slow motion. Diamond kept calling my cell but each time it rang, I sent it to voicemail.

I couldn't talk to her right at that moment—shit, I didn't know what to say. I had promised her that I would protect her and now it didn't look like I could. She was always so dramatic so I knew that it would turn into a long, drawn-out episode and I wasn't in the mood for the soap opera shit right then.

JB, Tommy, and Kenyon were waiting outside when I pulled up at the safe house. Like three soldiers they stood waiting for orders. With three totally different personalities and all from different backgrounds, they made the perfect army. JB was from uptown, an only child whose only parent was the TV. Most times he'd steal from the corner stores to eat. His mother had been locked up for armed robbery since he was seven and at ten he moved in with his drug-addicted aunt. Getting high was her main concern so her children were forced to grow up long before their time. JB refused to go back to foster care so he struggled to keep things in order when the social workers would come to visit. He met Kemp when he was seventeen while trying to get into the drug game. Kemp noticed his potential and quickly took him under his wing. Tommy was from West Philly and what I'd call a loose cannon. Tommy came from a two-parent middle-class home but stayed in so much trouble he was put in the youth study center at fifteen. He was released after his eighteenth birthday right into the arms of Kemp. Tommy didn't know any other way to survive since he had a criminal record. The fast life grabbed ahold of him and hadn't let him go ever since.

Last there was Kenyon—the brains is what I'd call him. He was much smarter than the average nigga and that alone made him the deadliest of them all. A single mother who always showed him the importance of education raised him. Yes, in school he was the nigga with straight As, but if you picked a fight with him, instead of fighting you he'd come up with a plan for you to hurt yourself more than he ever could. He got drafted into the game because of that. See, most of the niggas in the game will shoot first and ask questions later. Fuckin' with Kenyon, you'd put the gun to your temple and blow your own fuckin' brains out. He could say the slickest shit to get in your head and have you second-guessing everything you'd ever learned. He threw me for a loop when

I first met him because he always kicked that intellectual shit. I wondered how a nigga so smart could end up selling drugs. But the craziest part of it all is how he had just as much if not more money than Kemp and had never touched the drugs that got him there.

I parked and sat in the car for a few seconds before getting out. I wanted to build the suspense. I knew that they were wondering what I had planned.

"Yo', what's the deal, man? Who are we going to war with?" JB asked as soon as I stepped out of the car.

"Let's go inside," I responded, before walking toward the door.

We all walked inside the house. I was still silent. I knew as soon as I told them who I thought was doing everything they were going to go crazy. They'd never understand why, so I had to think hard on how I'd reveal my thoughts.

"So who burned down the store?" Tommy asked, while taking a seat at the kitchen table.

I stood there and stared at them. They all stared back, waiting to hear my response. They were like children in a classroom waiting to be taught. "Kemp," I answered in a low tone, hoping that they wouldn't hear me.

"Kemp? What the hell do you mean? He's dead!" Kenyon yelled immediately. I knew what reaction I was going to get from him. He was the type that didn't believe shit stunk unless you put it right under his nose.

"Yeah, that's what I thought too but we got this strange note that points to him and now this shit with Diamond and the store. In my heart, I know he's dead but the note makes me question that," I replied, hoping that I wouldn't have to go any further.

"What note? What did it say?" Tommy stood up and stared at me, probably wondering why I hadn't revealed the note sooner.

"There was a note sent to the office saying that he hoped Diamond enjoyed the past few months." I conveniently left out the part about checking his pulse. I wasn't ready to reveal the fact that Diamond had shot him. I didn't know how they would react if they'd found out and I didn't want to take that chance. They had all grown to respect her as their boss, but they would most likely feel betrayed if they knew the true facts of that night. How could they trust the person that robbed them of not only their leader but their friend? If it weren't for me, they would have probably all went separate ways, but I convinced them to stay on board. To find out what she'd done and then to know that I knew and did nothing about it, would only make things worse. I couldn't risk it. Especially when I didn't know who was out to get us. Every time I convinced myself it couldn't be him something inside made me think it was. The letter, to me, meant that someone was there and knew what went down. I didn't believe it myself at first and I probably wouldn't know if I hadn't seen it with my own eyes.

"What the hell does that mean? Why would he say some shit like? It doesn't make sense. We all know Kemp's dead, man—I was there. Why do you think it's him when you were right there with me? " Tommy asked with a puzzled look on his face.

"That can't be it and there has to be something that you're not telling us. Nothing you just said makes sense." Kenyon was seeing right through me but I had to keep it cool. I wasn't about to tell them the truth no matter how hard they pushed.

"I don't know what it is, Kenyon, all I know is someone is trying to take me and her under. I can't let that shit go down like that."

They all sat quiet and confused. If it were Kemp, how was I supposed to convince them to go to war with the man that helped them all get to where they were today? In reality, Kemp had helped us all. I waited for one of them to speak but they didn't. I didn't know what else to say. What I did know was that I wasn't going down without a fight and I damn sure wasn't going to let anyone hurt Diamond.

"So what are we going to do?" JB broke the five-minute silence that followed my last reply. Both Kenyon and Tommy turned to look at him with the stare of death. They had definitely always been loyal to Kemp and with just the thought of him being alive they were stuck between a rock and a hard place. Would they remain loyal to him or me, the nigga that was currently keeping their pockets fat if it turned out to be Kemp?

"What the fuck do you mean *we*? Nigga, I'm not doing shit until I know who the fuck I'm fighting. If it's Kemp, why the hell should I be fighting? His beef ain't wit' me," Tommy blurted out loud as he stood up from the chair that he was sitting in. JB stood up as well and was now standing face-to-face with Kenyon.

"So you just gonna bail out on Black after all the shit he's done? That's some sucka shit."

"Man, fuck you, I'm far from a sucka," he yelled back at JB, pointing in his face. I could see where things were heading so I stepped in the middle to try and calm them both down.

"Look, I know where you're coming from and I don't expect you to go to war with Kemp, but I gotta do what I gotta do. I'm not gonna just lay down and get killed," I said after they both sat back down. "Do what you have to, man, all of you, and I'll do the same." I turned my back and headed toward the door. As I was climbing into the car JB ran out to stop me.

"Yo' Black!" he yelled before reaching the rear of the car.

"What's up?"

"I'm wit' you all the way, I just want you to know that I got your back."

"I appreciate that, man, and I'll get up with you later. I have to go check on D." I reached out and gave him dap before getting into the car. He stood there facing me. I noticed Kenyon and Tommy standing at the door, watching. Now, not only did I have to worry about Kemp or some unknown killer, I had to worry about them too. Their loyalty was definitely to him and that wouldn't change. Even though they were working for me, to them, if Kemp were here I'd still be a worker just like them. Thinking back, I'd always been loyal to Kemp even if it got me caught up. One situation in particular showed just how loyal I was. It was 1995 and I had just gotten my first car. Shit, I was so happy you couldn't smack the smile off my face. It was a dark blue Acura Integra. I thought I was the shit! I was driving through all of the neighborhoods where the chicks were slower than the speed limit just to be seen. I had my Jay-Z, *Reasonable Doubt,* CD blasting as I bobbed my head with one hand on the steering wheel. Of course I'd purchased it courtesy of drug money. I hadn't been in the game very long but I vowed to purchase myself a car as soon as I got enough money to afford one. Kemp and Kenyon were standing on the corner in front of Papi's, the Puerto Rican store that we would get all of our candy and whatever else we needed. I pulled up slowly and rolled down the window.

"What's up, niggas?" I said loudly to make sure that I gained their attention. Kemp had his back turned but eased off of the car he was sitting on when he heard my voice. He was now facing me with a big smile on his face.

"I see you couldn't wait to spend that money, nigga. I like it. You trying to be a mini-version of me or something?" He burst into laughter. Kenyon joined in.

"Come on now, you know damn well I ain't tryna be you. You got too many hos with contracts on you." I grinned and pointed at him as he stood there laughing but underneath you could tell the comment rubbed him the wrong way. He definitely didn't find that funny. He'd screwed so many women over, one of them was bound to shoot his ass one of these days, I thought. I put on the hazard lights and opened the door to get out of the car. I couldn't believe it myself. Shit, I looked cleaner than the board of health riding around in that car. Kemp walked over and gave me dap as Kenyon followed up.

"This shit clean, nigga, you lucky I like you 'cause I'd jack your ass for this one," Kemp laughed.

"Yo' Kenyon, I'ma take a ride with him. I gotta holler at him about something. Meet me at the crib around six."

"All right," he replied before Kemp motioned for me to get back in the car. I didn't know what the hell he had to talk to me about but the look on his face told me that whatever it was he was going to make me listen—whether I wanted to or not.

Kemp got in the car and looked around without speaking. I did the same while I waited to see what it was he had to say.

"So what's the deal?" I asked, finally breaking the silence. He turned to look at me with a stare that said if looks could kill I'd be dead.

"You need to take this car back"

"Take it back? Why?" I was instantly pissed. I definitely respected Kemp and was appreciative for all that he'd done but he wasn't my father.

"It'll get too much attention."

"You're driving around in a BMW so why is that any different?"

"Because you gotta crawl before you walk. Shit, last week your ass was on the bus—now you got an Acura. If you want to have longevity in this game you have to use your head. I'm successful because I'm smart and you can be too if you play your cards right."

"So where are we going?" I asked changing the subject.

"Yo', did you hear what I just said?" His tone changed from one of concern to one of anger.

"Yeah, man, I heard you. I'll take it back and get something else." I was pissed but without this game I wouldn't be able to afford it anyway. I already knew that there wasn't any negotiating with him. Once his mind was made up there wasn't anything that could change it.

"Pull over!" he yelled. I wasn't even at a complete stop before he jumped out of the car, pulled out his gun, and ran over to a group of guys on the corner. A few of them scattered immediately. Two men remained and stood frozen. I jumped out the car and pulled out my gun just in case something popped off.

"Where's my money, nigga?" Kemp yelled with the gun against the man's chin. The man's name was Jojo. Jojo was a local Jamaican hustler who purchased weight from Kemp. Leading up to that day, Jojo hadn't been paying up, claiming that there had been a recent drop in sales. It was a bullshit story because one of his workers had recently told Kemp all about what he did with his money. The informant told Kemp how Jojo would take the product that he got on consignment, cut it in half—lowering the purity—and then doubled the price. He was making damn near triple what he'd have to pay Kemp for the original product. After Kemp heard about it, he stopped letting him get any more cocaine until he paid the back money he owed. Three months had passed since the last payment and this particular day was the first time he'd seen him since.

"I don't have it yet, man. Shit is still slow around here," Jojo replied while the other man stood still as a statue.

"Do you think I'm a fool? I'll shoot your ass dead right where you stand. Don't fuck with me, where's the money?" He started patting him down while still holding the gun just under his chin. He retrieved a wad of money from one of his pockets. "What do we have here? Looks like money to me, muthafucker," he yelled before hitting Jojo on the side of the head with the gun. Blood instantly poured from his temple. Some of the excess splashed onto Kemp's fresh white T-shirt.

"I'm sorry, man, I need that money to feed my family. I promise I'll pay up. Just give me another week."

"Feeding your family sounds like a personal problem. Nigga, you owe me. I'm going to take this as a down payment now but I want the rest of my money by Friday." He moved closer to Jojo and forced part of the gun up his nose. Jojo was damn near crying as his friend still stood behind him, not saying a word. "And if I don't have my money, next time your head won't be the only thing bleeding."

Kemp backed away toward the car. I knew that was my cue. I jumped into the car and drove off as soon as Kemp sat down. He sat unfolding and counting the money that he had just taken from Jojo.

"That muthafucker messed up my damn shirt," he said as he looked down, noticing the spattered blood pattern on the front of his shirt.

"You want me to drop you off at home?"

"Yeah, I told Kenyon to meet me at the spot at six so I still got a little time. I can probably sneak in a quickie or something while I'm at it." He laughed. I joined in the laughter. "But back to you, man, I need you to take this car back and get a Honda or something. This car is going to get you too much attention way too fast. Don't get ahead of yourself, you might fuck around and end up like that nigga Jojo back there."

I nodded, agreeing. I respected him and he'd been in the game much longer than me so he was definitely wiser. I followed his order and the following day, I went back to the dealership and took the Acura back. I drove off the lot in a used Honda Accord. It was nowhere near as flashy and wouldn't get me much attention. At the time I didn't really understand why, but I never understood a lot of shit Kemp said or did. It was sort of like a teenager and their parents.

They never understand why they have to obey them but later when it turns out to have been the best choice, they're thankful. That's how I felt but in that situation and many more that would come about in the future, mind over matter was how they worked. It was also a motto that got me where I was at that point. Being a boss took brains.

Chapter Thirty

Diamond

Fatherless

"Diamond! Hurry up and get down here for breakfast," my mother yelled through the house. It was almost 7:00 A.M. and the school bus would be there by seven-thirty. I hated waking up so early and I think my mother hated waking me up just as much. It was always a fight to get me out of the door on time. My dad was sitting at the table when I got there and as usual, him and my mom didn't have much to say to each other. Most days they sat across from each other without speaking a word. I walked to my father's side of the table and gave him a kiss on the cheek. For the first time since I was around five years old he didn't kiss me on my cheek as well.

"Is everything okay, Daddy?" I asked, still standing on the side of his chair. He set his newspaper down and looked me in the eye.

"Everything is fine, sweetie; Daddy's just got a lot on his mind, that's all." After his response he picked his paper back up off the table and resumed reading it. I knew that something wasn't right but I didn't want to ruin everyone's morning by probing him for more information. I slowly walked away and slid into my seat opposite his. There was a small bowl of oatmeal and a glass of milk sitting in front of me. The air in the room felt weird. I couldn't put a finger on what was different but I could feel it in the pit of my stomach. My mom was standing over the sink washing dishes as we continued to eat in silence. The date was October 13th and I remembered it because of a fire just a few blocks away. One of my best friends lived in that house and hadn't made it out alive. The date seemed significant to me at the time because of the loss, but by the end of that day I would not only lose my best friend but my father as well.

I had just scraped the last bit of oatmeal from the bowl and finished the glass of milk when I heard the school bus pulling up outside. I jumped up out of the chair and grabbed my book bag off of the floor. Just as I was about to head to the door my dad grabbed me by the arm and pulled me into a hug. The hug was much different than any other hugs because he wouldn't let go. I mean, he held onto me like it was the last hug that I would ever get. After he let go, I kissed him and walked out of the door. I glanced back before stepping onto the bus and noticed him standing at the door with a blank look on his face. That blank look was one that would haunt me for years since it was the last time that I'd see his face. We lost our house because my mother couldn't pay the bills. We were forced to move in with my grandmom, in a raggedy row home in North Philly.

I hated living there. I was used to having my own room and my own things. There, I not only had to fight for my things, I damn near had to fight for food. My cousins were bigger and much stronger than me so when it was time to eat I'd quickly be pushed aside and forced to eat the scraps that were left. Then my Aunt Cicely was the meanest bitch I'd ever known. Not a day went by where she wouldn't throw the fact that I wasn't really part of the family in my face. As if knowing it wasn't bad enough, I had to hear it every day. I would go to bed each night wondering why my real parents gave me away. From the day I found out, my mother tried her best to convince me of how special I was. I couldn't see it, since my biological father and the father that I'd always known not only left me but my real mother had as well.

Next there were the boys. I just couldn't get enough of them. I lost my virginity at the age of twelve and had sex with at least five boys by the time I met Johnny. Unlike the rest of them, Johnny couldn't care less about sex. I, on the other hand, was addicted. I loved the feeling of being wanted. The attention that they gave me somehow filled the void that my father had left me with. When one would leave, I'd quickly find another one to replace him. This cycle was one of the most reckless I'd taken part in my whole life.

The first time Johnny and I had sex, it was almost like I was a teacher and he was the student. Johnny, Mica, and me were watching TV in their basement. It was cold outside and not much heat was circulating. We were covered up with fleece blankets all piled up next to each other on the sofa. Mica had fallen asleep halfway into the movie and both Johnny and me were wide awake. Hidden underneath the blanket, my hand was rubbing his knee. Soon it was up to his thigh and next I was caressing his package, which was tightly nestled in his underwear. For once, he didn't stop me and since he hadn't, I took full advantage of the situation. He leaned over and began kissing me while palming my overdeveloped breasts at the same time. By now, I was unzipping his pants and sliding my hand into the opening. I could tell he was excited as his dick grew three more inches than normal. I prayed that he wouldn't stop me as he'd done the few times we'd made it this far. Mica was still sleeping, snoring loudly with drool slowly sliding down the side of her face. We were kissing and tonguing each other down so heavily that you could hear the smacking even over the TV. I stopped him just long enough to ease down on the floor. I motioned with my finger for him to join me. He obliged and within seconds we picked up where we had left off. Instead of getting completely naked I removed just my shorts. Johnny had his pants and underwear pulled down to his knees. I lay on my back as he crawled on top of me and struggled to find my warm opening. With one hand I grabbed hold of his dick and guided it inside of me. He let out a sigh immediately. I knew that he'd never had sex before so I didn't expect him to go very long. Surprisingly, he got into a rhythm and was still going fifteen minutes later. I guess some men are just born with it because for it to have been his first time he lasted longer than most of the boys I had been with. About twenty minutes later he was shaking and moaning on top of me. I covered his mouth with my hand to muffle the sounds that were escaping. After we were done, I hurried into the bathroom to wipe myself off and got back in position at the far end of the sofa. Johnny looked over at me and quietly said, "I love you" before focusing his attention back on the movie. I never wanted to tell Mica about our first time. I figured she'd be mad that we did it while she slept a few feet away.

Eventually, I had to tell her and everyone else when I found out that I was pregnant. My mother was pissed. I didn't understand how I'd managed to sleep with five boys, numerous times each and hadn't gotten pregnant. I was practically shaking when I told her that I had missed my period. She sat across from me, quiet, while continuing to smoke her cigarette.

"So you missed your period? I guess that wouldn't mean anything unless you were out there screwing. Is that what you're telling me? You've been out there fucking those little boys?" I was silent, afraid to look her in the eye. I was afraid of seeing the disappointment. What mother would be proud of her teenage daughter carrying a baby? "I don't hear anything. I just asked you a question." Her voice was louder than it had been a few seconds ago, which to me showed fury.

"I'm sorry, Mom, I didn't think I could get pregnant."

"Why not? Don't you learn that shit in school? As soon as you get a period you can get pregnant. I'm so disappointed in you, Diamond. I expected so much more from you."

Hell, I expected more from me. I also expected that I'd always have a father around that loved me, but obviously that wasn't the case. I didn't know what to say or do. I did know that I wasn't ready to take care of a baby.

"I'm not ready to take care of a baby, Mom."

"Who said anything about taking care of a baby? I'm taking you to the clinic first thing Monday morning to get rid of it. I'll be damned if you're going to embarrass me."

I sat there with tears forming in the wells of my eyes. I was scared. I didn't think she would force me to get an abortion. I thought we could probably give it up for adoption. I knew my mother very well and what she said was pretty much what happened. There wasn't anything that I could do to make her think any different. Then I thought about it a little more. It was the right decision for all of us. Johnny definitely didn't want me to have the baby. He felt that it would ruin both of us and he probably was right. That Monday morning when she dragged me down to the clinic in the frigid weather, all I could think about was getting my life back to normal as quickly as possible.

The clinic was packed and most of the girls there were around my age. I guess I wasn't the only one dumb enough to think I couldn't get knocked up. After filling out all of the paperwork, we sat in the waiting room for hours. It was almost noon when they finally called my name and we'd been there since seven-thirty in the morning. They led me down a long hallway that had bright white paint like you see on TV. My mother stayed out in the waiting area with the other mothers and young girls waiting for their turn.

The nurse took me into a small room that had two changing stalls and a bathroom. She handed me a clear bag that contained a hospital gown, socks, and a cap for your head. She instructed me to take everything off, put on the things in the bag, and fill it with all of my belongings. I could barely get my pants unbuttoned I was so nervous. I didn't know what was about to happen to me. They hadn't explained it to me, only saying that my mother wouldn't sign for me to be put under anesthesia. Was that a form of punishment? How could she force me to be wide awake when they ripped my baby from the womb? I almost thought about running out of there and hitchhiking a ride home. The nurse startled me when she returned and reached out for my bag of belongings.

"Come with me. I'll put your things in a locker. I'm going to take you into the procedure room and prep you. Do you have any questions for me?"

"Is it going to be really painful?" I was scared shitless, still unaware of what was about to take place. I mean, I knew that I was going to leave here not pregnant anymore but I didn't know what would happen between now and then.

"It will be a little painful but doing it without anesthesia is the best way to do it. You won't feel groggy or possibly have any bad after-effects. Don't worry, I'll be in there with you the whole time. You can hold on to me and squeeze my hand if you need to."

I felt a little better after that but I was still a little uneasy. The procedure room was freezing cold. There was a table in the center surrounded by a bunch of machines. I assumed that most of them were to monitor your vital signs and things of that nature. Just from TV shows and things I saw in school, I saw the resemblance. I lay down on the table and tried to relax as I placed my feet in the stirrups and scooted down to the edge of it.

The doctor entered the room a few minutes later in a blue gown and gloves.

"This will be over before you know it. Scoot down a little more for me."

I was so uncomfortable. A grown man who was a complete stranger had his face down in my young pussy. I had never even been to a gynecologist before so this was all new to me. I followed his instruction and slid down so that my butt was at the end of the table.

"Okay, now you'll feel some cold fluid. I'm cleaning the area. Now a little pinch."

I damn near jumped off the table. A little pinch, my ass. Whatever he had just done hurt like hell. "Okay just a few more pinches." I held in the screams as he continued to stick needles in me. Tears were rolling down the sides of my face and landing on the paper that covered the table beneath me. Next came a loud machine and then I heard what sounded like a vacuum. My stomach was cramping beyond belief. Not even my worse day of PMS felt that bad. After a few more minutes of cramping, the loud machine stopped and the experience was over. I was so weak that I could barely stand when the nurse helped me off of the table and into a wheelchair. I recovered for about an hour before I was allowed to get dressed and meet my mother outside. Once she saw me, she walked around to the driver's side of the car and got in. The ride home was completely silent. She hadn't even asked how I felt. I guess she didn't care since I'd gotten myself into the situation in the first place. I didn't even have the energy to try and spark up a conversation because she probably wouldn't have joined in anyway.

Following the abortion, Johnny was afraid to touch me. Honestly, I wasn't so anxious to have sex either. I'd be damned if I'd go through that shit again. Things between us remained the same and I was extremely happy that they did. I'd be lost without his love or the love of any man for that matter. Being fatherless screwed me up and pretty much set the tone for the way I'd search for a replacement. Of course I'd never find a man who would love me the way that he did, but at least I could dream about it.

Chapter thirty-one

Black

Me and My Bitch

Besides Diamond, Trice was the only chick that knew how to make me come back for more. Shit, pussy was pussy but every once in a while you run across one that's exceptional. I wasn't ready to go home just yet. I was still trippin' about Kemp and if I'd gone home that's all Diamond would end up talking about. I needed to relax and what better way to do so than getting some bomb-ass head. I'd spoken to her earlier that day and told her I'd be by later that night so I knew she'd be ready. I parked, hit the alarm on the keypad, and headed to the door. Trice opened it wearing a pair of tight-ass shorts where her ass was hanging out of the bottom and a T-shirt that showed her hard nipples. She hadn't even pushed the door closed before I stuck my tongue in her mouth and grabbed hold of her ass. I was horny as hell and anytime I wanted sex with no strings attached, this was the place to be. Trice playfully pushed me away. I stared at her as she backed away.

"You've been a bad boy. I'm not really sure you deserve this pussy."

I smiled for the first time in a few days. She knew exactly what I liked. I loved her playfulness especially when I needed a boost for the day.

"A bad boy, huh? Well, tell me how I can make it up to you because I definitely want the pussy." She moved closer to me as I now stood in front of the sofa. She gave me a push that forced me to sit down on the sofa. I sat looking up at her with a huge smile on my face. My dick was already damn near busting through my jeans. She slowly removed her T-shirt and shorts to revealed her naked body underneath. I wanted to grab hold of her and pull her on top of me but I didn't, I let her continue to lead.

"You see this? All of this is for you. Do you want it?"

"Of course I want it."

"How bad? I need you to make me believe it. If not, you won't even get to sniff it."

I let out a laugh. She was funny as hell but I knew that she meant it. As bad as she missed me, if I didn't convince her that I missed her just as much she wouldn't budge.

"More than ever, babe, I was thinking about you all day. Couldn't wait to get here."

"Oh, really, what were you thinking?"

"About those juicy-ass lips and that soft ass that I couldn't wait to touch."

She turned around so that her ass was facing me. "Go 'head and touch it."

I smiled and pulled her closer while rubbing my hands across her ass. It was soft as a baby's ass and I couldn't resist planting kisses all over it. She moaned and stuck it out a little further. I took one hand and massaged her clit from behind. Her juices were damn near pouring out. I couldn't wait to shove my dick inside of her. Her ass was still facing me as I stuck my finger inside of her. Within seconds her body began to tremble and the moans were even louder than before. I was afraid that she'd wake the kids, she was so damn loud.

"So that's how you feel?" she asked, smiling. I nodded but remained silent. She got down on her knees in front of me and loosened my belt before unzipping my pants and letting my dick breath. She put her lips on the head and planted a kiss that immediately made me sigh. She followed with one lick up the shaft and back down before deep-throating it, catching me off guard. That was damn near enough to make me bust right in her mouth. She smiled when she looked up and noticed the faces that I was making. I couldn't take anymore. I pulled her up from the floor, turned her around so that her back was facing me, and made her sit down on top of me. Her pussy was soaking wet as my dick made its way inside. I lifted up off the seat to meet her as she moved up and down on it. I knew

I was about to disappoint her because it felt too good to do a marathon that night. I held onto her hips and my cum for all of ten minutes before I exploded inside of her. My body shook uncontrollably for a few seconds. That was just what I needed to relax. I sat there on the sofa with my head back after she went upstairs in the bathroom. She returned with a hot washcloth, which she placed on top of my dick, which forced me to open my eyes. I was about to grab hold of it until she began to wipe me off. Damn, I thought, if I didn't love Diamond as much as I did, she'd be mine again.

I fell asleep and hadn't even looked at the time before I did. I felt my cell phone vibrating and knew it was Diamond before I even picked up. I let out a little sigh before rolling out of bed and pressing talk on the phone.

"Hello?"

"Why haven't you answered any of my calls?"

"Because I was busy, Diamond, what's up?"

"What's up? Nigga, I've been calling you for three fucking hours."

"I said I was busy, what's up?"

"Somebody's been calling here, threatening me."

"Did you call JB?"

"Why would I call JB, you're my man, not him!"

"I'll be there in a little bit Diamond all right. I'm sorry, okay."

"Not as sorry as that bitch next to you will be if you don't answer my calls next time"

Click!

"Wifey's pissed, huh?"

"Yeah, I gotta go but I'll holla at you later." I leaned over and kissed her before getting up to get dressed. I didn't want to argue with Diamond but I knew that it was inevitable. I thought that going over to Trice's would keep me relaxed but the second I felt the vibration of the phone the relaxation was over. Things were great with Diamond and me up until this shit with Kemp started up. I mean, I could definitely understand her frustration but, shit, I was in it just as deep as she was. Not that I was scared of Kemp, but I'd known Kemp a lot longer than she had, which meant I knew what he was capable of. I always felt that I was stronger than him in many ways because for one, I knew how to keep my anger under control and two, he had more enemies than any nigga I knew. To him, that was power but to me it was foolish. Not that I wanted to be everyone's friend— that wasn't it by a long shot—I just knew that when it was time to go to war it was better to have more niggas ready to fight with you then take your ass down.

I pulled up in front of the house and sat in there staring at the house. Kiki's car was in the driveway, which was never a good sign. See, Kiki was drama. Though she was Diamond's best and pretty much only friend she still got on my last nerve. At times she'd been the word of wisdom and I could appreciate that since Diamond normally didn't think before she made a dumb decision, but then there were times like these when I knew that she would only make things worse between her and me. I was hesitant going in but I had to make sure that things were under control. I knew that she was afraid and deep down I was afraid too. Not of what could potentially happen to me but what could happen to her. Regardless of the ups and downs, I cared about Diamond more than I'd cared about any woman. It just pissed me off when she didn't believe that I would do whatever I had to, to protect her.

Entering the house I could hear Kiki's ranting about me. I could hear Diamond, in a low voice, telling her to hush. I almost turned back around and left but I wanted to look her in the eye with a stare so she'd know I'd heard what she'd said. When I walked into the living room, she rolled her eyes and turned to hug Diamond before getting up and heading toward the door. I stood there silent before shaking my head and going into the kitchen. I opened the refrigerator door and as I bent down to grab a Corona from the shelf I heard the sound of Diamond's shoes tapping against the marble floor. I stood up, looked at her, and turned to open my beer. I brushed past her and walked toward the living room to sit down.

"So what are you planning on doing, Black?"

Damn, I didn't even get a second to plant my ass in a seat. She had already started. "I don't know yet, Diamond." I sighed as I spoke to let her know that I wasn't in the mood for this conversation.

"What do you mean, you don't know? You have to know. Are you just going to allow him to sneak up on you?"

"On me? Have you forgotten that you are the one that shot him? And you don't even know that it's him anyway."

"Who the hell else would it be, Black? It's the only thing that makes sense. When are you going to be a man and stand up to him?"

"What?" I was pissed. I got up from my seat, slammed the beer down onto the coffee table, and walked in her direction. I knew that she could see the anger on my face because she was backing into the corner of the sofa. "Be a man? Shit, I'm the man keeping your ass afloat. You wouldn't know what to do without me."

"Really? Well, you wouldn't have shit without me!"

Slap.

Before I could think about it my hand had landed clean across the side of her face. She placed her hand over her cheek, which had quickly turned red. For the first time since we'd been together she'd pushed me to the limit. Now she sat across from me crying and I felt like shit.

"Babe, I'm sorry," I tried to reach out and grab her.

"Get the fuck off me!" She pulled her arm away and stood up from the sofa. I was going to try and apologize more but she gave me a stare that said if looks could kill I'd be dead. I never wanted her to see that side of me. In the past I'd snapped a few times and hit a woman, which is something that I wasn't proud of. I didn't even know what to say to fix it. *Shit*, I yelled. I sat there for the next half hour not even looking at TV. My mind was going in circles. I was pissed that I'd let this nigga ruin everything.

I remembered the first time that I saw her—I couldn't wait to get closer. I knew that I was going to be with her from that moment. I had come too far to fuck it up. I knew that I couldn't make it up to her tonight. I was so fucked-up about it that I called JB and told him to take care of the pickups that night. I didn't want to leave for fear that she wouldn't be there when I got back. At one point I crept upstairs and stood outside of the door listening to her cry. I was close to turning the knob and going in but it would probably have just made it worse. I had almost drifted off to sleep when the telephone rung. I jumped up, and glanced at the clock that read 4:00 A.M.

"Yo'," I spoke in a low tone. I knew whatever it was at this time of morning it couldn't be good.

"These niggas are trippin' out here, B, you need to come through and handle this shit," JB yelled into the receiver.

"What niggas?"

"Down on the block. Kenyon then went and put some shit in they ear and now niggas are tripping talking 'bout they can't trust you and shit."

I was pissed, I wasn't trying to hear that shit but deep down I knew it was coming. I could actually understand how they could feel the way they did. But shit, I was the boss running things so either they would get down or lay the fuck down, and that was my word. "I can't deal with this shit right now, JB. I got so much going on man. This shit with Kemp is fucking up my home life and everything. The way I feel now, I'll fuck around and blow his ass away. I need you to be a soldier and take care of it."

"I'm sorry to bother you but I didn't know how you wanted me to handle it. Is Diamond okay?"

"Naw man, I fucking snapped and I didn't mean to. She's been upstairs crying for hours."

"Damn, man, maybe you should go stay with Trice tonight."

"I'm not leaving, I just gotta get my head right. Shit is getting out of control."

"All right, well, call me when you get up in the A.M. I'm going to do another pick up now."

"All right," I replied before ending the call. I heard Diamond coming out of the bedroom and going into the bathroom. I felt like this was my cue. I walked up the steps and stood outside of the door. She opened it and was startled by my presence.

"Diamond."

She turned off the bathroom light and walked past me toward the bedroom. I followed behind her but didn't speak. She climbed into bed and pulled the blankets over her body. I had never seen her like this. I knew about the relationship she had with her ex, Davey, and how he treated her. The way that he cheated and how they fought like cats and dogs. I could see by the way she looked at me how disappointed she was. I sat down in the chair opposite the bed and stared in her direction. As she closed her eyes and drifted off to sleep, I put my head back and closed my eyes too.

Chapter thirty-two

Diamond

Spoiled Rotten

I opened my eyes and noticed Black asleep in the chair across from me. I was still angry about last night but regardless of his fuck-ups, I still had a soft spot for him. I knew he was sorry since any other night he'd be out running the streets. I sat up on the side of the bed and the sound of the box spring woke him up.

"Hey babe, you feel any better?" he said as he sat straight up. I was tempted to ignore him but I wanted to just get on with the day and let it go.

"I'm fine."

"Can I get you some breakfast or something?"

"No, I'm not hungry."

"You sure, 'cause I can get JB to drop something off or we can go to IHOP or something."

"I said I'm not hungry, Black—damn!" I got up from the bed and walked toward the door.

"I'm sorry, D, for everything."

I didn't say a word. I walked into the bathroom and closed the door. I had already decided that I would do some shopping today since shopping was the only thing that could help when I was upset. I did the morning ritual of brushing my teeth and washing my face. Black was gone when I came out. I let out a sigh of relief. I walked into the bedroom and saw a blue sheet of paper with writing on it. Next to it was a wad of money. I bent down to grab it. The note read:

I know I fucked up, but I'm going to make it up to you.
I know shopping helps you clear your head when you're

angry so here's a few dollars for you. Buy something nice on me.

I smiled. He knew me well. Of course, I had my own money so I wasn't jumping for joy like I would have a few years back but I was smiling because he really wanted me to forgive him. I sat the note back down and grabbed my cell to text his phone. *I LOVE YOU* was all I wrote. I got dressed and headed out for my day of shopping. I opened the door and turned to close it and a tall, dark-skinned man was walking up the path. He was older, probably in his late forties. He had on a suit and dress shoes and was carrying a briefcase. I hoped my ass wasn't about to get subpoenaed to court or some shit.

"Hi, can I help you?" I asked, nervously.

"Yes, I'm trying to locate a Mrs. Diamond Brooks."

"Well, I'm Diamond, but my last name isn't Brooks any more. What can I do for you?"

"Don't I look familiar to you? Isn't there anything about me that looks familiar?" he said, as I stood there staring at him. I didn't really see anything that stuck out to me but there was obviously something he wanted me to see.

"No, really it doesn't. Is it supposed to?" I was still clueless.

"It's me, Diamond, your dad."

My heart dropped at that moment. I mean, with all the shit that I was going through at the moment someone would play a cruel-ass joke like this. I knew this couldn't be my father, I would have recognized him. Then he smiled, the smile that I couldn't forget, the same smile that I saw the day he disappeared from my life. *Was it really him?* What the hell was I supposed to do, hug him or slap him? I never thought that I'd see him again. I could have prepared what I would say but instead I stood in front of him, speechless.

"Are you okay?" he asked, breaking the silence.

I stood still, staring at him. I was trying to look deep inside of him, hoping I could get answers without asking. He'd been gone almost twelve years. Why would he come back now?

"I'm fine—actually no, I'm not. I'm trying to figure out why you're here." *Is that what I wanted to say?*

"I expected you to say that. You wouldn't be human if you didn't. I want to explain everything if you'll give me a chance to."

"How did you find out where I lived?"

"Through a private investigator," he replied.

"What? Why go through all the trouble? I mean, you left with no problem."

"I really want to explain and I don't think this is a good place. Could we go to lunch or something and talk?"

I wasn't truly ready to hear why he'd walked away. I had to figure out what to say to at least put the conversation off for another day. He stood there, waiting for my answer. The look on his face was so sincere, I could've almost been fooled, fooled into believing that he'd been there all the time or that he'd even been looking for me all of those years.

"I have an appointment in less than an hour, so could we meet tomorrow?"

He looked at me as if he were preparing to burst into tears. What was I missing? I mean, how could you miss me so much and stay gone so long? I wasn't trying to be mean at all but I wasn't going to be fooled into believing that I would have the void filled that had been empty for so long.

"There's no way you can fit me in today?"

I stood quiet for a few seconds before answering, I almost said yes. "Really, I can't. I have an important appointment that can't be missed."

"So is there a number I can call you at?"

"You've managed to find me this time, I'm sure it won't be hard to find me again." I turned and walked toward my car. I didn't want to turn around and see his face. Shit, I wanted him to feel the pain that I'd felt all of these years.

I got in the car, pulled my sunglasses down over my eyes, and drove away. Once I got around the corner, I let go the tears that I had held in the entire time I stood in front of him. I had to tell someone but I wasn't sure how much of a shoulder Black could be for me to lean on at the time so I drove over to Kiki's office. Kiki, of course, had always been one of my best friends and was there in my times of need. Once I got all of the money from Kemp's death I bought Kiki her own bar. I wasn't about to have my best friend continue to work for tips at someone else's bar. The bar was a success from the grand opening and Kiki was where she needed to be, in charge. I pulled up in front of her office, which was located directly in back of the bar in Center City. I saw her car in front of the door so I knew that she was inside. She opened it before I even had a chance to get out and knock.

"I saw your car pull up, what's up, girl? I was going to call you today too."

I took off my sunglasses and displayed the drying tears on my cheeks. She walked over and hugged me.

"What the hell happened, is that nigga still acting up?"

"Girl, you won't believe who showed up on my doorstep today."

"Who?"

"My father," I said in a low tone. It almost brought tears to my eyes again.

"What? Girl, come on inside so we can sit down and talk. Your father though? Where the hell has he been?" she asked, while entering the door. I followed behind her and sat down in the first available chair.

"I don't know where the hell he's been. He says he found me through a private investigator. I didn't even know what to say, girl, I was standing there like a damn statue."

"I can't believe he had the audacity to just show up on your damn doorstep. He could have wrote a letter or some shit to see how you felt about seeing him. I mean, damn, people don't even think. He didn't even know if you wanted to see him."

"I was so shocked, like it's been over ten years. I'm not sure what he expected me to say."

"Shit, he probably didn't expect you to say anything. I mean, how could he? I think that's so inconsiderate what he did. Did you tell Black?"

"No, I haven't talked to Black and now that you mentioned it, he didn't respond to my text. I'm about to call him right now." I dialed his number, which went straight to voice mail. I was pissed. After the shit that had been going on lately I couldn't understand how he could turn off his fucking phone. I screamed into the answering machine as soon as I heard the beep. "Just when I thought you were sorry you pull this shit!

Why is your fucking phone off, Black? Call me when you get this damn message!"

Kiki sat at the desk, shaking her head. "What?" I asked with my face in knots.

"I don't know when you're gonna learn that niggas ain't never been shit and ain't never gonna be shit! You can't let that nigga get you all upset and shit, it's not worth it girl. I see I still have to be the mommy around here."

"Everything is just so messed up right now, Kiki, I gotta look over my shoulders and hope Kemp doesn't come blow my head off. I can't keep worrying about him all the time. I have to worry about me."

"That's the right idea!" She laughed.

I smiled but inside I felt like shit. I was lying. I was worried about him and of course even more worried about myself.

"Well, I'm headed to the mall so I'll get with you later," I said, before getting up and hugging her.

"Okay and remember what I said."

"I will, girl."

As soon as I got inside the car I pulled out my cell to call him again. As I entered the number the phone began to ring. It was Black.

"Yo', what's up?" His voice boomed even over the loud music that played in the background.

"Why the hell was your phone off?"

"It wasn't off, somebody else was calling at the same time. What's the problem?"

"The problem is that every time I need you here lately you're not available!"

"What the hell are you talking about, Diamond?"

"I need to talk to you about something—could you just come home?"

"I can't right now, you know that."

"Just like I thought, 'bye, Black!"

"Diamond?"

"What?" I responded angrily.

"I'll be there in a half."

"Okay," I smiled before hanging up. I knew what to say to get him home when I wanted him to be. He got home about five minutes short of the half hour that he'd promised. I was sitting on the sofa with the lights off. My mind was spinning and I didn't know how to stop it. I always thought that the day I finally saw my father, I'd hug him and the empty void that was there for so many years would be closed. Nothing ever turns out the way that I imagine, which always ended up being a huge disappointment. When I was disappointed, I always made stupid decisions.

Black walked in, looking around to find me. Once he noticed me sitting on the sofa he turned on the lamp and walked over.

"Babe, why are you sitting here in the dark? What's going on?" He sat down next to me.

"My father showed up today," I replied in a low tone.

"What?"

"Yes, I was leaving out and he was walking up the path."

"Well, what the hell did he say? I mean, why did he show up?"

"I don't know, he wanted to go to lunch but I lied and said I had somewhere important to be. I didn't know what to say. I couldn't stand to look at him after the way he left me."

"Well you shouldn't have been put in that position. I'm sorry you had to go through that shit today with all of the other shit going on." He moved closer to me and didn't say another word. I mean, there wasn't really anything that he could say. Him being there next to me was good enough. I lay in his arms on the sofa and closed my eyes. I could feel myself drifting off to sleep within seconds.

Chapter Thirty-three

Black

Eyes Behind My Head

Boom . . .
Debris was everywhere. All I could remember was sticking my hand on the handle to open up the car door and hearing a loud-ass boom and a force unlike any that I'd ever felt in my life. I landed up against the wall. My eyes were closed and I instantly felt the back of my head throbbing. I rubbed the back of my head, which felt like it was bleeding. What the fuck? I yelled. My car was sitting just a few feet away from me on fire. This shit was getting crazy! At this point I wanted this nigga to just show his face so we could get this shit over with. I heard sirens in the background as I tried to peel myself off of the pavement.

"Are you okay sir?" The one paramedic asked.

I couldn't even respond. I was still in shock and I was dizzy as hell with a banging headache. I tried to get up again.

"Stay still, sir, we'll get you to a hospital."

"I'm fine, I don't need a hospital."

"Sir, you have to go to a hospital, your head is bleeding and you could have a concussion."

"I said I'm fine." I tried to force myself up and fell right back down. I was pissed. "Damn!" I yelled in frustration. This nigga was really getting the best of me. My head was spinning and my legs were shaking. Before long, I was being put on the gurney, strapped down, and rolled into the back of the ambulance. The whole ride I kept asking to use the phone and they wouldn't allow me to. I needed to make sure that Diamond was okay.

"Please, can I call my girl? Whoever did this could be trying to hurt her."

The male paramedic didn't budge while the female paramedic immediately looked concerned.

"Do you have your phone?" she asked. Her male partner turned to look at her with a frown. She wasn't fazed.

"Yeah, it's in my left pocket."

She went in my pocket and retrieved the phone. "I can't unstrap you for safety reasons but I can dial it for you."

"Cool, her name's Diamond. It's in the phone book."

She dialed the number and placed the phone near my ear. "Hello?"

"Babe, are you okay?" I asked, breathing heavily. I had never been happier to hear her voice.

"Yeah, I'm fine, what's wrong with you?"

"Somebody put a bomb in my car but . . ."

"A bomb! Baby, are you hurt?"

"I'm okay, they're taking me to the hospital now. Don't run down here, I'm okay."

"I'm coming now."

"Babe . . ."

"What hospital are you going to? It's not up for discussion, Black."

"I think Penn," I replied. I knew there wasn't any arguing with her at this point.

"I'll meet you there." *Click!*

I looked over at the female paramedic and nodded my head in thanks. We arrived at the hospital where they hurried me into trauma. The whole time I repeated that I was fine and wanted to go home. My requests went unheard. After an hour of trying to fight them, they sedated me. The last thing I could remember was seeing a long-ass needle and heavy eyelids. When I woke up, Diamond was sitting in a chair at the bedside.

"Hey, Babe, how are you feeling?" She got up from the chair and came over to sit next to me.

"I'm good."

"What the hell happened?"

"Somebody put a bomb in the car and . . ."

"A bomb?"

"Listen, don't get bent all out of shape. I'm okay as you can see."

"You could have been killed. We have to get away from here, babe."

"I'm not running from that nigga, fuck him! If he's coming, I'm waiting."

"You see what keeps happening? He's going to kill one of us." I could tell how afraid she was. What the hell was I supposed to say? There probably wasn't anything that I could say to ease her mind. I thought about what she said and it made perfect sense, getting away. I wasn't about to run but I needed to get her out of harm's way. Even if just for a week or two, it would give me time to sort things out.

"Look, I'm going to send you away for a couple of weeks. See if Kiki can get free and go with you," I said as I sat up in bed. I knew sending her away without me wouldn't be easy. I prepared myself for an argument.

"What? Why the hell would I go away and leave you here? If I go anywhere you're going with me."

"I'm not going to argue with you, D. I'm angry, my fucking car is blown to shreds, and my head hurts like hell. If you stay here you're a target and I need time to figure this shit out. I need you to listen to me for once and stop being so damn stubborn."

She sat there with a blank stare. I was waiting for her to yell, cry or do something other than sit in silence. I could see how this was affecting her. Diamond had always been strong, since I'd known her, anyway. That was one of the things that attracted me to her. I knew that she wouldn't let a nigga run over her. Now, things were different. She was falling apart and I didn't know how else to patch her back together other than killing this nigga. Soon a single tear formed in the well of her right eye, slowly rolled down her cheek, and dropped onto the sheets.

"I'm losing my mind, Black, I can't take this shit. I thought I was built for this. It's much easier when you're the predator. I can't believe that I was so stupid."

"Don't beat yourself up about the past, okay. I need you to think realistically, babe. You shot that nigga and he could have lived. Shit, if that were me, I'd be doing the same shit. I know him well and if it's him I know he won't stop until he gets what he wants. I would lose my mind if I lost you."

After a few seconds of silence she spoke again. "Okay, I'll go."

"I'm glad." I smiled as I reached over to hug her. I wasn't trying to get sentimental but on some real shit, I needed her in my life. She was the balance that I never had before. I know that it may sound fucked up since she was once and still may be my best friend's wife, but he didn't deserve her. Hell, he didn't give a fuck about her. I remember the first time they'd had sex up in the box at the Sixers game. No sooner than he closed the door behind her he was boasting. I had never been one to brag about getting ass, but Kemp, he needed to feel like a king. That day she had finally gotten his attention. She'd been trying for weeks and he knew it.

"I need to make her sweat. Shit, that gold-digging bitch ain't about to get a piece of me that easily." He laughed. "She's sexy as shit but I know the game."

"How you know she playing you? She could really like you."

"Bullshit, Black," he began to laugh. "That bitch just got out of jail, she's broke as hell and who the fuck goes around practically stalking a nigga if it ain't about money. You sound like one of them. You ain't getting soft on me now, are you?"

"Soft, come on man, I'm far from that. I'm just saying, you gotta stop treating every female you meet like a gold digger just because you rich."

He continued to laugh, "What you trying to say, it's real love out here?"

"That's exactly what I'm saying."

"Nigga, I've been married twice and I'm divorced. These bitches only see the dollars. If I was a chick I'd be the same way."

"You're divorced because you think like you do. You only got married 'cause you're selfish."

"And I already know that shit, man. I lock 'em down, that's how you gotta do it. And Diamond, she'll be number three.

If you know one thing about me it's that I keep my promises, and I promise you that shit."

He couldn't wait to clown her after he fucked her with all of us sitting a few short feet away. She left out of the room with a huge smile on her face. As soon as the door was closed, everyone but me burst into laughter.

"You ain't right, man," I spoke loudly. Everyone turned to look at me as if I was speaking in another language. To them, I was. There were just some things that I couldn't accept as right—shit, I had three sisters.

"Yo', you been acting like a bitch lately. You act like you want to fuck her. You know me, nigga, I don't cock block. If that's what you want by all means go for it," Kemp yelled. Everyone turned to look at me and soon erupted into laughter.

"Come on now, don't try to play me, nigga. You know it ain't that. I'm just saying, why you gotta come out here and boast. Everybody knows you get pussy!" I was getting annoyed. If it was one thing I hated, it was to be put on blast, especially in front of a bunch of niggas.

"Stop tripping, man, if it makes you feel any better I'll refrain from talking about pussy around you." He continued to laugh.

I didn't even respond. I just nodded my head and took a sip of my Corona. Soon the attention was off of me and back on the game. I sat there wondering how this dude even got to where he was at that point. I mean, he was street smart and he had the wit to get all of the shit he had, but keeping it—that was a whole different story. That took more than what he had and I could see him losing it even back then. I didn't envy Kemp but I did always want to claim his spot. Even as his friend, there was something in the back of my mind. I could see the future and was ready to jump in his place as soon as it was open.

Chapter Thirty-four

Diamond

Permanent Monday

Who the hell was at the door so damn early? I thought while crawling out of bed. Black was asleep next to me and hadn't budged even after the bell rang a fourth time. I put on a robe and headed downstairs. I looked out of the peephole and spoke.

"Who is it?"

"Hey, Diamond, it's your dad. Can I come in and talk to you for a minute?"

"Right now isn't a real good time, you should have called first."

"You didn't give me your number."

Damn, I wasn't ready to talk with him yet but I knew that he'd keep trying until I did. "Okay, let me put something on, give me a minute," I replied, hoping that by the time I got back down to the door he'd be gone. Once I got up to the room, Black was sitting up on the side of the bed.

"Who's at the door?"

"My father."

"Did you let him in?"

"No, not yet, I came up to get something on. He's still standing outside."

"You should have just let him in."

"I am going to let him in, damn!" I yelled. He looked at me and shook his head.

"I'm sorry okay? I know it's a sore subject."

"I'm sorry for snapping. I'm going to go see what he has to say to get this over with. He's not going to leave me alone until I do."

"Well, I'm going to jump into the shower and head out. If you need me, holla!"

"Where are you going? You're not supposed to be in the streets. The doctor said to rest for a week. It's only been three days, Black."

"Go ahead and talk to your dad. I'm fine, okay."

I didn't respond, I just grabbed my shorts and slipped them on before leaving back out of the room and down the stairs again. I glanced out of the peephole again to find him patiently waiting on my return. I took a deep breath and opened it.

"Thanks a lot for talking to me, Diamond. There are some things I just have to explain."

I took a few steps back to give him room to enter. As soon as he did he looked around with a pleased look. I guess he was proud of what I had accomplished—well, at least I hoped that he was. I always wanted his approval after he'd gone away. I blamed myself for his departure. I thought that I wasn't good enough. I prayed for him to come back so I could prove that I was. Maybe this was my chance and the longer I thought about having the satisfaction of being loved by him the happier I got.

"This is very nice, Diamond, you're doing well. I'm happy about that," he said as he walked into the living room and sat down.

"Thanks," I replied, joining him on the sofa. "So what is it that you wanted to talk to me about?" I went straight in. I'd waited for this day for so long and now that I was ready to know the answer I couldn't wait any longer.

"Well, it's about us and why I left."

"Us? What do you mean by that?"

"About me being your father."

I sat there still unsure of what it was he was trying to say. "Okay and what about that?" I asked with a confused expression on my face. I was hoping that he hadn't come to bullshit me. I wanted him to get to the point and stop beating around the bush.

"That I'm your biological father."

"What? Mom told me that I was adopted." Okay, so now I was getting annoyed. I wondered if this was just a ploy to get close to my money.

"You were adopted, by her."

"I still don't get what you're trying to tell me. Excuse me if I'm a little slow this morning, but I need you to get to the point."

"After your mom and I were married, I had an affair. It lasted about two years and I didn't tell your mother about the infidelity until my mistress became pregnant. It hurt her and I had never felt worse in my life. Well, Nila couldn't have children and she'd always talked about adopting. Pam, the woman I had an affair with, didn't want children but I convinced her to go through with it promising that I'd leave Nila. Once you were born she tried to be a mother, but it wasn't in her. She couldn't take care of you, especially without me. I couldn't and I wouldn't leave Nila at that time so we all decided that we'd let her adopt you and Pam would move on with her life." He stopped for a few seconds. By then, tears were flowing. If this was all true that made the fact that he'd walked away from me even worse. I was his biological daughter?

"I don't know what to say. I mean, that still doesn't explain why you walked out on me."

"Because I was in love with Pam and Nila promised me if I walked out on her I'd never see you again."

"So I'm assuming that means you chose her over me, right?" Now I was angry. I couldn't believe what I was hearing. Nothing was making sense.

"I didn't choose her over you, I love you and I've always loved you from the day you were born and I held you in my arms. I wasn't happy and I couldn't be the father you needed if I stayed."

"I still can't believe what I'm hearing. It really took you ten years to tell me this?"

Just as he was about to speak Black came down the stairs. My father stood up to greet him.

"Black, this is my father Jim, this is Black, my . . ."

"Fiancé, I'm Black her fiancé," he interrupted me, while reaching out to shake his hand.

My fiancé? Was I missing something? When the hell did that happen?

"Nice to meet you, Black, is that your real name?"

He had nerve, like he wanted to act like a father now. What the fuck did he know about being a father?

"Naw, my real name is Keshawn Black but everyone calls me Black."

"Oh, okay."

"Well, it was nice meeting you, Jim. Babe, I'm gonna run, call me if you need anything." He leaned in to kiss me. I didn't know what he was thinking but I'd definitely discuss it with him later.

"Okay," I replied. I didn't want to let on that I was upset. I was trying to be strong.

Black left and I immediately turned my attention back to my father. He had sat back down on the sofa but remained quiet.

"So what do you expect from me? I still don't understand the purpose of this meeting." I wasn't slow but I just didn't know how he could walk in here after all this time, tell me a story like he'd just done, and think I'd run and jump in his arms like I used to as a child.

"I wanted you to know the truth. You haven't asked about Pam—do you want to know what happened to her?"

"Why? She didn't want me. Why should I give a damn about her?" My face was twisted so tight my head was beginning to hurt. What kind of woman would do that? Here I believed that my mother was weak for falling apart like she did. Hell, who wouldn't under those circumstances?

"That's not true, she loves you."

"How do you know that?"

"Because I've been married to her for the past eight years, and she's only stayed away because she thought you wouldn't want to see her."

"That's bullshit! You know I can't believe that you all lied to me. My whole fucking life's been a lie." I stood up from the chair and paced the room. "So what's next, huh? I guess you're going to tell me you had kids, right? I mean that's next right?"

He was quiet. I shook my head and masked my tears with anger.

"I'm sorry, Diamond, I really wish I could turn back the hands of time and fix this."

"Get out!" I yelled.

"Diamond, please."

I turned my back and hoped that he wouldn't speak another word. Soon I heard his footsteps and the door closing behind him. I burst into tears as soon as the door shut. Just when I thought things couldn't get any worse he dropped that bomb on me. I didn't know what to do or who to call. My mind was racing. My biological mother—the one I never thought of seeing before—and my asshole of a father had left me out to dry. Where the hell was he when my mom was strung out on drugs? Where the hell was he when I fell into depression after Johnny went to prison? Where the hell was he every time I needed him? I was hurting and confused. I sat down on the sofa and placed my face in the palms of my hands. The phone rang a few minutes later and startled me. It was Black.

"Babe, how'd everything go?"

"Crazy, my mind is racing over here. I told him to get out. I can't believe the shit that he just told me."

"Do you need me to come home?"

I wanted him to be there, but honestly, I needed time alone to clear my head. I didn't want to end up taking my anger out on him. I was quiet for a second before speaking for fear that I'd say the wrong thing, which I often did when I was upset.

"Honestly, I just need to be alone right now. I appreciate you asking. I want to talk to you about it but right now I'm still trying to take it all in. I'll see you tonight when you come in and we'll talk then. Is that okay?"

"Whatever you want, babe. If you change your mind, call me. I'll call and check on you in a little while."

"Okay, I love you."

"I love you too."

I'd never felt a pain as deep as the one I was feeling at that moment. I knew he wouldn't listen and would probably be on his way back home to see what the hell was going on. Being alone was what I thought I needed but most likely wasn't the case. I thought about my mother and how special she was. I mean, a woman who could take care of a child that her husband went outside of their marriage and created was extraordinary. I loved her before but even more at this moment. I tried to fit in and it never really mattered. I continued to cry until Black walked through the door and held me. Breaking down was a sign of weakness and lately I felt myself slipping. I felt like something was taking over me and I hated it. I struggled to tell Black all that I'd just heard from my father. He comforted me until I was calm enough to begin drifting off to sleep.

Chapter Thirty-five

Black

New Money

"Yo', what's taking this nigga so long? He called over an hour ago. How long does it take to drive from G-town?" I was getting annoyed. I was waiting on Kenyon to bring me the money from last night's pickup. I should have stopped fucking with him the day I saw how he felt about Kemp but I let it slide because he was a good worker. JB and I were sitting inside the warehouse for way too long. I'd called his phone six times and hadn't gotten a response yet.

"You want me to call him again?" JB asked, noticing my frustration.

"I already called that muthafucker six times, he's gonna make me bust a cap in his ass for real!"

JB sat there quiet, glancing down at his phone. You could cut the tension in the room with a knife. I felt like I was losing control of them since they believed Kemp was alive. I had to figure out a way to get my soldiers back in line even if it meant permanently getting rid of the bad seeds. One thing that stood out about this situation was a comment Kemp once made to me. It was back in 2002 and things on the strip had never been better. We were killing all the other local crews in sales and were slowly taking over. Of course with more money comes more jealousy and envy. I always knew it but had never witnessed it myself. I thought that if there were any form of hate it would come from the outside. Everyone that worked for Kemp was paid pretty well—maybe not as much as he was or as much as they wished they should have been—but it was well in my books. They never wanted for anything, or at least that's what I thought.

Back then there was a runner named Tony that handled most of the money pickups. He'd known Kemp since they were kids and had actually been one of his best friends. Money began to come up short and it didn't take long to figure out where the money was going. Kemp confronted Tony when he came to the warehouse to drop off the money.

"How much is this?" Kemp asked. You could tell Tony was nervous but he tried to maintain his cool. Kemp remained calm.

"Ten thousand."

"Ten? You sure?"

"Yeah, I counted it myself before I came here."

"I called and got report and it should be thirteen so you sure about that?" Kemp got up from his chair. I was sitting in a chair off to the side, unsure of what was about to go down. Kemp wasn't one to discuss what he planned to do. Most times I don't think he even had a plan. He seemed to do things at the spur of the moment.

"I'm sure—who the hell said it was thirteen? I counted ten."

"It doesn't matter who said it, what matters is the three Gs that's missing."

"This is bullshit, Kemp, you know me better than that. Why would I steal from you?"

"I've been trying to figure that shit out and I'm stuck. I make sure you get dough and this is the thanks I get?"

"I keep trying to tell you I didn't steal from you. If anything's missing you need to holla at them niggas on the street." Tony was now raising his voice. If there was one thing about Kemp that never changed it was that once his mind was made up it was pretty close to impossible to change it.

"Well, I don't believe you," he shouted while reaching to the small of his back and retrieving his gun. "I trusted you, nigga, and I guess that was me being naïve. I'm not about to let you get away with that shit. No one steals from me." He was now pointing the gun in his direction. I was still sitting in the chair waiting for what would happen next. I mean, I was pretty sure what was about to happen but I wasn't sure what Kemp would do afterward.

"If you gonna shoot me then get it over with, you'll feel like an ass once you find out it wasn't me!" Tony yelled back. You could tell Kemp didn't really want to shoot him by the look in his eyes. He looked at him like a brother.

"Me feel like an ass? That'll never happen. You should feel like an ass for thinking that you could get away with this bullshit!" he yelled. His finger was now firmly on the trigger. His face was in knots and his eyes showed the anger that was flowing through his body. A few seconds later, he shot him twice in the chest. His body fell into the wall behind him and slid down to the floor. Blood was smeared down the wall and forming a puddle beneath Tony's body on the floor.

"Damn, this shit gonna fuck up my carpet!" Kemp said before putting his gun down on the desk. I still hadn't budged. I was waiting for him to give me an order. He walked over to the phone and dialed. I didn't know who he was calling at the time but I'd find out a few minutes later. "Help me wrap this nigga up, they're coming to get him in a few minutes."

I got up from the chair and helped him wrap Tony's body up in plastic. I was still in shock. I had seen Kemp kill before but never someone as close to him as Tony. He was trying to prove a point, which was that it didn't matter who it was—if he was crossed—they would be taken care of. To me, this was a valuable lesson, which would aid me in situations like these. Kemp taught me that you couldn't trust anyone regardless of how close you were to them.

As I stood here waiting for Kenyon, all I could think about was Kemp and this lesson. Though Kenyon wasn't close to me, he was one of the workers and I didn't trust him as far as I could throw him. He didn't respect me the way that he did Kemp and I felt like I had to prove a point. I wanted people to fear me the same way they feared him. My mind was racing as I dialed his number one last time. He still didn't answer. A minute or two later I heard footsteps nearing the door.

"Yo', what the fuck took you so long?" I yelled as soon as his face was revealed through the opened door.

"My bad, I got caught up with some personal shit. I'm here now, here's the money," he said walking over to the desk and dropping the black duffel bag full of money on the table.

"Personal? What personal shit would you be handling while you're carrying my money?"

"I said my bad, damn! All the money is there." He pointed to the bag.

I walked over to him and stood close enough where he could most likely feel the heat from my body. "Don't let that shit happen again."

"All right, it won't." He stood firm in his position as if he didn't fear me. This added fuel to the fire but I relaxed. I didn't want him to know he was pissing me off. "Do you need me for anything else?"

"I'm not done talking—why the fuck are you cutting me off?"

"I'm not cutting you off, I just have some shit to handle. If you don't need anything else I can go take care of it."

"I didn't say I was finished, I'm still trying to figure out why you would make a detour with my money."

"I've already said *my bad*, I'm not gonna keep saying it, man. It won't happen again." Kenyon was getting angry which only pissed me off more. Why the fuck was he angry? To me that meant he had something to hide.

"Who are you yelling at? You don't have any reason to be upset, you're the one lollygagging with my fuckin' money in the wings. You should have dropped that shit off first." I was repeating myself and I hated it. I just wanted to make sure this nigga knew not to play games with me.

"Look, I'm not no sucka Black, you're not gonna be talking to me like some fucking young boy. I told you what happened and that's that. You don't have to keep repeating yourself either because I heard."

I felt just like Kemp did when he faced Tony that day. I wanted to blow him away but I had to think about it. Was killing him going to prove anything? I couldn't let him disrespect me like that, though I would definitely lose more respect like that. I'd worked too hard to gain what I had and I'd be damned if I'd let one nigga ruin it. "I'll talk to you however I see fit. You work for me, nigga, don't ever forget that!" I yelled.

"How can I? You keep reminding me."

His sarcasm was taking me to a level of anger that I was trying to avoid. My fingers were gripped tightly around the .45 that was in my hand. Sweat was forming on my forehead from the adrenaline rushing through my body. JB was sitting there with his eyes glued to Kenyon's back. He was waiting for one of us to make a move. I couldn't even respond to what he'd just said. He didn't respect me and it didn't matter what I did at this point. For me, there was only one option: killing him. With a quick hand motion, I raised the gun and shot him in the chest. He stumbled before I released four more shots, forcing him down to the ground. JB didn't budge, almost as if he knew what I was about to do before I did it. I gave him a look, which meant get help to come take him out. I walked back to the desk and sat down. I placed the gun on the desk and grabbed a cloth to wipe the blood that I felt resting on my face.

JB left out of the office and shortly returned with a couple of the runners, some rope, and a bunch of plastic. I still sat silent at the desk. I hated the fact that I had to resort to murder. I hoped that I could keep him around regardless of his attitude toward me after he believed Kemp was alive. He actually was a good soldier his loyalty just didn't lie with me. After they wrapped him up and took him out of the room the female we used to clean up messes like these came in and begin cleaning up the blood that was left behind. I got up to leave the room and walked straight into JB, who was on his way back in.

"I know this ain't a good time, but it's somebody I want you to meet."

"You're right, it ain't a good time, so can we do this later?"

"I wish we could, but with Kenyon being gone I need you to meet this dude like yesterday."

"I just shot this nigga and you're already trying to replace him."

"Well, what am I supposed to do? I can't handle the work on both ends alone."

I stood there for a second thinking. He was right, I couldn't expect him to handle Kenyon's area. He had to be replaced or shit would get out of hand. At this point I had to think rationally if I wanted things to get back on track. Putting too much work on one person would only hurt the situation. "All right, where is he?"

"Out front, his name is Money."

"Money? I think I heard that name before. Is he the one that holds down the corner outside of Papi's?"

"Yeah, that's him," JB said as we walked toward the exit. I couldn't remember where I knew him from at the time but I knew that it would come back to me eventually. We exited the building where Money was standing, leaning up against a Ranger Rover. I was impressed; for a nigga that holds down one corner he seemed to be doing especially well. It also made me wonder what the hell he needed me for. Naturally, I was a suspicious dude but I figured I'd give him the benefit of the doubt since I trusted JB.

"Money, this is Black. Black, meet Money."

I reached my right hand out to shake his. I nodded my head before speaking. "So JB tells me that you want to work for me."

"Well, I was thinking more like a partnership. I do pretty well on my own block so I definitely don't want to work for anyone. I figured we could work together to knock all the other hustlers out of the box."

What the fuck is he talking about? I thought. Why the hell would I begin a partnership with a nigga I don't even know? I must look like a straight fool.

"A partnership? What makes you think I need a partner?"

"I didn't say you needed one, but you could only benefit from having me on your team. I know you don't know me and if a nigga I ain't know came to me the same way I'd be skeptical too. But on some real shit, I'm one of the toughest soldiers out here. You won't find another me, for sure."

"Maybe we can work something out. I'm not sure if it'll be a partnership but I'll figure it out once I get my head straight. I got a lot of shit on my mind right now and I can't really make that kind of decision. Give JB your contact information and I will get back to you by the end of the week." Though most of what I said was true. I wanted to wait until I did a little research. I didn't really trust what he was saying. I didn't want to hear too much more of his pitch because him being my partner was out of the question. Niggas like JB had been down with me from day one and I hadn't given them that opportunity. They'd look at me like an asshole if I let this nigga slide in so easily.

"Cool, I appreciate it," he said, reaching out to shake my hand.

"I'm out, JB, call me if something's up. I'll be back shortly." I walked over to my car and began my drive home. I had so much on my mind and so much to straighten out. I had just killed someone. In the past I'd shot at a couple of people and had hit a few but had never killed anyone. It was a different feeling, one of triumph. I felt like I could do anything at that point and I planned on using this no-tolerance method from that point on.

Chapter Thirty-six

Diamond

Where I Belong

I sat on the steps, both eyes full of tears. They had just handcuffed Johnny and took him off to jail. I was losing my best friend and there wasn't anything that I could do to stop it. Did I cause this? If I hadn't pushed him so hard maybe this wouldn't have happened. I could remember the blood all over him and he ran to my house to tell me what happened. It was a vision that I'd never be able to erase. I heard banging on the back door. It was almost midnight so I knew it could only be him. By the sound of the knocks I could tell that something was wrong so I hurried to the door to answer it. It was pouring outside and he stood there in jeans and a T-shirt soaked with rain and blood. He stood there frozen as I stood on the other side of the threshold with the same look.

"What the hell happened, Johnny?" I said as tears instantly formed in the wells of my eyes. I grabbed hold of him to make sure that he wasn't hurt.

"I did it, I couldn't take it anymore. I did it," he said as he walked through the door and began pacing. Water was dripping all over the place, leaving little blood-tinged puddles all over the kitchen floor. He was disoriented and filled with anger. I had never seen him so upset. Each time I tried to touch him he'd snatch away and keep repeating the same thing over and over again. I didn't know what it was that he'd done at that moment but I knew it couldn't be good.

"Babe, what did you do?" I was crying at this point. I wanted to console him but at the young age of sixteen I didn't know how. I thought about movies and TV shows to see if I could remember how they'd done it. My mind was drawing a blank and my instinct wasn't helping much either.

"I did it, I fuckin' killed him. I did it."

"Who did you kill?"

"My father, he can't hurt us anymore."

I couldn't believe what I was hearing. Did he just say he killed his father? The only thing I could think of doing was holding him. I wrapped my arms around him and held on tight as we cried together. I felt like my world was crashing down. He was going to be taken away and I'd probably never see him again.

"It's all my fault, I'm so sorry."

"It's not your fault. I had to. I couldn't let him keep abusing us. I had to stand up and be a man."

Stand up and be a man was what I'd always told him. I told him that he'd never be a man if he couldn't stand up for himself and protect his sister. I pushed him and now his life was over. I stood there holding him close without saying a word until I heard police sirens and saw flashing lights. A few seconds later there was banging at the door. I opened the door after Johnny gave me a nod. The cops pushed me aside and burst into the house, immediately putting handcuffs on him. My mother and aunt had since woke up and were standing in the living room with me. My mom was clueless as they dragged him out of the house. I cried and tried to free myself from my mom's grip to get one last hug. He was out of the house and into the car before I could get to him. I sat on the steps looking on as they drove away. My head was buried in my knees.

"Come on in, baby, and get out of those pajamas, you're soaked."

I didn't budge as if I was glued to the steps. My body felt like I was drained of the energy that I had. "Diamond, come on, sweetie it's late and you have school tomorrow."

School? Was she serious? I'd just witnessed something that would probably stay with me forever. The look in his eyes when he spoke those words reminded me of those serial killers in movies. There was no feeling behind it. It was as if he didn't care that the man he'd just killed was his father.

How could you murder someone and not give a damn? I know that he did it to save them from abuse but even still, he should have cared. After a while my mother just sat down beside me and placed her hand on my back. I sat there until I was all cried out and exhausted so much so that I had to lie down.

I didn't get up for school the following morning or the rest of that week. I cried all day and night. I wanted to close my eyes and wake up and it would all be gone. I wanted to be able to hold him at night when he'd sneak over and make love to me. I wanted to laugh with him and smile when he told me how much he loved me. I missed my best friend and letters would never fill the void.

Now all of these years later I realized how much I needed a father. I didn't know it back then but I knew now how important it was to have him around at times like those. My mother tried but I was never as close to her as I was to him. I missed him being there to console me when I was upset so when he walked away I felt the same way I did the night they took Johnny away.

I thought about it long and hard. I had to talk to my real mother and figure out why she gave me away. The explanation that my father gave me wasn't quite enough for me. I mean, I had come to the realization years ago that my mother didn't want me but with the information my father had given me I felt a lot different. I always prayed that I would meet her and finally feel like I was somewhere that I belonged, but once I heard the words that were coming out of my father's mouth I didn't quite feel the same. I was hurt. It was a hurt that I couldn't really explain. I couldn't imagine a pain much worse than this. To know that I was the result of an affair and then to be dumped by the woman that ruined a happy home was worse than just being rejected. Even if she had just given me up for adoption and disappeared I wouldn't have felt as bad as I did. She not only left me fatherless but motherless. The only mother that I'd known pretty much committed suicide because she was so stressed about their breakup. I believe that any woman would be devastated about taking care of her husband's love child to keep their marriage together only for him to leave anyway.

I told my father that I wanted to meet both him and Pam together. There were a lot of unanswered questions and some things that I needed to say. I wanted them to know how they ruined my life. I wasn't going to let them back into my life that easy. They needed to suffer the way that I had all of the years that they were gone. Black tried to talk me out of it, saying that I didn't want to dig too deep because I'd most likely find out things that I didn't want to know. I didn't care honestly, I needed to know where I came from. Even if it hurt, I'd figure out a way to get over it just like every obstacle that had been thrown my way.

I told them that I would come over to their house for dinner. I was nervous especially since I would be meeting Pam for the first time. What would she look like? How would she react to seeing me? There were so many questions going through my mind I could hardly relax on the drive over.

I arrived at a large row home in the Northeast part of Philly. There were two cars in the driveway, a black Lexus and a white Acura. *Somebody must be doing pretty well,* I thought. I wasn't going to jump to conclusions but if they were over here living well while we struggled in North Philly all of those years I'd be disgusted. I parked on the side street and walked over to the door. I almost turned back around but the motion lights came on. I didn't want to get caught running away from the door so I stayed. I rang the bell and heard footsteps nearing on the opposite side.

"Glad you made it," my father said, opening the door with a huge-ass Kool-Aid smile on his face. "Come on in," he motioned with his hand.

I slowly walked inside and took a quick survey of the area. Everything was perfect, not even a pillow was out of place. I moved in just enough for him to close the door and stood still.

"Don't be scared to go in further. We won't bite." He laughed.

I didn't join in. This wasn't a situation that I could laugh about. I didn't find anything humorous about meeting up with them.

"Pam, she's here!" he yelled out. A few moments later I heard shoes clicking against the hardwood floor. When I saw her face I knew—I knew that I belonged to her. She was beautiful and had a body that was pretty close to flawless. She had a bright smile with perfect white teeth and long, silky hair. I was almost her spitting image. I stared at her from head to toe. She was dressed in designer gear and flaunted diamonds everywhere. She looked exactly as I hoped I would when I reached her age.

Tears streaming down her face soon joined her smile. She walked over to me and wrapped her arms around me. I was hesitant about hugging her back. Eventually I gave in but it wasn't genuine, not on my part anyway. I felt like hugging her back was the right thing to do at the time.

"I never thought I'd get a chance to see you this way. I wanted this day for so long."

She backed away while holding onto one of my hands and looking me up and down. "You're so pretty, you look just like me when I was your age."

I still stood there, silent. I wanted to thank her for the compliment but something in me wouldn't allow me to.

"Come on in the living room so we can sit down and talk," she said slightly pulling me in the direction of the living room. I followed behind her and took a seat on the sofa opposite of the love seat where she sat. I still wasn't all that comfortable.

"Before you start to speak, I just need to say a few things." I had finally broken my silence. I wanted to just get it over with. "I want you to know that I'm angry first and hurt second. I'm angry because it took this long for you to reach out to me. I needed you both when I was a teenager getting into trouble because my mom was too busy getting strung out to pay me any attention. Or when my aunt would get angry and starve me all day while parading food in front of my face. Or when I fell for a worthless man and ended up spending nine months in jail. There were so many times in my life that I needed you and you were nowhere around. Looking around here, you seem to be pretty well-off, so it disgusts me that you would leave me in that tore-down neighborhood all of those years. Did you even know that I went to jail? I went to jail for nine months because I desperately wanted a man. I felt like there was something missing from my life. I needed a father and a mother. Yeah, my mother was there but she was high on drugs. You caused that and you should feel bad because now she's dead. The only mother that I ever knew is gone. I'm not sure what it is that we'd want to gain from this meeting. An apology would fall on deaf ears because it can't erase all of the crap that I went through." I paused for a second to catch my breath. I was finally getting the chance to speak my mind.

"I know that you said an apology wouldn't matter, but I am really sorry. I was young and dumb back then. I got caught up in an affair and wasn't ready for a child. I honestly did what I thought was best for you. If I could turn back the hands of time I would, but being with me might not have been the best thing for either of us."

I sat quietly and listened to what she had to say. Maybe there was some truth to what she said. I mean, who knows what would have happened if she would have kept me. Though I couldn't think of being in a more fucked-up situation than I was in, you never really know. I was trying to keep an open mind even though I was angry.

"Diamond, I never wanted to leave you but Nila didn't give me a choice."

"You can't sit here and blame it all on her. There's no way a judge would have left me with a drug addict and not placed me with my biological parents. So I'm not a fool, you can't try to convince me of that."

"I know you're not a fool. I believe that you're a very smart woman. But you have to believe me. I really wanted to take you away but one side wanted to keep you and the other side didn't."

"So I'm assuming the side that didn't want to keep me was her, right?" I spoke aloud.

"It's not that I didn't want you, I couldn't take care of you." Pam jumped in and spoke in her defense. "I really wanted to be with you and it killed me to watch you grow up from afar and not be a part of that. Though I wasn't around, I kept up with you. I always knew what was going on in your life."

I was starting to believe her. Either she was a good actress or what she was saying was truly genuine. "So how many other children do you have?"

"We only have one other child, his name is Javan."

"How old is he?" I was finally breaking the ice and slowly getting over the anger and wanted to know more about the life that I missed. Although I was kind of jealous I instantly felt close to him and felt an urge to meet him.

"He's nineteen, he goes to college at Temple."

"Wow, so I have a brother That's crazy." I was still taking the idea in. I always wished I had a sibling. I wanted that just as much as I wanted my father. "So when can I meet him?" I could tell by their reaction that they weren't expecting me to say that.

"You really want to see him?" Pam asked.

"Yes I do." I wasn't sure where I wanted to take this relationship with them but I did feel that it was important for my brother and me to get acquainted.

"So what does that mean for us?" my father asked. I figured that would be his next question.

"I honestly don't know. I wish that I could give you an answer but this is a situation where we'll just have to take things one day at a time."

"That's fair and I respect that. We just want a chance and if you decide to pull away we'll accept it," my father said grabbing hold of my hand. I almost pulled away but decided to allow the affection. After all, it's what I longed for.

"So how about you give me your number to give to Javan so he can call you. I'm so excited for him. He's always wanted to meet you," Pam said with a huge smile across her face.

"So he knew about me?"

"Of course, I never wanted to hide you. All of my family knows about you."

I felt myself warming up even more. I had a whole family out there that I didn't know anything about. I couldn't wait to meet them. "Well, I have to get going. I told Black that I'd meet up with him." I stood up and began to move toward the door.

"You're leaving so soon? I thought that you would have at least stayed for dinner."

"No, I have some things to do but I will come back. Now that I'm around we have a lot of catching up to do." I laughed. I was really interested in learning more about them so I planned to stay around.

"Well, drive safely," my father spoke quietly as if he was sad that I had to leave. I was actually sad I was leaving as well. I wanted to stay and find out more about them but I couldn't.

I gave them both a hug and headed out of the door, down the driveway, and into my car. They stood at the door, waving good-bye as if I was going off to college or something. The entire time I sat there talking to them I felt my anger slipping away. All my life I was bitter and angry with the people who gave me away. The fact that I didn't know the whole story didn't help. I wondered why my mother kept them away from me all of those years or why she never fully revealed the situations surrounding my adoption. I'd never know the answer to that and at this point it didn't really matter. I was where I belonged and where I should have been all along.

Chapter Thirty-seven

Black

Motives

"So where you from?" I was sitting at my desk opposite of Money. I still didn't trust him so I was trying to feel him out. I had started my research and I wanted to test him to see if I'd catch him in a lie. Word on the street was how much of a hustler he was. He was known to work hard to maintain. Never flashy, which was a good quality. He had a Range and a few jewels but he didn't over-do it like most niggas with money do when they get on. To me, that meant that people wouldn't be so fast to test him and if I was going to have him on my team I needed to know that I could trust him with my goods and money. He sat across from me with a stone-cold face. I figured he was trying to show me that he wasn't afraid of me.

"From Frankford, I hold down the block up there."

"You hold down a block where you live?" I replied. That was definitely the wrong move.

"Naw, I said that's where I'm from not where I live. I don't tell nobody where I live, not even you."

I was taken aback by that response. What the fuck did he mean, not even me? If I wanted to know I could find out. "How long you been hustling? You look pretty young."

"Shit, I've been on the block for three years. I'm not trying to make a career out of hugging the block, though. I just want to get enough ends so I can get out of town."

"So three years and you still on the same block alone. You should have people out working for you by now."

"I don't trust a lot of people and I'm not trying to pay niggas to do some shit that I can do better by myself."

"I can respect that," I said, nodding my head. "So what is it that you think you can enhance by being part of my team? If you've done so well working alone for all of these years, why partner up with someone now? Unless you have an ulterior motive or something, it just doesn't make sense to me."

He smiled. "Nothing like that. I have some connections that no one in Philly has. The product that I sell is like fifty percent cheaper than the lowest price you'll get."

"Fifty percent? I'd have to see that to believe it."

"I wouldn't bullshit you. That's why I manage to make so much money out here alone."

"I'm still confused. If the profit is so great why share it with me? You don't know me from Adam." I sat there with a dead stare. I was anxious to see what he'd come up with next. He'd answered most of my questions in a clever fashion, almost as if he'd rehearsed it. I couldn't quite put my finger on what was bugging me about this dude. Something was sticking out like a sore thumb and I had to figure it out.

"Yeah, I don't know you personally, but I've been watching you for awhile. I like your style. I mean, I think the way you took over after Kemp got murdered was remarkable."

What the hell? Did this nigga just say he's been watching me? I wasn't too comfortable with that. Then he makes a comment about Kemp. Where did that come from? "Watching me?"

"Yeah, not like no stalker," He burst into laughter. "From a distance and from the words off the street. I feel like I've known you for years and we just met. You remind me of myself and I like that."

I laughed a little myself. There wasn't anything else I could do but laugh. He was cracking me up and the fact that he was dead serious made it that much more comical. He didn't appear to appreciate my humor. "I like you, Money. And I'm cracking-up because I've never met one nigga that would have the balls to come at me the way you did. That shows me that you have heart."

He nodded his head as his frown loosened up a little bit. "Cool—so do we have a deal or what?"

"You gotta tell me the perks first. All you said was about a connection. You still haven't said what you'd gain from hooking me up with your connect."

"I mean, you have a huge customer base and that's what I'm trying to get. If we work together, shit, we can take over the whole city. You feel me?"

He was really starting to make sense now. I was down for a takeover. In fact, that had always been one of my goals. I had the power that I wanted now. I just had to figure out the best way to use it. "Cool, give me a few days to sleep on it and I will get back to you."

"Okay, well, thanks for meeting with me. I appreciate you hearing me out." He got up to shake my hand. I got up from my chair and obliged.

"I'll be in touch."

He nodded and turned to leave the office. JB rushed in no sooner than he made it out of the door. He closed the door behind him and came rushing to my desk.

"Yo', what the hell are you so hype for?" I asked. He was looking like a crackhead fiendin' for some crack.

"I'm just anxious to see how the meeting went."

"Why, are you getting a cut or something?"

"Come on man, I'm just looking out for you."

"For me?" I burst into laughter. Who the hell did he think he was fooling? "It's all love, man. The meeting went okay, I told him to give me a couple of days to sleep on it." I could tell JB wasn't too happy about my answer and I couldn't figure out why. Maybe I was being a little insecure or maybe my nerves were getting the best of me. I trusted JB as much as I possibly could in this situation.

"Okay, just don't let this good opportunity slip away."

"I'm no fool JB, I got this."

"All right then. I have to go make a couple of drops so I will get up with you later."

"All right." I reached out to shake his hand.

After he walked out of the office I sat there thinking about Money's proposition. I was definitely leaning toward going with his idea but I couldn't let him know so fast and seem desperate. With me, everything was planned. Shit, I even planned what underwear I'd put on. Every move had to be calculated because one slip could end it all. The phone rang just as I was getting up to leave the office. It was Trice. I hadn't seen or communicated with her in a couple weeks and I knew she'd be pissed.

"Hello," I said in a low tone.

"Where the hell have you been? I'm glad that you're alive, which lets me know you were just avoiding me for the past few weeks."

"I wasn't avoiding you, I just had some personal shit to deal with."

"Like what, Diamond?"

"Come on with that, Trice, I'm not gonna argue with you right now."

"I'm not going to either. You keep pushing me away and Diamond's going to end up getting her feelings hurt."

"What? Don't fuck with me, Trice, besides Diamond ain't the type of woman that'll let shit like that affect her. I don't even know why you're going there. You act like you are my girl or something."

"So what am I, then? What have I been for all of these years?"

"I'm not even going to answer that question, Trice. On some real shit, this conversation is giving me a headache."

"Don't come running to me when she leaves your ass!"

Click!

She hung up and I was glad. Threatening me damn sure wasn't about to make me run into her arms. I don't know why she believed that she was anything more to me than pussy and the mother of my child. I used her to ease my mind and to get a release when my mind was out of sorts. I couldn't focus on her at the moment; she'd be back. This was just one of her stunts. Every time she felt like I was neglecting her, this happened. I mean, don't get me wrong, Trice was the shit in bed and could potentially make a great woman but I had Diamond. See, Trice I met back when I first began hustling with Kemp. I was parked outside of the corner store laughing and talking shit with a few of the guys. She walked by with her friend Cherrie and everyone including Kemp was trying to holla. I stood in the back and gave her a few smiles and she threw a few back at me. She had a dark tone, smooth skin, and her body was the shit. Her curves fit her long, lean legs, and her breasts sat up like gravity hadn't taken its toll. I waited until she stepped away, allowing Kemp to talk to her girlfriend. I walked over and moved close to her. I wanted her to feel the heat from my body and smell the aroma of my Gaultier cologne. I could tell she was getting sucked in the minute I was staring her eye to eye.

"I saw you giving me the look so I figured I'd move closer so you wouldn't have to strain your eyes looking at me."

She giggled. "Up close and personal is the way I like it." She was flirting and I liked it.

"So what's your name?"

"Shartrice, but Trice is fine."

"Well, Trice, it's nice to meet you. My name is Black."

"I know," she said, smiling.

"How do you know that?" I asked, surprised. I know I was a well-known nigga but not like that.

"Everybody knows Black—you and Kemp are the talk of the town."

"Oh, really? Well, I guess that's a good thing." I hunched my shoulders. "So when are you gonna let me take you out to dinner or something?"

"Whenever you want."

"Well, what if I said tonight?"

"Then I'd say, see you later." She smiled and tapped me on the chest with her finger. She was turning me on. There was no way I could resist.

"Cool, give me your number and I'll call you around eight to come scoop you up."

She wrote her number down on a small sheet of paper and slowly placed it in the palm of my hand. She turned to walk away, giving me a perfect view of her ass. I called her that night but instead of going out to dinner, I ate her, if you know what I mean. It was on and poppin' after that with Trice. We were actually a couple at one point and I was ecstatic when she had my son. Shit just went down the tubes after that. We argued a lot, mainly because she wanted me to marry her and I wasn't into that shit back then. So she goes out and cheats and gets pregnant by another nigga. What type of shit is that? She actually thought shit between us would be the same after that. I was still angry about that shit but I did have genuine feelings for her that even my anger couldn't erase. Before I got with Diamond, I contemplated being with her but she couldn't handle my lifestyle. Diamond was used to it and she was the type of woman that could handle anything that was thrown her way. Trice would fall apart at the mere glimpse of drama. I had to have a strong woman on my team and though I felt bad for leaving her to raise my son, I did my part so that he'd never want for anything.

So I didn't believe Trice would do anything to mess up her life. But there's always a possibility, which was proven when Diamond called my phone an hour after I got off the phone with Trice.

"Why the fuck is your baby moms playing with me? I told you before to get that bitch in check because I will gladly go over there and whoop her ass!" she yelled into the phone.

"What did she do now?"

"This bitch called me talking about how you're still fucking her and you're planning on leaving me to be with her."

"That's bullshit, Diamond, I don't know why you even feed into her dumb shit. She's just mad because I didn't fuck her. I'll straighten her out later."

"No, you need to straighten her out now before she gets hurt. If it wasn't for your son I'd shoot that bitch! She's not going to keep disrespecting me."

"Calm down, Diamond, it's not that serious."

"It's not serious to you but it is to me! She's not calling you with the dumb shit she's calling me."

"How do you know she's not calling me?"

"Oh, so you've been talking to her?" she said with attitude. I could almost imagine the expression that she had on her face.

"Yeah, I talk to her, she is the mother of my child. Let's not do this, Diamond, please. My head is still hurting from arguing with her."

"Are you being smart?"

"No, Diamond, my head is hurting. I'm on my way home to lay down for a little bit."

"All right I'll see you when you get here."

Click!

Chapter Thirty-eight

Diamond

Love Lockdown

Since that last incident with Trice a couple of weeks ago things with Black and me had been better. I decided that I wasn't about to let him slip away or waste my time fighting with some chick that he didn't even want. In all actuality she wasn't any competition. There wasn't a chick around as fly as me. Yeah, she had his baby but I had his heart and I wasn't letting it go no matter how hard I had to fight to keep it. I realized how much his son meant to him and I wasn't trying to stand in the way of that but I had to get him where I wanted him. When it came to planning, I was the queen. Shit, she could try but I had a defense for every attack in the book. So I sat around thinking of a way that I could grab him hook, line, and sinker. I came up with the answer: having his child. I had never thought of having a child before now but I knew how much that meant to him. I wanted to keep the kind of control that Trice had. Shit, even if we weren't together he'd still be around. Unlike Trice, I didn't need him for money, I needed him for power. What we had took both of us to maintain. When Kemp died I was left with properties and numerous businesses, including an auto-body shop, a few corner stores, a barbershop and hair salon. Though I had more than enough money to keep up living the lavish life we were used to, Black needed to be in control. It's sort of like a boy waiting his whole life to run the family business. Black waited in the wings for the chance to walk in Kemp's shoes and now that the door was wide open there was no way I could pull him away from it. Honestly, I wasn't sure that I wanted to. There were some things about the business that I didn't like—the women, the late nights, and the threats. But just as I hated those things I loved the fact that it made him happy to finally be in charge. He was in his element, no longer having someone telling him what to do and how high to jump. I could never understand how he worked for Kemp as long as he had but I guess his loyalty meant more.

Finally knowing my family was also something that pushed me toward having children because family was more important to me now than ever. Now that I had a family I didn't want to let go.

I was on birth control for as long as I could remember. When I ended up knocked up as a teen my mom put me on pills. In a way, I was glad because I loved my life too much to have to deal with a child back then. I stopped taking my pills consistently right after the last argument we had about Trice. I'd flush one down the toilet every other day so he wouldn't find out that I wasn't taking them. I knew that it would take some time for them to work but I knew when I was most fertile and I made sure that we got it in during that time.

Two months went by and I was still getting my period. I was pissed. I felt like the longer this dragged on the possibility of it happening was slimmer. I decided to let Kiki in on my plan. It was hard for me to keep her in the dark. I pretty much told her everything even when I knew she'd try to talk me out of whatever crazy idea it was I had at the time. I drove over to her house unexpectedly and noticed JB's car parked in the driveway. *What the fuck?* Since when is Kiki cool with JB? I started to leave since she appeared to have company but after a few seconds of contemplating I ended up going to the door anyway. I knocked lightly and waited patiently. A few seconds later Kiki's voice screamed from the opposite side of the door.

"Who is it?"

"It's D, girl, open the door."

"Give me a second, okay."

Now I knew she was in there messing around. I laughed to myself as I stood outside of the door. Miss I-don't-date-drug-dealers was caught in the act. I wanted to see her lie herself out of this one. After five minutes I knocked again but this time not so lightly. Unexpectedly the door opened and JB was standing there putting his jacket on.

"What's up, Diamond?"

"I should be asking you that question." I laughed. He smiled and walked past me. Kiki was now standing at the door with a devilish grin on her face.

"Don't even say anything, girl, just get in here."

"I'm cracking-up inside, let me just tell you that. You are funny as hell." I smiled as I walked inside and headed over to the couch. "So what's the deal? You and JB—I would have never imagined that."

"Yeah, me either, girl, you know how I feel about them drug-dealing niggas. I don't want to have to sleep with one eye open waiting for someone to do a drive-by and shit. I'm lo-key. Damn shame he can lay the pipe, girl."

I burst into laughter. "JB, really? He don't look like the type."

"Well, his looks are definitely deceiving."

"How the hell did you even hook up with him? I never even saw y'all talking before."

"He was down at the club a few weeks ago and kicked a little game. I almost ignored his ass until he gave me a hundred-dollar tip. I figured I could at least go out with him. Going out turned into fucking and we've been doing it ever since." She laughed and slapped me a high five.

I was all for Kiki finding a man; she'd been single for a while now. It was good to see someone making her smile for a change.

"So enough about me, what brings you here? I know it wasn't to say hi—you never come all the way over here for that."

She knew me so well. "Well, I came over to tell you about my plan. I know you're going to try and talk me out of it but I can't keep secrets from you."

"You always got a damn plan girl. Your mind's always wandering. What the hell are you up to now? I hope it ain't anything illegal, you can't afford to go to jail again."

"No, not illegal, but conniving as hell."

She sat back in the chair and gave me a funny look. Her eyebrows were raised and her smile was a little smaller than it had been a few minutes earlier. "I stopped my birth control pills."

"What? Why the hell would you do that? You are in the prime of your life. You damn sure don't need to be dragging no baby around. Plus that shit drops your sexy ratings by at least two points."

"Sexy ratings? What the hell are you talking about, Kiki?"

"The way niggas look at you, duh!"

"Girl, I'm focused. I'm gonna have Black's baby and bump that bitch Trice out of the picture."

She laughed, "What? I know you can come up with a better plan than that. Shit ain't like that baby will guarantee he'll stay. The only thing that will guarantee is that you'll be tied up with a whining-ass kid every day. Girl, I can't even think about that."

"I didn't know you were so anti-child."

"I love kids—don't get me wrong—but just somebody else's."

"Well, that's my plan and I'm sticking to it. All I have to do is get knocked up."

"That should be the easy part. You really think that chick is going to give up that easily? I don't see it. She's stuck around even after he dumped her ass for you."

"It ain't about what I think, it's about what I know. And I know that bitch won't have a choice."

"Okay now we don't need no more murders."

"I'm not trying to go there, Kiki, but you know I will."

"I didn't know you cared about Black that much, honestly. I thought that shit was just another game."

"I love him and I know he loves me. Girl he called me his fiancée when I introduced him to my dad."

"Your dad? When the hell was that? I see you've been keeping me out of the loop lately." She sat up in the chair.

"I've just been busy. You know you're my girl, I can't keep shit from you."

"Okay then spill it."

"Well, I went over and met my mother and I look so much like her. I mean, I could almost be her twin. It turned out a lot better than I thought it would at first. I almost didn't go because I was scared of what I would see. I was actually surprised. I warmed up to them pretty fast. It felt like I belonged, you know." I was getting choked up just talking about it.

"Wow, I'm so happy for you D. I know that means so much to you."

"It does. I have a brother too, named Javan. I haven't met him yet but I did talk to him on the phone."

"That's so good."

"Yeah, but back to my plan."

"You never cease to amaze me." she laughed.

"I'm serious about this, I'm really ready to do this."

"I hope it works for you. I don't want to see you get hurt and to bring a baby into this world to be caught in the middle of all of that drama isn't good. But I got your back whatever you decide to do. You know that." She moved over to hug me. I felt better knowing that she had my back. I didn't doubt it but I still needed to have it confirmed. "So where are you off to?"

"Home to my man, girl, gotta get working on this baby!" I yelled. We both giggled as we walked to the door. I gave her one more hug before leaving. I dialed Black's cell and didn't get an answer so I left a message. I drove home hoping he'd call before I got there. I turned the corner and saw his car parked outside. I smiled. I parked, got out, and went inside. I went upstairs after calling his name a few times and found him asleep across the bed with the remote control in his hand.

"Babe," I said as I tapped him on the leg. He woke up, startled.

"What's up? Damn, I was knocked out."

"Yeah, snoring and all."

"No, I wasn't, stop lying," he said, smiling. I always picked with him about snoring. I told him I'd tape him one day so he could hear it for himself. He looked at me almost as if he could eat me. Hell, I wanted him to eat me, to be honest. I wanted to jump on him and make this baby that I wanted.

"Come here," he said reaching his arms out to grab me. His warm hands wrapped around my waist. His fingertips were caressing the small of my back and his lips were kissing my cleavage. I moaned a little, confirming how good he made me feel. I pushed him back onto the bed playfully. He smiled.

He loved it when I took control. I didn't say a word, only loosening his belt and unbuttoning his pants. His dick was already hard and practically busting through his jeans. Once I pulled his pants and boxers off and revealed his dick, my mouth began to water. I was extremely horny, so much so that my pussy juices were soaking up my panties. I grabbed hold of it and gently planted a kiss on the head of it. I kissed it a few more times before taking it in my mouth. As I sucked up and down I used one hand to jerk it and the other hand to massage his balls. I'd occasionally take it out of my mouth and spit on it. He said shit like that turned him on. He was begging me to stop but I couldn't—well, I wouldn't stop. I was too focused on getting every drop of his cum in me. After a few more minutes I stood up, removed my pants and panties, and climbed on top of him. His dick went inside of me with ease. I was so wet each time I'd slam my ass down a splashing effect occurred.

"This pussy is so wet," he moaned.

I didn't respond, I kept riding him, moving my hips in circles and fitting all of his length inside of me. I would occasionally stop for a second just to bend down and kiss him. He'd kiss me and as I'd go to sit back up he'd grab hold of me to kiss a little more. As we lay stomach to stomach I'd slowly lift my ass up and push it back down. I'd grind and moan at the same time. Though the moans were muffled by our passionate kiss you could still hear them escaping into the air. Over the next half hour and a continuous pace he erupted inside of me. Both of our bodies were shaking and exhausted. After I crawled off of him we lay there quiet. I was on my back staring up at the ceiling with my mind wandering. I hoped that this session of love making would get me the results that I yearned for. Black was quiet as well and I knew if he were ever quiet it meant that he was in deep thought. Most times I'd let him be rather than interrupting him but this time I wanted to know what was on his mind.

"Why are you so quiet? What's on your mind?" I said as I turned on my side and rubbed my hand across his chest.

"Just thinking about this dude named Money JB recommended to me."

"Money? That name sounds familiar."

"Familiar how?" He turned to look at me.

"I don't know, it just sounds like I heard it before."

"Well, he's trying to partner up with me and I'm leaning toward doing just that."

"Partner? Why would you need a partner?"

"I don't need a partner technically but he has some connections that will only benefit us in the long run."

"What's wrong with the connections that we already have? I mean, with this Kemp shit still lingering do you really trust dealing with somebody new?"

"I'm not worried about Kemp and this doesn't have anything to do with him and whoever is out here trying to scare us the shit ain't working. I'm not about to stop my money because of that shit. This can only put more money in both of our pockets. I know that you love money so what's the problem?"

"There isn't a problem. I just want you to be safe. I'd die if something happened to you."

"Nothing's going to happen to me." He turned on his side and was now staring me in the eyes. This was one of those sensitive moments that I treasured. He placed his hand on the side of my face and rubbed it gently. "I love you, okay. I'm not about to go down that easily."

I smiled and kissed him. I knew that he loved me and I had him where I wanted him. The pregnancy would seal the deal. With that, I'd permanently have his love locked down.

Chapter Thirty-nine

Black

More Drama

"Why the hell do I have to argue with you all the time? It's not like you want for anything!" I yelled. Trice was standing on the opposite side of the room with her hands on her hips and her face frowned up.

"Who said I didn't want for anything? I want us. I want things to be the way they used to be. I don't know what's so special about her. I tried to hang around hoping that you'd see her true colors and dump her ass but I can't do this anymore."

"What colors? You don't even know her."

"Not personally but I know all about her. How could you be with someone like her?"

"I'm not going to explain that, Trice. The bottom line is I'm with her and that's that."

She sat there with a sad look on her face. I never wanted to hurt her but what the hell was I supposed to do. Don't get me wrong I did love Trice but not enough to go back. That's partly what made me look at her as if she were just a piece of ass when I needed some. I could admit that her actions were partly my fault since I never told her how deep my relationship with Diamond really was. I was going to marry her and it was probably about time I told her.

"I can't accept that."

"Well, you'll have to because soon I'm going to marry her."

She stared at me as if she was ready to cry. I'd just broken her heart in a million pieces. How did things get this way? I still couldn't figure it out. As men, we make some of the dumbest choices when it comes to dealing with women. Not saying that being with Diamond wasn't the right choice, just saying that leading Trice on was. Unexpectedly she grabbed a vase off the table and threw it at me. It just missed my head by inches and crashed against the wall behind me, breaking into pieces. Tears were pouring out of her eyes.

"Get the fuck out!" she screamed.

"Trice, I'm . . ."

"Just get out, please. I can't stand to look at you right now."

I turned to walk toward the door without a fight. She'd come back around eventually, she always did. I opened the door and said, "I'm sorry," before walking out. Once I got inside the car I reached in the glove compartment and pulled out the little black box that I'd just picked up from jewelers row. Inside was the five-karat engagement ring that I bought for Diamond. I didn't think that the time was right to propose to her because if Kemp was in fact still alive, she couldn't marry me anyway. I took the ring out the box, glanced at it for a few seconds, and put it back inside. What was I going to do? My mind was going in circles as I looked up at Trice standing in the window. We made eye contact for a few seconds before I turned on the car and backed out of the driveway.

Kemp was now on my mind more than ever. Almost three months had passed since the car bomb. Not that I wanted something else to happen but I was ready for war. I was tired of waiting around like a sitting duck for him to sneak up on me. I was ready to go to war and get the shit over with. I pulled my cell phone from my jacket pocket and dialed Tommy. I hadn't seen him much in the past few weeks. Kenyon was his right hand, so with him missing I knew he'd probably blame me.

"Hello!" he yelled over the loud music in the background.

"Yo' it's Black, what's the deal?"

He turned down the radio. "Nothing, man, what's up?"

"I should be asking you that question, where you been? I ain't seen you in a minute. You got that much dough you ain't gotta work no more?"

"Naw man, I was just feeling under the weather. Had to take some time to get myself together that's all. I'm gonna get back on my job this week."

"Is that right?"

"Yeah, I wouldn't bullshit you."

"For as long as I've known you, you've been about money, so this disappearing act seems pretty strange to me. This wouldn't have anything to do with Kemp would it?"

"Kemp? Hell no, I don't believe everything I hear in the streets. I really don't believe he's alive. If he were alive he would have showed his face by now."

He was right; Kemp wasn't afraid of no one. I couldn't see him doing all this shit and hiding in the background. Kemp was more on point too—shit, if he wanted me dead I would have been dead by now. My mind was seriously playing tricks on me.

"All right man, just get with me this week."

"I will, yo', have you heard from Kenyon? I've been calling him and I ain't get no answer."

"No, I haven't. I was just about to call him too," I lied.

"Last time I spoke to him he was on his way to see you."

"Damn, well, I ain't never see him. Did you stop by his crib?"

"Yup, his car ain't even there."

"Well, I'll ask around too, if you hear anything let me know," I said, acting as if I was concerned. I knew exactly where he was, in the damn river where he belonged. That nigga should have been more loyal and the way Tommy was acting he'd probably end up right there with his ass.

"Cool," he replied before ending the call.

I had one more stop to make before going home. I looked in my rearview mirror and noticed a black Lincoln behind me. It was almost eight o'clock so it was dark outside. I could see that there was just one person in the car, the driver. I felt like I was being followed because each time I switched lanes or made a turn they did the same thing. When I'd speed up they would be right on my bumper. I was getting angry. I got on the highway to head to South Philly rather than taking the streets. It was Saturday so the roads wouldn't be so empty. If someone was in fact following me I didn't think they'd be bold enough to do something in front of all of those cars.

I got on and merged into traffic. The black car followed right behind me. I knew for a fact they were following me at that point. I drove at a steady speed until I reached my exit and as I was going off I was hit in the back. I almost lost control but I got it together quickly. Glancing in my mirror I now saw two people when there had only been one the last time I looked back. I sped off, even going through red lights and all. I was nearing one of my stores when the passenger leaned out of the window and began firing shots. One pierced the back window then a few more hit the body.

"Fuck," I yelled. I grabbed my cell phone off the seat while trying to speed through traffic. I dialed JB. I was close by the block that he ran so I knew he'd be around. He picked up on the second ring.

"Hello."

"These niggas is shooting at me. I'm coming around the block now." I dropped the phone. I knocked my driver-side mirror off. I was making it through small streets while they were still following behind me. Where the fuck were the cops when you needed them? As I neared the block I looked behind me and noticed the car was gone. I didn't even notice that they had turned off. My heart was racing. Just when I thought this shit was dying down it comes right back. JB and a few niggas were standing on the corner when I pulled up. You could smell burning rubber from the tires. I jumped out of the car as they all ran over to examine it.

"What the fuck happened? Who was following you?"

"Hell if I know. When I first noticed the car it was one nigga. I get hit in the back, lose control for a second and look back it's two niggas in there." I was pacing and yelling. I was so mad. I could've been shot that time. It could've been all over for me. I wasn't even about to tell Diamond what happened so she could get all upset.

"Damn man, you gotta start riding with someone until this shit gets straight. Did you see what kind of car it was?" JB asked, now angry himself.

"It was a black Caddy. I'm so fucking mad right now. I'm going to need to use someone's car. I can't drive this shit home like that. D will have a fit."

"Take mine. I'll get that shit fixed for you in the A.M."

"All right, I'll get up with you in a few hours. I have to take care of something real quick."

"All right," he responded before shaking my hand.

I jumped in his car and quickly sped off. I was pissed. What the hell were they going to do next? How many times would I be able to escape death? I'd been lucky so far but maybe JB was right, I needed to have someone riding with me at all times. I felt like a sucker needing a bodyguard but I wasn't ready to die. I wasn't going down that easily. I couldn't even think straight; I completely forgot about the stop, but fuck it, I'd just get to it later. I had to go regroup. I was paranoid, looking in the rearview mirror every few seconds. I pulled up in front of the house and sat there for a minute or two to get myself together. I didn't want Diamond to know something was wrong. I had always been pretty good at hiding things from women but lately it hadn't been working out that way. Before I could get out the car and up to the door she was standing there with the door wide open, tapping her feet on the ground.

"What's wrong with you? Why are you sitting out here like that?"

"Nothing is wrong, I was coming in."

"You never sit out here like that unless something is wrong. What's going on, Black?"

"I said nothing, D, chill out."

"I'm not going to chill out until you tell me what's going on. Did Kemp try to get at you again?"

"What? What the hell would make you say that?" I tried to fake it, hoping that sooner or later she'd give up or believe me. At least that was what I was hoping for.

"First of all, you're in JB's car and you were sitting out here with your head down like something heavy was weighing on your mind. I'm not a fool, Black."

"I got a flat so JB let me hold his car until the morning, okay? Stop reading so much into everything. I said that there wasn't anything wrong." By this time I had brushed past her and made it into the house. She was still standing there with the door open. "Could you get in here and close the door, please?"

She closed the door but still kept a frown on her face. I walked over to the sofa and sat down. I wasn't going to give in and tell her what had gone down. I'd have to hear her mouth all night if I did.

"I'm not slow, Black, I know you too well," she said before coming over to the sofa and sitting beside me. I was sitting there with my head back and my eyes closed. I loved Diamond but I hated the fact that she could never leave well enough alone.

"Diamond, please, I have a headache and you're not making it any better."

"Well, let me go get you some aspirin," she said getting up.

"Thank you," I replied.

She returned to the room a few seconds later. I soon felt cold water and a bottle of aspirin hitting my face.

"I'm not an asshole, and just 'cause you get in some fight with your little bitch out there you don't have to act all funny with me."

"What the hell is wrong with you, Diamond?" I yelled, sitting up and wiping the water off of my face. Where the hell did she get that? "This doesn't have anything to do with anyone, Diamond, my fucking head is hurting and I thought I could lay my head down for a little while. Obviously I was wrong when a nigga can't rest in his own fucking house," I yelled. "And thanks for the aspirin," I said before throwing them back at her and heading toward the steps. I turned back to look at her before I walked upstairs. She was standing there still angry. I sighed and shook my head as I took the steps. I felt bad for snapping but not bad enough to apologize. She had to stop being so damn persistent before she got an answer that she didn't want to hear. I went up to the bedroom, shut the door, and lay down. I was trying to clear all of the drama out of my mind at least for an hour or two. Surprisingly, Diamond allowed me to rest without bothering me. When I woke up to head back out to the house she was asleep on the living room sofa. I left her untouched and snuck out the door. It was time to get back to work and it was also time to finish this war that had begun. I wasn't going to hide and I damn sure wasn't going to run. I'd get at him and whoever was down for him. Just like Kenyon, Kemp and his help were going down.

Chapter Forty

Diamond

Emotional

My moods were so up and down. One minute I was laughing and shedding tears the next. It was like something out of a horror film. I felt like one of those psychiatric patients that you see on TV. I was sitting in the tub relaxing. Black was out working as usual and lately we'd argued more than usual. I wasn't sure if it was the stress or if it was someone else. I mean, I knew he fucked around but it seemed like this situation was weighing him down. I had to do something to get his mind back on me, which is where it belonged. Then I thought about it, I hadn't gotten my period yet. I hurried and washed up and got dressed quickly so I could drive to the CVS and grab a pregnancy test. With all of the arguing I had completely forgotten that I was trying to get pregnant. Plus, I'd been unsuccessful for so long that I thought it wouldn't work anyway. I had a big smile on my face as I went to the counter to pay for it. The chick at the register gave me a funny look. Instead of snapping like I normally would I killed her with kindness.

I couldn't get home fast enough I was so excited. I dropped my purse downstairs and hurried up to the bathroom. I paced for the few minutes it took to show the answer that I was hoping for: pregnant. Though I had been waiting for this moment for the last few months I never knew how I'd feel once I found out. I hadn't prepared that part of the plan. How could you really prepare yourself mentally for something like this? Within five minutes I'd went from anxious to happy to nervous. *What the hell was going on with me?* I thought. I had to pull myself together. I was always a fighter. I always stuck to my plans no matter how crazy they might have seemed.

I had to let it sink in for a few more days before telling Black. I decided to run by Kiki's to let her in on the news. As I was leaving out of the house, my cell phone rang. It almost startled me. It was a number that I didn't recognize. I almost didn't answer it but I said what the hell and picked up.

"Hello."

"Can I speak with Diamond?"

"Speaking, who's this?"

"This is Trice," she said loudly. *How the hell did she get my number?* I thought. I damn sure wasn't in the mood to be fighting with this chick.

"How can I help you?"

"Look, I know that we haven't gotten along in the past but I wanted to know if we could meet somewhere and sit down and talk."

"Talk? About what? Any other time you're jumping down my throat or screaming obscenities."

"And I'm trying to move past that."

I didn't trust her one bit but with all of the other shit going on in my life I could stand to lose one enemy. I wondered if this reconciliation was an act or was it truly genuine.

"Well, I'm pretty busy this week but maybe one day next week."

"Are you sure that you can't squeeze it in this week?"

What the fuck was the rush? I felt like she was up to something. I didn't know Trice too well but she seemed desperate and I wasn't in the mood for any tricks.

"No, I can't," I replied sternly. Shit, if she wanted to meet it would be on my time.

"All right then, I'll give you a call back next week. Oh, and could we keep this between us? Black will swear I'm up to something." She gave a girlish giggle.

Was she serious? Don't tell Black? She was definitely up to something now. She'd just confirmed it for sure. "Okay, no problem," I lied. I was damn sure going to tell him. I wasn't a fool. I hung up and shook my head. I couldn't even wrap my mind around what had just happened. Now she's trying to be all friendly. A week ago we would have been in a full-blown argument before I got a chance to say hello. Thinking back, her hatred never had anything to do with me. I definitely believed that Black was dipping and dabbing though he'd swear to God he wasn't. I mean, unless you were a total nutcase you wouldn't bring so much drama for nothing.

When Black and me first got together I made sure that everything was on the table. If there was one thing I hated, it was surprises. He told me that he didn't have a woman but his son's mom was one of those die-hard women that wouldn't let go. Of course I was cocky and I felt that even if he was going back and forth what I had would keep him with me. Besides, when they were together she went and had a baby by another dude. I thought for sure he'd never want her. The more she called and tried to cause drama between us the more I saw how much she cared about him. It didn't matter how many times he'd cuss her out or throw me in her face, she'd keep coming back for more.

I left out of the house and got in the car. On my way over Kiki's I was blasting my new Beyoncé CD. I was singing along like I was in a full concert. I stopped at a light on Broad Street and for a second I thought I was seeing things. I saw a female that looked just like Mica. I swear she could have been her twin. The car sped by me; it was a blue Camry. I was still trying to look back at the car when the car in back of me began to beep because the light had turned green. I was losing my mind. I laughed out loud as I pulled off. I made it to Kiki's in record time and of course I damn near knocked the door down banging. I was always impatient when I had something to tell her.

"I knew it had to be you. No one else has the balls to knock on my door so damn hard." She laughed.

"I have something to tell you—well, actually I have a few things to tell you. Girl, you know I saw some chick that looked just like Mica when I was on my way over here?" I was babbling on as I made my way into her apartment and closed the door behind me. She'd walked into her living room before me and sat down on the sofa.

"Mica? Girl, I know you're tripping. That girl is cremated and poured out in the ocean. I know that ain't what you came all the way over here to tell me," she said, lighting up a cigarette.

"Girl, you need to stop smoking. You saw that damn commercial with all the people falling out in the street and shit. That's gonna be your ass if you don't quit. You're gonna be just like that man playing the guitar with the electronic voice." I burst into laughter. I was laughing so hard tears came to my eyes.

"That's not funny," she replied.

"Well, how about Black's baby mom called my damn cell phone talking about she wants to meet up so we can talk. I don't know what the hell she has up her sleeve but she don't know me. She's gonna fuck around and get herself hurt. Shit, I'm the queen at this conniving shit—she betta ask somebody," I said, slapping Kiki a high five.

"I can't believe that she called you. She's up to something, you better tell Black to get her ass in check."

"I know right. I'm so sick of that girl I don't know what to do."

"I mean, when is she going to get the point?"

"Oh, she gets the point now, that's why she's trying to be my friend."

Kiki and I both laughed. "So when the hell is he going to get you a ring? Shit, he's already claiming you as his fiancée."

"Well, that leads to what else I came to tell you. It worked girl, I'm pregnant!" I yelled. She sat there for a second before responding.

"Wow, I can't believe it. You really did it, you are nuts, girl!" She put her cigarette into the ashtray and blew out some smoke before reaching her arms out. "Well, looks like I'm going to be an auntie. I'm so excited!" She yelled as she hugged me.

"I thought I'd be jumping for joy when I found out but it was weird. I couldn't get my emotions together. I'm actually afraid to tell Black."

"Why, he'll be happy. He loves you, girl."

"I know but I'm not sure if now is the right time. Maybe I was being selfish, you know. I felt him slipping away. I can't lose him to her."

"Her who? His BM? Girl, if he wanted to be with her he would be."

"I know—well, at least I hope," I said as I put my head down.

"Girl, don't sit around here and get sad after that good news. That's the best thing I've heard all day." She laughed and slapped me on the leg. She was right, it wasn't a reason to be moping around.

"I just have to figure out how I'm going to tell him."

"Shit, just tell him. Catch him off guard with it."

"Oh, it's going to be off guard. Shit, I never even mentioned wanting kids before."

"So are you sure you really want this baby or is it primarily to keep him?"

I sat quiet. Really, I didn't know the answer to that question. In a way I wanted to do nothing more than have a baby with the man that I love but I did want to keep Black. So was I wrong for deciding to do things this way? I was the type that would do whatever I have to do to get what it was that I wanted.

"I would say that it was a combination of the two."

"Well, you know that I'm always here for advice and hopefully it leans more toward the side that you're doing it because you want to."

"It is," I lied. That wasn't really the case but I felt like saying that it was would end the conversation. I wanted her to be happy for me just as much as I wanted to be happy myself. Was I really happy? I don't know, but that was something that I would have to explore. I couldn't change my mind now since it was already done. I wasn't going to get an abortion after all of the trouble that I went through to get pregnant in the first place. That would most likely bring back some old memories that I'd worked hard to suppress anyway. I stayed and chatted with Kiki for about another half hour before I hugged her good-bye and left. I decided that I would just get it over with and tell Black. I couldn't wait to hear what he'd have to say. I dialed his number before I pulled out of the parking spot.

"What's up?" he said into the phone. He sounded like he wasn't in such a good mood, which might have been even better. I should be able to brighten up his day with this news.

"You don't sound too happy to hear from me, what's up?"

"I just got a lot of shit on my mind that's all. What's up?"

"Well, I have some good news."

"What's that?" he said blandly. This wasn't going to be as easy as I thought. Whatever was on his mind must have been really bothering him.

"We're having a baby," I said, excited. He didn't respond. That definitely wasn't the reaction I was hoping for. "Did you hear me, I said we're having a baby."

"I'm going to call you back in a little while. I have to handle something."

Click!

What the hell? I thought. Did he just hang up on me or was my mind playing tricks on me? He didn't just do that. I stared at the phone hoping that it would ring again. I felt like bursting into tears. Was all that I've done in vain? I felt like a damn fool. I couldn't even think straight. I was hyperventilating at one point. I'd gotten so worked up I had to pull over. I mean, I was at the point of no return. What could I do if he didn't want this baby or if he didn't want me? That wasn't an option. Maybe I was overreacting and something really important caused him to end the call so abruptly. I sat there in the car for the next ten minutes before I calmed down enough to maneuver through traffic safely. I made it home and was still out of sorts when I got there. I slammed the door and stomped my feet up to the room like a twelve-year-old. Now been holding on to it until the right time and what better then almost forty-five minutes since he hung up on me. I wouldn't give in and call him again. I wasn't a weak chick, I wasn't even an emotional chick so I didn't know where the hell all of it was coming from. Wait, yes I did, this damn baby was taking me over. I got up to the bedroom and lay across the bed. I was exhausted and I hoped that maybe if I took a nap by the time I got up he'd be here apologizing for dissing me.

Chapter Forty-one

Black

Take This Ring

I sat there staring at the phone and feeling like the biggest asshole on the planet. Did she just say we were having a baby? How the hell did that happen? I wasn't ready for that. Not that I don't love kids but with so much shit going on it wasn't the time to bring a baby into the world. Shit, I still had to look over my shoulder every time I took a step to make sure someone wasn't sneaking up on me. I knew she'd be pissed but even more hurt the way that I reacted but at the time I couldn't think of anything else to say. I figured not saying anything at all was better than saying the wrong thing. If she was pregnant and planned on keeping it, there wasn't anything that I could say to change her mind. With Diamond that was virtually impossible. Now, I not only had to worry about keeping her safe but a baby as well. And what would Trice do? That was a whole different issue in itself. I could see her becoming more conniving once she got a whiff of the news. JB sat across from me trying to figure out what the hell was going on. His lips were moving but I could no longer hear him.

"Hello, is anybody in there?" JB said, waving his hands in front of my face trying to break my stare.

"Yeah I'm here," I said shaking out of it for a second.

"Yo', what happened? Who was that on the phone?"

"That was Diamond, I just did some dumb shit."

"What? I was sitting right here and I didn't hear you say anything but you'll call her back."

"Yeah, that's the problem, I didn't say anything. She just told me that she was pregnant and I hung up on her."

He sat back in his chair with a puzzled look on his face. "Damn, that's heavy."

"Tell me about it. I didn't mean to diss her like that, she just caught me off guard. Now I feel like shit because it came across like I don't want it and it's not even like that."

"Well, call her back and explain it. That should settle it, right?"

"Man, that shit ain't going to just go away like that. You don't know her like I do and she's not that easy to smooth over when shit gets rough."

"I don't know what else to tell you, can't say buy her some shit 'cause she can buy anything her damn self."

"Let me show you something," I said as I opened up the drawer and removed the black velvet ring box that I'd locked up inside. I sat it on the desk in front of him without opening it.

"Is that what I think it is?" He asked with a surprised look on his face.

"Yeah it is, open it."

He sat up and grabbed the box off the desk and opened it. "Damn man, this shit is tight. Why didn't you give it to her?"

"Because it didn't make sense. We still haven't straightened out this shit with Kemp that's lingering on and realistically she couldn't marry me if she's still married to him."

"So you really believe he's still alive?"

"I don't know what to believe anymore. I do know someone is out there trying to kill me."

"I mean, we were both at the funeral. I know damn well I saw them put his body in the ground. Unless he has a twin, he's dead. I think someone is trying to fuck with you and by the looks of it they're succeeding. You can't let this shit put your life on hold. If you love her, marry her. She's having your seed now too—you have to keep it moving."

What he said made total sense. Here I was tripping about a nigga that I knew for a fact was dead. This whole situation had gotten out of hand and the more I let it get to me the worse things got between me and Diamond. He was right, that's exactly what they wanted to do. Fuck it, I was going to give her the ring and I was going to do it tonight. I wasn't waiting around any longer.

"You're absolutely right," I said, laughing. "Why am I tripping, I know what needs to be done."

"What about the baby?"

"I'm actually excited about that, believe it or not."

"Well, congrats then, nigga," he said, standing up to give me dap. I grabbed the box back off the table and instead of tucking it back inside the drawer I put it in my pocket. I'd been holding on to it until the right time and what better time then the present.

"So a quick change in subject, I talked to Money and he's going to get with you sometime this week. We're moving forward with this partnership."

"Word, I'm glad you thought it over. I trust him, he's a good dude."

"Well, if not, I'll have you to blame for it." I said, sternly. Though JB and me were cool, business was business and if for any reason this nigga Money fucked me over, I'd be on his ass. He looked at me as if he wasn't expecting it.

"Why you coming at me like that? You know I'd take him out my damn self if anything shiesty comes up," he said, putting his hand on his chest.

"I'm not coming at you, I'm just saying, you brought him to my attention so if something happens it's partly your fault."

"I'll accept that but I gotta run, I have a few stops to make. I'll get with you later." He reached over to shake my hand.

"Okay, cool." I replied, as I extended my arm to shake his hand.

Once he left the room I dialed Diamond. Surprisingly she didn't pick up. I thought for sure she'd at least answer and curse me out. I didn't bother to leave a message, I just headed home to straighten this out. As I pulled up to the house and turned into the driveway a blue Camry quickly sped off from the opposite side of the street. Normally I wouldn't pay something like that any mind but they peeled off so damn fast they left tire marks in the street. Plus, with all of the shit that had been going down lately I had to be extremely careful and pay close attention to my surroundings. If I didn't, that would definitely give them the advantage and I wasn't going to go that route.

I got up to the door and opened it. It was pretty quiet but I knew she was home because her car was in the driveway.

"Diamond," I yelled out through the house. I didn't get an answer so I thought she might have been asleep. I walked into the bedroom and saw her stretched out across the bed. She looked peaceful but as I walked closer I could see the dry tear tracks on both sides of her face. Seeing the evidence of her tears made feel even worse than I had before I got there. I stood there holding onto my pocket wondering if it was the right time to pop the question. I wasn't sure if I was ready and now that I was standing there I was more nervous than I would have imagined I'd be at this point in my life. I stood there for a few more minutes almost afraid to wake her. She must have felt my presence because she woke up and noticed me before I was able to leave the room.

"Hey babe, I didn't mean to wake you." I turned to face her. She didn't respond, only getting up from the bed and heading into the bathroom.

"Diamond, can we talk?"

She stopped in her tracks and turned to walk back to the door. "Talk about what? How you just dissed me? I told you I was having your baby and you hung the phone up!" she yelled as she paced back and forth. She had every reason to be upset.

"I'm sorry, okay, it just caught me off guard and I wasn't dissing you, I would never do that to you."

"Maybe you didn't want to but that's exactly what you did. That shit was low for you, I never thought you wouldn't be able to take care of your responsibility."

"I can take care of my responsibility. It's not about that, it's really about nothing. I said I was sorry."

She stood there staring as if there was something that she wanted to say but couldn't. She shook her head and turned to continue her trip into the bathroom.

"Diamond," I called out to her.

"What?" she yelled with her back still facing me.

"Could you turn around, please? I need to show you something." I pulled the ring box from my pocket and opened it.

She turned and looked at me, still angry. Not immediately noticing the ring, she said, "What is it Black, I'm really not in the mood for . . ." She was now staring at the box in my hand.

Her frown quickly turned into a smile and tears soon followed that smile. "Are you serious?"

"Dead serious," I said as I walked over to where she was standing. Diamond was never the mushy type and now that I knew she was pregnant that said it all. The mood swings and the arguments—I mean, it was all out of character for her. Honestly, some of it I could get used to. Assuming how she felt was what I'd done in the past—knowing sure felt a lot better. I guess this pregnancy had its pros and cons after all. I removed the ring from the small velvet box and placed it on her finger as she held out her hand for me. Tears were still flowing as she moved in and kissed me.

"I'm sorry I'm so emotional, this isn't me. I love you so much, I'm happier than you know." She hugged me.

I felt good, and I hoped that the feeling would last. In the past, I've been known for losing interest in women after a while but I didn't see that happening with her. Regardless of the ups and downs she was actually one of the only women I felt this strong of a connection to. After a few seconds the smile that brightened her face became dim.

"What's wrong?"

"I'm just thinking about Kemp—we can't get married if he's still alive."

"Look, I honestly don't believe that it's Kemp. Someone else has to know what happened and just wants to fuck with us. I think I know him more than anyone and if he really wanted us dead, trust me, we would have been dead by now. That's real talk, D, I don't see it, I just don't." I shook my head.

"How would someone know what happened? I would have been in jail by now if that was the case."

"Obviously they want something from us, I just have to find out what the hell it is."

"I'm just scared, with the baby coming and all, I don't want anything to happen."

"It won't, trust me, you've believed in me this long, don't stop now. I'm not going to let anything happen to you. I promise." I reached out to hug her and she obliged, wrapping her arms tightly around me.

I had to find out who it was and I had to find out sooner than later. I wasn't about to let this shit ruin my future. The business was being affected as well and I couldn't have that either. The workers were turning against me, niggas were stealing money, and people didn't fear me in the streets. I'd worked too hard and too long to let shit slip away now.

Chapter Forty-two

Diamond

Knock You Down

There was a loud knock at the door. I never liked the sound of that in the wee hours of the morning. I glanced to the left and the time on the alarm clock read three-thirty. Black still hadn't made it home yet. I figured that out when I felt the untouched spot next to me in bed. I got up and grabbed my robe from the back of the bedroom door before going downstairs. As I neared the door, the knocks got louder. It was raining out too and the sound of the water beating against the windows didn't even muffle their knocking.

"Who is it?" I yelled, hoping that they'd stop.

"Ma'am, it's the police. We need you to open the door, please."

"The police?" I looked through the peephole and saw two male officers standing outside. One was black and the other was white. I slowly unlocked the door and opened it. "Can I help you?"

"Yes, we're looking for Diamond Brooks, is that you?" the black officer said immediately.

"Yes, that is me, my last name isn't Brooks anymore but how can I help you?"

"We need to take you down to the station for questioning. I need you to go get dressed."

"Questioning? At three o'clock in the morning? What do you have to question me about?"

"The death of your deceased husband and one Mica Thompson."

"What? Why would you need to question me now—that happened over a year ago." My heart dropped to my stomach. What the hell was going on?

"Please ma'am, just get dressed so we can take care of this."

"What if I say no?"

"You don't have a choice, we can come back with a warrant if you'd like," the white cop added.

I was pissed and I was afraid. I couldn't go back to jail. I was pregnant. I wasn't about to have my baby behind bars. The officers were pretty clear so I knew that the only option I had was to go along with it. I motioned with my hands to allow them in from the rain. They came in and stood near the door as I headed upstairs to throw something on. I was afraid to call Black since they were probably standing downstairs listening. Instead I sent a text message to his phone explaining what was going on. I hurried into a sweat suit and sneakers and ran back downstairs. I followed them out of the door and into the police car that was waiting at the end of the driveway. My heart was pounding and my entire body was trembling. I didn't know what was going to happen to me at this point but whatever it was it couldn't have been good. It took us about fifteen minutes to reach the station. Once inside they placed me in a room alone. The room was cold and small. The walls were painted dark gray with white around the edges. There was a small wooden table in the center of the room with one chair on each side. There was also a large mirror on the wall opposite the table, which I assumed they could view me from the other side. I tried to keep my cool and not look all nervous because I was sure I was being watched. If I looked guilty they'd be sure to use it against me when they had the opportunity.

Twenty minutes later a plainclothes white detective entered the room. He looked to be in his late fifties, early sixties. His hair was mixed with gray and he was dressed in black dress pants and a white button-down shirt. He had a smirk on his face that rubbed me the wrong way. I still remained calm.

"Hello, Ms. Brooks. Is it okay if I call you Diamond?"

"That's fine," I said, blandly.

"Okay Diamond, my name is Detective Hill."

I sat silent.

"I'm sure you want to get down to business so I won't keep you waiting any longer. We've recently gotten some information that indicates you as a suspect in the murder of your husband and one Mica Thompson." He sat down in the chair opposite me.

"That's ludicrous, I didn't have anything to do with that. It was a home invasion and robbery, everyone knows that."

"Well, we have a witness that tells us otherwise."

"Well, your witness is mistaken. I wasn't even anywhere near the house when it happened. When I came home the cops were already at my house."

"I'm going to give it to you straight. They claim to have video that will back up their story even though we already have evidence to put you away as an accessory to murder."

"An accessory? You just said that they said I was the murderer."

"That's not what I said, I said that you were implicated in the murder. The charges are against your boyfriend, Black."

"What?" I yelled. Who the hell would try and put everything on him? He had nothing to do with it."

"What we believe happened is you walked in on the murder and you ended up covering for him."

"That's so far from the truth it doesn't even make sense." My heart was pounding even harder than it had been a few minutes earlier. "Where are you getting your information?" I asked as if he would really give me the answer to that question.

"That's confidential. The bottom line here is that if you choose not to tell us what happened, we'll lock you up right along with him."

"Neither him nor I had anything to do with it and that's the truth. I don't know why someone would tell you that. I loved my husband. I would have never hurt him and Black was his best friend."

"His best friend that you're now in a relationship with? That's extremely suspicious, especially when you inherited all that he had."

"I was his wife. Who else was it supposed to go to?"

"I'm going to walk out of here and give you a few minutes to think, okay? I'm not going to sit here answering your questions and you haven't been able to answer any of mine."

"But . . ."

"There is no but, you need to talk or you're going to jail."

"Well in that case, I need to call my lawyer," I replied. I knew that they didn't have anything concrete because my ass would have been in a cell rather than sitting here doing a damn survey.

"I figured you'd say that, that's what all criminals say!" he said as he walked out and closed the door behind him.

I was pissed. What the fuck did he mean by that? Okay, I know that I was the one that committed the murder and I couldn't let Black go down for that. I had to somehow let him know what was going on. I was praying that he hadn't rushed down here to the station like I'd asked in the text because they'd probably never let him go. I didn't know what to do but I knew that I had to get my lawyer on this if I wanted to walk out of here. After a few more minutes of waiting, they took me out to the desk so that I could call my lawyer. After I called and left her a voice mail they took me right back into the box that I'd been in for the past two hours. Black had to have been worried sick and I refused to call him. Then I thought about it—Kiki. I could call Kiki so that she could somehow get a message to him. Just as I was about to sit down I told him that I had figured out who I wanted to call. The officer looked at me as if I'd pissed him off but I didn't give a damn, I needed to make my phone call.

The phone rang a few times before she picked up. "Hey Kiki, it's D, I need you to do me a favor."

"Girl, what the hell do you need me to do at five in the morning."

"I'm down at the police station, girl, they . . ." I turned to look at the officer who was standing behind me. I gave him a look like *Damn can I get a little privacy* and he sighed as he turned his attention toward the other things going on around the precinct. "The cops came to the door this morning saying they have a witness that fingers Black as the one who killed Kemp and Mica."

"What?" she yelled. "Who the hell is the witness?"

"I don't know but I need you to get a message out for me, I can't really say because they're watching me like a hawk but I'm sure you know what I mean."

"I got you, Diamond, don't worry, girl, everything will work itself out."

"Thanks Kiki, I love you, girl."

"I love you too."

I hung up and was then walked back into the interrogation room. I was tired, cold, and annoyed. I kept my fingers crossed and hoped that this would all go away as some type of misunderstanding. I had to figure out how to get myself out of this one. I waited and the longer it took for them to return the angrier I got. I heard the doorknob turning and prepared myself for the worst.

"So, have you thought it over?" the detective asked with a smirk on his face.

"Look, where's my lawyer? I'm not talking to you anymore until she shows up."

Just then Ms. Baker, my lawyer, walked through the door. I instantly felt a little bit of weight being lifted off of my shoulders.

"Sorry it took me so long to get here," she said as she walked around to the side of the table where I was seated. "What are you charging my client with?"

"She's been fingered as an accessory to two murders."

"Fingered? So I assume that means you haven't pressed charges yet?"

"Not officially, but we will very soon."

"Well, then we're finished here. Diamond, come on, you're free to go."

"Just like that?" I asked, shocked.

"Just like that!" she replied as she headed toward the door and motioned for me to follow.

I jumped up out of that chair faster than a cheetah. I wish I would have known I could have left because I would have done that hours earlier. I turned and looked back and gave the detective the same smirk that he had been giving me each time he'd walked into the room. He gave me a look that said a thousand words. Like this wasn't over and I wasn't going to get over that easy. I walked out of there and Ms. Baker offered me a ride home. I knew that she'd pick my brain on the way.

"Now, what's going on here, Diamond?"

"They are accusing me of being an accomplice to the murder of my husband and my best friend. They're saying that Black was the one that murdered them. There isn't any truth to that whatsoever but they claim that they have a witness."

"Witnesses can be broken so don't worry yourself too much about that. Have you spoken to Black?"

"No, I didn't want to call him and risk him being dragged down there with me."

"Good, well believe this, if their witness was as strong as they claim they are, you'd both be locked up. They haven't arrested you yet because they don't have enough evidence."

"Thank you so much for getting down there. I know it was before business hours."

"Don't worry about that, Diamond, I work for you and believe me, you'll get through this, I'll make sure of it."

By then we were pulling up in front of my house. I got out and waved good-bye. I hadn't even made it up to the steps before Black was coming out of the front door.

"Babe, what the hell happened?"

"The cops came and knocked on the door saying that they needed to take me down to the station for questioning and then when I got there they were saying that they have a witness that is fingering both you and me for Kemp and Mica's murder."

"What? A witness? How the hell could they have a witness?"

"I don't know, but it probably has something to do with the person who's been terrorizing us."

"What did Ms. Baker say?"

"She said that their case must not be strong or else both of us would be in jail. She says not to worry about it."

"Not to worry? Someone is trying to put us under and I'm not going to rest until I find out who the fuck it is!"

"Babe, don't go out there and get hurt. Please don't do anything crazy—we have a baby on the way."

"I know that, but these muthafuckers are taking me for a joke. I'm not about to get knocked down and not get the fuck back up. This shit is getting way out of hand."

"I'm just afraid, I'm not trying to have this baby behind bars."

"You're not going to. Look, if no one else understands, I do. I know why you did what you did and I never bashed you for it. Yeah, Kemp was my friend but all is fair in love and war. Shit happens and if you hadn't shot him when you did, trust me, someone else would have."

I stood there silent. I hadn't even made it into the living room. I was still standing near the door. My heart was pounding. I couldn't relax and I was beginning to feel sick to my stomach. My head was spinning and it was becoming hard to breathe. "I need to sit down, babe, I feel like I'm about to faint," I said, placing one hand on my forehead.

"Come on," he said, grabbing my hand and leading me over to the sofa. "You have to calm down. You can't let this wear you out."

I had reached the sofa and sat down but I was still feeling sick. "Babe, I feel like I'm . . ." I threw up right on him and all over the sofa and the floor. He didn't even budge; he sat there next to me with his hand gently rubbing across the top of my back. "I'm so sorry, I didn't have enough time to warn you."

"It's okay come on, let's go upstairs so you can lie down and rest. I'll clean this up in a little while."

I agreed and got up from the sofa and followed him upstairs. My nerves had gotten the best of me. Once I got up to the bedroom I went into the master bathroom to wash the throw-up off of me. My shirt was soaked and the smell of it almost made me do it again. I sat down on the side of the tub and put my face in the palms of my hands. What the hell had I gotten myself into? If I thought things were bad in the past they were definitely only going to get worse.

Chapter Forty-three

Black

Falling

"What the hell do you expect me to do, just wait around and let them lock my ass up for some shit that I had nothing to do with?" I yelled at JB. I didn't normally take my anger out on him but he was pissing me off.

"That's not what I'm saying, I'm just saying the way that you are approaching the situation is only going to make things worse."

"Well, this is the only way I know how to handle shit and if I have to keep shooting mothafuckers until somebody tells me who the fuck the culprit is that's what I'm going to do. Nigga, I got kids and a woman to think about."

"I know, but . . ."

"But what? There is no *but,* you said that you would ride for me and you had my back—now that's what the fuck I need from you."

JB sat across from me with a frown on his face. No man likes to be spoken to like a child, but hell, he wasn't getting the point. I was angry, but I knew if I had to go around town putting a gun to people's head for information I would. This shit was stressing me because I couldn't go to jail—I had too much shit to live for. Money entered the room a few seconds later and he must've felt the heat in the room.

"Damn, is everything cool?" he asked, barely shutting the door before he spoke.

"Hell no, everything ain't cool, someone is out here trying to sabotage me and I'm not having that shit."

"Well, anything you need me to do, I'm here. It ain't even going down that easy."

I could see sweat building up on JB's forehead. Money and I had gotten close since this partnership and slowly but surely JB was taking his self out of the equation. All of that *you're like my brother and I wouldn't let anything happen to you* shit wasn't much more than words and it was just making me angry in times like these. Money had been stepping up to the plate the past few weeks and I respected that. JB continued to give him a stare of death while I continued to pace back and forth.

"Look, I'll put every nigga that run with me on it for you. We're going to find out who it is, I put my life on that."

I stopped in my tracks and turned to look at him. "Thanks man, I really appreciate that shit." I stuck out my hand to give him dap and he obliged.

"It's no problem. You've looked out for me that's the least I can do. I'm going to get on that right now and I'll keep you updated."

"Cool, thanks again."

He walked out and even though I felt a little better knowing that niggas had my back I still continued to pace across the floor. It was quiet except for the sounds my boots were making on the floor. Without that you could hear a pin drop.

"Yo', I know you're going through it right now but you have to use your head on this one. I'm starting not to trust this nigga Money. I mean he just met you a few months ago and he's ready to ride for you like he's known you his whole life. I don't like that shit."

"Why, because you ain't doing the same thing? Don't hate on him now when you're the one that was on his dick from jump," I yelled.

"On his dick? I wasn't on his dick, I just saw an opportunity that's made you more money."

"Me? Nigga, it made *us* more money, not just me."

"Look, I'm going to let you calm down a little. I know how shit feels when the walls are closing in but you know I ain't going to let shit happen to you. I just think that once you calm down and think about the shit a lot of the moves you want to make now won't seem so smart."

Maybe he was right, maybe I did need some time to calm down. Maybe I needed to get away for a little while to ease my mind. I didn't know who to trust and which way to turn. I had to protect what was mine and that included my family.

"I'm going to take a trip for a few days, you think you and Tommy can handle things until I get back?"

"Of course, man, I think that's a good idea. A few days away from this drama will do your mind good, I guarantee that."

"All right, I'm going to bounce and get home to check on D. I'll probably ride out tomorrow or Friday."

"All right, let me know if you need anything."

"All right." I said before he got up to leave the office. I left out shortly after that to go home and check on Diamond. I had two workers sitting outside of the house to make sure she was safe. I pulled up in front and gave both of them a nod. I went in the house where Diamond was laying on the sofa watching TV.

"Hey babe, what brings you home so early?" she said, sitting up.

"I wanted to come and check on you plus I wanted to tell you to pack a bag so we can go to Vegas tomorrow."

"Vegas? Tomorrow, why?"

"Because I need to get away from all of this bullshit for a few days. I need to make some precise moves and dealing with all of this is clouding my mind."

"Well, who's going to run everything while we're gone? We can't trust everyone to keep things in order."

"We're only going a few days and I think that it will be good for both of us. You could use a vacation too."

"Yeah, you're probably right," she said with a slight smile.

"Plus we can get married too if you want," I said in a low tone. I thought that she might not have heard me but she definitely did.

"Are you serious? I would love to but I don't want you to rush into it because of everything that's going on now."

"I'm not rushing, I know where my heart is and I know that's what will make you happy."

"Well, I'm down then, nigga!" she said, bursting into laughter. We both laughed together and for a moment we forgot about all of the drama.

"I have to go back out but I just wanted to check on you. Do you need anything before I go?"

"No, I'm cool, I'll start getting my stuff together now. I'm excited, I've never been to Vegas before." She laughed.

"Okay," I said as I laughed with her. I gave her a hug before I was on my way back out the door. Just as I began to back out the driveway two police cars pulled up behind me with flashing lights and sirens blaring.

"Turn off your vehicle and step out of the car with your hands in the air," one of the police officers yelled as he stood with his door open and his gun in hand.

I got out of the car with my hands up as he'd requested. I was pissed though I knew what this was about. I knew that they'd come for me sooner or later. Diamond came running out of the house yelling.

"What are you doing? He didn't do anything," she cried.

"Stop right there, ma'am," the officer from the other vehicle yelled.

I looked around and the two workers were standing outside of the car most likely waiting on a signal from me. I gave them a look that kept them calm.

"Diamond, listen to them, please. Call the lawyer and tell her to meet me down at the station. Don't worry, babe, they don't have anything to hold me on."

The officer had handcuffed me and began walking toward the car and reading me my rights. I'd heard those rights before in the past but I still couldn't get used to it. Diamond was standing at the top of the steps as the officer got in the car and began to drive down the street. She still had tears streaming down her face. Even though I wasn't the one that murdered them I'd take the rap for it rather than have her locked away. I cared about her too much. Once we reached the station I was thrown into a holding cell, a small-ass box with a metal door and a small window, I felt like I was suffocating it was so damn hot in there. I sat down on the metal bench and leaned my head up against the wall. I prayed that my lawyer would get here fast and straighten everything out.

Chapter Forty-four

Diamond

For You I Will

It was time for his arraignment and Ms. Baker was confident that she could get him off. I was standing outside of the courtroom pacing. Ms. Baker met me in the hall where I stood nervous and feeling sick but I was going to hold it together until this was all over with.

"Stop worrying so much, it's going to be okay," she said, placing her hand on my shoulder. "Let's go head inside; they should be bringing him out shortly."

"Okay," I replied as I followed behind her.

The courtroom was packed with people. I remembered this all too well since I'd been in the same position just a few years ago myself. I found a seat and waited patiently, though my nerves were shot. When I saw him walking out with the officer behind him I smiled. I was so happy to see him even in these circumstances. I wished that I could hug him—my body had been yearning for his touch. He looked around the room as if he was trying to see if I was there. I stood up just before he turned around and blew him a kiss. He smiled and sat down.

"The Honorable Herbert Johnson, judge presiding. Please be seated and come to order," the clerk, said, standing over to the side of the bench.

"Good afternoon, ladies and gentlemen. In the matter of the people of the State of Pennsylvania versus Keshawn Black. Counsel, your appearances please," the Judge said loudly as he took his seat on the bench.

"Good afternoon, Your Honor, Rob Spencer and John Wilks on behalf of the people," the district attorney said, standing.

"Your Honor, good afternoon. Trisha Baker, attorney on behalf of Keshawn Black, who's present in custody before the court."

"All right, and with you?"

"Your Honor, this is Mr. Joseph Rake, an investigator, who will be assisting in the case."

"All right. Mr. Spencer, are you ready to proceed in this arraignment matter?"

"Yes, Your Honor. At this time the people would file, with this court, a ten-count complaint against defendant Keshawn Black, date of birth, February 8th, 1975. The people are filing five counts, one of them murder, the first count charges the defendant with murder with gun allegations pursuant to 12022.53, as well as special circumstances pursuant to penal code 190.2. The remaining counts are four counts of attempted murder, premeditated attempted murder, all with the gun allegations, again pursuant to penal code section 12022.53. The remaining counts are assault with a firearm charges, again with the attendant gun allegations. We are filing this complaint in this court due to the fact that the defendant personally killed the victim in these crimes."

"Mr. Black, how do you plead?" The judge turned to look over at Black.

"Not guilty," he responded.

"Okay, Mr. Black, to your plea as the court has recorded them, not guilty to all of the counts in the indictment," the clerk said.

"Thank you and you may be seated Mr. Black," the judge instructed. "Now, due to the severity of the charges here, there will be no bail set."

"Judge, my client is a respected business owner and is not a flight risk. I ask that some sort of bail be made for my client."

"The charges are A felonies, Ms. Baker. I'm sure you are aware how dangerous that would be to allow him to remain free during trial preparation and trial."

"Judge, my client is not a danger to society and we will prove that the charges against my client are bogus. The state claims to have one witness and no solid evidence."

"Is this true, counsel?" the judge asked, turning toward the district attorney.

"We do have one witness, Your Honor—it's actually one of the victims, Mica Thompson. We have her testimony that Mr. Keshawn Black shot both her and Lolan Kemp on the evening in question here. She's actually present here today."

My heart dropped to the floor. Black looked back at me and as I was looking around I spotted Mica off to the left side of the courtroom. She'd survived. Then I thought back to that day when I swore I saw her driving by me. How did this happen? Why would she accuse Black and not me? Black looked shocked as if he'd seen a ghost. She looked over at me with a look that could kill. We were staring each other down like we were about to go to war. Then she gave a devilish grin and sat back down.

"Ms. Baker, my decision stands, there will be no bail set at this time. We will revisit it later as we get closer to trial."

"Thank you, Judge," she said as she sat back down.

"So that's it, I'm going to be stuck in jail?" Black said in anger as he turned to Ms. Baker. "I didn't have anything to do with this."

"I know, Black, but there isn't anything that we can do at this time. We will talk later, okay?"

Black was pissed and I could see the anger in his face as the officer grabbed him by the arm so he could stand and be escorted out of the courtroom. I silently cried as they took him away. What the hell was I supposed to do now? Ms. Baker and her assistant walked toward me and motioned for me to come with her.

"What is going on? He can't stay in jail, I need him," I said as soon as we were outside the door.

"I told you to trust me, he's not going to be there very long. Just give me some time to straighten things out."

"I can't believe this. I . . . ." I stopped in my tracks as Mica walked out of the courtroom. I wanted to say something but I couldn't find the words to speak. She slowly walked toward Ms. Baker and me.

"Well, well, well. If it isn't Ms. Diamond Diva. Long time no see, congrats on the baby. Too bad you're going to be a single parent."

"Don't respond," Ms. Baker jumped in.

"I'm not because she's not worth it."

"Tell that to your man when he gets locked away for the rest of his life!" She yelled.

"You know what, Mica, you're going to get what you deserve, believe that."

"Is that a threat? Because if it is, I'll have you locked up right along with him."

"Diamond, come on, let's go."

Mica laughed loudly as we headed toward the door. I turned to look back at her before making it through and she was still laughing. She took her hands as if she had a gun and pointed it at me while still laughing. I turned around and walked out of the door. I was furious. I got in my car and picked up my cell to dial Kiki. My hands were shaking and I felt like I was going to lose everything I had, including Black.

"Hello," Kiki said in a low tone.

"Mica is alive," I yelled.

"What?"

"She's alive, she was in court today. She's the witness that they have. Black is going to go to jail for what I did. What am I going to do, Kiki?"

"What do you mean, she's alive? They had a funeral for her and everything."

"It was a memorial. Damn, Kiki, how did this happen?"

"I don't know D, do you think that she had something to do with all of the stuff that's been happening to you and Black?"

"You know what, now it all makes sense—it has to be her. I knew I wasn't crazy. Kemp is dead—it's been her all the time. Someone has to be working with her, I can't see her doing all of that on her own."

"Who do you think would be helping her?"

"I don't know, but that's what I am going to figure out. I'm not going to just sit back and let Black rot in jail. If I have to kill that bitch, I will, and this time I won't make the mistake of not checking her pulse," I yelled in frustration. "I have to call JB and tell him what's going on. I'll call you back, Kiki."

I hung up.

Instead of calling I decided to drive down to the warehouse. When I pulled up a few workers were standing outside. They all turned to look at me at the same time. Probably all anxious to see what was going on with Black.

"Hey D, how did everything go at court?" Tommy was the first one to speak.

"Not good, not good at all. Is JB here?"

"Yeah, he's inside. Is there anything that you need us to do?" Money stepped up and asked. I didn't even know him that well but I didn't get a good vibe from him. I felt like he was up to something from the moment that Black introduced me to him.

"No, I'm fine," I replied as I opened the door to go inside. JB was sitting in Black's office on the phone. He was quite comfortable with his feet on the desk and his chair leaning back. He jumped up as soon as he noticed me and quickly ended his call. I didn't know who to trust, but Black told me if anything ever happened, JB was the only one I should talk to.

"What happened down at court?" he asked as soon as he ended his call.

"They kept him and they wouldn't give him a bail."

"Why not?"

"Because Mica is alive and she's saying that he's the one that shot her and Kemp."

"Wait a minute, she's alive?"

"Yes, I think she has something to with all of the shit that happened. The fire, the car bomb, all of it."

"Are you serious?"

I gave him a look that said it all. I wished that I wasn't serious. I wished that it was all a dream that I would wake up from.

"Well, what do you need me to do? Whatever it is, I'll handle it."

"I need you to find out who's helping her and I need her ass eliminated. Without her they have no case. If she's dead they'll have to let Black out." I meant every word of that. I was going to do whatever I had to do for him. I had to because I knew that he'd stay there if it meant keeping me out. We not being together just wasn't an option.

"Okay, don't worry about it, I'll take care of everything for you."

"Thanks, JB, I really appreciate it. He's gonna need you to continue taking care of things out here until he gets out."

"No doubt, I got it."

"Okay," I said as I headed back out to the car. Money walked over to me just as I was about to get in.

"Hey Diamond, I'm sorry about Black. I just want you to know that if you need anything—I mean anything—I'm here for you." He reached his hand out and touched mine. I quickly pulled my hand away.

"Thanks, Money, I'll keep that in mind." I tried not to be rude but I hoped that he wasn't coming on to me.

"Okay, well, I won't hold you. Here's my number, make sure you use it."

I didn't even respond as he gave me a devilish grin and began to walk away. Black would kill him if he even thought he was looking at me too hard. That wasn't the first time that he'd said or done something that I didn't feel too comfortable with but I still hadn't told Black. I was too focused on getting him out of jail. I got in the car and saw through the rearview mirror that he was still standing there as I drove away. The drive home seemed especially long because so much was going through my mind. I pulled up to the house probably in about twenty minutes but it felt like an hour. I parked, got out, and walked up to the door. Just as I turned the knob someone called my name.

"Diamond," a female voice yelled.

I turned around to find Trice standing there with her and Black's son holding her hand. What the hell did she want? I thought.

"Yeah," I replied.

"Look, I know I don't know you but since Black's been locked up I've been struggling and since you're his girl you have access to his money. I need some money for his son."

"I'm sorry you've been struggling but I don't have access to his money, so I can't help you."

"I'm trying to be nice here. You don't know how hard it was for me to come here today. When I found out you were with him I was furious and then when I found out you were pregnant I hated you. Then I felt like an ass for it. I don't know you but I know Black and regardless of the badass street persona he's a good dude and if he loves you then I can't hate you. I'm really just asking for some help—whatever you could do would help me."

She was melting my heart. How could I not help her and the little boy who looked just like the man that I loved? This pregnancy was definitely changing me because if she'd said these same words to me before I was pregnant this conversation would have gone a whole lot different. If I turned her away I'd be the bitch that I used to be and the bitch that only cared about getting to the top and being in charge. I wasn't that person anymore and I honestly liked this person a lot better. I stood there quiet, trying to take it all in. I must've stood for a minute too long because she turned around and began to walk away.

"Trice," I called out to her. "Come in, let's sit down and talk. Let me know what you need and I'll make sure you get it."

"Thank you so much," she said, turning around and walking toward me. She followed me in to the house. I stood at the door for a second looking at the sky before I closed the door. Maybe this good deed would help things go right for me. At least that's what I hoped anyway.

Chapter Forty-five

Diamond

Emergency

Two months had passed since the day of Black's arraignment and I still hadn't heard any news of him getting out. JB had been unsuccessful in finding Mica because they'd obviously had her in a witness-protection program. I hadn't seen her again since that day in the courtroom and honestly I wasn't trying to. The next time I saw her I wanted it to be in a casket. I was just two months shy of giving birth to the baby and I couldn't wait to get back to myself. Lately, Trice and I had become pretty cool. Kiki hated the idea but, shit, Kiki hated anybody she thought would take her spot as my best friend. I didn't plan on being friends with her but shit happens. She was actually fun to hang around; I could see why Black cared about her. She reminded me of myself—well, the way I used to be.

I hadn't been to Gia's in two weeks and I was in desperate need of a touch-up. I didn't have an appointment as usual but Gia would always bump me to the front of the line, pissing all the other girls in the salon off. I pulled up in my freshly cleaned BMW and parked right in front. There were a few random people standing outside on the corner and I could tell before I got inside that it was packed. I walked in and headed to the back.

"Hey girl," Gia yelled as she normally did when she saw me. She immediately stopped curling the girl's hair in her chair to give me a hug. "Look at you, all prego, I never thought I'd see the day," she laughed.

"Yeah, tell me about it, girl, I can't wait until this is all over so I can get back to normal."

"What you getting done today?"

"The works, my hair is a damn mess." I laughed, pointing to my head.

"Well, you can go 'head in the back to the shampoo girl, I'll do you next."

"Okay, cool." I walked in the back where the shampoo bowls were. I sat down and waited for the girl to come over, which took a little too long but shit, I just jumped in front of a bunch of chicks outside. I couldn't be so impatient. She walked over to me with a smirk on her face. This was a new shampoo girl who I had never seen before. I wanted to know what the hell she was smiling about but then I remembered my ass was big and pregnant.

"You're Black's girl, right?" she asked.

What the hell was she asking me that for? I didn't know this girl from a can of paint so I wanted to know what the hell her motives were. "Yeah, why?" I asked with a straight face. I wanted her to know that I wasn't one to play with.

"I just wanted to say that it's fucked-up how he's stuck in jail. I know how it is to have a man behind bars. My dude's been in jail for three years," she said in that ghetto tone that I hated. What the hell was she saying? I mean, I knew what she said but I wasn't sure what her angle was. I didn't trust females too much anyway, especially ones like her. I knew that I had a lot of haters out here and I had to always be on point no matter where I was.

"So what are you saying?" I asked honestly. She gave me a stare, like she thought that I was trying to play her in some way. Shit, I was just asking a question.

"I'm just saying, keep your head up when times get hard."

"Times won't get hard for me. I'm pretty well off on my own."

"Oh, excuse me if I hit a soft spot. I was just making conversation. Shit, it's hard being a single mom no matter how much dough you got." She laughed as the other women at the other stations shook their heads, agreeing with her. This chick must have me confused.

"It's not a soft spot, sweetie, and this ain't no talk show so I'm not going to sit here and entertain you and the peanut gallery over there. I simply need my hair washed and a hot oil treatment. Thank you very much."

She put her hand on her hip and sucked her teeth. I didn't want to have to put her in her place like that but I didn't have a choice. None of these bitches were on my level. "Matter fact, I'll wait until Gia's done so she can wash me," I said, sitting up from the bowl. She looked at me one last time and rolled her eyes before going up to the front. I guess she didn't know I could have her ass fired right then but like she said times were hard and I wasn't trying to snatch food out of her baby's mouth. Gia came back a few minutes later and laughed.

"You always start trouble when you come in here, girl. You lucky I love you!"

"No, they lucky I love you 'cause I'd be tearing this shop up!" I laughed. I was dead serious though. Back in the day I would have whipped her ass in here.

"So what's up with Kiki? She ain't been in here in a minute," she asked as she pulled me back toward the sink and turned the water on.

"She's good. She's busy running that bar but you know Kiki she won't be gone too long."

"I know, girl, I missed you too. Your ass then got knocked and you don't visit a bitch no more."

"No, that ain't it, I've just been super-busy. I got so much to catch you up on, girl. We're going to have to go out to dinner or something one day."

"Cool, because I got some shit to catch you up on too."

"I bet you do." I burst into laughter. Gia always keep up with the rumor mill. I could always come to her when I wanted to know what was going on in the streets. I was out of the shop about an hour later and on my way home. This baby kept me exhausted and I needed to take a power nap. It was hot as hell outside. It was mid-summer and I hated the heat. I was trying to hurry up and get in the house near the AC. My cell phone started to ring and I fished through my bag to grab it. The phone dropped on the floor of the passenger side. I went to grab it and before I could sit back up . . .

Boom! That was the last thing I heard before my body experienced a numbing pain. Glass was everywhere. I had been hit on the driver's side so hard that the air bag deployed. I could feel blood running down from my head to the side of my face. I felt a sharp pain coming from my stomach and fluid running down my legs. I yelled out for help. The driver from the other car was now standing outside of my car window on the phone with a 911 operator. I kept yelling out that I was pregnant. I didn't care about anything but the baby at the time and though I never had a baby before I knew that I was in labor. It was too early, I was two months away from my due date. I cried each time a contraction hit and the other driver kept saying how sorry he was and asking if I was okay.

The ambulance arrived and came to my car immediately. The female opened the door on the passenger side and put a brace around my neck. "How far are the contractions?" she asked.

"I don't know, they're really close, please don't let me lose my baby," I cried.

"Don't worry, we're going to get you out of here."

Fire rescue had arrived as well and were on the driver's side, trying to pry the door open. Each movement hurt as I continued to cry in agony. I kept crying over and over to save my baby. I'd done too much to have this baby and I'd changed so much from it. It couldn't all be over now. It just couldn't. They had me out of the car and into the ambulance faster than I'd expected. They placed an IV in my arm and checked all of my vital signs. I couldn't hold in my tears, I was falling apart. I couldn't even call Black to have him run to the hospital and be by my side. I begged for them to call my father. I needed him since I had no one else.

We reached the hospital and they immediately rushed me into the trauma room. There were hands everywhere. My clothes were being cut off from every angle. The whole room was in a commotion.

"Ma'am, what's your name?"

"Diamond," I replied.

"Do you know where you are?"

"At the hospital."

"Do you know what year it is?" the doctor asked as he held open my eyes and waved a flashlight across them.

"It's 2008."

"How far along are you?" he asked, continuing the survey that was getting on my nerves. I wanted to know if my baby was okay.

"I'm thirty-two weeks, is my baby going to be okay?" I cried.

"We're going to do everything that we can to make sure of that." They were putting ultrasound gel on my stomach and wrapping the monitors around it. I could hear my baby's heartbeat. That sound was music to my ears. "We're going to try and hydrate you, this is just some fluid to hopefully stop the contractions," he said as he hooked a bag of fluid up to the IV. "Where are you in pain?"

"My head hurts and my left knee, and besides the contractions my left side is really hurting."

"If we can't stop the contractions we're going to have to take you in for an emergency cesarean. We're giving you some steroids just in case. The steroids will help the baby's lungs and breathing."

Everything was a blur, I was in so much pain. I couldn't really think straight. I just prayed that it would all be over soon. The contractions were slowing down, which I assumed was a good sign. The number of people that were in the room had been cut down drastically. There was someone cleaning out the gash on the side of my head and putting some sort of stitching in it. My leg was still throbbing in pain even with the pain medication they'd given me.

"Once she's done we're going to get you up to X-ray and take some pictures of your leg. We think your knee may have been shattered."

"I just want my baby to be okay," I replied. Even after all that had happened and all of the pain that I was in, I just wanted my baby. I couldn't bear losing her.

"We're doing our best, you just relax. We're taking care of you now. Your parents are out in the waiting area. After we get your X-rays we'll bring them in so you can see them for a brief moment."

"Okay," I replied with a sigh of relief.

I was taken up to X-ray a few minutes later and brought back down to the emergency room where the doctor confirmed that I'd need knee surgery. All of this because I went to pick up a damn phone. I didn't even know who the hell had been calling. The pain medication was working wonders because I wasn't feeling any pain. I was happy to still hear the fast heartbeat of my baby. I was going to go into surgery the same day but they called Pam and my dad in to see me before they took me to the operating room.

"Are you okay? I was so scared when I got that call," my dad said, moving close to the bed so he could kiss me on the forehead.

"I'm so glad you came. I'm okay but I'm going to have surgery on my knee."

"Well, you can come stay with us when you come home. I'll stay home to take care of you," Pam said after reaching over to give me a hug.

"No, you don't have to go through the trouble, I'll be okay."

"Knee surgery takes time to heal. You're going to need help and it's not any trouble; that's the least I can do. I owe it to you," she replied, rubbing her hand across mine.

"I'll think about it, I promise."

"Well, they won't let us stay but we'll be here waiting for you to come out of surgery." My dad bent down to kiss me again.

"Okay, I love you . . . both," I said with a smile. Pam looked back at me as if she wasn't expecting to hear those words. Honestly, I wasn't expecting to say them but she'd grown on me and she was actually stepping up to the plate and making up for lost time.

They left the room and I was soon being prepped for surgery. The nurse came in and wheeled me up to the operating room. She gave me a few shots of something in my IV that had me on cloud nine.

"Think of going somewhere nice, like Aruba, that's where I want to go," she said as she pushed the gurney next to the operating table. It was ice-cold in the room and there were a few people with blue gowns and caps on their heads. I felt my eyelids getting heavier by the second. I listened to the nurse and tried to think of Aruba—shit, anywhere was better than that emergency room.

Chapter Forty-six

Diamond

A Piece of Me

I heard an unfamiliar sound and my throat felt like I'd swallowed sandpaper. I woke up and noticed that I was still in the hospital. The sound that I heard was the nurse pressing the buttons on the machine that was hooked up to the IV. I felt different, like something was missing. I didn't hear the heat monitor. The sound that comforted me, which was my baby's heartbeat, wasn't there anymore. I rubbed my hands across my stomach, which was flat. My huge baby bump was gone. I panicked.

"Where's my baby, what happened to my baby?" I cried, trying to sit up in bed.

"Calm down, Diamond, your baby's fine, she's in the newborn intensive-care unit. During the knee surgery you went into labor so the doctors had to do an emergency C-section. You're baby's fine, don't worry. She's premature but she's a fighter."

"I need to go see her, I need to see her," I continued to cry.

"You can't go right now, you have to keep that leg flat until tomorrow. But I knew you'd want to see her so I had the nurses over there take this picture for you." She pulled a Polaroid photo out of her lab jacket pocket.

I held the photo in my hand. She was so small and beautiful. I rubbed my hands across the picture before picking it up and kissing it. "I love you, baby, I can't wait to hold you in my arms. Thank you so much for this."

"No problem, the number is written over there on the white board. You can call anytime to check on her and this red button here, you can press whenever you need anything." She pointed to the cord that was wrapped around the arm of the bed.

"Okay, I'm really thirsty. Can I have something to drink?"

"You can eat these ice cubes. You'll be able to drink in a few more hours. Call me if you need anything, I'll be right out at the desk." She began to walk away. "By the way, what's the baby's name?"

"Dior, her name is Dior." I looked down at the picture once more.

"That's beautiful," she replied before leaving the room.

I put my head back against the pillow and thanked God that she was okay. I wished Black could be here to see her and be the support system that I needed. I felt comfortable resting; I believed that she was in good hands. I closed my eyes and was just about to drift off to sleep when I heard a knock on the door.

"Come in," I yelled as loud as I could with all that I had been through. Kiki burst into the door with a huge smile on her face.

"Girl, I'm so glad to see you, I almost died when I heard about the accident. They were about to lock my ass up in the lobby because they wouldn't let me up to see you. How are you feeling?" She was talking a mile a minute. I was happy that she came though she had my head spinning with all that she was saying.

"I'm okay, look at a picture of the baby." I still held it in my hand. I didn't want to let it go even for her to see.

"She's beautiful, D, when are you going to get to see her?"

"Hopefully tomorrow, I just can't believe all of this happened. I was reaching for the damn phone girl and that car smacked right into my door. I was in so much pain I just kept hoping the baby was okay."

"I'm so glad you both are okay. I know we haven't talked much lately but how's things with Black, any news?"

"No, that bitch Mica is in a witness-protection program. I had JB trying to find her and he didn't have any luck getting close to her. I'm so angry, girl, because it's all my fault. Now shit's falling apart with him gone, these niggas don't respect me. Who respects a woman like a man and a pregnant one at that. I don't know what to do but I can't lose everything. I have to figure something out."

"Well, right now you have to focus on getting better. You can't be in here stressing about that shit. You have a little baby to worry about now. Black will take care of it, you know they can't hold him on some shit they have no evidence on. They're just buying time hoping that something will pop up. They have nothing and they won't find anything, so don't stress."

"It's easy to say that from the outside looking in—look what's happened. Me and my baby could have died today while he's in jail serving time for something that I did." I began to get upset just thinking about it.

"Let's change the subject because I need you to get some rest. I just had to see your face and tell you I love you. I'm here if you need anything," she said, coming closer to me on the bed. "Everything will work out, trust me." She smiled.

"Thanks Kiki, I love you too, girl."

"All right I'm going to run, I have to get down to the bar, but make sure you call me if you need anything."

"I will."

She bent down, kissed me on the forehead, and headed out of the room. Eventually I couldn't fight the pain medication and I was off to sleep. I woke up the next morning ready to get up to go over to the nursery. As soon as the morning nurse came in I asked what time I'd be able to go. She told me around lunchtime, which put a damper on my day. I was ready to go at that moment in pain and all but I listened. Lunchtime couldn't have come fast enough and though it took me tons of tears and pain to get from the bed into a wheelchair I held it together long enough to be wheeled over. Once I got there and the nurse took her out of the warmer and put her in my arms I let go of the emotions. I could admit that in the beginning my plan to get pregnant may have been for the wrong reasons but as time went on I knew that it was meant for me. I was meant to be a mother and the mother of Black's child. There wasn't any other explanation for the joy that I felt as I looked down at the four-pound replica of him in my arms. Everything was going to be okay, I finally believed that. She was a piece of me and she turned me into the woman that I always hoped I'd be.

Chapter Forty-seven

Diamond

Back on my Feet

"I see nothing can hold you down, looking like a diva even in a hospital bed." Money laughed as he walked through the door of the hospital room. He was carrying a huge bouquet of flowers and three get-well-soon balloons. I was still nervous around him and I still hadn't been able to put my finger on what it was about him that bothered me.

"Thanks, Money," I said with a smile.

He walked over and sat the flowers on the ledge of the window and let the balloons loose. He came over to the bed, grabbed my hand, and kissed the back of it. What the hell was he doing? I didn't get this guy at all. I slowly pulled my hand away but not fast enough to let him know how much it bothered me.

"You look a hell of a lot better than I thought you would—you look just as beautiful as you always do." He gave a devilish grin and sat down on the edge of my bed. There were four chairs in the small room and instead of sitting in one of them he had to sit up close and personal with me. I could admit that he was sexy but I couldn't let that affect me. I'd gotten myself wrapped up before doing the same exact thing.

"So what's going on out there, how's business?" I quickly changed the subject.

"Everything's good, everything's falling into place."

"That's good to hear, I was worried."

"I'm sure, but I ain't come here to talk about work."

"Well, what did you come here for?" I asked, both shocked and confused.

"I'm being straight up with you, your man's going to be in jail for a very long time, if not forever. What do you plan to do, be celibate?"

"No, because my man will be home very soon, I'm sure of that."

"What makes you so sure of that? They have his victim ready and willing to point him out. You live in a fairy tale if you think he can get off from that."

"Maybe I like fairy tales." I shot back. I was getting annoyed. I knew Black was coming home soon. I wasn't going to let anyone rain on my parade.

"That's cool too, but what about reality? I'm a nigga that can make you feel good all over. I can fuck you mentally and physically so good you'll forget all about him. You haven't had love the way I can give it."

Was he serious? Niggas weren't shit, they'd turn on their partners in a heartbeat. He didn't crack a smile the entire time.

"I've been through this before—with Black, as a matter of fact. I can't let temptation ruin what I have with him."

"Temptation, huh? So I guess that means you're tempted to get some of this reality?"

"I didn't say that, I just said that I've been in a similar situation before."

"Well, I won't keep pressuring you, but you know how to find me when you get tired of using your finger to pleasure yourself."

"Wow, I see you hold nothing back."

"Never. It'll kill you if you let it."

I couldn't even respond. He was so bold about it that it was almost scary. The thing about it, though, his confidence was a turn-on. I didn't want to make a mistake and do something that I would regret but I could honestly admit since Black was away I'd needed sex, I'd yearned for it, but I held it together feeling like I had no other choice.

"I'll let you rest, if you need anything make sure you call me," he said as he got up and walked toward the door. I still sat there in shock. I didn't know what to do. The phone rang and startled me out of my stare.

"Hello?"

"Hey it's Trice, just called to see how you were."

"I'm okay, thanks for calling. How are things with you? If you need any money for Keshawn I'll have someone drop it off for you."

"I didn't call you for that. I actually believe we've grown to be friends and I wanted to check on you to see if you needed anything."

"No, I'm fine, I just want to come home but I can't bring the baby anytime soon so I'm a little sad about that."

"Aww, Keshawn is so excited, he wants to see her."

"Well, she'll be out of here soon enough. I have to stay for two more days then I'm going to stay at my dad's for a week or two before I go home."

"That's good. Well, I will call you again later to check on you, I just wanted to see how you were."

"Okay thanks a lot." I said before hanging up.

Immediately my mind drifted back to Money and what he'd said. I still didn't know what I planned to do but either way I had to do something because he wasn't going to give up until I either went through with it or I made it clear that I wanted nothing to do with him. Option two I wasn't so sure of. There was a part of me, the old me, the part that loved danger and attention. I still got a high from doing what I knew I had no business doing and resisting was one of the hardest things I'd ever have to do.

Two days later I was packed and ready to leave the hospital. I sat and held Dior for an hour before I left. My father had come to pick me up and take me over to their house. I wasn't too excited about it but I knew that I needed all of the help that I could get. I was surprised when I was wheeled out to the car and Javan was there as well. I knew that it was him because he looked exactly like my father. He was standing on the side of the car leaning up against it, looking around when he noticed me.

"Wow, you do look like Mom," he said, walking over and bending down to hug me.

"I'm so glad you came, this is such a surprise."

"Yeah, I'm sorry about the accident. I didn't want us to meet up this way but now that we have no choice we'll make the best of it." He laughed as he helped me into the backseat.

"Well, look at it this way, now I have a lot of time to catch up with my family." I smiled. Now that Javan was going to be around I felt better about spending time with them. He made it that much more interesting. We began the drive over and engaged in conversation on the way. Once we reached the house Javan and me sat in the living room and talked for what seemed like an eternity.

"So how's school?"

"School's great but enough about me, let's talk about you. What do you do? Where's your job?"

"I don't work, I have a lot of businesses that I inherited from my husband when he died."

"So you're like rich or something?" His eyes grew wide.

"Something like that," I laughed.

"That's great, I always hoped that you were doing good. Though we never met I felt close to you. Mom never stopped talking about you. I even had your baby picture in my wallet. I waited for the day that we'd get to sit down and talk like this."

"I'm sad that I never knew about you but I have the rest of my life to enjoy you now."

I learned so much more about him as well as my mother and father and their families. I couldn't wait to meet them. I was losing the anger more and more each day and gaining love. I didn't stay but a week before I went back home but in that week a new world opened up for me. I was getting back on my feet and I planned on making a lot of changes for the better.

Chapter Forty-eight

Diamond

Money on My Mind

I was headed up to the sixteenth floor of Hahnemann Hospital as I did every morning to go visit Dior. I could get around on crutches against the wishes of my doctors but I had to go. I wasn't the type to lie down and let other people take care of me. I'd always been able to get up and do whatever it was I had to do for myself no matter what condition I was in. I waited on the elevator and as I stood there I saw a familiar face. It was Deidra, Mica's cousin. I almost wanted to avoid her; in a way I felt guilty about what I did, but then when I thought about the reason I did it, I didn't feel so bad. She caught a glimpse of me and walked over to where I was standing.

"Diamond, is that you?"

"Wow, Deidra? I thought that was you. How are you?"

"I'm good, I haven't seen you in so long. How have you been? I see you on crutches—what happened?"

"I was in a car accident, unfortunately, but I'm okay."

"You're all grown up now, last time I saw you, you were a teenager."

"I know, time flies."

"Yeah, I wish Mica was still here. I know she would have loved to see you."

I stood there quiet. I assumed that she didn't know what happened between her and me. Did she even know that she was still alive? I didn't know how to approach that question so I decided not to even mention it at all.

"Well, I don't want to hold you up, it was nice seeing you," she said in my moment of silence.

"You too," I quickly responded to avoid any suspicion. She waved and walked away. I pressed the elevator button and waited for the next one to come. I stayed for my normal one-hour visit before going home. I was surprised when Money's car was parked in front of the hospital rather than JB's. JB was supposed to pick me up and give me a ride home because my mom and dad were both working.

"Where's JB?"

"He had to take care of something so I offered to come pick you up."

"Why?"

"Because I wanted to, why are you making things so difficult? A nigga can't be nice to you, I see."

"I didn't say that a nigga can't be nice, but we both know that you are not just being nice. You have an ulterior motive."

"That's not completely true."

"Well, what part of it is true, then?"

"Well, of course I'm aiming for something but it's real. I'm not gaming you up, though, if that's what you think."

"Honestly, I do."

By this time we were in the car and heading the short ten-minute drive to my house. I was practically staring a hole in the side of his face. He hadn't even blinked. I didn't know what it was about him but I was definitely drawn to him and I knew that sooner or later the shield that I had up would crack. Right now, though, I had to focus on getting my health back.

"Well, what do you need? I'm here at your feet, your wish is my command, if that's what it takes."

"You're really serious, huh?"

"As a heart attack. I'm a pretty straightforward dude and I hate to keep repeating it, but your man Black ain't going to be around and you're going to need somebody to help you run those businesses. Who better than me?"

"So that's it? You just want to take his place with the business—it really has nothing to do with me?"

"You're misreading me, it has everything to do with you. I'm trying to be that strong nigga that you'll need when you come to your senses and see that this shit ain't a game. He's not coming home."

"Why are you so sure that he's not coming home?" I was beginning to get annoyed with him again. I wasn't giving up on Black until I knew that for fact. Even then I still wouldn't stop loving him. No one could take that away. It didn't matter how much game he spit or how much attention he gave he wasn't Black and he'd never be no matter how hard he tried.

"I'm sure of it because I know how that shit works. It's okay to have hope—don't get me wrong. Who wouldn't in your situation? That doesn't mean I'm going to sit in the background and not go for what I want. Yeah, I want his spot but it's his spot with you. It ain't all about the money. I got plenty of that."

I sat there still staring at him. I was so confused. My mind, heart, and body were all being pulled in different directions. Maybe what he was saying was the truth and Black would never be home. What the hell was I supposed to do, lose everything? Or find a strong man to take his place? Then I thought that this could all be too premature. I was known in the past to let my body run my decisions but would it be the worst thing to give him a chance?

"I hear you, but you have to understand that until that's a proven fact I'm not going to just give up on him."

"And I don't expect you to."

"So what is it that you expect?"

"I expect you to let me in."

We were pulling up in front of the house at that moment and I felt that it was perfect timing. I wasn't ready to give him a decision. Once he parked I still sat silent. He looked over at me and didn't say anymore. He exited the car and walked around to the passenger side to help me get out.

"Thanks a lot for coming to get me."

"No problem, I can come in and help you out if you want me to." He smiled. He knew damn well I wasn't going to let him in.

"I'm fine, I can manage."

"I figured you'd say that but don't forget that I'm here," he said, walking back toward the car after I made it to the steps.

He got in his car and drove away. I made it inside and though he was gone he still lingered on my mind. I was trying extremely hard and it wasn't working. He'd made a mark and now that it was down it wasn't going to be easy to erase. Money, can't live with it, can't live without it. That statement was ringing louder than a school bell at eight A.M.

Chapter Forty-nine

Diamond

Two Temptations

Letters weren't enough and I still hadn't been able to see Black. I missed him desperately and I didn't know how long I could hold off. My knee was healed enough to get around without crutches. I'd gone back home and was doing pretty good. I was just on my way to head out to Gia's when the doorbell rang. I opened it to find Money standing there with flowers in hand.

"Wow, you're back to normal, I see. I wanted to come by and personally drop these off."

"You don't have to keep doing stuff like this, Money, you really don't."

"I know I don't have to but I want to. Is it all right if I come in?"

"Well, I was just on my way out, actually."

"Just for a minute, just long enough for you to put these in water." He passed me the flowers.

"Okay, I guess that's fine." I walked into the house, letting him in behind me. He followed me into the kitchen. I grabbed a vase from the cabinet and turned on the sink to fill it up as I took the flowers out of the plastic. "So how are things going at . . ." I hadn't even finished my sentence. I turned around and was met by a kiss. His lips were soft as cotton and they felt so good against mine that I couldn't resist. My mind was saying that this was wrong but my body was saying you need this. His arms had since wrapped around me and began caressing my back. It was sending chills through my body. You would have thought this was the first time that I'd been kissed. I was nervous about moving forward because

I didn't know what would become of this. I wasn't ready to move on from Black but I was ready for the attention that Money wanted to give me. I closed my eyes and instead of fighting my body any longer I gave in and relaxed. He continued to kiss me intensely. His thick tongue was massaging mine as his hands moved from my back to my hips then the front of the jeans that I'd be wearing for only a few more seconds. He'd unbuttoned them, pulled them off, and placed me on the kitchen counter all within one minute or less. His face was then buried in my pussy and his tongue was massaging my clit as it had done my tongue before. My legs were wrapped around his head as I leaned back with both hands on the counter, bracing my body.

I moaned continuously. I wasn't sure if it was because I was deprived for so long or if it just felt that damn good but I was so loud the neighbors could probably hear me through the walls. I grabbed hold of his head just as I was about to erupt.

"Oh, shit, I'm about to cum," I yelled as my body shook uncontrollably. If I'd wrapped my legs around his neck any tighter I might have smothered him. He kept up the pace and I continued to shake, I couldn't stop. I wanted him to keep going but I wasn't sure how much more I could take. I had never been one to run away from some good loving but this felt different and maybe because it was so wrong. He stood up and licked his lips as if he'd just got finished eating a good steak. I smiled for the first time since we'd begun. He stared at me without speaking. His eyes were piercing with a sort of unknown agenda, but it continued to turn me on. I was still sitting in the same position as he removed a condom from his pocket, dropped his pants, and put the condom on his large, stiff dick, which was pointing in my direction. He walked over to me, opened my legs wider, making the path he was going for more accessible. I let out a sigh as he entered me. I was tight as vise grips and I could tell that he was enjoying the feeling of my tight pussy being wrapped around him. He grabbed hold of my waist and used his grip as leverage to push harder and harder. I could feel the juices coming out of me and running down onto the counter beneath me.

"You like this shit?"

"I love it," I moaned.

"Tell me again."

"I love it."

"You love what?"

"I love this dick," I yelled. I was in heaven and I realized how much I'd been missing with each passing second. He continued to move seamlessly in and out of me, picking up speed. I could feel myself reaching yet another climax. When I reached the peak, he suddenly stopped. The throbbing of his dick against my G-spot finished the job for him. I bit my bottom lip as I trembled in his arms. He stared at me for a few seconds and then starting pounding all over again.

I was exhausted but it felt too good to give up now. I sat there moaning and taking every inch of it for the next twenty minutes when he finally let go of me and pulled away, giving me the same silent stare that he'd given me before he moved in on me.

"The bathroom is at the top of the stairs to the left."

He didn't respond but walked away and headed up the steps. I didn't get it but I wasn't going to worry myself trying to figure it out. Money was definitely different than any of the other men that I dealt with in the past. Here he went from talking all of the game in the world to silence. I got down off the counter and began to clean it off when I heard him coming back down the steps. I continued to clean, waiting for him to come back into the kitchen. I heard his footsteps and then I heard the front door open and close. Did he just walk out of here? What the hell was up with this dude? I went into the living room and called out his name. I didn't get an answer. I walked over to the window and peeked through the blinds. He'd gotten in his car and drove away. I felt used. I felt angry. I also somehow felt like I deserved it. I shouldn't have let the temptations get the best of me. I don't know what the hell I was thinking and if Black found out he would be furious. I hurried up the stairs to the bathroom and into the shower. I needed to clear my body of any scent that he may have left behind. My mind was wandering, I hadn't seen the baby and now I felt guilty about what just went down. Maybe going up to the hospital would make me feel better than I did now. I went out to the car and was just about to get in when his car sped around the corner and stopped next to mine. He jumped out of the driver's side, walked over to me and kissed me. He held on to my waist and stared into my eyes. I was too caught off guard to react. I wanted to slap him and yell for the way that he left out with not even a good-bye. Instead I let go of the tension in my body and enjoyed the kiss. He backed away with a devilish grin on his face.

"I'll be here tonight at nine, we're going on a date."

"What?" I threw my hands in the air I couldn't figure this guy out for the life of me.

He didn't respond, only smiling as he got back in his car and drove away. I didn't know what to say or think. I knew that I still felt used and that was something I wasn't used to dealing with. I drove down to the hospital and spent about an hour visiting before I went to the mall to find something to wear. I didn't want to get too jazzy because if anyone saw us out together I could play it off as a meeting. I didn't need word getting back to Black for fear that I'd lose him. What the hell was I thinking? I had to think about the situation logically. Was Money really into me or was he just into what he could get from me? I was going to figure it out one way or the other and going out with him would be the perfect way to do that.

I was dressed and ready at nine. I was actually ready by eight because I needed to give myself time to get my nerves together. I didn't want to seem like a teenager on her first date nor did I want to seem like a detective so I had to calm myself down enough for this date to go off without a hitch. Nine o'clock came and went. It was almost ten and I was pissed. I should have known better by the way he acted earlier in the day. I was just on my way upstairs when I heard a horn beeping. I walked over to the window and pulled the curtain and saw his black Mercedes double-parked in the middle of the street. I grabbed my bag off of the sofa and walked out of the door. I wanted to give him a piece of my mind as soon as I got out of the door but then I figured that would just give him the impression that I was really interested in him. I was interested but not solely in him. I was more interested in finding out what the hell he was up to.

I walked around the front of the car and gave him a look that said it all. I wanted him to think that I was upset; maybe then it would be a little easier to break through this shield that he was obviously holding up. I got in the car where he still seemed unfazed by the attitude I was giving off. He was cocky, but I liked it. It was something about a man with so much confidence and a challenge was something that I would never turn down.

"Nine o'clock, huh?" I said as soon as I planted my ass in the seat.

"Had some shit to do first but I'm here now so don't bitch about it when you can make the best of it."

Who the hell did he think he was talking to? Obviously me, because I was the only one in the car but I wasn't about to go out like that. No matter who it was, no one would talk to me like shit and get away with it. "Excuse me?"

"You heard me right. It doesn't make sense to bitch about it if you are still here with me. If you were that pissed then you should have stayed in the house."

"Where the hell do you get off talking to me like that? I don't know what type of chicks you are used to dealing with but I'm not one of them."

"I know you're not one of them because if you were you would have never seen me again after I fucked you. So obviously you're different. Now, let's just go out and have a good time and forget about it."

Wow, I was shocked. Even though he made the comment in the rudest possible way that he could, it was cute. I got the point and what that meant was that I was more than a piece of ass. Not that I needed confirmation of that but it sounded good coming out of his mouth. I didn't respond. I didn't feel the need to make it bigger than it was. We arrived down on Delaware Avenue at the Chart House. I wasn't really all that excited about the food I was more excited about finding out more about him. We walked into the restaurant and were seated immediately. Money sat down and was still pretty silent.

"So tell me something about yourself."

"Tell you what?"

"About you. I don't know anything about you and we're practically partners."

"There ain't much to tell or much that I want to tell."

"Why, why is everything so cold and secret with you?"

"Because that's just the way that I am, it's not intentional it's just the way that it is." He was still cold as he picked the menu off of the table and began flipping through the pages.

"Don't you think you should change it? Or do you want to be alone all of your life?" I was staring at him so hard you'd think I could see through him.

"Alone is cool, at least when you fuck up you can't blame nobody but you. I like it that way."

"You are a strange character, I don't think I've ever met anyone like you." It was becoming a joke, and I was really beginning to think he was a comedian.

"What's so funny?"

"You, you are really cracking me up. I find it hard to believe you could be like this all of the time."

"So what do you think, I'm being hard for you?"

"Yeah, I think that you probably are trying to avoid falling for me."

"What?" He burst into laughter at this point. "You have to be kidding me, I don't have to put on an act for that. This is me and this is the way that I have always been."

"Well, even the strongest glass can be broken so don't think that it's impossible."

The waiter came over and took our order. That was the first time he smiled besides when he burst into laughter a few minutes earlier. I guess that last statement made him think about what I was saying. After the waiter walked away, I went right back in.

"When's the last time you've been in a relationship?"

"I'm in one now."

"Oh, really? So why are you here with me?"

"Because I want to be, it doesn't have anything to do with that. Shit, you have a man, so why are you here with me?"

"Because I want to." I laughed.

"All right then, that makes us even."

"I guess you're right."

The rest of the night went much better than it began. After dinner we went over to my house where we ended the night with mind-blowing sex and this time a hug good-bye. Maybe I was breaking through that shell and would get some of the information that I needed. I knew that there was something that he was trying to get from me and though at first I gave in to temptation and had sex with him, I was now on the hunt and Money was the prey.

Chapter Fifty

Diamond

What am I Missing?

"I'm on my way, just be ready when I get there. I have something special planned," Money yelled over the loud music playing on his car radio.

"Okay, I'll be waiting at the door," I replied with a huge smile on my face.

"All right."

Click!

This thing was turning into something much more than I'd expected. I was actually beginning to enjoy his company. I still missed Black and I hated the fact that I couldn't see him but the letters that he'd send me were comforting. They made me feel like there was still hope for us. I hadn't accepted the fact that he was in jail waiting on a murder trial for something that I did but I knew that I was going to get him out of there some way, somehow. I was beginning to trust Money and I wanted to see how or if he could help me get Black off. I didn't know how to approach the subject since we'd been seeing each other so much. He pulled up in front of the house and beeped the horn as usual. I still hadn't gotten him to break that habit. I hurried out to the car, excited about what he had planned.

"So what is it that you have planned that's so special?"

"It won't be a surprise if I tell you. Don't worry, you deserve it."

"Okay," I said smiling. I was a sucker for surprises.

"So I got a letter from Black today and he wanted me to ask you if you'd help me with getting him out of jail."

"How the hell am I supposed to do that?" He seemed annoyed.

"Well, there's this chick named Mica who's pointing the finger at him. She's the only witness they have. Without her, they'll have to let him go. She's in the witness protection program so we haven't been able to locate her. He said with your resources, you'd probably be able to."

He turned to look at me with a serious look on his face, "With my resources? What the hell does he mean by that?"

"Hell if I know, but that's what he said in the letter."

"Well, I'll see what I can do but I can't promise anything."

"Okay."

I wasn't sure where we were going but after that question the air in the car felt different. It had suddenly gone cold again like the first night that we were together. I felt like an ass for even bringing it up.

"So where are we headed?"

"You'll see," he quickly responded.

I sat back and kept quiet the rest of the ride. We arrived at a house in the Mount Airy section of the city. It was a pretty large house as all of the houses around it were. I felt special. I was finally going to see where he lived. I was glad that I had my gun with me, though. I remembered that he said he was in a relationship and I wasn't about to have his girl bust up in there acting a fool and not be able to protect myself. All of the lights were off inside the house but there were two other cars parked in the driveway, a blue Toyota and a black Mazda.

"Whose cars are these?" I asked as soon as I shut the car door behind me.

"Mine."

We walked up to the large wooden door quietly. I still wanted to know what the hell was going to happen that was so special that he couldn't tell me but I figured I could wait a little while longer if I waited this long. The house was huge inside but was so dark I stood still for fear that I would walk into something.

"Why are you standing there like a statue?"

"Because it's dark as . . ."

Just then the light came on. I laughed instead of finishing the sentence that I had started. He walked over to the radio and turned it on. The sounds of Raheem Devaughn, one of my favorite neo-soul singers, filled the room.

"This is a very nice place, you live here alone?"

"Why are you always giving me a survey? Just chill and have a seat. Your surprise will be here very soon."

I stared at him and his smile. He was so damn sexy it should be a sin. His hair was always perfect and he always smelled like Jean Paul Gautier cologne. His body was nice too. It wasn't as sculpted as Black's but it was pretty much running neck and neck. It was almost mouthwatering. I wanted to jump on him and get busy right then and there but I had to play his game. I walked over to the sofa and sat down. Crossing my legs, I began to shake my legs as if I was waiting impatiently.

"You crack me up, I'll be right back," he said laughing and heading out of the living room.

I sat there quiet, waiting for him to get back. I'd occasionally pick with my fingernails or run my fingers through my hair. I was bored as hell so the time seemed to be moving in slow motion. I heard his footsteps coming back toward the living room behind me. Out of nowhere I felt a hard hit on the back of my head. I tried to get up but my head was spinning. I fell back down in the chair.

"Hurry up and tie her up."

"I am hurrying, shit, stop rushing me, she's here now right where we wanted her."

I tried to open my eyes; my head was hurting like hell. When I was finally able to open my eyes I couldn't move my arms, they were tied behind my head. What the hell was going on? I tried to focus. There were two people standing in front of me, Money and Mica. What the fuck?

"What the hell is going on?"

"This is your surprise."

"What?"

"You really thought you could shoot me and get away with it? I knew you were cocky, but come on. You should have been more careful, now you're going to die and your boyfriend is going to spend the rest of his life in jail while we run his business."

"What do you mean *we*?"

"Oh, you still don't get it? Money is my man, I'm sure he told you that he had a woman, right? But that never stopped you before."

"It never stopped you either!" I yelled while trying to get my hands free.

"You're in no position to talk, remember that? I thought it would be good to watch you squirm like you watched me that day in the warehouse."

"I was the one that talked him into letting you go, so how can you compare that to this?"

"I'm not comparing it to that, I just thought that it would bring back memories. It's definitely bringing them back for me."

"What the hell do you want from me?" I yelled. I was getting angrier by the second. Mica wasn't the rough type so I knew she wasn't going to kill me.

"I want to watch you suffer and then I'm going to kill you. It's a shame your little baby is going to be parentless."

"Fuck you Mica, don't even talk about her. You're not going to kill me and you know it. You can try all that thug shit if you want. It won't work, because you of all people don't scare me."

"I'm cracking up over here. You probably thought my man really wanted you, huh? How does it feel to get played?"

"He did want me."

"Don't fool yourself, okay, he just talked a good game to bring you here today."

"That's what he told you?"

"That's what I know."

"Yeah, well, don't fool yourself because your man's been fucking me for weeks."

"Wow, you are a comedian." She laughed. I knew that I was getting under her skin.

"I'm dead serious and you're in denial. He's lying to you, sweetie, he just fucked me yesterday, as a matter of fact."

"Bitch, stop lying!" she yelled as she ran over to where I was seated and slapped me across the face. I laughed hysterically, which pissed her off even more. I was getting to her when her plan was to get to me. She'd never watch me squirm. I'd die before I'd give her that satisfaction.

"What are you doing, Mica? Calm down," Money yelled and grabbed her by the arm.

"What am I doing, what is this I hear about you fucking her? Is that true, Money?"

He turned and looked at me and then back at her, "No, she's lying," he said.

"I'm lying? So now I'm lying? You didn't say that shit when your face was buried in my pussy!" I yelled.

"You bitch," she yelled and tried to get back over to me but Money stopped her in her tracks.

"Look now, calm down, I didn't fuck her, okay. That bitch is lying. Now we have some shit to handle and Deidra is pulling up outside."

"I'm done with you, bitch, you better believe that shit," she yelled as she headed toward the door. Money was still standing there staring at me as if he wanted to tell me how sorry he was. "Let's go, Money, now!"

He followed behind her and walked out of the door. Soon I heard footsteps walking toward me and then Deidra appeared.

"Oh, my god, Deidra, I'm so glad to see you. Could you get me out of here?"

"I can't do that, baby girl."

"Why not, I though we were cool? You always told me that I was your little sister. What happened to that?" I pleaded.

"What happened? You tried to kill my flesh and blood. All of that shit went out the window the moment you shot her."

"It wasn't like that, Deidra. I never meant to hurt her, honestly. I was trying to kill Kemp and she just got caught in the crossfire. I didn't intentionally shoot her." I lied, hoping that I could get her to let me go.

"I wish that was true, Diamond, I really do."

"Well, what are you going to do? Be Mica's little flunky? I thought you were the older one here?"

"I'm not anyone's flunky and you know that. You can say what you want but pissing me off is not going to get me to let you go."

I sat there quiet for a few seconds. She was right; it wasn't going to work, so I had to figure something else out. I had to get her to let me go before Mica and Money returned.

"I'm sorry okay, I'm losing my mind here I need to get back to my baby."

"Baby? What baby?"

"I have a little baby. Her name is Dior. She was premature so she's still in the hospital. Remember I saw you that day at the hospital? I was visiting her."

"I didn't know that. She never told me you had a baby."

"I do and I need to be there for her, you have to help me, Deidra. Black's already in prison for the murder and assault—why isn't that enough? My daughter is going to suffer for this."

Deidra sat there as if she was debating what her next move should be. I could see that I was getting to her heart and that was where I needed to be. Though it was the truth I was laying it on thick and it seemed to be working. Deidra had always been a good person and I didn't see that changing. I could always talk to her and though Mica and me were close, my relationship with Deidra felt more real. I felt like we were family and she treated me as if I were really related to her. She would also do what she had to do to protect her blood so I could see how Mica would use that to her advantage.

"Are you going to help me?"

She looked at me for a minute or two but still remained silent. She got up from the chair and paced back and forth, looking at me every few seconds. I continued to beg her to let me go as she continued to pace the room. I knew that I was most likely running out of time the longer this went on. I had no idea what time they were coming back but I knew it would probably be pretty soon.

"I'm going to help you," she finally responded.

I smiled and began to work in my head what I was going to do to get out of here. She went to look out of the window before coming back to the chair where I was sitting. She untied me and gave me the keys to her car.

"You have to tie me up, this can't look like I willingly let you go." She grabbed hold of my arm.

I looked in her eyes and saw fear. Though I wanted to get out of there as fast as I could I had to do it. I couldn't let her take the heat for having the heart to let me go. I agreed and as she sat in the chair I tied her up. I hugged her before grabbing my purse from the table and running toward the door. Just as I was turning the knob I heard a car pulling up—it was them. What the hell was I going to do now? I ran back into the room and looked around like I was trying to find somewhere to hide. There didn't seem to be a back door that I could run out of either. I noticed a closet under the stairs. I ran over to it and hid inside. I heard them come into the living room where Deidra was sitting tied up in the chair. The door on the closet was wood and had slightly opened panels, sort of like a mini-blind. I could see out but you couldn't see in. I sat there quietly.

"What the hell?" Mica yelled, running over to Deidra. Deidra had her head down and picked it up just as she got down on her knees and touched her own leg.

"She got away, I'm sorry Mica, she got away."

"How the fuck did that happen? Did you untie her?" Money yelled. I could hear the anger in his voice as he paced back and forth. "Damn, Mica, I told you we shouldn't have left her here alone."

Mica was untying Deidra while Money was looking out the window, probably trying to see if I was outside.

"I'm sorry, Mica, she tricked me into letting her loose, then she overpowered me."

"Deidra, this is all messed up. What the hell are we going to do now?"

Money continued to pace the floor. He now had retrieved his gun from the small of his back and was waving it around in the air. "I'm going to kill her, I'm going to fucking kill her."

I thought that was the plan anyway. Maybe they weren't going to kill me and were only threatening me to see what I'd give up. I still didn't know how I was going to manage getting out of the house but I stood quietly in the closet, barely breathing. Even if that wasn't the plan in the beginning it was definitely the plan now.

Deidra was sitting in the chair crying what seemed to be real tears. I prayed that she wouldn't have a change of heart and rat me out. "I didn't mean to cause any trouble Mica, I really didn't. She was just going to use the bathroom and . . ."

"Don't worry about it, Deidra, I know you didn't mean to. We'll take care of it, okay." Mica helped Deidra up to her feet.

"You're damn right we'll take care of it. Come on, let's get out of here and go find her." Money walked toward the door and motioned with his hand for them to follow. I waited until I heard the sound of the cars pulling out of the driveway before I came out of the closet. I slowly opened the door and walked out into the living room. I pulled my cell phone out of my bag and dialed JB.

"Hello?"

"JB, it's Diamond. I need your help, where are you?"

"I'm at the office, what's up?"

"Money tried to kill me, him and Mica."

"What? Where are you?"

"I'm going to come to you, I can't risk them coming back and finding me."

"Okay, well, meet me at the office."

"I don't want to do that either, I'm afraid he's going to come there looking for me. Meet me at the warehouse. I'll get a cab to bring me there."

"Cool, I'll be there."

I hung up and ran out of the front door. I walked for blocks until I saw a cab riding by unoccupied and flagged it down. I sat low in the seat just in case they happened to drive by. We made it to the warehouse about twenty minutes after the cab picked me up. I jumped out of the car and paid the fare. JB was standing outside of the door when I got there.

"What the hell happened?"

"Money drove me to this house where they hit me over the head and tied me up. I thought they were going to kill me."

"Why were you with him in the first place? I told you I didn't trust him."

"I thought he was a good dude but it was all a setup—everything from the beginning. From the moment he met you and got close to Black it was all in their plan."

"What plan?"

"They wanted Black to go to jail then they were going to kill me and take over everything that we have."

"I should have known that muthafucker was up to something. I didn't see how shiesty this nigga really was. Damn, this shit is all my fault."

"It's not your fault. You didn't know."

"Black's not going to see it that way. I'm the one that brought him to his attention."

"Damn," he yelled. He was angry and rightfully so. I think that he was more angry at himself than he actually was at Money.

"We have to get rid of them, if not they won't stop and Black will end up in jail for the rest of his life. We can't let that happen, JB."

JB sat there staring into his hands as if he was trying to come up with a plan in his head. I hoped that he'd come up with a plan because I couldn't think of anything to do to take care of them. I needed his help and I prayed that he would come through for Black and me. I shouldn't have been so fast to jump in bed with Money. I should have listened to my heart and not let the lust win. Maybe then I would have been able to see through the facade and been able to protect myself. They could have killed me and left my baby an orphan. It was time that I started being smarter about what moves I made. I had to be certain that I didn't miss anything anymore that could potentially have such a devastating effect on my life. Especially now that my life wasn't just my own.

JB assured me that he'd get Money by acting as if he didn't know anything about what happened with me. He wanted me to hide out and he'd have everyone out in the streets looking for me, including Money. We still had to figure out how to get to Mica. Now that I knew where she stayed it shouldn't be as hard as it was before. I went out of state to a house Black and I owned by the shore. I planned to stay there for a few weeks until things blew over back in Philly. I arrived at the house and everything was covered in white sheets just the way we'd left them. I hadn't been there in months and every sheet was covered with dust. I took a deep breath and I stepped inside. I felt like for once I could rest. I went in my bag and pulled out a photo of Dior. I told the hospital that I would be gone for a few weeks but I'd call everyday. I said that there was a family emergency so that they wouldn't report me to child services.

After I cleaned up a bit I sat down on the sofa and lay my head back. I closed my eyes and thanked God that I was still here. He'd given me another chance and I wasn't going to take it for granted any longer. I curled up with a blanket and the photo and tried to fall asleep.

Chapter Fifty-one

Diamond

One Last Breath

The ringing on the phone was extremely loud. I attributed that to the fact that it was so quiet in the house. I was losing my mind and I couldn't wait to get back to my life, civilization, as I called it. I rolled out of bed and grabbed the phone off the nightstand.

"Hello?"

"It's done, you can come back now."

"What's done, JB?"

"Money, I took care of him."

"What about Mica?"

"I need your help for that, I need you to show me where she is."

"I can tell you, JB, I'd really rather stay away until everything is taken care of."

"I need your help, Diamond."

I sat quiet for a minute. Hearing that Money was dead and gone was like music to my ears. I felt like there was a weight lifted off my shoulders but I knew it wasn't over. It couldn't be over until Mica was with him. There was no way we could get Black out of jail with her still alive.

"Okay, I'm coming home. I'll be there later on today."

"Call me when you're back in town, we can get busy as soon as you're here."

"Okay."

I hung up the phone and looked around the room. I wasn't sure if I was ready to face her again. I hadn't done such a good job the first time I tried to kill her. I kept thinking back to that night and how she managed to slip away. I kept blaming myself for all of the trouble that Black was going through. I blamed myself for everything. I hadn't been able to do one thing right with my life. From the outside looking in it seemed that I had everything and that I was always lucky. But my life was in shambles. I was never happy regardless of how much money I had and it took me this long to figure it out. It took me to almost lose everything to appreciate the one thing that I always had. I always had life and I'd always had good sense, I just chose not to use it.

I gathered up my things and packed them in the car. I was on my way back to Philly and back to snatch my life back. Once I got back home, I called JB as he'd instructed. He came over to the house immediately. I heard the knock at the door and hurried to go answer it.

"Hey, come in, I just have to grab a couple of things." I walked away from the door after I answered it. JB followed me into the house after closing the door behind him.

"So that was pretty quick, I didn't expect you to get home so fast."

"Well, I want to get this over with, I need to see my man walk out of that prison."

"That's not going to happen."

"What do you mean . . ." I turned around to find JB standing there pointing a gun at me. What the hell was going on? "What's going on, JB?"

"I'm sorry you got caught up in this, Diamond, but this is the way that it has to be."

"What do you mean?"

"I mean, I wish that I could keep you alive but I know you'll never go along with this. I thought that we could be together but then you started fucking Money. Why did you go and do that, Diamond?"

"How did you know about that?" Tears started to form in my eyes. I never expected JB to be the one out to get me.

"He told me. We were working together to get rid of Black; you were supposed to be with me but you went and fucked him like a whore." He was yelling and waving the gun around. I was standing still, crying.

"Please, JB, don't do this, we can be together, we just have to go get rid of Mica, remember."

"That bitch is already dead. I took care of her and her man."

"How are you going to get what you want without me? Black is going to get out of prison now that she's dead."

He stared at me. He hadn't thought that far. He'd killed the only witness keeping Black in jail so unless he planned on killing him too his plan would never work.

"Fuck Black," he yelled. "You think I'm scared of him, I will kill that muthafucker so fast."

"I didn't say you were scared of him, I said that we can be together. You and me can do this." I was trying to get his confidence. I was still crying but I was trying to mask it, but it wasn't working out like I thought it would.

"Do you think I'm stupid? You actually think you can fool me? I'm not an asshole, Diamond. I know that you're only saying this so I can let you go."

"I mean it, I mean every word, JB. We can be together."

"I don't want you now, I know that you're a fucking whore. You cheated on Black with Money and Black hadn't even done shit to you. I know your kind and there's no way this shit would work now."

"Yes, it can work, you just have to give it a chance." I moved close to him and tried to win him over by looking in his eyes. He wouldn't look at me, only backing away the closer that I got. "Please give us a chance."

I saw a shadow behind him but I didn't want to focus on it. That shadow turned out to be Tommy. He put his finger up to his mouth as to say be quiet. JB was starting to warm up to me. I could tell because he wasn't backing away any longer.

"I'm sorry for what I did, I didn't know that you wanted to be with me."

"You're not sorry, you were willing to throw it all away for some dick," he began to yell again.

"I am sorry, I wish that it was you."

He turned to look at me again. Just then Tommy's shoes made a sound. JB turned around with his gun drawn. Tommy shot him twice before he had a chance to shoot back. I dropped down to the ground and burst into a hysterical cry. Tommy walked over to me and pulled me up from the floor. I grabbed hold of him and continued to cry. He walked me over to the couch where I sat down. He dialed the police on the house phone and reported the shooting.

"What are you doing, Tommy, you're going to go to jail!" I tried to grab the phone out of his hand.

"Look, take this gun. You're going to say that you shot him after he burst into your house and tried to attack you. Everything will be fine, I promise."

I'd heard that line too many times in the past few weeks. For once I wanted to believe it. I shook my head and agreed to tell the story to the police. The sirens and red and blue lights were flashing within ten minutes. The cops ran in with their guns drawn. I was still sitting on the sofa with the gun in my hand. Tommy had left out of the back door before they'd arrived.

"Ma'am, are you hurt?"

"No, I'm not hurt."

"Drop the gun, please."

I obeyed. I sat the gun down on the floor. The officer ran over and kicked the gun over. Another officer reached down to check JB's pulse and looked up, shaking his head, confirming that he had no pulse. I was in a daze. I still wasn't grasping what had happened. The cops left me on the sofa while they began marking the scene. I was taken down to the police station where I gave them the story of what happened at the house. I stayed for a few hours before they released me. I couldn't even sleep when I got home. I got up in the middle of the night and went over to Kiki's house.

Instead of giving me words of wisdom, she gave me comfort. I fell asleep in her bed finally after an hour or so. She lay next to me holding my hand. The day had been such a traumatic day and I still didn't know what was to come. I was still afraid. I didn't know who to trust. The person that Black trusted the least had been the one to save my life. Everything was so out of control. At that point, I didn't know if they could ever be the same.

Chapter Fifty-two

Black

Home Sweet Home

Finally, I was going home. I told Ms. Baker not to tell Diamond, I wanted to keep it a surprise. I hadn't seen her since the day that they dragged me out of the courtroom. I never wanted her to run up here and see me in this cage nor did I want my child witnessing that. I wasn't allowed visitors and letters still hadn't been enough. I missed her and I wanted to get home to feel her again. I'd heard how things were on the streets and I couldn't believe how JB turned on me. Jealousy and envy will make people do some strange things and that was definitely true with that situation.

What went wrong? Niggas were trying to kill me, my girl, and take my spot. When this shit first started JB was the main one, saying that he had my back no matter what happened and it turned out that he had more than my back in mind. I would have never thought that he'd turn on me. I would have thought Tommy would have been the one. When the Kemp shit started he was sure that Kemp wasn't alive. I guess it made sense now that he had so much confidence because he knew damn well he wasn't alive. He knew because it was him and that nigga Money all the time. Tommy made it his business to get word to me and I owed it to him for saving Diamond's life.

Tommy picked me up from the bus where they'd left me. I looked like shit and there wasn't any way I was going to show my face to her looking the way that I did. Tommy got out of the car and walked over to me. I stuck my hand out to shake his. Instead of shaking my hand he hugged me, which caught me completely off guard.

"It's good to see you, man."

"Thanks so much for all that you've done."

"No problem, man, I told you I was here for you."

"I need you to do me a favor before you take me home. I need to get a haircut and get some gear. I can't go home like this."

"Already got that shit lined up, got some jeans and shit in the back for you. Nigga, I know you too well." He laughed.

"My man, thanks!" I gave him dap.

We drove down to the barbershop where I got a fresh haircut, then he drove me over to his house so I could shower. I felt like new money when I got out of there. I was ready to go home. We pulled up in front of the house and I was more nervous then I'd ever been. I felt like I was going on a job interview or some shit. I didn't know what to say to her. I hoped that it would come natural. Tommy pulled out as I made it up to the door. I knocked lightly. It was strange knocking on my own door but I almost felt like a stranger visiting for the first time.

"Coming," she yelled as she neared the door. My heart was pounding a mile a minute. I couldn't wait to see her face. She opened the door and stood still as a statue. Tears came out of her eyes before she moved out of the door to wrap her arms around me. "How did you get out? Why didn't they tell me?" She cried and smiled at the same time.

"I wanted to surprise you, I missed the hell out of you." I grabbed hold of the sides of her face to bring her into a kiss. I wanted to make love to her at that moment and I would have if I could.

"The baby's inside, come on in so you can see her."

We walked into the house. I dropped my bag near the door and followed her upstairs toward the baby's room. She was asleep but as beautiful as a porcelain doll. I didn't want to wake her so I didn't reach in to pick her up. I just stood there looking at her, then looking at Diamond.

"Why are you looking at me like that?"

"Because I never would have imagined you being a mother. I'm sorry I couldn't be there for you."

"It doesn't matter, you're here now and everything is going to be okay."

I believed it. I was focused and there wasn't anything that was going to mess this up. We'd come too far for that. I pulled her out of the room and into the bedroom. I couldn't wait another minute to touch her. She smiled as I moved closer to grab hold of her. She helped me by taking off her clothes. I stared at her body and it was perfect, just as I'd left it. I'd heard about her and Money but I didn't care. I knew that everything she did was to get me out of jail and I couldn't let that affect me.

She lay on top of the bed as I undressed. I wasn't even fully naked before I opened her legs, got on my knees, and met her clit with my lips. It was as sweet as honey and I was savoring every drop. She was moaning as I continued to fuck her with my tongue. She used her hips to grind harder against it. I stuck two fingers inside of her pussy as I used my other hand to slide my boxers off. My dick was as hard as a brick and after months of jacking off I could finally feel her wrapped around it.

I got up from the floor and slid my dick inside of her. She gasped for air as if she wasn't expecting it. I pulled her legs up around my neck and fucked her like a racehorse for the next half hour. I erupted all inside of her and fell down on her like I'd lost every bit of my energy right along with the cum that was now running out of her.

She got up from under me and headed to the bathroom. I was still laying across the bed when she turned on the shower. For once I felt like I didn't want to hurry out of the house. I wasn't thinking about work but instead I was thinking about her. I got up off of the bed and jumped in the shower with her.

"You really do miss me, huh?" She giggled just before facing me then going down to her knees and taking my dick into her warm mouth. I grabbed onto the side of the wall and let out a sigh similar to the one that she'd let out earlier. Her lips wrapped around my dick with the water pouring all over her turned me on more than I'd ever been with her. It wasn't long before I bent her over and fucked her for another fifteen minutes. Finally, I allowed her to shower. She kissed me before leaving me in there alone. I washed up before jumping out and getting dressed again. She was downstairs in the kitchen making the baby a bottle.

"Trice is on her way over, I called her."

"What? Why would you call her?"

"Because your son wants to see you and Trice is cool. There won't be any drama, trust me."

"Since when have you two become friends? I see I've missed a lot more than I thought I did. I would have never imagined that."

"Right after you went in, she came to me and let me know that she needed some help. I wasn't going to turn her away, so I helped her and we've been cool ever since."

"You should have told me she was coming. I have to run out and meet Tommy back at the warehouse," I lied. I wasn't really ready to be in the same house with both of them. I thought of it as being a very uncomfortable situation.

"Babe, you just got home. Just see him and then you can go."

Damn, I was going to have to deal with it sooner or later so I thought, fuck it, I might as well get it over with. It wasn't long before she was ringing the bell. I opened the door and my son ran right to me, hugging my legs. Trice smiled and gave me a quick hug.

"Good to see you, he missed you a lot," she said, walking into the house. Diamond had come out of the kitchen and was standing in the hall.

"I have to run, but I'm going to spend a lot of time with him this week, I promise. I just have to go take care of some things right now. I didn't know that you were coming until a few minutes ago."

She looked disappointed. I wasn't trying to upset anyone but I really did have some shit to handle. I needed to get back to the office to begin rebuilding.

"It's cool, I know you have to go work. We'll hang out here for a little while but I'm going to hold you to that. He needs to be with you."

"And he will be."

I hugged him again and kissed Diamond before I left out of the house. It actually wasn't as bad as I thought it would be. I grabbed my keys off the key rack and hopped into the car. I was on my way down to the office. I had so much on my mind.

There was so much to do and now that Money, Mica, and JB were gone, there wasn't anything to worry about. Everything should be smooth sailing from that point on. I was back at home where I needed to be and the sweet smell of success was flowing up my nose as I drove up the expressway with the windows down. A change was coming and I was going to embrace it.

Chapter Fifty-three

Diamond

Trust

I was worried that Black would find out about Money and me. I enjoyed making love to him every night since he came home but it wasn't the same. It was almost as if he knew but didn't want to tell me. I wanted to just lay it out on the table but that most likely wasn't the right thing to do. He hadn't said anything about marrying me either. Maybe he changed his mind and decided that I wasn't marriage material. I was driving myself crazy worrying about it. I felt like I had to come clean so that we could move on. I would have to accept whatever was thrown my way afterward but I couldn't keep it inside any longer. He came home and I was sitting in the living room with the lights on but nothing else was on.

"What's wrong?" He could always tell when I was upset. I was beating myself up all day and I was probably about to make a huge mistake.

"There's something that I have to tell you. I have to be honest and I can't move forward without telling you." I could feel the tears forming in my eyes; it was going to kill me to hurt him but I didn't see what other choice I had.

"Look, Diamond, I just got back. There's no need to go into all of that. Let's enjoy this time that we have together."

"No, I have to tell you and I have to tell you now." I was determined to get things off of my chest.

"If it's about Money and you, I already know and I don't care."

I looked up at him, stunned. I wasn't sure if I'd heard him right.

"You don't care?"

"No, I don't care and I want to forget about it."

"But how can we have trust after that?"

"Diamond, I trust you and I'm not questioning you about it because I understand how that could have happened. I love you and I'm going to marry you. I don't care what happened when I wasn't here. I'm worried about what happens from this point on."

Was he serious? I've never found a man who could trust a woman after they'd cheated. I mean, I dealt with him even after I knew about all the women he chose to sleep with but that was different. That's what I thought I was supposed to do.

"Are you really going to marry me?"

"I just said I was, why do you think I bought you that big-ass ring?" He laughed. He pulled me close to him. "Look, I'm not perfect and I know that I've done some things in the past. I'm not going to leave you for doing the same shit that I did. We are going to start fresh from this point on. Fuck the past."

"Sounds good to me," I laughed as I hugged him.

I was happy the way that things were turning out. They were actually going better than I could have imagined. I thought for sure once I told him about Money we would be over. Following that day things were good. Black and I planned to get married in the spring and things couldn't have been better. The business was going great and I had even talked Black into making Tommy a partner. Tommy was strong and he'd saved my life. I had to find a way to pay him back. What better way to say thank you than running a major drug empire?

I thought back to all of the things that I'd been through in my life. It was always good to reflect on your past to appreciate the things that you've learned along the way. We all make mistakes and every mistake teaches us something. Whether we learn from them or not is up to us. That night, I lay in bed thankful for my life and all that I had to look forward to. There had been a lot of bumps along the way and I'd still been able to succeed. There were times that I felt like I didn't deserve to be here, but now, I knew that I did. I'd done a lot of wrong in my life but maybe that was also a part of the plan that was laid out for me. I believe all of it was even down to my teenage years. I closed my eyes with Black nestled next to me and reminisced.

I thought about Johnny and how things could have been different for us. Maybe if I hadn't pushed so hard he wouldn't have spent the rest of his life in jail. Maybe Mica and I wouldn't have fallen out either. At one time we were the best of friends. She never forgave me, even though the day I walked in the warehouse and found her tied up, I saved her life. I felt that once I saved her she'd forgive me for ruining her life but she never did.

I thought about my mother and how I left her to fend for herself when I met Davey. I still believed that if I'd helped her get out of that neighborhood instead of only worrying about me maybe she would have still been alive. I missed her and I felt like I was cheated out of time with her. There could have been so much more to our relationship but we both let temptations on the outside keep us apart. I was lured by the money and she was lured by the drugs, two different things, but both highly addictive. I felt like I lost a part of me the day that I found out she was gone. I hadn't even had a chance to say good-bye or kiss her one last time. Drugs robbed me of telling her I loved her.

I thought about my Aunt Cicely and how evil she had been my entire life. I felt bad for the way I treated my grandmother because of things that she said or did to me. She couldn't control the things that she did and it took me this long to realize that. She was the only grandmother that I'd known and she was always there for me when other people weren't. I planned to make things better between us even though I was still angry that she didn't tell me about the funeral, I still didn't understand how they'd bury my mother and not think I needed to know. How anyone could be so cruel I'd never know. I knew that it wasn't all her doing and I put most of the blame on Cicely but she didn't try to reach out to me so that made her just as guilty. I still had to forgive and the situation with Black showed me that it was definitely possible.

I thought about Davey and how my life took a turn for the worse. I let him take advantage of me in ways that damaged me as a woman. I knew that I wouldn't have made a lot of choices in my life if it weren't for things that I allowed him to do to me. I loved him with all of my heart and he stomped on it every chance that he had. I was happy that I was finally able to move on and find love in myself.

Kiki, my best friend, had always been there for me regardless of the dumb decisions that I made. I was lucky to have her in my life and she'd always be an important factor. There wasn't any one like her and that's what made her special.

I thought of Kemp. He was one of the men that I didn't give a chance to show his full potential. I went into that relationship in a bad state of mind. Maybe he wasn't perfect but maybe things could have worked out differently had I given him the chance and loved him the way that he intended on loving me. I was sorry that I took him away from his family and his child. Now that I had my own child and faced death, I know how devastating that must have been. Maybe all of the things that I went through I deserved because of what I did and I've accepted that.

I thought about Money and how I fell right into his trap. How could I have been so stupid believing that he really wanted to be with me? I'd been a fool more times than I could count on my hands but I could admit that being with him was one of the biggest mistakes I made in my life.

Then there are my parents. I hated them for years because of what I assumed they should have done. Who's to say that my life would have been any better if they'd kept me after all? Javan turned out okay but things could have been different for both of us if I would have been there. Maybe leaving me was best and I'd finally come to that conclusion and stopped hating them. I was finally accepting the way things were and loving them for who they are and not the people that they were in the past.

Then there was Black, the man that I loved more than any man that I'd been with my entire life. I hadn't found a man that loved me the way that he did. When I met him I never would have thought that we would be where we were at that point. We had evolved into a relationship that I'd always dreamed I'd be in but never thought I'd see.

Dior, my beautiful baby girl who'd changed me from the moment she fluttered in my stomach. The old conniving Diamond was an object of the past and I'd matured into a woman and a mother. The path that I took to get where I am today was a long one and it was a rough one. Everyone that I'd encountered in my life had all added to the person that I've become. Looking back, if you'd ask me would I take any of it back and my answer would be no. I wouldn't change a thing because changing one thing in the past would alter the future and my future was with Black and Dior.

Chapter Fifty-four

Black

Our Way

"So how does it feel?" Tommy asked, raising his glass to mine.

"It feels good, man, it feels damn good." I laughed. We were out celebrating because business was back on track. Money was flowing in and the soldiers were all in line. I never thought I'd be enjoying this moment with Tommy. Thinking back, all I could think of was Kemp and how he promised me that I was destined for greatness. I used to feel bad about being with Diamond but now I didn't. I knew that this was the way that things were supposed to be. I remember sitting with Kemp when he made a million dollars. We were sitting in his living room and we had a bottle of champagne sitting on the table. We were both pretty drunk.

"A million muthafucking dollars, do you believe that shit, nigga?"

"I knew you'd do it, you always said that you would."

"I sure did and you're getting to enjoy it with me. Being on top is a wonderful thing and you'll be here one day."

"I feel you and I'm happy to witness this shit for real."

"I'm king of the world, nigga, ain't that what they say!" He was standing on top of the sofa with a glass in his hand.

"That's what they say." I was cracking up. This nigga was drunk as hell and spilling shit all over himself and me.

"On some real shit though," he said, sitting back down next to me. "When I'm dead and gone, you're the only nigga that I'd want to have this shit. Even down to my bitch, you can have it all. I mean that shit man, I love you like a brother."

"I love you like a brother too."

"Let's drink to that shit then," he yelled as he grabbed the bottle off the table and instead of pouring it he toasted my glass with it and drank the rest of it. I laughed that night but I believed that what he said was true. If there was anyone that he wanted to have all that he accomplished when he was gone, that person was me. I felt good knowing that he wouldn't have wanted it any other way.

Now, I had it all. Everything that was his, even his woman was mine. Tommy looked at me and began waving his hands in front of my face to break my stare.

"Yo', what the hell are you thinking about, man?" He laughed as I turned to look at him.

"I was just thinking about Kemp and something that he once said to me. He told me that I would have everything that was his when he was dead and gone."

"What the hell made you think about that?"

"Because I used to feel bad about being here and I felt like I didn't deserve it."

"Man, if anybody deserves it, you do. You deserve it all, even Diamond."

I looked at him and just nodded my head. At least there was someone on this earth who felt the way that I did. I looked back on my life and the way that things had turned out. I was satisfied with that and I was looking my future in the eye ready to take it head on. Now looking at Tommy and knowing what he'd done for me, I could see how Kemp felt the way that he did back then. I lifted my glass and turned it in Tommy's direction.

"In the words of Kemp, when I'm dead and gone there's no one that I'd want to have everything that's mine. Even my woman or bitch as he'd say," I laughed. "On some real shit, Tommy, that person is you. When I'm not here it's all yours and I mean that shit from the heart." He looked at me as if there was something that he wanted to say. I wasn't sure what the look was for but he sat silent for a minute or two before he raised his glass to mine, looked at me and said, "That's real shit, and I'll handle it with care!"

Chapter Fifty-five

Feels So Right

September 2010

"I can't believe it's been two years already," Black said as he stood up, facing the many family members and friends who quietly sat at the surrounding tables that filled the first floor of the Park Avenue Banquet Hall. The room was darkened with a bright light shining directly on to Black and Diamond's table, which sat in the front of the large room.

Some of the attendees looked on and smiled in happiness, while some displayed evident looks of envy, wishing they could be as successful as the two guests of honor. Diamond and Black were celebrating their second wedding anniversary as well as their recent departure from the drug business. As planned, they'd invested in enough legal business to move on from the dangerous world that almost ripped them to shreds. They'd survived his imprisonment, her affair with Money, her near-fatal accident, as well as the attempt on both of their lives. After all that they'd been through, their relationship had blossomed into something much greater than anyone could have ever expected. They were the epitome of true love and, in current times, true love wasn't easy to find. With his glass raised in the air, Black looked over to his right and smiled at Diamond as she sat in a daydream taking it all in.

"I want to make a toast to the woman who has made this life worth living. Looking back I would've never thought that I'd be where I am today. I have a beautiful wife and a daughter I adore. I truly have everything that a man could dream of." He smiled while holding his glass up, thinking back to the moment he'd first laid eyes on Diamond. That was also the moment he knew he had to make her his wife. Realizing that he was getting more sentimental than normal he picked his speech back up. "Now, I'm going to stop being so mushy up here so we can get this party started." He laughed as the guests joined him, raising their glasses and toasting them with the others seated at their tables.

After a few seconds of laughter, the DJ increased the volume on the music and gradually people began to get up from their seats and migrate to the dance floor. Black sat down next to Diamond and stared at her for a few moments before she leaned in and broke the silence.

"That was beautiful, Black." She smiled. Her body was completely filled with joy. She couldn't remember another time in her life where she'd been this happy.

"Well I meant every word. You know you mean the world to me," he admitted while rubbing his hand across her cheek.

"Can you believe what we've accomplished? I mean things could have been disastrous for us but look how things turned out."

"That's because it was meant to be." He leaned in and kissed her softly on the lips.

"Uhhh, ummm, sorry to break you two lovebirds up but would you mind if I stole the man of the hour for a dance?" Trice said as she grabbed Black by the hand.

"Not at all, as long as you promise to return him safely," Diamond replied, motioning with her hand and giggling.

"Scout's honor." Trice laughed and tugged at Black to pull him from his seated position. Trice, the mother of Black's son, had become one of Diamond's best friends. A few years back Diamond would have been ready for a fight but Trice had since moved on and was happily married herself. For the sake of the children, they'd all maintained an alliance that closely resembled a family. As Diamond watched Black and Trice bopping on the floor Tommy slid into the barren chair next to her.

"I know Mrs. Diamond isn't being a wallflower at her own party now." He laughed.

"Not at all, I'm just taking it all in. Besides, you know I'm the truth on the dance floor. You know you don't want to see me get busy." She burst into laughter.

"That's a sight I wouldn't mind seeing." He shook his head as the literal thought of Diamond "getting busy" crossed his mind.

"You are crazy, Tommy," she said and playfully shoved him.

"I'm serious." He laughed as she bashfully turned away.

Tommy secretly had a soft spot for Diamond, but out of respect for Black kept it to minor flirting every now and then. Diamond knew that Tommy felt something for her but she always managed to convince herself that he was just being a clown. She also had a place in her heart for him due to the fact that he saved her life when Mica and Money conspired to kill her. But she wasn't about to make the mistake of sleeping with the best friend of husband number two. The reality of the situation was that she actually loved Black and her new life. At that point she truly believed that there was nothing that they couldn't overcome.

"So what's up with you and your girl Alyssa? I thought you'd be marrying her for sure by now." She changed the subject.

"Yeah, right." He burst into laughter and flagged her with his right hand. "You know damn well that girl ain't the marrying type."

"Hell, I thought that's the kind of woman you like, that's all I ever see you with." She laughed.

"That's because the woman of my dreams isn't available at the moment." He gave a devilish grin.

Black came over to the table and interrupted the conversation. Diamond, relieved, quickly stood from her chair and grabbed Black's arm as he led her out to the dance floor. Tommy sat in the chair, sipping his Hennessy and Coke. As Black spun Diamond around on the floor and a crowd formed a circle to cheer them on, Tommy stared at the couple, imagining standing in Black's spot. He'd already taken the reins running the drug business, but Diamond would be the icing on the cake. Tommy was confident that the time would come when she'd need him and he would patiently wait for that day. For him, that would be the ultimate accomplishment.

As the time neared 2:00 a.m. the crowd began to disperse, and some of their guests grabbed trash cans to assist with the cleanup. Black sat drinking the last few drops of his Grey Goose vodka while Diamond and a few of her friends walked into the bathroom. Kiki, noticeably absent, had decided against attending the event after an argument with Diamond days earlier. Usually, the two had been able to squash their squabbles but this argument had morphed into more of a dual. The two had never been so distant and angry at one another. Though Diamond wanted everyone to believe she didn't care, the separation had taken a toll on her. She'd lost the one person she had always been able to talk to. She was now forced to keep all of her concerns, wants, needs, and aspirations to herself. Their small circle of friends had been waiting all night for the perfect time to question Diamond about her missing BFF. Finally, as they all headed into the ladies' room, they would get the chance that they'd been waiting for.

Diamond stood in front of the mirror re-touching her makeup and making sure her hair was perfect. The group of women stood at different spots, all with the same question lingering in their minds. Diamond was always pretty quiet when it came to her personal business and not one of them was sure what they could ask without pissing her off. But, as they stood around the room appearing as if they had huge question marks over their heads, it was pretty evident that something was on their minds. Diamond realized that they were all just a bit too quiet and decided to break the silence to see what the hell was going on. Though she knew that most people didn't know how to approach her, she still believed that she was one of the easiest people to talk to.

"If someone wants to ask me a question, just do it. Standing there staring at each other won't get the answer that you are looking for." She paused to pucker her lips and apply her lip gloss. "I know it's about Kiki so what is it that you all want to know?"

All of the women appeared shocked and shook their heads as if they weren't concerned. Jasmine, the older of the bunch, stepped up and walked closer to where Diamond was standing. If there was one of them bold enough to go toe to toe with Diamond, it was Jasmine. The other three—Sydney, Palace, and Octavia—weren't as outspoken.

"Well yes, we do have a question. Kiki is supposed to be your best friend right? So, we really can't understand what could have been so important that she would miss your anniversary celebration."

Diamond shook her head briefly before grabbing a paper towel to dab off some of the excess gloss. "Jasmine, I think you just answered your own question with that statement, 'supposed to be.' Obviously she isn't, if she would miss one of the most important days of my life. Now, I don't cry over spilled milk because, honestly, she'll need me long before I need her. It's just sad that she would let a minor disagreement ruin our friendship after being my friend for so long. That makes me believe she was never really my friend to begin with." Diamond was now using her comb to tame the fly-aways in her hair.

The group of girls remained quiet, not wanting to press the issue any further. It was clearly a sore subject and rather than causing Diamond to feel as if she was being attacked, each of them believed it would be best to just drop it for the moment, knowing that it would all come up again in the future.

Jasmine, just as quickly as she asked the "Kiki" question, changed the subject. "Well, now that that's settled, what I really wanna know is where the hell the after-party is going down because I'm still fired up. I'm not ready to call it a night just yet. And besides, I need to find a nice piece of meat to go home with if you know what I mean." She giggled while swirling her hips.

"I know that's right," Palace, who was also Jasmine's sister, agreed and slapped Jasmine a high five.

"I don't know but I'm sure Black isn't ready to go in either, so follow us and we can make sure wherever we decide to go everyone makes it into the VIP section," Diamond said as she returned all of her beauty tools to her bag and headed toward the door.

The group followed her as she walked through the ballroom and out of the front door, where Black and all of the other partygoers were standing. Luxury cars lined every edge of the street and they were so amped you could hear their chatter around the corner. Diamond loved seeing her man happy and it was at that moment she realized that they did the right thing by leaving the drug game. Her eyes were locked on Black as she switched as hard as she could and walked in his direction.

Once he noticed her, he rubbed the hairs on his chin and smiled. He had every intention of bending her over and waxing her ass all over their home that evening. His dick was getting hard from just the thought and he quickly adjusted his pants, hoping that no one noticed his quickly growing bulge.

"So where are we headed, babe?" she said, standing so close to him he could feel her breath tickling his skin. The sweet scent of her Juicy Couture Viva La Juicy perfume was flowing freely up his nostrils. "The girls were hoping we could swing by Vault since they are open until three-thirty. I know I'm not ready to call it a night so I was hoping that you weren't either." She smiled as he caressed her arm softly with his hand.

He was silent for a few seconds as his mind was totally consumed with how much he loved her. He'd never met a woman whom he would die for, literally. There was no limit to the things that he would do for her and he was positive that she felt the same way. "That's cool with me if that's what you wanna do," he finally replied.

"That's not *all* I wanna do, just what I wanna do at the moment." She giggled and playfully tugged at the bottom of her dress.

"Is that right?" he asked, adjusting his pants once again to hide his protruding manhood.

She laughed as she looked down at his crotch and back at his face. "Well let's go, before we end up ass naked in the back of this car."

"Yeah, we better." He smiled as he stood up off of his car. "Yo, Tommy, let's roll out, man. The ladies wanna hit Vault before we take it down."

Tommy nodded and obediently walked over to his car and ordered everyone else in their crew to do the same. Just like a funeral procession they all drove off one by one with Center City their destination.

Diamond sat in the passenger seat comfortably as they made their way through the city. Every so often she'd glance over at Black and smile. If there was anyone on this earth that she loved more than her baby girl, Dior, it was Black. Visions of their past flashed before her eyes. She felt blessed to be where she was at that moment, especially after all of the wrong that she had done to get there. If you would have asked her three years ago where she thought she'd be today she would've most likely shrugged her shoulders and said she didn't know, but if you asked her this day where she would be in three more years she would say happily ever after with Black.

Unfortunately, when you were on top there was always someone at the bottom clawing at your cuffs to pull you back down. With a jagged past and more enemies than they could keep up with, there could be someone lurking behind every corner, waiting for that brief second when they'd let their guard down. Diamond knew that they still had a lot more to do before "officially" being done with the drug life, but she wanted to enjoy this bliss as long as she possibly could.

Chapter Fifty-six

Brass Knuckles

Two men occupied a small eight-by-twelve concrete cell. Photos of hip hop video vixens and scantly clad female emcees covered the walls, with small pieces of tape holding them in place at each corner. One of the men was sprawled out on a metal-framed twin bed with a thin polyester mattress so hard it almost resembled the metal frame that lay beneath it. The man—dark skinned, weighing 230 pounds, all muscle, and standing six foot three inches tall—was resting his left hand behind his head and on top of the pillow. In his right hand, a book, *Strength to Love* by Martin Luther King Jr., had his full attention. One quote rang true: "All progress is precarious, and the solution of one problem brings us face to face with another problem." As he dragged his eyes across the pages of this 1963 release, he could only compare the statements to his own experiences. For him, every moment in his life was precarious and even the most detailed plan could crumble at any given moment, which was why he always prepared a plan B in the event that things went horribly wrong.

The second man, a mix of Puerto Rican and African American, almost resembling his cellmate in height and weight, was sitting up on the edge of his neatly made bed, with a black-and-white composition book in his right hand and a pencil in the other. On the pages were handwritten notes. The meaning of the notes was only understood by the two men who'd shared living quarters for the past two years.

"Yo, why are you always reading, man? Hell, at least read some shit that's interesting," Reed blurted out, breaking the eerie silence that had filled the room for the past hour.

"'Cause it ain't shit else to do. Might as well learn some shit while I'm still on this earth," Johnny replied, still keeping his eyes on the book.

"Aww, man, it's plenty to do like going over this plan, my nigga. I'm trying to make sure this shit is airtight. I don't want to end up back in here rooming wit' your ass." He laughed.

"Right now ain't the time for that shit. You see niggas walking up and down the block don't you? If you don't keep that shit on the low you'll definitely end up back in here. I'm going to die in here so I ain't got shit to lose. You on the other hand are just weeks away from freedom so keep that in mind."

Reed shook his head and closed the notebook before stuffing it under his pillow. He thought about how close he was to freedom and compared it to the life he'd lived for the past two years. Before he was booked his life was as close to perfect as a life could get. He was well known in the streets and had a team who ruled the drug game in Philadelphia, New Jersey, and Delaware also known as the tri-state area. Now, his wife was out there fending for herself after his team dispersed to different sets. Without a leader, the empire that he'd built from the ground up quickly crumbled to bits and pieces. Luckily, he had a few loyal men who had maintained his relationships with his suppliers and kept a steady flow of narcotics and cash flowing while he was away. He was anxious to get back on top and with Johnny's help he was going to do just that.

Thinking back, he reminisced about the good times. Hanging out partying, spending money, and sexing beautiful and exotic women left and right. Now, a normal day consisted of washing dishes, playing basketball, working out in the yard, and hanging out in the cell with Johnny. He had no privacy—he couldn't even shit in peace. Even worse than boredom and the lack of serenity, he was being tested on a daily basis by other inmates who thought he was weak, or just felt like he had something that they wanted. Unfortunately for them he proved that he was far from weak each time he laid them out flat on their asses.

Unlike Johnny, Reed had a lot to live for; his wife, Raquel, and his five-year-old princess, Alyia, were all the inspiration he needed to keep going every day. A photo and vivid flashes of memories were all that kept him sane and it was them who were also what kept him from copping a murder charge behind bars. As the day neared when he could walk out of the hellhole that he'd been forced to call home and return to Philly to get things back on track, his anxiety became more evident.

His plan went beyond the tasks that Johnny wanted him to complete. He knew that he had to have another plan since Johnny's motives were that of pure revenge. Making decisions on that alone could land you six feet under, or in prison for the rest of your life. Reed was determined to stay out of prison by any means necessary. He refused to be one of those statistics that you see on TV. Living with Johnny had taught him a lot. It showed him just how little a nigga with a grudge cared about the things he stood to lose. In his mind, he figured that it was a lonely place—one that he never wanted to take a trip to.

After a few minutes of dullness, Reed retrieved the note-book from under his pillow again but decided to read it silently rather than asking Johnny about it. He felt like a student preparing for a final exam or turning in a term paper. He wanted to be certain that he'd crossed every "t" and dotted every "i." As he read the codes, which were scribbled on the pages, the symbol that represented the name of his main target stood out: *Diamond*. He wondered how a woman with a name so beautiful could wreak so much havoc on a man's life that he'd want to destroy everything that she loved. He hadn't seen a photo of her just yet, but by the way that Johnny described her he could imagine her without even one glance.

"So can I ask you a question, man?" Reed once again broke the silence and interrupted Johnny's concentration on the book that he was reading.

Closing the book and sitting up on the edge of the bed, Johnny asked, "What, man? It's obvious that you aren't going to let me finish my daily reading so go ahead and ask. This shit better be good, too, for you to interrupt me twice while I'm gaining some knowledge," he said, annoyed.

"Were you ever in love with this girl? I'm just curious because there has to be some sort of feelings in order to hate a person so much." Reed could tell by the look on Johnny's face that he was annoying him but he didn't care; he just wanted to learn as much about her as he could.

"Yeah, I loved her. She was my first love, hell my only love. Shit she was my girlfriend when I got arrested. Shit, I thought we would have been together forever. I thought she would stay down for me while I was locked away but it wasn't until my letters went unanswered that I realized how far from reality that actually was." He paused and shook his head. "My sister was my life and I felt like the biggest asshole on the planet when she told me how different Diamond had turned out to be. She looked me in the eye and said the girl I once knew and loved was long gone and would never return."

"So, I'm still a little confused, because I still don't get how a teenage love lost could cause so much anger and rage," Reed replied honestly.

"Man, this ain't got shit to do with teenage love. This bitch took away the one person who always had my back. My sister is dead because of her and now my mother has lost both of her children. I'm gonna die in here, man. If it's the last thing I do before I take my final breath that bitch is gonna pay for what she's done."

Reed looked at him still longing for more information. He wanted to know what role she played in the death of his sister. He decided not to ask him any more questions at that moment because he could tell Johnny was on the verge of breaking down. Though all of his siblings were still living he could feel his pain. He knew, if put in the same situation, he would feel the exact same way.

Johnny looked over at Reed and let out a laugh. The laugh was intended to downplay the seriousness of the conversation with the hopes that he wouldn't ask him any more questions. "Is that sufficient enough for you?" Johnny blurted out.

Laughing, Reed replied, "Yeah, man, for now, but we still got a lot more to talk about, especially if you want me to risk my life to settle a score that isn't even mine to begin with."

"That's fair enough, and I promise you will know everything there is to know about me, my past, and little Miss Diamond before your departure from Hotel Hell," he said and extended his hand to shake on it.

Reed obliged and with that he closed the composition book once again and placed it back underneath the pillow for safe-keeping. He wasn't 100 percent satisfied with the information that he was given, but he knew that it made no sense to keep pressing a man who obviously had something to hide. "It's cool, man, I'll drop it for now, but we only have a few weeks to get things straight. Just keep in mind, I don't like going into any situation blind, so I need any and all information no matter how small or unimportant it may seem to you. In order for me to do my job right you have to supply me with the proper tools. You know what I'm saying?"

"I know exactly what you're saying and I got it. I hear your concerns loud and clear," Johnny replied. With just a short time left before Reed would be released, Johnny knew he had a limited amount of time to give him a suitable explanation for taking a life. Saying that she was the reason Mica was dead wasn't the same as her being the one who murdered her. Death by association clearly wasn't enough for Reed, and Johnny had to cleverly lay out the clues without allowing Reed a moment to feel sorry for Diamond and change his mind. This was Johnny's last chance since his health was quickly deteriorating and he never knew which day would ultimately be his last.

Reed lay across his bed and drifted off in deep thought, awake but with closed eyes. Quietly, he was thinking more about his own plan than Johnny's. He knew that he needed to go through with it all in order to get the money that he needed to purchase the weight necessary for his own survival. As many times as he tried, he couldn't figure out how to get the money without extortion or murder. Though he didn't *know* Diamond, he did know his own wife and daughter, and because of that he couldn't get completely comfortable with taking a mother away from her child, or vice versa. The way that he saw it, Johnny would be dying soon anyway and as far as he knew, he had no drug or gang ties to make any noise out on the streets. So, the key would be finding a way to make

Johnny believe that the job was done just until he could take the money he needed and run. He also contemplated what he'd do if Johnny was actually setting him up to take a fall or, even worse, be murdered. He felt confident that his street smarts would assist him if he had to fight tooth and nail for his own life. However, there was always a chance that he could be blindsided and he had to expect the unexpected.

Johnny sat on the other side of the room with similar thoughts. Something in his heart told him that Reed would try to screw him if he got the chance, and he had just the thing for him in the event that things went totally left. As much as he didn't want to believe that Reed's betrayal was a possibility he had to prepare himself for the worst. His backup plan would allow him to deal with Diamond and Reed if necessary. In the past two years, the pair had become close friends, or so they liked to think. They'd even fought numerous bloody battles in the yard when fellow inmates attacked without warning. They'd always looked out for one another, but Johnny's time in the penitentiary had shown him how important it was to keep your friends closer than your enemies, since they were the ones to drive the dagger into your back as soon as you were caught slipping. That one lesson was the realest lesson he'd learned and not one book in any library could have taught him that. Learning how to grow eyes in the back and both sides of your head was *priceless*.

Soon, you could hear the correction officer's signal and then the lights went out. After a few minutes of chatter among the inmates, a few of them spewing obscenities at the guards and other inmates, the block was filled with silence. Johnny and Reed relaxed in their own private darkness until they drifted off to sleep, both men armed with a handy pair of mental brass knuckles in case there ever came a time when a secret weapon was needed, both prepared to go to war at the drop of a dime.

Chapter Fifty-seven

Frenemies

"All I'm saying is she wouldn't have shit if it weren't for me. I mean seriously, I went out of my way to make sure she lived more than comfortably. Shit, she was living in a small-ass apartment, going from hustla to hustla trying to score a kingpin when all she scored were some wet panties and a cold bed. If I wanted to be a real bitch, I could shut that fucking club down," Diamond said with an abundance of attitude, as she sat and ate dinner with Black at their tulip tree–wood dining room table.

"I don't get women, man, y'all two were the best of friends and now you're ready to shut her whole life down because of some he said, she said shit? Diamond, that's just crazy and I'm sorry, babe, I love you more than life itself but I have to disagree with your actions on this one." He shook his head before taking a bite of his slice of supreme Pizza Hut pizza.

"So my husband is just going to take another bitch's side over mine?" She raised her voice as she visibly became more annoyed. Both of her eyebrows were raised and her lips were twisted.

"I didn't say I was taking her side, Diamond, I just said you're being a bit childish. I don't understand why you two can't just have an adult conversation and straighten this shit out," Black replied before taking a swig of his Pepsi soda. "You can sit and twist your face, pout and all that shit, Diamond, but you can't be right all the time. If you were ever really friends you would be able to squash it."

"First of all, I'm not pouting, and can we just change the subject? Because I feel myself getting angry and I'd hate to report to my anger management counselor that I murdered my *second* husband," she said, rolling her eyes.

"Oh, so you're gonna murder me, huh?" Black asked before wiping the excess pizza crumbs from his mouth with his napkin.

Diamond sat mum as he placed the napkin down and slid his chair out from under the table. With seriousness written all across his face, he walked behind Diamond's chair and placed both of his large hands around her neck. "I didn't hear a response. You plan on murdering me?" He tightened his grip.

She pushed his hands off of her neck and quickly rose from her seat, turning around to face him. "I will if I have to," she replied.

Without speaking Black pushed the chair that sat in between them to the floor, and threw Diamond's plate of uneaten pizza to the floor, causing the glass to crack into bits and pieces all over the area rug. He stood face to face with her for a few moments, staring her in the eye as she tried her hardest not to blink. Unexpectedly, he grabbed both of her ass cheeks and picked her up on to the table, and with a quick hand motion his hands went under her dress and ripped her thong off of her. He threw them to the floor and grabbed her by the neck.

"Let me hear you say that again," he breathed into her ear while dropping his lounge pants to the floor and thrusting his rock-hard dick inside of her moist pussy, which welcomed him with opened lips.

"Ummm, damn baby," she moaned while grabbing hold of the tablecloth that lay beneath her.

Black continued to fuck her, using every muscle in his legs to push all ten inches of his thick meat inside of her. "You like that shit?" he asked while lightly squeezing her neck with one hand and using the other to pull her closer to him for a deeper penetration.

"I like it," she whispered.

"I can't hear you. What did you say?" he yelled while pumping harder and harder. You could hear his thighs slapping up against the table echoing through the house. Her pussy juices were pouring out of her and forming a small puddle underneath her. She loved when he was forceful—it turned her on.

"I like it," she said one octave louder than she had previously.

Black, still not satisfied with that answer, began to fuck her faster and harder. Every time he'd pull himself out of her, he'd leave just the head in, bend his knees and stand back up with force, almost lifting her ass one inch off of the table. "You said you like it, is that it? You only *like* this dick huh?" His deep voice was rumbling through the house.

"Ohhhh shit, Black, I'm about to cum. I'm gonna cum all over this fucking dick," she yelled as her legs wrapped tightly around his waist, grinding the tip of his stiff dick right into her G-spot and causing her body to shake uncontrollably, releasing her cum all over the entire shaft.

"Damn, baby, this pussy is soaking wet," he whispered, feeling himself nearing an eruption.

Diamond used her hands to lift herself off of the table. With her legs still wrapped around his waist she forced her pussy onto his dick continuously, while moving her hips in a circular motion.

"Baby, ooh shit, goddamn, baby, here it comes," he yelled as he released his cum inside of her for what felt like an eternity. His legs became weak and his arms could barley hold on to the table.

Diamond released him from her leg grip so he could sit down. Once he sat in the seat, both of them burst into laughter.

"We have to do that shit more often, damn!" he said aloud.

"Well now that we got that out the way, I guess I can take your advice and try to iron out this issue with Kiki," she spoke through twisted lips as she slid off of the table, trying to fix her ruffled clothing.

"That's my girl." Black smiled as he looked down at his dick, which was still rock hard. "Now let's take care of this before you go."

She smiled and walked over to him, bent over, and grabbed hold of his dick before getting in a squatting position and wrapping her thick lips around it. From behind, you could see her voluptuous frame and well-rounded ass cheeks moving up and down. Her sculpted calf muscles were glistening from the beads of sweat forming all over her body. She was working overtime, using every trick up her sleeve to satisfy her man.

Feeling himself nearing an orgasm he firmly gripped the arms of the chair with both hands and slightly lifted his butt off of the chair to push his dick deeper down her throat. A few moments later he was in pure heaven as he released every drop that he had left into her mouth. Without hesitation, she quickly swallowed his juices, not allowing any of it to slip from the sides of her mouth. His body was still shaking seconds later when she stood over him and stared him in the face.

"Are you okay?" she asked with a giggle, while she attempted to fix her disheveled clothing.

"I'm good, as a matter of fact I'm greeeeaaaattttt," he jokingly replied, imitating the voice of Tony the Frosted Flakes tiger.

The two laughed in sync before Diamond headed upstairs to shower. Her intention for the following day was to contact Kiki and see how they could get past this hurdle that they were experiencing. Black was right: at some point one of them needed to be mature, and if Kiki wasn't going to be the one to take the first step it wouldn't kill Diamond to do so.

The following day Diamond went about her normal routine, getting Dior off to daycare and doing her morning runs. She knew Kiki was usually working by twelve noon so she figured that would be the perfect time to go and talk with her, assuming that she was there alone.

Diamond arrived to find only Kiki's car in the parking lot of the club. Diamond took a deep breath before heading to the entrance to ring the bell. A few moments later she could hear the sound of Kiki's stilettos nearing the door.

Kiki could see that it was Diamond on the camera and was at first hesitant before opening it. She wasn't in the mood for a physical confrontation and she'd known Diamond long enough to know how she got down. But, she knew that it was probably wise to just get the conversation over with, as it was long overdue. The two women definitely had some things to hash out so she sincerely hoped that they could do so like mature adults.

"Long time no see. You're not hiding a gun behind your back are you?" Kiki asked jokingly, attempting to break the thick ice.

"Naw, if I had a gun I certainly wouldn't hide it." Diamond laughed.

"Come on in. I just got here." Kiki waved with her hands.

Diamond entered the building and made her way through the corridor that led to the office. She stepped inside after noticing the rest of the club was darkened besides that small office. She helped herself to a seat on the plush leather sofa, which sat in one corner of the room. She patiently waited with her legs crossed as Kiki made her way into the room.

"So what's been up, Ms. Kiki? I figured it was time that we talked," Diamond blurted.

"Same ol', just trying to stay afloat, and yes, it was definitely time that we talked. I mean I can't believe that we went this long without having a conversation." She sat down on the edge of her desk.

"Well, Black insisted that I come straighten things out. I mean, honestly, I can't even remember why we weren't speaking," Diamond replied.

"Well my issue with you started after the whole murder plot against you. It really hurt me when you accused me of knowing something about it. Yes, I was sleeping with JB but he never let me know about a plot to set you up. He used me the same way he used you and Black. I would never conspire with Mica to have you murdered and if I had known I most certainly would have told you. I thought that our friendship was stronger than that. I just couldn't get past that, Diamond, that shit hurt like hell," she said in a low tone.

"I apologized about that, Kiki. I mean you have to understand what I was going through. I didn't know who I could trust. I felt like everybody was out to get me. I can't take back the past but I am sorry that I hurt you; that was never my intention. That was the worst time of my life, one of the lowest points. I thought that we had worked through that, Kiki." She sat there confused.

"I thought we did, Diamond, but when your new circle of friends came in the picture I felt the distance between us.

Everything changed. You never talked to me about anything anymore. It was like I always had to hear shit from other people. You were shutting me out."

"And it wasn't intentionally. I was just so unsure of everything. My world had been turned upside down."

"I know that, Diamond, I was a part of your life. Did you ever stop to think how my life has changed? Did you ever think of how it all affected me?"

Diamond sat silent, pondering the questions that Kiki posed. She was absolutely right; she'd never thought about how Kiki felt. When things came crashing down the only people she thought about were herself, Dior, and Black. Sadly, Kiki never crossed her mind. Maybe it was a bit selfish, and that was something that she'd always been told about herself. It was something that she worked to change, but she wasn't perfect, so there would be times that slipped through the cracks.

"You're right, Kiki, I didn't think about you and I'm sorry. I love you, Kiki, you are the closet thing to a sister that I have. I never wanted to shut you out and I can swear on a stack of Bibles. I need you back in my life. I feel like there's a piece of me missing without you," she said honestly.

Kiki sat relieved. She was hoping that things would turn out this way. It made her feel like a huge weight had been lifted off of her shoulders now that she'd been able to get Diamond to see that she was wrong. Instead of responding with words Kiki eased off of the desk and walked over to hug Diamond. As Diamond stood to hug her, both of them held in tears. Regardless of the outer appearances the two had portrayed during their time apart, they loved each other and both women were silently thanking Black for nudging Diamond to move on from the past.

"Now, when can I see my goddaughter? I know she is so big now!" Kiki laughed.

"You can see her whenever you want!" She smiled.

The two women sat and caught each other up on life and what they'd missed. Within minutes it was as if they'd never been separated to begin with. The two frenemies were back to being friends.

Chapter Fifty-eight

Back Against the Wall

Reed stood at the exit of the prison, waiting for the gates to open to let him out on to the street. So many thoughts were running through his head and not even the anticipation of seeing his family could steady it. He wanted to enjoy his freedom but he knew that it wouldn't immediately be something to celebrate. He looked back over his shoulder one last time before taking the steps through the large metal gate to find his right-hand man, Romeo, waiting patiently, posted up against a brand-new Mercedes-Benz CL-Class, all black with shiny rims. Though he expected his wife to be there to pick him up he was happy to see Romeo. It instantly brought back memories of better days and moneymaking escapades. He smiled as he put some pep in his step in order to reach his chariot in record time.

"Daaaaaaamnnnnnnnn, I see life is treating you well. Nigga, this ride is the shit. Can't wait to get back up, man." He reached out to Romeo to engage in their signature handshake and hug. They patted each other on the back a few times before finally separating.

Romeo looked at him with a huge grin before replying, "You like this shit, man?"

"Like? Nigga I *love* this shit, man. You can't get a better Benz than this. This shit is top of the line."

"Well it's yours, man," Romeo said before pulling a set of keys from his pocket and dangling them in the air in front of his face.

"You bullshittin' me?" he asked with a laugh.

"Have I ever bullshitted you, man?" He paused, waiting for an answer, knowing he wouldn't give him one. "Now take these keys, hop in, and let's get the fuck outta here. I got warrants and shit. I can't be out here too long if you know what I mean." He laughed and dropped the keys in the palm of Reed's hand.

Reed opened the door and threw his bag of belongings in the back seat. He couldn't wait to feel the gas pedal under his foot and watch the sight of the prison slowly disappearing from his rearview mirror.

"How does it feel, man? I know it's been a long time coming. I know how that shit felt when I was locked up and, shit, that was only for six months! Nigga, I would lose my damn mind if I had to be caged up like that for two years." He laughed.

"Shit, man, all I could think about was coming home. The past few weeks couldn't come fast enough for me. Those days felt like months. I can't wait to get home to my wife, man. I told her not to visit so she wouldn't have to see me caged in, but I regretted that shit because I missed her like crazy." He shook his head in excitement.

"I wanna talk to you about her, man. Shit's done changed since you've been away." Romeo's tone went from happiness to seriousness in a matter of seconds.

"What the fuck you mean shit's changed? And don't beat around the bush; just give that shit to me raw!" His smile had diminished and turned to a frown.

"Yo, about a year into your bid she started fucking with the young gun Brook. She put your crib up for sale and moved to Jersey, man. I took the money down to the Realtor to buy that shit so you wouldn't lose it."

Rage instantly flowed through Reed's veins. To avoid causing an accident, he slammed on the brakes, as he needed a few minutes to process what Romeo had just said. Romeo sat quiet waiting for Reed to say something but his eyes were looking down at the floor as both of his hands were firmly gripping the steering wheel. He couldn't even think straight. He'd never wanted to kill someone as much as he did at that moment. He was certain if he saw Brook it would take at least ten men to keep his hands from choking him to death.

Just the thought of another man having sex with his wife was almost enough to make him vomit. The woman he'd devoted everything to for the majority of his adult life had betrayed him in the worst way possible. *How could she?* he thought. If it weren't for him she'd still be a ghetto project bitch living off government assistance. She would have never had the pleasure of riding around in luxury cars or wearing jewelry that cost more than people's homes. His friends had clowned him for marrying her because they were certain that she poked holes in the condoms to ensure her ticket out of the hood. Regardless of how they tried to influence him to leave her ass stranded at the altar, he couldn't live comfortably knowing that he'd left the mother of his child to struggle when he lived in a $300,000 house on the hill.

"Do you know where they stay at?" Reed asked through clinched teeth.

"Naw, not the exact address; I know the area, but I can find out for you. I got some niggas who owe me a few favors."

"And, what about Alyia? Does this bitch have my baby girl shacking up with some random wannabe thug?"

"Naw, she's with her mother. I take money over there every month, man, just like I promised I would. I would've wrote you while you were gone to update you but I didn't want you to get all angry and shit and fuck up your probation. I made sure your baby girl was good but Raquel, I haven't given her a dime since she did that slimy shit, man."

"Does she know that I was coming home?"

"I'm sure she does, you know how fast word gets around in the streets. I haven't seen her in the hood but that don't mean shit. I haven't seen that nigga Brook either but he certainly ain't untouchable."

Romeo hated to be the bearer of bad news. Even though he'd prepared himself to spill the beans, he didn't expect to see the hurt in Reed's eyes. He'd known him since grade school so he could see right through his anger. "I'm sorry, Reed, real talk. I wish this shit was all a joke and your homecoming could've been a bit more welcoming. I hate to see you hurting."

"It ain't your fault that I married a conniving bitch, and eventually I'm gonna deal with her. I just need to handle some other shit first." He twisted the key in the ignition and began the drive toward his home. He was happy that he had at least one true friend in the world to make sure that he could live comfortably once he was released. "Since I still have a home to go to, let's be on our way. I hope you got some alcohol and some bitches lined up for me, too. I ain't smelled pussy in two years. I'm wayyyyyyy overdue." He laughed, attempting to hide how angry and hurt he actually was.

"You know I got you covered; it wouldn't be me if I didn't." He joined in laughter with Reed.

The remainder of the ride went pretty silent besides the few times they passed a group of people they knew on the streets. Just like a celebrity or a rapper, Reed still got the same respect that he did prior to his arrest. After each wave or yell he felt good for a brief moment until the realization of his broken home popped up in his mind. After finally reaching the cul-de-sac that led to his home, his nerves began to go wild. Most likely the thought of life being totally different shook him up a bit. When they arrived at his driveway they noticed a white Porsche Cayman S parked behind Romeo's Range Rover. Romeo used his arm to signal Reed to slow down and approach the driveway cautiously.

"Yo, I think that's Raquel's car parked right there. What the fuck is she doing here?" Romeo asked, annoyed by the sight of the gold digger who he truly believed was the biggest mistake in Reed's life.

"Word? This bitch has balls the size of King Kong to roll up here after the shit you just told me." He stopped just short of the driveway and, without turning the engine off, he swung the door open with force and jumped out of the car.

Raquel opened her car door and swung her legs around, planting her Jimmy Choos on the ground before standing. She was dressed in a black jumpsuit that hugged her curves and created a camel-toe effect in her crotch, which under different circumstances would normally turn Reed on. She looked like a runway model with her long hair flowing freely and blowing in the wind. With one hand, she removed her Luxuriator Style 23 shades from her eyes. She looked like a million bucks, literally, as the cost of the car and her attire would set a low-grade hustla way back trying to keep up. But as beautiful as she was, it wouldn't erase the fact that she'd hopped on the next dick smoking when the going got tough. That was an unforgivable offense that would be punishable by public stoning in other countries.

Reed began to walk toward her with Romeo following closely behind in the event that she had goons lurking in the background.

"So I see not much has changed since you went away. As usual you have an obedient guard dog by your side." She laughed.

Reed laughed to try to avoid lunging at her neck and slowly choking the life out of her. He remained as cool as he possibly could under the circumstances since he certainly didn't want to be hauled back to prison. "I can't believe that you have the audacity to show up here after you abandoned all of my property and our daughter for some punk-ass dealer who was practically a servant of mine for years," Reed replied, as he now stood about three feet away from her.

"That's funny that you can stand here with a straight face and say some shit like that. My shades cost more than half of what this house is worth. Obviously he's worth more than you ever were."

"Bitch, let me explain something to you real quick," he said as he pounded his left fist into his right hand as most men did when they were trying to get a point across. "I should've left your trifling ass in those filthy, pissy-ass projects. That shit could've saved me years of stress and aggravation."

"Well, you didn't, and if you regret it then that's just too damn bad. I didn't come here to engage in small talk and as much as I would just *love* to catch up on the past two years I have some official business to take care of." She reached into her car and retrieved a large manila envelope before holding it out in his direction.

"What the hell is this?" he asked, snatching the envelope from her hand.

"Open it and see," she snapped.

He opened the envelope to find divorce papers citing irrec-
oncilable differences. Almost instantaneously he felt nothing
but disgust and hatred for the woman he vowed to stick with
for better or worse. He shook his head before being brutally
honest about his feelings for her at that moment. "You know
you are the most vindictive and trifling bitch I've ever laid
eyes on. If you were a man you'd be snoring on the concrete
right now after I'd knocked you the fuck out. I should break
your fucking face to pieces to disfigure you just enough to
knock you off of that high horse you're sitting on. You can
take these damn divorce papers and shove them up your
pretty little ass. I wish I would give you the pleasure of taking
what's mine. Bitch, I don't owe you shit," he yelled with spit
flying from his lips. His body was filled with so much rage that
it was becoming more difficult by the second to contain it.

"Well I suggest you hire a good lawyer because I can't
stay married to you another day. I have a man at home who
provides more for me physically and emotionally than you're
capable of."

"I couldn't care less about your suggestions, or anything
that has to do with you for that matter. You can take your
stuck-up, gold-digging ass back to your bitch-ass man and tell
him I'll be seeing his ass around real soon," he yelled.

"Yeah, we'll see how much of bitch he is when you meet face
to face." She laughed as she turned to walk back to her car.
"I'll be seeing you soon, smooches," she said before puckering
her lips into a kiss.

He stood there shaking his head in disbelief. He couldn't
believe that this was the same woman he'd fallen in love with
so many years ago. The ride-or-die-chick façade was proving
to be faker than a thirty dollar bill. He turned to look at
Romeo, who was shaking his head as well.

"Scandalous-ass bitch," Romeo yelled. He could feel Reed's
pain as he, too, had been through many women in his day;
you always had to get through a bunch of rocks before you
found a diamond.

"What a homecoming, man." Reed laughed.

Romeo walked over to his car to remove it from the driveway to allow Reed to pull his car in. As Reed sat in his car he

used the silence to reflect on the choices that he'd made in his life. He wondered if this was punishment for all of the wrong that he'd committed. Reed parked and exited his car.

Romeo rolled down his window. "I'm gonna come in with you to do a walk-through, then I have to go handle some shit."

"Cool, I have some shit to handle myself," Reed replied before walking over to the front door.

Romeo exited his car and walked behind Reed as he entered the house. Turning on the light Romeo took a quick surveillance.

"Home sweet home. I thought that I'd be opening my front door and having my baby girl running into my arms."

"I know, man." Romeo patted Reed on his shoulder. "Everything happens for a reason. I'm a strong believer of that shit. It's a good thing you saw that shit now, man. I'm gonna roll out now to make a few runs but I'm gonna swing back around eight, 'cause I got a lot of shit planned for you tonight."

"All right, I'll be ready for sure."

"And wipe that frown off your face; fuck her for real. It's plenty of bad bitches out here. Seriously," Romeo said before reaching out to shake Reed's hand. Reed walked Romeo to the door and slowly shut it behind him. "Home sweet fucking home," he said aloud as he shook his head in disbelief. He walked around the house, looking at the things that were the same as well as the things that were different. He was glad to be home but he was frustrated that things weren't going to be the way that he'd left them. Walking into his kitchen he remembered the mornings where his daughter would sit eating her breakfast and swinging her legs in her high chair. He pictured her little face and her smile. Even with her mother being the bitch she was, he could at least thank her for giving him the daughter he loved more than life itself.

He headed upstairs to the master bedroom and found a fresh pair of Prada sneakers with the matching leather belt, a black button up, and crisp dark blue Rock & Republic jeans. He smiled, knowing that Romeo was probably the only person on this earth who knew him better than or just as well as he knew himself. It was certainly going to feel good to rock designer threads instead of prison blues. He hurried to shower so he could get started on his stops to make it back in time to meet Romeo at eight. Though his day hadn't started out as well as he would have liked, he was going to make the best of whatever was thrown his way. The hot water, steam, and the smell of Zest body wash filled the bathroom with a relaxing aroma, just what he needed to prepare him for the night ahead.

Chapter Fifty-nine

His Little Secret

"So, how are things with your new boo?" Diamond asked, playfully nudging Kiki on her shoulder.

"Who said he was my boo?" Kiki laughed.

"Well you said that you had a friend. I mean excuse me if I *thought* that was what you meant." She laughed as she shook her head.

"I'm joking, girl, yes, he is my boo and things are going great."

"I'm happy for you. I really hope things work out."

"Shit, me too. Lord knows I've had my fair share of assholes along the way." She took a sip of her juice.

"So how are you enjoying life away from the game?"

"It's nice to have the weight off of my shoulders but I miss the control. It's nothing like being the boss of an empire like that. That's a once-in-a-lifetime situation. Plus Black is only eighty percent out of the game. I still sit up at night waiting for him to come home. I always worry that some jealous-ass nigga is going to try to take him out as soon as his back is turned."

"I thought you were officially out."

"Yeah, I thought so too, but Black is still in the streets more than he's home. He claims that there are things that he has to wrap up and it's taking a lot longer than he expected. I think it's bullshit, he probably never had any intention of leaving the game in the first place."

Kiki sat shaking her head, clueless. Though she hadn't been around for a year, she'd heard through the grapevine that they were done. She wondered why he'd make promises and plans that he never intended to keep. She wasn't sure what to say to her friend, as it was obvious that there was trouble in paradise. She remembered being envious of their relation-ship. She remembered how much they were in love and how Black doted on her. If there was any couple that would last forever, it was them. For as long as she'd known Diamond she couldn't remember a time when she was happier than she was with Black. "But are things good between you two?" Kiki asked after a few seconds of silent thoughts.

"I mean things are okay, but not as good as I would like them to be," she admitted. If there was one thing that Diamond hated, it was to look like a failure. She would do anything in her power to avoid that.

"Aww, D, I am sorry things aren't turning out the way that you planned."

"Girl, don't be sorry, it ain't your fault." She flagged her, attempting to brush it off. "You know me though, I've got a strategy. I refuse to lose my man." She cracked a smile.

"Oh I know you always think on your feet. I'm just worried, D. I know how much you love him and how much you went through to keep him. I just hope that you are as important to him as he is to you."

"I don't doubt that, Kiki, not one bit. I just think that he has his priorities a little screwed up, but he'll get it together."

"Well, hate to cut you short, baby girl, but I have to go open the club. If you need to talk call me, okay?" she said before getting up and walking over to hug Diamond. After the two embraced, Diamond walked Kiki to the door. Just as she was leaving Black pulled up in the driveway. "Speak of the devil," she said with a big smile.

"What does that mean?" Black asked, rubbing his hands across his beard as he normally did when he was deep in thought.

"I was just chatting with the missus that's all." She turned to look at Diamond as she stood in the door. Black stared at Kiki without saying a word. Diamond stood at the door, looking on. Kiki put her sunglasses on her forehead and twisted her lips. "Don't get your boxers in a bunch, Black, I kept quiet."

He looked at her and then looked over at Diamond before turning his attention back to Kiki. "I knew you would, espe-cially if you want to keep breathing," he responded through clinched teeth.

Kiki began to laugh before giving Diamond a final wave and walking toward her car. Black nodded and made his way to the door. He kissed Diamond before she spoke.

"What was all that about?"

"Oh, she was just thanking me for pushing you to contact her." He lied, knowing if she knew the truth he'd practically have to take a lie detector test to keep their relationship together. Deep down, he felt like the biggest asshole on the planet. He wasn't prepared to lose his family and he would do whatever it took to make sure of that. In his eyes, Diamond was still the woman he fell in love with and wanted to spend the rest of his life with.

After entering the house, Black made his way upstairs without saying much to Diamond. Their relationship had gradually been changing and she couldn't figure out why. As she watched him walk up the steps without any conversation she remained in the living room shaking her head. At first, she was going to let him have his space and get through whatever it was that he needed to do, but this had been dragged out long enough. She noticed Black sitting on the edge of the bed, finishing up a phone conversation when she walked in the room.

"What's going on with us, Black?" she said in a low tone.

Black turned around and shot her a look of seriousness. "What are you talking about, Diamond?"

"You know what I mean, Black. Three weeks ago we were fine, now it's like we barely talk. I'm trying to figure out what the issue is so that I can fix it."

"Diamond, you know what I'm trying to do and what's consuming my time. I'm just tired that's all. You're thinking too much and turning nothing into something. There isn't an issue to fix, okay? Nothing is wrong."

"Black, please don't shut me out," she pleaded with a single tear dropping from her right eye. She knew Black like the back of her hand and she knew that there was something wrong. Diamond stood there, lost, trying desperately to figure out what was bothering him.

Black looked over at her and noticed her tears. He hated to see her cry, especially when he was the one causing the pain.

"Diamond, why are you crying? I just told you there wasn't anything wrong. I just have a lot on me right now that's all. I wish you would start taking my word instead of coming up with your own ideas."

Figuring that she'd never be able to get him to come clean, she shook her head and walked out of the room. She had a gut feeling that there was another woman and now she needed to devise another plan to regain his attention. Over the years she'd learned how to use what she had to get whatever it was that she wanted, and this time wasn't any different.

Confident that she was out of ear's reach, Black pressed redial on his phone. "Sorry I hung up on you but she was coming in," Black whispered into the phone while walking to close the bedroom door.

"Yeah, I figured that," the female on the other end responded. "So when can I see you? I miss you like crazy. It's killing me."

"Tomorrow for sure. I have some shit to handle early in the day but I can swing by after five if that's cool."

"Of course. At this point I will take what I can get. I know you have to split your time and I'm okay with that, as long as I get some of your time."

Black laughed. "Well I will see you tomorrow. I'm about to take a quick nap before I head back out."

"Okay, well, sleep well."

"I will," he said before ending the call.

Diamond quietly stood outside of the door, devastated. The conversation confirmed her suspicions. She wanted to burst into the room and let him know that he was caught red-handed, but she now had a burning desire to find out who the other woman was. She believed that if she figured that out she could eliminate her from the equation. She couldn't stop the tears from streaming out of her eyes, or the smoldering sensation she now felt in her heart. But, instead of making a fool out of herself or causing him to walk out, she headed back downstairs as if she'd never heard anything. Grabbing her cell phone and walking outside for some privacy, she dialed Kiki. She needed her words of wisdom to steer her in the right direction. After three rings Kiki picked up. Diamond could barely hear her over the loud music in the background.

"Hey, girl. I know you just left but do you have a minute? I could really use your advice right now," Diamond yelled into the receiver.

"Hold on," Kiki said, turning down the music in her car. "Hello?"

"Hey, Kiki, it's me, Diamond. Are you busy? I could really use your advice on something," she repeated.

"Oh hey, girl, what's up? I have a few minutes before I get to the club."

"Girl, I think Black is cheating on me again," she said after a sigh and a short pause.

"What? Why do you think that?" she asked, shocked.

"Because I confronted him right after you left about the distance between us and of course he denied it. Well then he goes upstairs and makes a phone call. I can tell by the way he was responding that he was talking to a woman."

"That doesn't mean he's cheating, D. In his line of work I'm sure that he has to talk to women."

"Yeah, but not like that!" she replied.

"Not like what?"

"He was whispering and shit. Who does that if they aren't trying to hide something?" Diamond yelled.

"I don't know, D, but I mean unless you have concrete proof I wouldn't just go accusing him of anything."

"Damn, Kiki, I *thought* you were my friend. If I didn't know any better I'd think that you were taking his side."

"Diamond, what are you talking about? I'm not taking his side. I'm just saying be rational here," Kiki responded with annoyance in her tone.

"You right, Kiki, sorry to bother you. I will talk to you later."

"Diamond," Kiki yelled to silence, as Diamond had already hung up the phone.

Diamond sat looking at the phone, shaking her head and hoping Kiki wouldn't call her back. She wasn't in the mood for any more lecturing. She was looking for a confidant and it was obvious that Kiki had changed during their time apart. She'd have to figure this one out on her own.

Chapter Sixty

Second Time Around

"Didn't I tell you I had you covered?" Romeo yelled over the loud music, which filled each corner of Club Onyx, an upscale gentleman's club in the south part of Philadelphia. "It has wall-to-wall bitches in here, man, and I'm not even talking about the stripper hoes. It's always more chicks in here than niggas, all of them ready to give up some ass." He laughed as he patted Reed on the shoulders and pushed him through the entrance of the club.

Reed immediately noticed the large stage, which had three poles and lights that lined the entire edge. On stage was a stripper who was skillfully working her way down the pole with her legs only. Reed shook his head, thinking how she had the strongest legs he'd ever seen. "Drop and Gimme 50" by Mike Jones was blasting though the sound system and the stripper known as Montana was working the stage, commanding the attention of every person, male and female, in the room. Reed was in a daze, almost frozen in the spot where his feet rested. Things had definitely changed; he certainly remembered this a lot different before getting booked.

"I see. I definitely can appreciate the abundance of pussy all up, down, and around here." Reed laughed and slapped Romeo a five. "Damn it feels good to be home." He continued to laugh, looking at the many asses jiggling and bouncing around. All he could do was shake his head in amusement. He felt like a kid in a candy store as his eyes wandered wildly and he held in drool that was slowly making its way to his lips. He was positive that any man who'd ever been in prison before could totally relate to the overwhelming feeling of adrenaline that was rushing through his veins.

"I got us a VIP section in the back," Romeo yelled, regaining Reed's attention.

The two men made their way over to the far rear corner of the club. The section was filled with plush upholstered arm-chairs and featured mini coffee tables that were adorned with white runners and large stainless-steel wine buckets. Some of the dancers walked around from hustler to hustler, grabbing a quick lap dance and a few dollars. Reed tried to hold it together as he didn't want his dick to begin bursting through his pants, bringing any extra attention, but he knew there wasn't any way he could make it through the night without it. Just the scent of the women was sending his senses wild.

"You all right, my nigga?" Romeo yelled, laughing at the faces Reed was making.

"Yeah, I'm good, just happy to be home you know. Can't wait to get up in some pussy, man, straight up." He laughed.

Romeo laughed at his friend, knowing exactly how he felt. He looked over at a dancer named Lucky as she entered the room with her stallion strut. Her caramel skin glistened in the colorful lighting, which flashed continuously from the ceiling. He was familiar with what she was capable of so he knew she was the perfect dancer to pay Reed some extra spe-cial attention for the evening. He raised his left hand in the air and waved her in their direction.

She nodded and began walking over to where the two men were seated. She bent over with her ass pointed up in the air and her long twenty-seven-inch ponytail extension draped to one side. Her pink thong panties were pulled down to the center of her ass, making it appear even plumper.

To Reed, the two round cheeks that sat inches away from his face looked as appetizing as a well done piece of porter-house with a coat of Jack Daniel's Barbeque Sauce. He was tempted to reach out and grab it but he knew that was an offense that could have him ejected from the club. Instead, he sat patiently, waiting to see what Romeo had up his sleeve.

As Reed bobbed his head to the music he noticed Romeo pointing at him from his peripheral view. A few seconds later, Lucky was bending over, slowly whispering in his ear.

"You wanna head to the private room with me?" she asked, seductively licking her lips.

Reed looked up at her and quickly replied, "No doubt," smiling from ear to ear. He stood from the chair, looking down at Lucky's ass, and began to follow her lead. Before walking out he reached behind his back and gave Romeo dap followed by a quick nod to thank him.

The two went into the back, where she was prepared to put on a show worth every penny of the five crisp one hundred dollar bills that Romeo had secretly slipped into her bra top. As he sat down he could feel the bass of the music vibrating through his body. The sexually charged track "Ride It" by Ciara appropriately boomed through the speakers.

Lucky stood in front of Reed and slowly began to gyrate her hips, swaying them from side to side, front to back, against the beat of the song. He instantly began to feel his dick throb and growing hard as a brick. The sensitivity of the head rubbing against his boxers and jeans kept him struggling to stay still in his seat. She moved closer to him and quickly turned around and moved to a seated position with both of her hands gripping the arms of the chair. The aroma of her perfume was tickling his nostrils with delight; even the scent of her hair smelled like something you'd want to eat for dessert. Lucky was a skilled dancer, not the run-of-the-mill ass shaker. She moved in ways he'd never seen or even knew were possible. He almost felt like a virgin staring at his first piece of ass. At one point, she even did a spilt over the chair handles and dipped her ass all the way down to the crotch of his pants and then up in front of his face. All he could imagine was him getting inside of her.

After twenty minutes of being tortured he thanked Lucky for the entertainment and began to head out of the room. He turned to look back at her but she had already disappeared through the door in the rear of the room. He shook his head and let out a laugh. He knew it was against the rules for the two to exchange numbers or make promises to meet at a later time. Though he was horny as hell he wasn't one to fuck up another person's cash flow, especially if he wasn't prepared to foot the bill. Shit, he had so much to do to get the streets back in order, a relationship, other than the one he thought he'd come home to, was the furthest thing from his mind.

He walked out and returned to the VIP section to find Romeo drunk as hell and grinning like a Cheshire cat. The sight was pretty comical and was just the laugh that he needed.

"So how was it?" he asked as he struggled to keep his balance.

"Torture, man." He laughed. "Naw, thanks, my dude, it was all good, just wish I could've taken her home."

"Awww come on. I know you ain't had no ass in a long time but you ain't T-Pain and you can't be falling in love with no damn stripper." He laughed.

"Love? Nigga, please, I'm just tryin'a get rid of two years worth of build up." He laughed.

"Too much information, nigga, way too much." Romeo laughed. "Let's get out of here. I'm hungry as hell. You wanna hit South Street Diner before I run you home?"

"Yeah, your drunk ass needs to sober up a bit anyway." He laughed. "Let's roll." He reached into his back pocket to grab his wallet to leave the hostess a tip. He felt a loose bill and retrieved it, not remembering putting any money into his pocket. He unfolded the crisp one hundred dollar bill and noticed a telephone number and a kiss in bright pink lipstick. Beneath the kiss was a note that read: "Call me . . . Olivia aka Lucky xoxo." He smiled, folded the bill, and put it back into his pocket. After tossing twenty dollars on the table he gave Romeo the signal to head toward the door.

The two men exited the club and walked toward Romeo's car. Before entering, Reed caught a glimpse of a black Range Rover riding by with twenty-four-inch rims and dark tinted windows. The car pulled over and the driver and two passengers emerged. The driver—a tall, thin, dark-skinned man—appeared to be in charge. You could tell by the attention that he commanded and the way that everyone followed his lead. Reed was used to being the center of attention so he found himself interested in the identity of the ringleader. Romeo looked up from flipping through his cell phone as the rumbling in his stomach was digging a hole into his back.

"Yo, what's up, man? I'm starving like Marvin over here," Romeo yelled.

"Who is this nigga over here? The tall black-ass nigga," Reed said, pointing across the street at the group of men who were now surrounded by groupies and wannabe hustlers.

"That's that nigga named Black, used to work for that nigga Kemp who got merked a couple of years back."

"Oh, yeah? I remember that shit clearly. When this nigga get all flashy and shit? I remember this nigga riding Kemp's coattail and shit," Reed said, as he remembered exactly who he was. Prior to his release, he thought the name and description that Johnny gave sounded familiar, but it wasn't until that moment when he could see his face that he realized exactly who he was. Thinking back, he'd even had a conversation or two with Black but he knew him by a different name. "Keyshawn or some shit like that," he said aloud.

"What?" Romeo asked, confused as to what the hell Reed was talking about.

"That's his real name, Keyshawn or some shit like that."

"Yo, why are you so fascinated with this nigga, man? I'm hungrier than a hostage and you over here worrying about a motherfucka's government. Don't tell me the pen got you turning sweet on me, man." Romeo laughed aloud.

"Man, fuck outta here. I'm far from sweet, nigga. I damn sure ain't fascinated either—I just got some shit to take care of that involves him, that's all," Reed replied, still focused on Black and his entourage. He took mental notes, trying to get as much information as he could without it being obvious that he had a hidden agenda. After a few more seconds of glaring he shook his head, turned to open the driver-side door, and sat down inside.

"Now can we go eat? I feel like I'm losing pounds by the second over here, nigga." Romeo laughed.

"Yeah, man." He shut the car door, turned the key in the ignition, and drove off. At that moment, he had two things on his mind—getting more information on Black and getting back on top, where he belonged. He was positive that this time around he would remain on top by any means necessary.

Chapter Sixty-one

Forbidden Fruit

Black pulled up in front of a large single home in the Mount Airy section of the city. The house was aligned with neatly kept flowerbeds and trimmed green grass. The house, which he'd visited on many different occasions, looked different for some reason this particular day. *Maybe it's my mind playing tricks on me,* he thought. Over the past year he'd spent a lot of time here—time that he should have spent at home. Nothing about it was right but he couldn't seem to pull himself away no matter how much he wanted to. Just like anything else that was forbidden, it was always the most tempting and hard to resist. Black hadn't been strong enough to walk away. In the past, he'd made some choices that he regretted, especially those that brought pain to those he loved. He never did anything to intentionally hurt Diamond, but somehow he couldn't avoid it.

So, he sat there in his car, deep in thought, wondering if he should follow his heart and drive away or follow his mind and go inside. The way he saw it, the damage was already done and one more time wouldn't make any difference; if Diamond found out her reaction would still be the same. He sat there staring at the door of the house until the door opened and a female stood in the doorway waving in his direction. He took a deep breath and released a loud sigh before getting out of the car and heading her way.

"What took you so long? I thought I was going to end up wasting this outfit," Kiki said, pulling her robe open and revealing her Frederick's of Hollywood ensemble.

Licking his lips Black admired her curves. Her thirty-six double-D breasts were spilling out of her bra and her fat pussy was forcing a camel toe into her panties. He moved in close to her and touched her lips with his and grabbed her waist with both of his strong hands. She backed into the house, pulling him inside. Black used his feet to push the door closed as the two were engrossed in a French kiss. Piece by piece she began to undress him as they made their way toward the living room. As she unzipped his pants his rock-hard dick made its way through his boxers. She didn't waste any time getting down in a squatting position and wrapping her lips around it. She used both hands to massage the shaft in different directions while using her tongue to kiss the head.

"Damn," he moaned, enjoying every stroke. His knees almost buckled at one point, as Kiki knew exactly how to make him feel good; not that Diamond didn't, but sex with Kiki always went to a level he hadn't yet experienced with Diamond. Most likely, that was because everything about it was so wrong.

Kiki continued her rendition of the greatest blowjob ever while Black fought to remain on his feet. He struggled to keep himself from an early eruption by focusing on something else but after a few minutes of fighting he pulled himself from her grips.

"What's wrong? Too much for you?" She laughed.

"Come here," he said, pulling her from her squatting position. She smiled and quickly obliged.

Standing face to face they stared at each other silently with different thoughts: Kiki thinking about the relationship she wished she had with Black; and Black thinking about the pain that this would cause Diamond. Kiki looked in his eyes and could tell what he was thinking and she didn't feel sorry for her actions. Diamond had done so much wrong to so many people she truly believed that she didn't deserve a man like Black. Black was the kind of man she needed in her life. Over a year ago when this affair began she felt that she belonged with him, but with most men, there was just something about Diamond that kept him holding on to her. Regardless of her faults and flaws Black loved her just as much today as he did when he married her. Kiki knew she didn't possess what he wanted in a wife so she was willing to settle for whatever he would give.

"Kiki, look," Black began to speak.

"Black, I understand," she began to respond but was cut off by Black quickly putting his right index finger in front of her lips.

"Don't talk, just listen. I enjoy being with you and I don't ever want you to think that I don't. Mentally, this is draining me because I love my wife and it's really no reason for me to be treating her this way. Now, I care about you and I'm not saying that I want this to stop, however, I don't want you to think that I am going to leave her because I'm not." Black paused. "I don't want to hurt either of you."

Regardless of the way things appeared he was sincere. He didn't want to hurt either of them, and though it might have seemed stupid he knew getting them back on track as friends was probably the only way he could keep this affair a secret. By keeping them close, he could keep them both at arm's reach.

"I get it, Black. I never expected you to leave her," she lied. "I'm happy with what I can get. Now, can we stop with all of the chatter and get to screwing? If I get any wetter there is going to be a puddle on the floor." She laughed.

Black laughed with her and then leaned in to kiss her. Feeling satisfied with their arrangement, his hands made their way to her wet mound. He parted her lips with his index and ring finger and slowly massaged her clit with his middle finger. She moaned as delight oozed from her skin and filled the room. Black's dick remained hard and would occasionally bump up against her stomach as he fingered her wet pussy.

"Fuck me please," she begged, eager to feel him inside of her.

Without a word Black picked her up and palmed her ass cheeks as she wrapped her legs around his waist. Using his strong leg muscles to stand firm, he guided her up and down on his dick with force. Her ass slapped up against him loudly echoing in the quiet room. "Oh, Black, shit." She moaned.

"Is it good, baby?" he asked, gaining speed.

"Yes," she yelled.

"Do you like it?" he asked.

"Yes, I like it," she screamed.

"Do you love it?"

"Yes, I love it," she answered with a moan and a sigh. She could feel her body began to shake as he hit her G-spot continuously. Her legs were tightly wrapped around his waist. He could barely move she was holding him so tightly.

"How does it feel?" he asked. It turned him on knowing that he was doing all that he could do to make her reach her sexual peak. He loved conformation and she loved giving it to him.

"Black, I'm about to cum," she yelled.

"Yeah?" he asked while forcing his dick deeper inside of her.

She wrapped her arms around his neck and stuck her tongue into his mouth, forcing a kiss. Her body bounced up and down until she erupted and her juices were running down the shaft of his dick. The warmness of it caused him to follow suit as he quickly let loose all that he'd tried to hold on to. His legs weakened and he grabbed hold of the sofa to brace himself as all of his energy left his body. She unwrapped her legs and slid off of him. Still facing him, she thought about having the moment last a little longer, but the reality of it all was that he would be leaving and going home to his wife.

"Black, I love you," she said without thinking. She'd wanted to tell him those words for months but had never mustered up the courage to say it. After she said it and he stood silent, she felt as if she'd made a mistake.

Black stood there, staring at her for a few seconds without replying. He hadn't figured out what this thing was but he couldn't hide the way he felt about her any longer. "I love you too, Kiki," he spoke softly.

A huge smile formed on her face, as that was all she needed to hear. Without speaking another word Black picked up his clothing from the floor and headed to her bathroom to clean up before heading back out. Once in the bathroom he turned on the sink and stared at himself in the mirror. "What the fuck are you doing?" he asked himself aloud. He shook his head before grabbing a washcloth and soap. After he was dressed he kissed Kiki good-bye and went on his way.

His next destination was to meet up with Tommy. Earlier that day, Tommy left him a message saying they needed to meet and it was pretty urgent. Tommy was patiently waiting for Black in front of one of their safe houses when he arrived. He quickly exited the car and greeted him with their signature handshake.

"What's good, man? Sorry I'm late. I had to take care of girlfriend number two," he joked.

"You a wild boy," Tommy said as he shook his head. "Let's step over here for a second." He nodded his head over to the left of the building.

The two walked over to the dimly lit side door where they could talk in private but still be seen by the armed gunmen who watched the doors.

"So what's the deal? What so urgent that I had to rush over here?" Black asked immediately, as he was anxious to hear what Tommy had to say.

"You remember the nigga named Reed from up west? He got locked up a couple years ago in that big-ass bust the feds did up Wynnfield."

Black shook his head, trying to picture him. "Naw, I don't remember him."

"You remember, the nigga who had the young nigga Brook who used to run with him. He over Jersey now."

"Oh yeah, I remember now, I thought that nigga name was Chance or some shit."

"It is but they call him Reed. Well he just got out of jail and word on the street is he's trying to move in on our turf."

"Where the fuck you hear that?"

"A bunch of niggas, you know I always got my ear to the streets. I don't know if it's true but I'm saying that's what I hear. I just don't want this nigga to creep up on us and we're not prepared."

Black stood there, rubbing his hands across his beard deep in thought. If the information was true they needed to come up with a plan to throw him off.

"So what do you wanna do?" Tommy asked, so anxious he could barely stand still.

"I'm thinking, calm down." Black raised his voice an octave.

"I can't calm down when a nigga is trying to wreck the shit I live off of."

"Being all hype is what these niggas want. All they need is to catch you slipping and bam! Your ass is grass. You gotta use your head, man. I know you're upset. Don't think I'm not, I just like to think logically and come up with a strategy rather than going in with my heart all angry and shit," Black replied, trying to calm Tommy down. He hoped that Tommy would use his head.

"I get it, Black, I'm just trying to see what you want me to do. I don't trust these niggas. I feel like they are planning some shit and I just don't want our shit to crumble. We've worked too hard to let a nigga walk in and take what's rightfully ours."

"Could you set up a meeting with your sources? At least that way I can hear all that they've heard."

"Yeah, I can do that. When do you wanna meet?"

"As soon as possible. If you can get them together by tomorrow night I can swing by here and then we can go from there."

"All right, cool. I will just hit you up tomorrow when I confirm everything."

"Cool," Black said, reaching out to shake Tommy's hand. Tommy entered the building while Black got into his car to drive home. He grabbed his 9 mm handgun from under the seat and placed it on his lap. In the event someone approached he would be prepared for them. Now more than ever he was going to have to look over his shoulders, at least until they were certain things were under control.

Chapter Sixty-two

A Game of Chess

Reed sat outside of a large warehouse, patiently waiting for his seven o'clock meeting. Every so often he'd glance at the time, which was brightly displayed on the car radio, before turning his attention back toward the huge grey metal door guarded by two tall, husky men. Both wore all black from head to toe including their leather gloves, Skullies, and Timberland hiking boots. The two men were engrossed in conversation but aware of their surroundings at the same time. The clock read six forty-five the last time Reed checked but he couldn't stop himself from looking again at six forty-eight. He wasn't being impatient, but more so anxious to get this over with.

The past three weeks had been all about this vendetta that Johnny had against Black. He hadn't even been able to focus on his own plans, or even enjoy his freedom. As he began to think about all the things he wanted to do once this was all over with, two men emerged from the warehouse doors. After shaking the hands of the two guards the men began to make their way over to Reed's car, which was parked on the opposite side of the street. Both of the men entered the car, one in the passenger seat and one in the back. Reed turned on the car and immediately began pulling out of the parking spot and heading down the dimly lit street.

"Any word from Johnny?" Reed asked, looking over at the man in his passenger seat.

"Yeah, the thirteenth is the day. We can get in, take care of this nigga, Black, and get the fuck outta there," Justice replied in a deep, raspy tone. Justice was the only one of the two who Reed kept in contact with. The other passenger, Dex, was there in the event that things went awry.

"So what about the girl, Diamond?" Reed questioned. From the conversations that he'd had with Johnny while behind bars, she was the main target but, somehow, the focus seemed to have shifted totally on Black.

"What about her?" Justice asked, turning toward Reed.

"I'm saying, what are we supposed to do about her? I thought she was supposed to be taken care of as well, so I'm a tad bit confused here."

"Listen, I'm just as clueless as you, dog. Johnny told me that we needed to get the money and get rid of Black, that's all."

Reed shook his head and kept quiet to avoid saying the wrong thing. This was exactly the kind of shit he didn't want to happen. Most importantly, this was exactly why he had a backup plan. There was something about the two men that didn't sit well with him. It was almost as if he could feel the knife touching his back ready to stab him as soon as he was caught slipping. He didn't plan on going out like a sucker, nor did he plan on being used as a pawn in Johnny's game of chess.

"All right, well, what time is this all supposed to take place?"

"We'll figure that out next week. What we need to take care of right now is figuring out who is taking care of what." Justice changed his tone to one of seriousness.

Reed kept his composure, knowing that his responses could be the difference between life and death. Losing his cool would only cause turmoil and he didn't trust either of them as far as he could throw them.

As Justice sat across from Reed he tried to read his movements and expressions. Johnny always told him to study people, especially those you did dirt with. You never wanted a man who could wreck your life to have one up on you. You always needed to pay attention even when everyone else didn't. Though he didn't know Reed personally, he'd sat with Johnny on many visits and he'd read a lot of letters where Reed was the topic of discussion. Though Johnny was just a teenager when he was locked away, being in prison turned him into a man quickly. It also made him more streetwise than he probably ever would have been at home.

"Okay, so what is it that I am supposed to do? Because you still haven't been clear about that, or really anything for that matter," Reed blurted after a few moments of silence.

"Your job is managing any bystanders, including the girl. We'll take care of getting the money and we'll take care of Black."

"And when will I get my cut?" Reed asked.

"We'll meet after a few days and give you what's owed to you."

Deep down Reed was feeling less comfortable by the second. He had to figure out a way to use his own man as backup. He knew something was wrong. It was just a gut feeling and most of the time his gut was right. By the way Justice spoke, it was almost as if he believed Reed was a pushover or a punk, and he was neither. Justice continued his speech as Reed sat quietly, thinking of his own strategy. After a few more minutes of driving and conversation Reed was pulling back up in front of the warehouse where he'd picked them up. The two men exited the car and Justice quickly shook Reed's hand before walking across the street toward his own car, which was parked on the corner.

Reed watched as he opened the door and got inside. He was thinking that he'd gotten himself into a situation that might not have been in his best interest. Thinking back to the day that he agreed to taking care of this for Johnny, he wasn't 100 percent sure of what made him say yes. Yeah, he wanted the money, but he didn't need it. Things were pretty much set for him financially. Was it greed? Or, was it just the excitement of it all? He asked himself these questions over and over again because he was the type of man who needed to make sense of anything that he did, even if it didn't make sense to anyone else.

As he began to drive off his cell phone rang and the name "Lucky" flashed across his screen. He'd called her a few times since the night that she'd first given him her number, but he'd been so busy the past few weeks that he hadn't gotten around to actually hooking up with her. He lifted the phone from his lap and pressed the green call button and cleared his throat before speaking.

"Hello," he said in a deep baritone.

"Is Reed available?" Her voice oozed sexiness through the receiver.

"This is Reed, who's this?" he asked, though he'd already saved her number and knew who she was before he'd even answered.

"This is Lucky, the dancer you met at the club," she reminded him.

"Oh, okay. I erased your number from my phone when you never called me back," he lied.

"I'm sorry, I was working like crazy. Trying to pay my tuition for school. It wasn't intentional at all. I definitely wanted to talk to you."

"Is that right?" he asked, smiling but maintaining a serious tone.

"Definitely, I have never given my number to a customer. First of all, it's against the rules, but besides that, you're the sexiest man I've seen in a very long time."

Reed shook his head, knowing that she'd probably spit the same game to other men on different occasions. Here she was, a stripper trying to act like an innocent schoolgirl. There was something about her that intrigued him and because of that he entertained the conversation a little longer than he normally would.

"So, what are you getting into tonight? I'm assuming that you're going to work."

"Actually, I didn't work tonight. I took a 'me day' for some much-needed relaxation," she replied, hoping that his next question would involve meeting him and hanging out for the evening.

"Relaxation, huh? So I guess that means your full of energy then?" He laughed.

"Yup, Energizer Bunny!" She let out a girlish giggle.

"Well, what are you trying to get into? You feel like hanging out?"

"Depends on what you have in mind."

"Well, I'm a man who likes to surprise. If you're not up to it, I totally understand, but if I tell you everything you won't appreciate the details as much."

"Well, how much detail could you possibly whip up on such short notice?" she asked, shaking her head. She wasn't impressed but she was eager to hear more. She got comfortable in her seat and waited for him to answer.

"You'd be surprised what a man like me could do with a little bit of time. I can make the impossible very possible. Believe me," he replied with confidence. He didn't have a clue what he wanted to do but he had to make it sound good if he wanted to keep her attention. "And if you don't know about me now, you will by the end of the night. That's for damn sure." He laughed.

"Well, we're wasting time talking. I should be getting ready for you to pick me up," she said with a huge smile on her face. She couldn't remember the last time a man had made her this anxious to see him. She couldn't wait to get off the phone to hurry upstairs to pick the flyest outfit in the closet.

"You're absolutely right. Well you get ready, text me your address, and I will see you in an hour. Is that enough time or are you one of those two-to-three-hour women?"

"Please, I am naturally beautiful. I can be ready in less than an hour and still look like I stepped off of a magazine spread. I'm the shit, boy; don't doubt me." She laughed.

"All right then, I'll see you in a bit."

"Okay, I'll be waiting."

Lucky sent her address to his phone as requested before running to the bathroom to jump in the shower. She made sure to pay extra attention to the hot spots in the event that things turned physical.

She stepped out of the tub and realized that she had used up twenty minutes in the shower. She ran down the hall to her bedroom and rummaged through her drawer to find underwear. She settled on a black lace bra and thong. Black was always sexy, especially on her size-eight curvy frame. She'd been blessed by the best with a full thirty-eight double-D cup, twenty-seven-inch waist, and forty-two-inch hips. A Coke bottle didn't have shit on this brick house. It didn't stop at the great frame either—she also had a face as beautiful as a porcelain doll. Her skin was a glowing caramel and remained blemish free. Unlike some of the other dancers at the club, Lucky could quickly transform from the stage to the classy woman you would love to carry on your arm or to meet Mama. Naturally, she was great in bed, using her dancing and stage skills to make a man lose his mind. She worked hard at perfecting her lovemaking skill to ensure that her future husband would be satisfied.

After slipping into her all-black Badgely Mischka mid-thigh-length dress, which generously accentuated her curves, and putting on her Christian Louboutin glitter daffodil pumps, she was dressed to impress without a minute to spare. As promised, Reed rang her bell at exactly one hour, and Lucky loved a man of his word. She hurried to the door but stopped just short of it to look at herself in the floor-length mirror once more to be sure that everything was still in place. Once she was satisfied with her look she opened the door with a huge smile and one hand placed on her hip.

Reed looked her up and down and rubbed the hair on his chin before speaking. "Damn, you look even better with clothes on. I didn't know that shit was even possible." He laughed while Lucky did a quick spin to give him a full 360-degree view. "I would've planned something a little more fancy if I knew you would come out with your Sunday's best on." He continued to laugh.

"This isn't hardly my Sunday's best. More like a Saturday night special, and I can change if I'm gonna be wasting a good outfit," she said, twisting her lip.

"I was just playing. Come on now, you need that outfit just to walk with me." He laughed. "But I wouldn't have you get all dressed up for nothing. I'm not that dude."

"I would hope not." She smiled, feeling a little better.

"Did you pack an overnight bag?"

"An overnight bag? Who said I was staying overnight with you?"

"I did. Trust me, after a night with me, you won't want to come home tonight. Hell you may not ever want to come home for real, for real."

"Oh, *really?*" she asked. She wasn't sure if it was confidence or arrogance; either way, it was a turn-on. Reed stood there, silent, as Lucky stared at him waiting for a response. After a few seconds she broke the silence. "Okay, give me a few minutes. I'll go pack a bag."

Reed laughed to himself as Lucky disappeared into the house to gather enough things to last a weekend. She made sure to grab sexy underwear and smell-goods. Reed was patiently waiting for her when she returned to the door with her bag in hand.

For most of the ride the two rode in silence until Lucky initiated an inevitable conversation. "So, Mr. Reed, I've never seen you around before. Where were you hiding?"

"I wasn't hiding, I was locked up," he answered honestly. "Got locked up on a drug charge but that's the past, you know. I'm home now, back on top where I need to be."

"I see. I was about to ask how you can just come home to a fly-ass car, clothes, and money to throw around like there's no tomorrow."

"Well, I have good friends."

"What about a woman? Do you have one of those?"

He laughed. "I was waiting for that one, actually. I have a wife, but when I came home she served my ass with divorce papers. Soon as I was away she jumped on the next thing smoking, shipped my daughter off to her relatives, and rolled out to live the glamorous life."

"Wow." Lucky shook her head in disbelief.

"Yeah, wow is right. That's what I said when I came home and found out. That was my welcome home gift. But it's all good. But enough about me, let's hear about you, Miss Lucky. How did you end up dancing for a living?"

"Money is the root of that evil of course. I needed money for college. I wasn't blessed with parents who could send me to school or a man who had the funds to assist so I had to get it on my own. I'll be done with school in eight months and I can say that I don't have any student loans to pay back when I graduate."

"Do you like your job?"

"Of course not, but it pays the bills," she said with attitude.

"Don't shoot me, I was just asking an honest question. I mean, there are people out there who actually like what they do. No disrespect, you do your job very well, so usually when women take the job that serious, it's because they like it."

"Well for me, anything that I decide to do I make sure I am the best at it. If I'm not going to put my best foot forward then I'm not going to do it."

"I respect that. I respect that one hundred percent," Reed responded.

"Good, 'cause I didn't wanna have to shoot you," she said before they both burst into laughter.

Soon they were pulling up in front of Reed's home and parking in the driveway. While Lucky had expected going out to a nice restaurant for dinner she wasn't surprised that he'd brought her here instead. She shook her head, thinking, *why the hell did I think anything different in the first place?* She went to exit the car and Reed stopped her.

"I'm just going to drop off your bag, grab some money, and then we'll be on our way."

"Okay," she replied, caught off guard but in a good way. She was immediately excited and anxious about what he was planning. Here she was giving up on him before he had a chance to show and prove.

Reed returned to the car a few minutes later and began the drive to their next destination. A half-hour later they arrived at a beautiful restaurant in Rittenhouse Square in downtown Philadelphia. The small, cozy restaurant was just the atmosphere that they needed to tip off a romantic evening. The night had been going well so far and both of them were looking forward to ending it with a bang, both figuratively and literally. The restaurant was sparsely filled with couples of all different ages and nationalities.

The couple was seated and immediately served a bottle of the best champagne. Lucky wasn't a huge fan of champagne but she figured she'd make an exception for the special occasion. She was very interested in finding out more about him. To her, he was mysterious and she'd always wanted that in a man. She watched his every move and listened to his every word as they went through the three courses of their meal. Though she'd enjoyed the dinner and conversation she was excited to move on to the next portion of their evening.

Soon the two were on their way back to Reed's house, both anticipating what was next. Reed was planning on giving her every bit of the energy that he'd had backed up for the past two years and Lucky, well, she was planning on receiving it.

Chapter Sixty-three

Foolin' Around

"So what did you find out?" Black asked Tommy as he sat down in the plush leather chair, which sat behind his large cherry-wood desk. Three days ago he learned of Reed, a man who was on a mission to come up in the drug game. He wasn't scared but he hated to be blind in any situation, especially one that threatened his life. He couldn't rest easy until any potential threat was eliminated.

"Nothing really. I really don't see him as a threat. He isn't really making any noise. He's trying to come up but not takeover nothing that we own," Tommy replied while sitting down in the chair that sat opposite Black.

"So you ain't found out nothing in three days? That's all you have to tell me?" Black asked, visibly annoyed.

"I asked around, man, nobody knows anything. Dude is pretty low-key, he doesn't cause too much noise." Tommy leaned forward in the chair.

"I hope you're right. I really do." Black shook his head. "You know niggas are constantly trying to move in and attack. I have a family, man. I need to be here for them and I can't watch my own back. That's what I have you for. I feel like you've been slipping lately."

"Now I'm slipping? I'm the one who brought this shit to your attention. I know this shit is stressful, man, but come on—there is no need to start throwing unnecessary jabs. I've always had your back."

"I'm just saying, you should be up on this shit. There shouldn't be any room for mistakes if you cross all your t's and dot all your i's," Black yelled.

"There won't be any mistakes, Black," Tommy responded, raising his voice. He was frustrated with Black's tone. Not once did he ever think Black would doubt his ability to handle business. Regardless of the situation, he had always come through. He wanted to just chalk it all up to stress but something inside of him wouldn't allow him to. Honestly, he felt like his time with Black was almost up and, soon, he'd have to do his own thing. "I don't understand you, man. Who was the one who saved you and your wife? Me! I have always been there to shield you from harm." Tommy was now standing as his adrenaline began to pump through his veins.

"Yo, sit down, man, you taking this shit too personal. This shit ain't about no friendships or any other shit like that. This is about my life and my family. I can't allow a nigga to move in and take what's mine. Yes, you were there in the past but back then you took your job more seriously. If I'm wrong then, okay, I'll be a man and apologize, but right now this shit is business. I need to know more about this nigga and his master plan. Now you can either help me or keep bitching, one or the other," Black said, pounding his closed fist against the desk.

Tommy stood on the opposite side of the office and stared at Black. His stare was direct and his eyes were piercing. It was almost as if he could see right through Black. So many thoughts were running through his head. He was growing angrier by the second, but he tried as hard as he could to conceal any obvious signs of it. He stood steady in the same place for a few more minutes before walking back over to the chair where he'd originally been seated, and flopped down in it.

Black shook his head as he wondered what Tommy was thinking. He was sure by the look on Tommy's face that it wasn't something positive, but it didn't scare him or ruffle his feathers in the least bit. He had to worry about himself and his family—babysitting wasn't an option.

Tommy was still quiet, trying to figure out what to say next. He didn't want this to turn into a war but he didn't want to seem like a bitch either. Though he worked for Black he wasn't a servant and wasn't going to bow down like one either.

"So what are you planning on doing?" Black asked, restarting the conversation that had sat dormant for the past five minutes.

Tommy shook his head before speaking. "I'm going to do the best that I can to find out what's going on."

"All right, well, I'll get up with you later. I need to go take care of some other shit," Black said before walking around the desk and giving Tommy dap and heading toward the door.

As he walked toward his car he noticed a black Mercedes near the corner with tinted windows. He watched the car as he got inside of his car. He refused to move and be followed if something was up. He wanted to make sure they knew he wasn't afraid or running scared. After a few minutes the car pulled out of the parking and sped off down the street and around the corner. Because of the dark tinted windows, he couldn't see who was inside. After all of the shit that he'd been through the previous year, shit like this instantly put him on edge. A few moments later, his cell phone rang, breaking the silence and startling him. Looking down at the caller ID, Diamond's name flashed across the screen.

"Hello," he said dryly.

"Where are you? I thought you were coming straight home, Black. It's been three hours since I last spoke to you."

"Diamond, I'm a grown-ass man, okay? Stop clocking me like a fucking child."

"What the fuck is your problem lately, Black? Is it that bitch you're cheating on me with?" she screamed into the phone.

"Good-bye, Diamond," Black said, attempting to end the conversation and avoid the inevitable conversation. He knew it was only a matter of time before Diamond would figure it out but he wasn't in the mood for the discussion at the moment.

"Oh so you're gonna hang up on me? That's real mature, Black. I know what you're doing and I don't deserve it. I haven't done anything but try to be the best wife I can be and this is how you repay me," she yelled as her voice began to quiver.

Black was quiet, not knowing how to respond. She was right, she didn't deserve it, and the reason that he was wrapped up in an affair didn't have anything to do with her. She had been a good wife but for a reason that he couldn't quite explain he slipped again.

"Cat got your tongue?" she asked with evident pain in her voice. She wanted to burst into tears but her pride wouldn't let her show him how this was affecting her.

"Diamond, I'm really not in the mood for this shit right now. It doesn't really matter what I say, you still won't believe me, so what's the point?" he responded.

"You know what, Black, fuck it! Have a good night!" She hung up the phone and screamed. She was furious. Deep down she'd hoped that he would respond differently and reassure her that his heart still belonged to her. Unfortunately, the conversation went left and she felt even worse than she did before she called.

Black looked at the phone and shook his head. Instead of going home, he made a U-turn and took the on-ramp to I-76 to head to Kiki's house for the evening. He pulled up in front of her house twenty minutes later and dialed her cell phone to be sure she didn't have any company before ringing the doorbell.

"Hello," she breathed into the phone.

"Did I wake you?" Black asked, noticing the harshness in her voice.

"Yeah, but it's okay. What's up?" She perked up after hearing the sound of his voice. She was always happy to hear from him.

"I'm outside. I don't feel like going home tonight. Diamond's in bitch mode."

"Okay, I'm coming down," she replied before getting out of bed. She walked downstairs and opened the door wearing only a T-shirt and a red thong. Black smiled when he saw her. It was almost as if she'd taken Diamond's place keeping a smile on his face. As she backed into the house he grabbed her around the waist and pulled her close to him. Her skin was soft as silk as his large hands caressed both of her exposed cheeks.

"I see somebody missed me." She laughed.

"I definitely missed you," he replied, feeling a relief from all the drama at home.

"How much?" she asked, backing away from him. "This much?" she asked, holding her arms apart, creating a space with her hands.

Black took off his jacket and set it down on the chair near the entrance of the living room. Gently, he pushed Kiki back so that her butt rested on the arm of the sofa. In a swift motion, he got on his knees and pulled her thong to the side, revealing her perfectly shaved pussy. His thick tongue licked her clit with just enough pressure to send her into an instant orgasm. She'd never erupted so prematurely but her feelings for Black mixed with adrenaline made it almost impossible to hold it back. She rested her legs on his shoulders and nestled his head in place. He sopped up all of her juices and French kissed her lips, making a loud smacking sound. Slipping his right index and middle finger inside of her, he continued to suck on her clit while massaging her G-spot with his fingers. She rocked her hips and used her hands to brace herself as she pressed her pussy harder into his face.

"Right there, baby, that's it," she moaned, letting him know that he was in the right spot. She leaned back and lifted her cheeks slightly to give him more room. He removed his finger from her wet tunnel and used his hands to wrap them around her thighs and pull them farther apart. Hearing her delight only fueled his fire and he used every trick in the book to give her exactly what she was yearning for. "Oh shit, Black," she screamed as she reached yet another orgasm and her body began to shake uncontrollably.

Black pulled himself away and stood up from the floor with a huge smile and a rock-hard dick trying to make its way out of his boxers and jeans. Kiki still had her eyes closed, trying to regain her composure. He laughed a little at the sight of it, which turned him on even more. He quickly loosened his belt and unzipped his pants, allowing them to drop to the floor. With her legs open wide he moved back in close to her and touched her lips with his before grabbing hold of her neck and ramming his long dick into her pussy, causing an instant release of juices from inside of her. He fit inside of her like a glove as he maneuvered his way around her insides like a well-lit racetrack. He pulled himself in and out of her slowly and made sure to push every inch of himself inside of her. She continued to moan as he remained focused on reaching his sexual peak. From the floor his cell phone began to ring but both of them ignored it. He figured that it would be Diamond and he wasn't going to let her ruin the nut that he was anticipating. He pumped harder and with each stroke Kiki moaned louder. She wrapped her arms around his neck to pull him closer and used her tongue to lick his left ear.

"Oh shit," he moaned, feeling all of his energy rushing to the head of his dick.

She continued to suck and lick on his ear as he fucked her as hard as he could. Within minutes he was releasing what felt like eight ounces of cum inside of her. The head of his dick was instantly so sensitive that he didn't want to back away. She laughed, knowing why he was still holding on to her so tight.

"What's so funny?" he asked, keeping as still as he possibly could.

"You, sir." She laughed, moving her hips and forcing him to quickly pull his semi-soft dick from her pussy.

"That's not funny at all," he replied before sitting down on the chair.

His cell phone began to ring again. He grabbed his pants from the floor to retrieve it. Looking down at the caller ID he wasn't surprised to see Diamond's name flashing across the screen.

"Is that who I think it is?" Kiki asked curiously. She could tell by the look on his face that he wasn't happy and figured that it could only be her.

"Yeah, she keeps calling back and I swear I don't feel like fighting with her."

"Well, turn the phone off then," she suggested.

"I can't turn it off. You know I get business calls at all different times of the night."

"Well, answer it then, Black. She's not going to stop calling so you might as well get it over with."

He took a deep breath before answering the phone with an obvious attitude. "What?" he yelled.

"Is that how you answer the phone for your wife?"

"Yeah, when you're getting on my nerves," he replied. "What do you want, Diamond?"

"Are you coming home?"

"No, Diamond, I will see you tomorrow. I need time alone tonight." *Click.*

Diamond looked at the phone, hoping that he didn't just hang up on her. Realizing that the call was ended tears began to drop from her eyes. She realized that she was losing him and she wasn't prepared for that.

She went upstairs and looked in on her sleeping daughter. *How can he do this to us?* The situation was turning out to be a lot harder to figure out than she'd expected. Either way, she wasn't going down without a fight. She closed the door and walked to her bedroom, where she crawled into bed and soon fell asleep clutching her cell phone in her hand, hoping that he would call.

Chapter Sixty-four

Breath of Fresh Air

"What's on your mind?" Reed asked, looking at Lucky as she lay looking up at the ceiling.

"Nothing really," she replied. "Just happy that's all." She smiled. Being with him the past few weeks was turning out to be more exciting than she'd expected. She'd never met a man like Reed who was so strong yet so caring. He always made sure to keep a smile on her face and she could appreciate that. Even in his thug state he was gentle.

Reed sat up from the bed and stared her in the eyes. He was trying to read her mind, knowing that there was more to her silence than she was letting on. She was beautiful both inside and out, unlike his estranged wife, Raquel. He saw something in her that he hadn't seen with any other woman. She wasn't afraid to let him in, almost as if she'd never had her heart broken. Most women would resist, especially with a man like him, who could have almost any woman that he wanted. Lucky was almost the perfect woman and he didn't plan on letting her go anytime soon.

"So what are you so happy about?" Reed finally asked, breaking the brief silence.

"Everything. My life is going great now and it's all because of you." She smiled.

"I'm just glad that you're allowing me into your heart. For real. I know things with us are moving fast, but when something feels this good, I don't see a reason to slow down," he said sincerely. "I mean what I say, so I hope that you don't think I'm gassing you up."

She laughed. "No, I don't believe that. You haven't lied to me. Well, I haven't caught you in a lie, so I can only trust that what you are saying is the truth."

"Caught me?" He laughed. "I'm as real as they come, you can believe that."

He leaned in to kiss her, satisfied with the conversation and where the relationship was going. She met his lips without the slightest bit of resistance. The two locked lips for a full two minutes before his cell phone began blaring, rudely interrupting their moment of passion. Reed ignored the annoying ring tone and slowly forced his tongue through her lips and began massaging her tongue. The phone continued to ring, forcing them to break their connection.

"You might as well just see who it is. Doesn't look like they are planning to stop calling," Lucky said, hoping that answering the call would give them whatever it was they were calling for.

Without looking at the caller ID, Reed answered the phone with an attitude. "Hello," he yelled.

"Is this Reed?" A deep male voice boomed through the receiver.

Reed pulled the phone away from his ear to glance at the caller ID, which conveniently read, "Unknown." Returning the phone to his ear he added extra bass to voice before responding, "Who wants to know?" His face was balled in a knot.

"Damn, it's been that long?" The caller laughed. "Well, this is Brook and, believe me, I'm not calling to reminisce. I need to find out what's holding up your signature on those divorce papers." He finished with an even tone.

"Are you fucking kidding me?" He removed the phone from his ear once more and looked at it with anger written all across his face. "I can't believe that you have the fucking balls to call me with this bullshit!" He shook his head. "I didn't even have beef with you about her 'cause I don't give a fuck about that trifling-ass bitch. That shit doesn't have anything to do with you so you need to stay in your fucking place!" he yelled, furious, as spit flew from the sides of his mouth. He stood up from the bed and began pacing the floor.

"My place? Yeah, all right, muthafucker. This ain't back when you got booked. You don't run shit, nigga. I'm tryin'a let you breathe but if you want to make shit difficult I can make it so she'll be filing for a death certificate instead."

Reed was screaming and pointing at the phone. He was practically foaming at the mouth by this point. "Try it then, muthafucker. You know where to find me." He ended the call and slammed the phone down on the bed.

Lucky sat up, almost afraid to speak.

"This nigga wants to fuck with me? I will kill that muthafucker and that bitch," he yelled, pacing. He walked back over to the bed and grabbed his cell phone and immediately dialed Romeo on the phone.

"Yo, I need some niggas to take care of this muthafucker, Brook. This nigga had the fucking balls to call my phone threatening me and shit."

"What?" Romeo yelled back.

"Yo, I'm so fucking pissed right now, I want this nigga buried. You hear me, man? Six fucking feet under," he yelled.

"All right, calm down. Where you at?"

"I'm home."

"I'll be over there in a half-hour. Just sit tight, all right? I don't wanna talk too much on this phone," Romeo replied as he grabbed his jeans from the back of his chair and began to put them on.

"All right," Reed replied before putting the phone back down.

Lucky was still sitting up at the top of the bed, quiet as a mouse. She was afraid to speak for fear that she'd say the wrong thing and piss him off even more.

Reed turned to look at her and immediately noticed the fear in her eyes. He walked over to her and sat down beside her on the bed. "I'm sorry about that, okay, baby? I don't want you to worry about that or me. Everything's gonna be okay." He softly rubbed her right thigh.

"I don't want anything to happen to you," she spoke softly, holding back the tears that were forming in the wells of her eyes.

"Nothing is going to happen to me. Come here," he said, pulling her close to him and wrapping his arms around her.

She breathed in his scent and felt secure in his arms. Things were going too good for everything to be snatched away. She was just getting used to life with him.

"Do you have somewhere that I can take you while I go take care of this? I don't feel comfortable leaving you here alone right now."

"Yes, you can take me to my aunt's house."

"Okay, get dressed and I'll be downstairs," he said before kissing her and getting up from the bed. He grabbed a pair of jeans from his closet and quickly threw them on with a pair of sneakers and headed downstairs to wait for Romeo.

Romeo arrived twenty minutes later along with Mike, one of their closest friends. They drove in silence until Lucky was dropped off and safely inside. Reed returned to the car stone-faced.

"So what do you want to do?" Romeo asked. He already felt like Brook would be a problem once Reed was home. He expected things to happen exactly the way that they were. After Reed was arrested, a lot in the street changed. Jealousy and egos quickly turned things upside down, forcing a separation in the crew. Brook was always known as a hothead but his attitude was always controllable with Reed around. Now that he could stand on his own financially and he had his trusty followers, he felt like he was untouchable. Dealing with Reed's wife was a slap in the face but Reed wasn't too concerned with that. The fact that she'd be out of his life was a good thing and it would give him great pleasure to watch her suffer when Brook was taken care of.

"You know what needs to be done. I can't have a fucking loose cannon running around while I'm trying to get shit back in order. I need this nigga to be officially wiped out. All the way off the fucking map! Whatever you have to do to handle that, handle it," he spoke, pounding his fist into his hand.

"I'll take care of it for sure. I was waiting for this day anyway. I already knew this nigga would start some shit. I was just waiting for your word," Romeo said while heading on to I-95.

"I can't believe that he really called you with that bullshit, man. This nigga really grew King Kong balls," Mike blurted as he shook his head. "I kinda wish I would've rocked that nigga to sleep years ago. Punk-ass muthafucker."

"It's all good though. I was having a nice night and shit wit' my baby and this bitch-ass nigga calls me." Reed spoke with a smile when thinking about Lucky.

"Sounds like shit's working out with her." Romeo laughed. "Your ass is really falling in love wit' a stripper." He chuckled.

"I guess I am." Reed smiled.

The car was now pulling up in front of one of their drop spots. All three men exited the car in sync and began to walk toward the entrance of the building. Without speaking, each of them nodded and gave dap to the two men guarding the door. Walking inside they headed toward the back of the building to the meeting room. Reed and Romeo entered the building alone while Mike remained outside in front of the bolted door. Reed and Romeo sat down at opposite sides of the table.

"You know I never thought shit would turn out the way that is has, man. It's crazy how your life can be turned upside down in the blink of an eye," Reed said, shaking his head.

"That's real shit, man, but you don't have to worry about this shit. I'm going to make sure that I take care of it." Romeo spoke with seriousness written across his face. He loved Reed like they were brothers and sisters and he vowed to always have his back. Most people looked at Romeo as if he was a servant of Black's, but the reality of the situation was that he'd never be his subordinate; he'd always been a partner. He was comfortable with his position and there wasn't a time that he felt the need to defend it.

"I should've listened to you, man, and never married that bitch. She is the true definition of hell on wheels." He laughed to mask his anger. He felt like screaming he was so pissed.

"Can't say I know how you feel but I know how it feels to want to kill a nigga," he responded.

"Well, I'm gonna jet so I can clear my mind. I just need to mentally put some shit in prospective." He stood from the table and walked around to the side of the table where Romeo was sitting. Romeo stood up from his seat to give him dap before tapping on the back of the door to let them know that they were about to come out.

"I'll get up with you in a few hours, all right?"

"Cool," Reed responded before walking out of the door and into the hallway.

Quietly, Reed headed out of the building and to the car, making sure to check his surroundings before pulling out of the parking spot. His mind was racing a mile a minute, thinking about everything that had led up to this very moment. Naturally, he regretted a lot of his decisions. He couldn't totally regret his decision to deal with Raquel since he'd gained a beautiful daughter he loved with all of his heart. He wasn't about to let her ruin his life and he'd do whatever he had to do to make it known.

Chapter Sixty-five

A Dose of Reality

Diamond sat on her sofa, looking out of the window. Her heart was filled with so much worry as the family she'd worked so hard to maintain was slowly slipping away. For the first time in her life she didn't know what to do. She felt like she was completely alone. Though she and Kiki were talking again, things still weren't the same. She figured that the time that they spent away from each other was the reason for the obvious distance. She thought back to some of her other friendships and as much as Kiki had bashed Mica's actions when it pertained to her, she was becoming a mirror image of her. She didn't even feel comfortable talking to Kiki, or any of her other friends for that matter, about her relationship with Black. She never wanted anyone to see it as an opportunity to slide in between, especially when things weren't at their best. The only person she'd been able to talk to was her mother, Pam.

Since meeting her a couple of years back, the two had actually become really good friends. Pam was now the shoulder that she could cry on and the person she could confide in when she need someone to talk to.

As she continued to stare off in thought she saw Pam's white BMW pull up in front of her house. She got up from the sofa to open the door and let her in. As soon as she saw Pam's face she began to cry. Without saying a word Pam reached out and hugged Diamond. After closing the door the two women walked into the living room where Diamond returned to her seat on the sofa.

"Can I get you anything to drink?" Diamond asked, trying to look past her mental state and play the perfect hostess.

"No, I'm fine, baby. When you called I came right over. What's going on? You know I hate to see you cry, makes me want to cry and I absolutely hate messing up my makeup." She laughed, trying to lighten up Diamond's mood.

"I'm just so stressed right now. Nothing is going right for me. I thought that Black and me had a relationship that was unbreakable but now I'm realizing that what we have isn't much different than any other relationship," Diamond replied.

"What's the problem though? I mean is there anything that you can think of that may have caused a distance?"

"No. I mean a month ago we were fine then all of a sudden things changed. I know in my heart that he's cheating on me. I stood outside the room and heard him talking to a woman on the phone. Then he hasn't been coming home every night."

"So you know for a fact that he was talking to a woman?" Pam asked, trying to figure out where things went wrong.

"I mean no, I don't have concrete proof. I wasn't on the line but I can tell by the way that he was talking that he wasn't talking to a man. I just don't know what it is that I did to make him feel like he needs to cheat. It makes me think about the time that he cheated with Trice. You know I had to intentionally get pregnant to keep him?" Diamond blurted by mistake. Besides Kiki, she'd never told anyone that she purposely got pregnant.

"So in other words you trapped him? Did you ever think that he might have found out?"

"No, I don't think that he's found out and even if he did I don't think that would be a reason to cheat." She paused.

"Well, men don't always have the best reasons to cheat but they don't think with their brains at those times either."

"I just need to figure out what's going on because right now I'm so lost. At least if I knew what he was upset about I could work on fixing it but right now he won't tell me anything."

"Sometimes men will shut you out, but if you truly want to be with him and keep your family together you can't give up. There were times that I thought my family was being torn apart. You know I've been on both sides of the fence, the mistress and the wife, so I know how it feels. I never expected my relationship with your father to be all peaches and cream because of the way that it started. Nothing that starts out that way goes on without a few bumps in the road. It all takes work whether good or bad," Pam said, rubbing Diamond's arm, trying to console her.

"So do you think I should approach her?"

"No, I think that you should approach him," Pam quickly replied.

"I've tried to confront him but all he does is push me away."

"Well, you have to keep trying. I know I didn't raise you, Diamond, but I didn't birth any children who are wimps. I have fighter genes and I know that you have it in you."

"You're right, I am a fighter. I'm not going to give up on my family just yet. I worked too hard to have it to just let someone come in and steal it all away. Thanks for being here for me. I truly appreciate all that you've done for me."

"You don't have to thank me, you're my daughter and I love you too much to just allow you to cry without a shoulder to lean on. You can always call me when you need me," Pam said with a smile.

Diamond extended her arms to hug Pam. The conversation with Pam was just the push that she needed. Pam stayed for a few more moments before leaving. Diamond immediately picked up her phone and called Black.

After the phone rang a few times, Black answered, immediately letting out a sigh before speaking. "Yeah."

"Are you coming home today? I really want to sit down and talk. I don't like the way that we are right now. Black, it's killing me."

"Yeah, I will be home later, Diamond," he replied in a lighter tone.

"Okay, I will see you then."

"All right," he said before ending the call.

She smiled, as he didn't give her the usual brush-off response that she was expecting. His reaction made her feel as if things weren't done and there was a strong chance for reconciliation. She headed upstairs to her room and took a shower before patiently waiting for Black to arrive. She'd fallen asleep waiting for the time to pass and was awakened by a tap on her foot and a whisper of her name.

"Hey, I fell asleep waiting," she said as she rubbed her eyes to get a clear view of him. He was standing at the bottom of the bed.

"Did you still want to talk?" he asked before sitting down on the edge of the bed.

"I'm just trying to figure out what's going on with us. I feel like we're falling apart, Black, and I don't want to lose you," she said as she scooted to the edge of the bed to sit next to him. "Is it something that I did? I mean if so, let me know and I will fix it."

"It's not you, Diamond. I just have a lot of shit on my mind. I'm trying to straighten out all of this shit that's going on in the street and keep you happy at the same time. It's hard, Diamond, because you have a tendency to over think things and push when it isn't necessary."

"I only act that way because I care, Black. I love you too much to lose you."

"You just gotta give me a little breathing room, Diamond. I don't need you on my back all the time like my mother. I need a wife. I need the wife I fell in love with."

"So what are you asking me to do, Black?"

"I don't know, Diamond. I'm just tired of the bickering and arguing for nothing. It used to be fun coming home, now I almost dread it." He spoke sharply.

Diamond sat silent for a few minutes, thinking about what he'd just said to her. She never wanted him to dread coming home and it was never her intention to make him unhappy. She wanted to ask him about the phone call but she was afraid he'd cut the conversation short. "Black, I understand how you feel completely and I'm sorry, okay? I just want things to go back to the way that they were," she pleaded as she placed her hand on top of his right hand, which was resting on his thigh. "Please, Black, I need you," she said softly as she grabbed his chin to turn his face toward her. Without allowing him to respond she kissed him.

He grabbed her around her waist and pushed her back onto the bed. All of his emotions rushed to the surface of his skin as if they'd never left. There wasn't any doubt that he loved her, but as a man he struggled with his thirst for other women.

He lay on top of her and caressed every inch of her skin, which was revealed. Her skin was soft as cotton and carried the scent of Victoria's Secret Love Spell. Soon, his kisses moved from her lips to her neck and from her neck to her breasts, which were protruding from the center of her black lace bra. After treating them with equal attention he moved down to her belly button, slowly sticking his tongue in and out of the center. Every so often she'd let out a moan as she fought to hold in the evidence of ecstasy. With one hand he pulled her panties down as she lifted up a little to allow an easy removal. With her pussy fully exposed he didn't waste any time burying his face in between her legs and sticking his thick tongue into her moist opening. With all the energy that she had bottled up just the slightest tickle nearly caused an orgasm.

"Oh shit," she moaned as he slid the middle and index fingers of his right hand inside of her. She began to sway her hips as he pulled his fingers in and out while using his tongue to focus on her clit.

Black remained silent as his dick was growing more and more by the second. With her moans providing the soundtrack and the sensitivity of his stiff dick, he was fighting to hold in his own eruption. He was positioned in front of the bed on his knees with her legs folding over his shoulders. After a few more minutes of fondling her G-spot he felt the rush of her juices on his fingertips run down to the palm of his hand. Her body shook uncontrollably as her legs briefly tightened around his head, firmly holding him in place. Her release was his cue and he simultaneously unzipped his pants, slid his boxers down, and thrust his long dick deep inside of her. Her body immediately tensed up as he placed both of his hands under the arch in her back on both sides. Getting a rhythm going he picked up speed, filling her walls completely. He looked down at her as she stared at him, biting her lower lip. The small beads of sweat that formed on different areas of her face illuminated her beauty. She was just as stunning if not more so as the day he'd met her. She could tell by the look on his face that even in this moment of passion he was deep in thought.

"I love you," Black blurted as he continued to move in and out of her. It was at that moment that he felt sorry for all that he'd done and made a decision to do his best to make things right between them. He continued to force himself as far as he could go before leaning down to kiss her. She stuck her tongue through his lips and began to massage his tongue. Knowing that he was nearing his peak she wrapped her arms around his back and held him tightly. After a few more thrusts every ounce of his cum was flowing out of him, inside of her, and then out on the bed, forming a small puddle underneath her. The two lay connected without saying a word for the next five minutes before he pulled himself from inside of her, gasping for air as the sensitivity of his semi-hard dick almost erupted again.

He got up and gathered his clothing from the floor while she still lay on the edge of the bed not sure of what to say. Knowing their lovemaking session wouldn't solve all of their problems, it was a start. She could hear the shower come on in the bathroom and immediately she assumed that he would be right back on his way out. Surprisingly, after he was done showering and she followed him, he was asleep on his side of the bed when she reentered the room. Quietly, she climbed into bed, moved near him, and wrapped her arm around him.

Chapter Sixty-six

Mr. Perfect?

"What do you mean you're quitting?" Lucky's best friend and confidant Alisha asked, concerned that she was making too drastic of a decision.

"I mean exactly what I just said, I'm quitting and I'm moving in with him," Lucky said as she folded articles of clothing and stuffed them into suitcases and bags that were lying open on her bed.

"Why are you rushing, Lucky? You just met him. How could you possibly know that much about him to be comfortable enough with quitting your job and moving in with him? What about your tuition? I mean is he going to pay that? I would hate to see you mess up school. You've come too far for that."

"I know how far I've come, Alisha, and obviously I wouldn't let anyone mess up my education. You of all people know how important that is to me. He knows how important that is to me, Lish. I know that you don't know him at all but give him a chance. He's a good man. I feel it in my heart and usually my heart doesn't steer me wrong, even when my body and mind try to. Come on, you've always been supportive and I still need you. Don't back out on me now regardless of how foolish the decision may seem. The reality of the situation is, if things don't go as planned, which I'm not going to even think that way, but if for some reason that happens, I'm going to still need you to have my back."

Alisha sat there shaking her head, feeling like her friend was making the biggest mistake of her life, but she knew that once her mind was made up it was almost impossible to change it. She also knew to continue to try could ultimately cause damage to their friendship, so she realized that sitting back and being supportive was the best thing that she could do.

"So when do I meet Mr. Perfect?" she said, breaking the ice. "I mean I need to at least meet the man before he steals my best friend away." She laughed, trying to make light of the situation, although deep down she wasn't happy at all.

She was still worried. She remembered the last time Lucky had made a swift decision like this with a man that almost ended her life. His name was Jeff, Jeff Pearson, and she was head over heels in love with him quickly. The two met after a basketball game and kept constant contact but immediately what Lucky saw as love Alisha saw as insecurity, and slowly but surely his true colors shined through. It wasn't long before Lucky became pregnant with his child, which Alisha swore was all in his plan to begin with. Leave it up to Jeff the condom broke by accident, but Alisha truly believed that he poked holes inside of the condoms to ensure that she'd bear his seed.

To make matters even worse, he became abusive, and there were many nights the two were sitting in the ER nursing a busted lip or a bruised body part. Regardless, Alisha was there by her side and she always tried to encourage her and support her decisions, despite how foolish they were. Ultimately, the beatings led to a miscarriage, and even though that was the saddest that she'd ever seen her friend, she realized it was probably the best thing that could have happened to her. The loss of the child was just the thing to force Jeff to walk away, and though it devastated Lucky and would take months to get her back on track, she had been the best that she'd ever seen her since then. So she wasn't selfish at all; she was worried that she would end up seeing a replay of 2007: the year of hell, as she called it.

After a few moments of hesitation Lucky responded to her question. She let out a sigh and finally replied, "Soon enough, you will meet him. And why do you have to call him Mr. Perfect? Don't start, Alisha, okay?" She pointed toward her friend with a bit of sassiness.

"Okay, okay. It was just a joke, Lucky. I get it, you're in love, and I'm happy for you, don't get me wrong. But I love you and you know I don't want to see you hurt. You know I'd kill a nigga over you." She laughed but was dead serious.

"I know and I appreciate it, but you can't breastfeed a baby forever. At some point you gotta snatch the titty away!" She grabbed her breast and made a popping sound.

Alisha mugged her and knocked her onto the bed and both women burst into laughter. There wasn't anything that could break these two apart and there had been plenty of people, things, and situations that had tried.

"Can we stop all this packing and shit for a minute? I need a drink, girl, a real one!" Alisha blurted, getting up from the bed.

Lucky rose from the bed and threw the handful of clothing she had in her hand down onto the suitcase. "Sure, I can use a drink myself."

"Okay, then, let's go."

The two gathered their things and headed toward the door to go to the corner bar to get a few drinks. Alisha exited before Lucky, who was locking the door when a white Porsche pulled up in front of the door. Both women looked at each other, unsure of who the driver was. The windows were darkened so they couldn't see who was inside until the car's ignition turned off and the driver exited. A woman dressed expensively from head to toe headed straight for Lucky and Alisha. Lucky looked the woman up and down as she removed her sunglasses before speaking.

"I'm looking for a woman named Lucky," Raquel spoke in an assertive tone.

"I'm Lucky, how can I help you?" Lucky stepped forward, making sure the woman knew she wasn't intimidated.

"How are you doing?" She extended her hand to shake Lucky's hand. "My name is Raquel. I'm married to Chance, the guy you're currently seeing."

Lucky looked confused.

"Oh, Reed, sorry. I guess that's the name you know him by. Chancellor Reed is his full name, in case you didn't know. Well, I'm his wife. I'm sure he told you he was married but I'm not here to rain on your parade not one bit. I'm here because I've moved on totally and the problem is he's contesting the divorce. I figured, if he had a new relationship and all what's the point of holding on to the past you know? I'm just here to see if you can talk to him to speed things up, because I have a man who's waiting to marry me and I can't do that until he signs those papers you know." She giggled.

Lucky stood there stone-faced. She was certain this woman had other motives for finding out where she lived and approaching her besides some fucking divorce papers. "Okay, so excuse me if I'm confused here. You really came all the way to my home to tell me that Reed, excuse me, I mean *Chancellor Reed* won't sign divorce papers?"

"That's exactly what I'm telling you, hun. Listen, I don't want him and I certainly don't want to impede your relationship with him. Honestly, I'm ecstatic that he was able to come home and find somebody to love because I was done with him a long time ago. I just want him off of my back that's all. I came here on some woman-to-woman shit hoping you could see where I was coming from."

"Actually I don't see where you're coming from . . . uhhh what's your name again?"

"Raquel. Raquel Reed."

"Okay, well, Mrs. Raquel Reed. I will make sure that I pass the message along to him but that's all that I can promise you."

"And that's all that I ask. I appreciate your assistance, Lucky. You ladies have a good evening." She placed her shades back on and walked back to her car.

Both Lucky and Alisha stood there staring at her car until she pulled off and turned the corner. Alisha immediately looked at Lucky and spoke. "Really? Was she fucking serious?"

"The sad part is I think she was," Lucky responded, shaking her head.

"Well what are you gonna do?"

"I don't know, do you think I should call him? I mean I don't even know how I should feel about it. She wasn't really disrespectful."

"Oh the bitch was disrespectful by coming to your house, that shit was out of fucking line, Lucky. Seriously. I tried to fall back but you know me, the ghetto was about to come out. I wanted to punch that bitch in her face!" Alisha yelled.

"You know I'm not immediately hostile, Lish."

"Well, you should be, that shit was crazy. I would be calling his ass right now snapping the fuck out. I mean really, is this what you have to look forward to? Ex-wives—I mean *wives*—showing up at your door and shit," Alisha said, pacing back and forth. "Shit if I could use a drink before I *really* need one now."

"Well, let's go get a drink so you can calm down then because I'm calm. I'm not going to let her ruin my evening. I will discuss it with him later." Her cell phone began to ring and caught both of them off guard. It was Reed. "It's him," she said, looking at Alisha to figure out what to do.

"Well, answer it," Alisha said, motioning with her hands.

For some reason she was nervous about picking up the phone. It was almost as if her fairy tale had somehow been tarnished. She knew about his wife but she was hoping that everything he'd told her from the beginning was true. She wanted so much to believe in him. The last thing that she wanted was for Alisha to see their relationship at odds, especially after she'd made him seem like Prince Charming. So she wasn't sure if it was a good time to have the inevitable conversation regarding Raquel, but she didn't want to ignore his call either.

"Hello," she said in an unruffled tone.

"Hey, babe. Did Raquel just stop by your house?"

"Yes. Actually she just left, how did you know?" she asked.

"I'm so sorry about that, babe. She called my phone laughing about how she'd spoken to you. Are you still home?"

"I'm outside of my house on my way to get a drink with my friend Alisha."

"Are you still moving some of your things over tonight?"

"Yes," she replied without hesitation.

"Okay, well call me when you're done with your friend and I will come by to pick you up. I have some things to talk to you about."

"Okay, I will call you when I'm done," she said before ending the call.

"Well what did he say?" Alisha asked anxiously.

"He asked me if she had come by here and we would talk later on when I'm done with you."

"That's it?" Alisha asked with one hand on her hip.

"What do you mean *that's it?* Girl, you are a mess! Let's go to the bar please and pick this conversation up another day," Lucky said, nudging Alisha on her shoulder off of the steps.

"I'll drop it for now." She laughed.

The two women headed to the bar and had their drinks without incident. They managed to have girl talk without Reed or Raquel being the topic of conversation. The two hung out at the bar for two hours before walking back to Lucky's house and parting ways. Lucky obediently called Reed to let him know that she was home, and soon he would be arriving to pick her up.

She was packed and ready when he rang the bell. She opened the door with a smile as he stood looking as delicious as well-done steak.

"Is this all you're bringing?" he asked, looking down at the small suitcase she had with her.

"For now." She smiled. "You look yummy." She leaned in to kiss him. "What, you have a date or something?"

"As a matter of fact I do. I have a date with your backside. I'm gonna hit it all night long." He laughed.

"Is that right?"

"Oh yeah," he said, tapping her from behind as she walked toward the car.

She quietly got inside and waited for him to get in. She wasn't about to be the one to bring up Raquel; she was waiting for him to say what it was he needed to say about it. The whole situation was pretty awkward for Lucky. She'd never dealt with a man who was married, and even though he was in the process of a divorce, legally, he was still married.

Reed closed the trunk and climbed into the car and rubbed the back of her hand. Inside, he was dreading having the "Raquel conversation." He was angry and frustrated but he didn't want her to think that things were out of his control. He'd quickly fallen for Lucky and he wasn't about to let his past ruin his future. He'd been honest with Lucky about his relationship with her and he hated the fact that she was attempting to put doubt in her mind.

"So what did Raquel say to you?"

"She said that she served you with divorce papers and you have yet to sign them. I mean I thought you wanted a divorce, Reed?"

"It's much more complicated than that. Trust me, I don't want anything more than to be divorced from her, believe me. I have been honest with you about my situation with her from day one. I have not lied to you. The reason that I haven't signed the papers is because she's trying to get half of everything that I own and I refuse to let that scandalous woman do that to me. She's taken so much from me and she's still trying to take like a fucking leech. You know she hasn't done shit for my daughter. She doesn't even call her, it's like she doesn't even exist. All she wants is money."

Lucky sat attentive, taking in everything that he said. She wanted to make sure that she didn't miss anything, to avoid the deer-in-headlights look that she displayed when Raquel approached her earlier that day.

"I want you to trust me. I would never ask you to quit your job and leave your comfort zone if I was on some bullshit. I'm through with her. I'm just trying to protect what's mine, you feel me?" He grabbed hold of her hand and looked her in the eye.

She felt a sigh of relief. Hearing him say that he was finished with her was the confirmation that she needed. Her fairy tale was still a fairy tale and he was still Mr. Perfect.

"Do you still trust me?"

Without any hesitation she replied, "Yes, I still trust you. It's gonna take a lot more than that to get rid of me."

"Well, I'm glad to hear that, 'cause I was worried for a second when you came out with one bag. I know you have way more shit than that."

"I wanted to scare you a little bit." She laughed.

He laughed with her and turned on the ignition. Both of them felt much more relaxed then they had before. Reed was even more determined to deal with his situation with Raquel as quickly as possible before she ruined his life any more than she already had.

After reaching his house he reluctantly told Lucky that he had to make a run once he received a phone call on his cell phone that he took in the other room.

"I promise, I'll be back before you know it." Reed spoke before kissing her on the forehead.

"I guess I need to get used to it if I'm going to be living here, right?" She smiled.

"Sure, you're right," he replied, smiling from ear to ear. With that he kissed her on the forehead once more before heading out of the house and jumping into his car.

Soon, she heard the loud boom of his car radio and his car speeding down the street.

Chapter Sixty-seven

Open Season

Click, Click . . . Even in her sleep, the sound was all too familiar. It was a sound that almost ruined her life. The sound that altered the path that her life would take and every twist and turn that would follow. Because she knew what followed the sound, she was afraid to open her eyes.

She lay there in bed, still hoping that the noise was only part of a horrible dream. Instead she opened her eyes to face the barrel of a 9 mm handgun.

"Don't scream, don't speak, or I'll blow your muthafucking brains out, bitch!" The deep tone boomed through the black ski mask that accompanied the all-black attire the stranger wore.

Tears instantly began to fall from Diamond's eyes. She kept her weeping silent as he slowly pulled her from the bed and dragged her down the long hall that led to the stairs. She wondered where the hell Black was as flashbacks of the day she murdered Kemp came to mind. She could clearly see his lifeless body falling to the floor as if it had just happened yesterday. She tried to focus and obey his commands as they headed down the stairs, but she needed to know if Black was okay.

"Where is my husband?" she asked in a low tone.

Without a response, he used the butt of the gun to hit her in the back of the head. The hard steel instantly sent her tumbling down the stairs. She hit almost every step before reaching the bottom, where she cried in agony. She couldn't move but she could hear his footsteps nearing the spot where she was lying.

"Learn how to follow directions! You'd think a fine bitch like you would have the brains for this, especially a bitch who likes to murder niggas." He laughed.

How the hell did he know that? she thought as she continued to lie in pain on the cold cherry-wood floor. She knew that he would have to know her personally to know what she'd done. She wished that she could rip off the mask that he wore to find out who he was, but out of fear she tried to relax.

"Get the fuck up!" he yelled.

She struggled to get up from the floor but every part of her body ached from the fall. After realizing that she might not be able to stand alone, he grabbed her by the arm tightly and pulled her up. They headed toward the dining room where Black was seated at the head of the table, tied up. There was duct tape across his mouth and blood running down both sides of his face.

"Oh my God, baby, are you okay?" She tried to run over to him but the guy who had been leading her into the room wrapped his arm around her neck and pulled her back to the other end of the table. He pushed her down into the chair as she rubbed her neck. It was at that point she realized that they really meant business. Not that she didn't believe it when they pulled her out of bed, but deep down she hoped that it was all a dream. She knew now that it wasn't and she was wide awake and in pain all over. She said a silent prayer for them to make it out of this alive. Black was sitting there with blood all over his face and shirt. They had really done a number on him. She wanted to just get it over with and give them whatever it was that they wanted so that she could get back to her life.

"What did you do to him?" she asked as he forced her into the chair that was near where she was standing. The man hit her on the back of the head again. It was still throbbing in pain from the hit she'd received a few minutes back.

"Yo, I'm going to kill this bitch in a minute. She won't shut the fuck up!" he yelled to his partner as he began pacing back and forth behind her.

"Calm down," yelled the taller, leaner guy who stood near Black.

Black sat there, looking at her, shaking his head. She figured he was most likely trying to tell her to obey their commands but she couldn't. She couldn't just sit there not knowing what the hell it was they wanted from her. If she was going to die she was at least going to know why. She'd never been one to go down without a fight and she wasn't about to start now. Her mind was all over the place. She was looking around the room to see if there was any way that she could get them out of there.

"Please tell me what you want," she cried. They all began laughing as if she'd told a hilarious joke. She didn't see what the hell was so funny.

"Look, bitch, common sense would tell you we ain't drop in to say hi. We know that you stashed up some money when you left the game and we're here to collect."

"We don't have a lot of money. Most of it is tied up in real estate."

"She just doesn't get it, I see," the taller one yelled before punching her on the right side of her face.

She felt like he'd broken her jaw instantly. Blood was now running out of her mouth.

"Now we're going to try this shit again. We know you have that money. Y'all living in this big-ass house, driving these fly-ass cars, jewels and shit. Bitch, I wasn't born yesterday. We want five hundred thousand dollars by Friday."

"Friday? You can't be serious, there's no way I can get that to you by Friday."

"Does it look like we're laughing?" The armed guy behind her bent down and yelled into her ear, "Hell, those cars you drive, you might want get rid of those, that's a start."

"And what if I can't come up with it?" she asked.

"You really wanna see how serious I am?" Without flinching, the man who was standing near Black raised his gun and shot Black in the head at point-blank range. Blood and brain matter covered the ivory-colored walls. Black's body slumped over and blood poured from the gaping wound in his head.

Diamond screamed so loud it echoed throughout the house and probably throughout the neighborhood. She pulled away from the grips of her captor, who didn't try to hold on to her.

He was shocked himself and currently yelling at the gunman for shooting Black. "What the fuck are you doing?" He stormed over toward the gunman, who raised the gun in his direction.

"Yo, back the fuck up, nigga, and control this bitch before I shoot her ass too."

Diamond was kneeling next to Black's lifeless body and cradling his face in her hands, which were both covered with blood.

"Get that fucking gun out of my face." The two men were now standing face to face as Diamond wept below them. The gunman backed down, then proceeded to pick Diamond up from the floor himself and pushed her across the room.

She slammed into the wall, causing a loud thump. She immediately bounced off of the wall and fell to the floor. Her body was racked with pain and sorrow. After all that she'd done and all that she'd been through she never imagined that things would turn out this way. Though she'd done a lot of wrong to a lot of people she always hoped that the good that she'd done would somehow outweigh the bad. As she lay there with her face buried in the hardwood floor, tears seeped into the cracks. She was shaking uncontrollably as visions of Black's brain being splattered across the room played in her mind.

The other man was now standing near Diamond and looking across the room at the gunman who was visibly annoyed. He was frustrated, as the evening's events weren't going as planned and the gunman appeared to have plans of his own. Not only was he part of a robbery; he was now a part of murder.

"Can we wrap this shit up?" he yelled, directing his speech at the gunman.

"Certainly, get her ass up off the ground." He pointed at Diamond.

The taller masked man picked Diamond up off the ground and moved her over to the chair. She closed her eyes to avoid seeing Black. The gunman made his way over to the end of the table where she was seated and stood in front of her. He wanted to make sure that she was clear on what they needed and when then they needed it.

"Now, what is it that we need and when do we need it?" he asked as he bent down in front of her and grabbed her chin, forcing her to look him in the eye.

"Five hundred thousand dollars by Friday."

"Good girl," he said, patting her on the top of her head with the tip of his gun. "Now just in case you're thinking about doing something stupid, we have some insurance. Your little girl—"

Diamond jumped out of her chair to attack him and was immediately knocked back down by the gun-toting masked man.

"Don't do it. If you ever want to see her again you'll calm the fuck down."

Diamond sat in the chair, sobbing. She'd just lost her husband and now faced losing her only child as well. It was all too much to handle and she didn't care about living without them.

"Your little girl will be returned safely once we get our money."

"How will I find you?"

"You won't. We'll find you, and if you have all of the money, we will return your daughter as promised."

"And what if I can't get the money?" she asked honestly, as she didn't know where or how she was going to get $500,000 on such short notice.

"Well, then you can kiss your little girl good-bye. I'd hate to be a child killer so I know you're going to do everything in your power to get the money to us."

"Can I just see her? Please, I just want to make sure that she's okay. Where did you take her?"

"She's safe, don't worry about that. I'd like to think I'm a man of my word and I'd also like to think that you're a woman of yours. So as long as those statements are true then neither of us has anything to worry about."

Diamond continued to plead with him to allow her to see Dior. Without Black, she was the most important thing in the world. Her mind was spinning and the physical pain that she'd felt before was now masked by adrenaline. She knew that she had to do whatever it took. Even if she had to rob, steal, or commit another murder she would if it meant she would get her daughter back in her arms. Her survival instincts kicked in and suddenly her tears dried up and tremors ceased. Without even the slightest tremble in her voice she spoke, "Okay, so what am I supposed to tell the cops about his body?"

The masked men looked at her, then looked at each other before the leader of the pack spoke. "Tell them exactly what happened, three niggas broke in your house, shot him, whipped your ass, and kidnapped your daughter for ransom."

"And then what? If I tell them she's been taken for ransom they'll be on me like flies to shit. I'll never be able to get the money together with them on my back."

"You're a smart girl, Diamond, you got away with murder. I'm sure you can figure this shit out. This should be as easy as taking candy from a baby."

Diamond stood there deep in thought. He was right—she'd gotten away with murder before and if she made it through this shit alive she was damn sure going to try to get away with it again. There was no way that she was going to let them breathe after what they'd put her through. She kept a stone face as the other two men headed toward the door and the leader of the group looked her in the eye and gave her a smirk before extending his hand to shake hers. She looked down at his hand as if it were diseased, but she knew that she needed to play along to avoid pissing him off.

"Pleasure doing business with you," he said while firmly gripping her hand. He pulled her close enough to whisper in her ear. "Just remember what I said and you'll be fine." He released her hand and followed the other two men out of the door.

As soon as the door shut she slid down to the floor and began to sob once more. She stared at Black and began to apologize to him. She blamed herself for everything, thinking that this was all somehow tied to Kemp's murder. *Again,* she thought, *it's all coming back to bite me in the ass.* The pain from all of the punches that she'd sustained was now coming back with a vengeance. Her body was stiffening as she attempted to get up from the floor to crawl over to the phone to call 911. She dreaded speaking to the police about the night's events because she would have to twist the truth in an attempt to save her daughter's life. She took a deep breath before dialing; within a few seconds the female operator's voice came through the receiver.

"Nine-one-one, what's your emergency?"

"I need an ambulance and the police, my husband's been shot. I've been beaten and my daughter's been kidnapped. Please send help, please hurry." She dropped the phone to the floor. In the distance she could hear the operator through the receiver.

"Ma'am, are you there? Ma'am, if you're there please pick up the phone."

Diamond sat with her back against the wall with tears streaming down her face as she waited for the police and ambulance to arrive. As her husband lay dead less than four feet away from her, she watched the clock ticking on the wall, knowing that every minute counted. Every minute that passed was a minute wasted, and by the looks of things, she didn't have any minutes to spare.

The police were the first to arrive and the ambulance arrived moments later. Black was pronounced dead at the scene and Diamond refused medical treatment each time it was offered.

"Ma'am, you really need medical treatment. Your jaw could possibly be broken and you could have internal bleeding from some of the blows that you sustained," the male technician pleaded with Diamond, but his case was sadly falling on deaf ears.

"What part of no don't you understand? I already told you that I'm not going to the hospital. My child is missing and I need to do everything that I can to find her. Sitting up in a hospital just won't do," she yelled. "Now could you please hurry up and wrap up these cuts because I really need to get out and look for my child."

Black's body had since been taken out of the house by the medical examiner and different sections of the house were now taped off with yellow police tape. It almost resembled something that you'd only see on TV. There was a large pool of blood on the floor under where Black had slumped off the chair and there were remnants of his brain matter splattered all over the walls and other surfaces. Her home was filled with detectives and other crime scene personnel.

Outside, there was a huge crowd forming as the tenants of the high-class cul-de-sac weren't used to such a large police presence, and they most definitely weren't used to home invasions and children being taken for ransom. The news vans from channels three, six, ten, seventeen, and twenty-nine were parked outside of their house as well. The spectacle was all too much for Diamond as she was becoming more frustrated by the second, but she continued to try to hold it together to evade any suspicion.

"How long is this going to take? I really need to make some calls."

"I'll be done in a few minutes, please just bear with me," the technician said as he shook his head and mumbled under his breath. He was a father so he knew that, put in her position, he'd probably feel the same way, but he also knew that there was a proper way to handle every situation and it was his opinion that she was going about things totally wrong.

Diamond, on the other hand, believed that she was doing what was right and that there wasn't any other way to handle a situation like this one.

"Okay, all done. Now, make sure you come in to the hospital tomorrow to get these two stitched up. If not, you'll risk infection and the scars will take a lot longer to heal."

"Okay, got it, now are you done?" she asked with sarcasm. Immediately she got up from the chair, grabbed her purse, and headed toward the door.

"You can't leave, Mrs. Black. You have to be around in case the kidnappers call," the lead detective spoke, catching Diamond heading out of the door.

"Last time I checked I wasn't a child, you weren't my mother, and I wasn't under arrest. So unless you plan on shooting or arresting me, I'm leaving. I have to find my child."

"No, you're not under arrest, yet, but you can be for obstruction of justice. We still need to go over the rest of the details of the events that led you here, and we also need to talk to you about any enemies your husband might have had, or anything that may be useful in our search for your daughter as well as your husband's killer. I know it's tough and I can't imagine what you're going through, but your husband would want you to do this right. I'm sure he wouldn't want it any other way," the female detective spoke, attempting to place her hand on Diamond's shoulder.

Diamond quickly snatched her arm away from her. "First off, you don't know shit about my husband and you damn sure don't know shit about me, so you can't begin to tell me what he would've wanted. Now again, if I'm not under arrest I really have to go." Diamond looked the detective up and down, waiting for her response.

"Well, if you want to do this the hard way so be it. Officers, arrest her please for obstruction of justice." She flagged the two uniformed officers in their direction.

"What? No, you can't do that," Diamond yelled, causing a scene.

The spectators outside of the house looked on in confusion.

"Cuff her," the detective instructed.

"Please, you can't do this," Diamond screamed, trying to pull away from the officer's grip.

"You have the right to remain silent. Anything you say can be held against you in a court of law. You have the right to an attorney. If you cannot afford an attorney, one will be provided to you free of charge. Do you understand these rights as they have been read to you?" The female detective read her Miranda rights clearly and distinctively.

"Please, my daughter will die if you do this. Please don't arrest me." Diamond began to cry as her temper had just written her a check that her ass couldn't cash.

"Do you understand these rights as they have been read to you?" she repeated.

"Yes, I understand, but please don't take me to jail. I need to be home to find my baby." She pleaded as tears were pouring from her eyes.

The female detective stood looking at her, wanting to stop her from being taken away, but knowing that she had a duty to find out who was guilty of the bloodshed that had taken place that evening. She watched Diamond sob as the officers escorted her out of the house, placed her in the back of the car, and shut the door. She had no intention of keeping her in prison more than she needed to; however, if she refused to cooperate she wouldn't have a choice. The detective looked over at her partner, who stood behind her just as confused as she was.

Shaking his head he spoke, "There's definitely more to this than meets the eye."

"Oh, I'm sure of that."

Both of them reentered the house to wrap up before heading down to the station.

Diamond rode in the back of the police car with many thoughts running through her mind. She silently prayed that things would work out for her. The sooner that she could be released from their custody, the better. *How did things get so out of control?* she thought. Just a few hours earlier she was looking forward to getting her relationship with Black back on track. Now as she rode in the back of the police cruiser it was evident that nothing in her life would be the same or even resemble anything from the past. The man she thought she would spend the rest of her life with had been stripped away. It was almost as if her heart had been ripped out of her chest and stomped into a million little pieces. Realizing that crying wouldn't save her daughter, she knew what she had to do. After her last tear fell, she gently placed her head on the back of the seat and closed her eyes.

Chapter Sixty-eight

The Ties That Bind

"You waited up for me?" Reed asked, entering the bedroom and noticing Lucky sitting up at the head of the bed watching an episode of *CSI: Miami*.

"Of course I did. I wanted to make sure that my man made it in safely." She smiled.

"Well, I need you to wait up just a little bit more. I want to jump in the shower. I've been out running the streets all day." He smiled while leaning on the bed to kiss her.

"Yeah, that would be a good idea. You definitely smell like you've been *outside* all day." She laughed.

He playfully pushed her shoulder, making her fall onto the bed. "It's cool, a nigga knows when he stinks." He laughed while heading to the bathroom. Once inside the bathroom he quickly removed his clothes and placed them inside of the trash bag and tied the bag in a knot before tucking it under the bathroom sink. After turning on the shower he looked at himself in the mirror.

"What have I gotten myself into?" he said while shaking his head. Things hadn't gone as planned and now he wasn't sure what move he should make next. He tried to keep the situation a secret from Romeo but after Justice put a gun to his chest he realized that Brook might not be his only enemy.

He got in the shower and stood under the hot water, hoping to rinse away all of his sins and any remnant of blood that may have been left behind. After leaving the shower and going back into the bedroom he kept as quiet as possible, noticing Lucky sound asleep. Instead of waking her and creating dialogue that he wasn't ready for, he climbed into bed, avoiding any physical contact that might disturb her peaceful sleep. With one hand behind his head and the other across his chest, he stared at the ceiling, replaying Justice calmly pulling the trigger and killing Black. Though he'd witnessed many murders, he'd never witnessed one that, in his heart, he believed was unjust. He couldn't for the life of him figure out why Black needed to die or why the hell their daughter needed to be taken. So many decisions appeared to have been made without thinking about what effect it could have had on his life. It was almost as if all of his plans for getting his own life straightened out had taken a back seat to what Johnny wanted. The more he thought about it the more he wished that he'd never agreed to get involved in the first place. He had to figure out a way out of it before it damaged his life and any plan that he had for himself. Realizing how exhausted he truly was, he allowed his body to relax, and soon he was drifting off to sleep.

The following morning he woke up to the smell of bacon and, after looking over to his right at the empty space that was occupied by Lucky the night before, he smiled. He loved a woman who catered to her man. He immediately thought about Raquel and how she used to do things to satisfy him until she got the ring on her finger and things quickly changed. She was more interested in designer clothes and handbags than making him happy, and eventually he began to feel the same way. He'd been raised to honor and respect his wife, and he tried his best to be the man his mother would have wanted him to be. He was enjoying his time with Lucky, but naturally he wondered if he was taking things too fast. He hadn't even gotten his divorce and the last thing that he wanted to do was hurt Lucky. Raquel was unpredictable so he had to make sure to be prepared for anything that she threw his way.

He got out of bed, and after brushing his teeth he joined her in the kitchen, where she had a plate ready with a tall glass of orange juice on the side. Looking even more delicious then the feast that she had prepared, Lucky stood naked with only an apron covering her curvy frame. He'd have to resist the temptation to jump her bones and make it through breakfast.

He leaned on the frame of the kitchen doorway, looking her up and down while licking his lips.

"I thought I was gonna have to come drag you out of bed." She laughed, walking over to him and kissing him on the lips. "Come on and see what I made for you," she said, grabbing him by the arm and dragging him over to the island where the meal awaited him.

"This looks good, baby. I can't believe that you did all of this for me." He smiled.

"I don't know why not, you know you're my boo." She laughed.

"Well are you going to join me? I only see one plate here," he said, sitting down on the high stool.

"No, I'm not a big breakfast eater. Besides, I'd rather stand here and admire you enjoying all of my hard work." She walked around to the opposite side of the island and leaned her elbows on the countertop.

"Well, then it's probably best that you stay on that side of the counter or I won't be dining on this food for damn sure." He laughed.

"Why, is my outfit that irresistible?" she asked, standing straight up and turning in a circle to give him a full view of the lack of clothing she was wearing.

"You knew exactly what you were doing when you put that shit on, but it's cool. I'm going to eat this good food here, and then I'm gonna eat that good pussy, so I hope you're prepared for it 'cause I'm gonna get busy, you hear me?" He laughed as he bowed his head to say a silent prayer before grabbing his fork and practically swallowing the food without chewing.

Lucky stood on the opposite side of the island, laughing so hard that tears were quickly forming in her eyes. "Don't choke. I'm not CPR certified." She continued to chuckle.

"Oh, I can eat very well. I'm definitely not going to choke, so you don't have to even worry about that." He smiled before taking a bite of his bacon.

"Oh, I know you can *eat*." She smiled, getting a slight chill just thinking about the things that he could do with his lips and tongue. He was certainly blessed by the best in the lovemaking department.

It took Reed all of five minutes to demolish his food, and after going over to the sink to rinse his mouth of excess food, he turned around, ready to pay extra special attention to his woman. When he turned to face her she was already sitting on top of the island counter, naked, with her legs crossed and the apron hanging from her finger. His dick stiffened immediately at the sight of her.

"Wow," he said, grabbing the crotch of his boxer briefs to adjust his bulge.

Lucky looked down at his boxers and licked her lips before looking him in the eye and biting her bottom lip. She uncrossed her legs to reveal her cleanly shaven pussy, giving him a full view of the treat that he was about to receive. Without speaking another word Reed walked over to her and got in position in front of her pussy. Sticking out his tongue he gently teased her clit, flicking it up and down and then winding it in slow circles. She used her left hand to lean back and her right hand to palm the back of his head. Every so often he'd let out an "Ummmm," savoring the taste of her juices.

Her body was experiencing chills all over as he reached spots with his tongue that no one before him had ever been able to reach. He grabbed both of her ass cheeks to pull her body closer to the edge and allowing him to stick his tongue deeper inside of her moist walls. He was feasting on her pussy like it was his last meal on death row.

"Right there, you're about to make me cum all over you," she whispered. Grabbing his head tighter she moved her hips in a circle and pushed her pussy harder into his face, feeling the early signs of an arising orgasm. It was as if she were running a race and seeing the finish line at arm's length. Just as her body began to shake he slowed down his pace and placed her clit in between his lips and sucked it as if he was French kissing it. She screamed as pure pleasure ran through her veins. She was shaking so much that her movements mimicked a seizure. He pulled himself away, wiped the excess of juices from his face, and quickly revealed his dick before stroking it. She smiled once she was able to open her eyes and focus on him. His dick was the largest that she'd ever seen it and she couldn't wait to fill every inch of it deep inside of her.

"What you know about this?" he asked, referring to his stiff eleven-inch dick. He continued to stroke its length to maintain the hard appearance. He was well aware of her bedroom skills but a little taunting always went a long way. "Bend that ass over so I can get in it," he directed.

Without hesitation she got down off of the counter and turned her ass to him before bending over and arching her back as much as she could. He walked up behind her and pushed her right leg up so that her knee rested on top of the stool. With his left hand he massaged the head of his dick in between the lips of her pussy to feel the wetness before plunging all eleven inches inside of her. A loud moan escaped her lips as her tight pussy gripped his dick. With both hands he grabbed hold of her breasts and with each thrust he'd squeeze them lightly. With her back still arched she pushed back on him as hard as she could to make sure that the head of his dick connected with her G-spot each time he was all the way inside of her.

"Yeah, that's it, tell me how good it feels," he instructed.

"It's more than good, it's great. The best I've ever had," she moaned, stroking his ego.

The sound of her voice intertwined with the sound of his body slapping up against her ass created a melodious atmosphere. He moved in and out of her with ease, making sure to use just enough force to cause just the right amount of friction. He continued the rhythm until she could feel the throbbing of his dick, alerting her of his pending eruption. Soon he held on tight and released every drop of his cum inside of her, which was followed by a loud moan and intermittent tremble. Slowly separating himself from her warm insides, he laughed unexpectedly.

"What's so funny?" Lucky asked, turning around with a look of confusion on his face.

"Just thinking about how good that shit was and the fact that I actually have Raquel to thank for it." He continued to giggle.

"Raquel?" she asked, placing one hand on her hip.

"Yes, because if she wasn't such a bitch I would've never met you." He smiled.

"Oh." She smiled, allowing her hand to ease off of her hip.

"You got me. I'm not going nowhere, all right?" he said before moving close enough to her to kiss her. "All right?"

"All right." She smiled.

"I gotta run out this morning. Romeo is picking me up so you can use my car if you need to go anywhere."

"Okay," she replied.

She watched him disappear into the hallway and soon heard his footsteps going up the stairs. She shook her head and continued to smile, thinking about how happy he made her. She hadn't smiled this much in a very long time and it truly felt good. She was glad that this time she listened to her heart, and after the great morning she planned to make it official and go gather some more of her things to surprise him when he made it back home.

Chapter Sixty-nine

Choices

"You really should have allowed them to take you to the hospital. Those men really did a number on you," the female detective spoke, entering the interrogation room where Diamond had impatiently sat for eight hours.

"Is this even legal, keeping me here? I mean how many times do I have to go over the story? While my daughter is out there somewhere you're asking me the same questions over and over again," she yelled. She was more than frustrated.

"Listen, if you would have cooperated from the beginning you would have never been here in the first place. If it were me, I'd be doing everything that I could to get my daughter back."

"Sitting here is not going to get her back. I don't have a fucking clue who those men were and I sure as hell won't figure it out locked in this damn room."

"Okay, so let's go over this again and this time I might think about letting you leave."

"I was woken up out of my sleep and beaten. I've told you this. I was taken downstairs where my husband was tied up and beaten. The men made requests for money and I told them that I didn't have any. They murdered my husband right in front of my face." She paused. "Then they told me that they had my daughter and I would only get her back if I came up with five hundred thousand dollars by the end of the week. I didn't think that it was possible then but the likelihood has been cut down dramatically since you've kept me in here, wasting time when I could be trying to gather up the money. The story isn't going to change because that's what happened.

I don't understand why you keep asking me over and over again." She stopped and looked at both of the detectives who were sitting on opposite sides of the table.

"So what happened with your first husband? He was murdered too, correct?" the female detective chimed in after a few seconds of silence.

"What does that have to do with anything?"

"Same thing, an intruder right?"

"I wasn't there so I wouldn't know," she yelled.

"What I'm trying to figure out here is how you have such horrible luck that both of your husbands would meet the same fate. Especially when you claim that you didn't have anything to do with it."

"You can't really think I would have my husband murdered. Really, if that were the case would I let them beat me like this? Do you see my face? I look a fucking wreck!"

"I mean I've seen it before. I've seen people get shot or even shoot themselves to cover up a murder. So it's not that uncommon or impossible," she replied, adjusting her position in her chair and leaning forward on the table.

"It's not impossible for a person like me to end up with two dead husbands either. Do you see where I live? There are envious people all over. I loved my husband with all my heart and every time I close my eyes I see his brain being splattered all across the room. There is no way that I would ever order something like that. I love him too much." She said as a tear slowly rolled down her left cheek. She quickly wiped it from her face.

"Listen, I'm really sorry that this has happened to you. I am trying to do everything I can to find your daughter. I want you to believe that, okay? I know she doesn't belong to me but I am a mother and every missing child is just my priority," she said, placing her hand on top of Diamond's hands, which were folded in front of her.

"Please let me go so I can find my daughter. She's all that I have left," she said sincerely while looking the detective in the eye. She realized that being angry hadn't worked so it was time to show her that she wasn't as hard as she appeared.

"I'm going to let you go, but we can't allow you to go out there looking for your daughter alone. After seeing what they did to your husband I don't doubt that they will kill you and your daughter. These people mean business, you have to know that."

"Yes, I know that. I also know that I can't have the police following me around. They'll never give her back. I need to do what they asked of me and provide them with the money. I don't know how I am going to get it but I will figure it out. I just need you to let me go."

"We are experienced with this kind of thing, Diamond, you just have to give us a chance. We've seen a lot of situations turn back real fast when people didn't allow us to do our job. We can set things up so that they will never even know that we're there. We don't have to follow you but we just need to be in the vicinity in case things go bad. We can conceal a wire on you so that we can hear everything that is being said, and we can give you a word to use to signal us if you run into trouble."

"A wire? Hell no. They will probably pat me down and if they find a wire they will kill me for sure. I can't risk that. I need to do it alone."

"If you want your daughter back you will do it our way, Diamond. I understand what you are going through. I know that you feel the urge to protect your daughter but you don't want to be the reason that she winds up dead, do you?" she asked in a concerned tone. She was hoping that her speech would get through to Diamond. She didn't have any evidence to hold her any longer and she couldn't force her to wear a wire, but she knew that it was for the best.

Diamond sat thinking about what the detective said and she was absolutely right, she didn't want to be the reason that her daughter ended up dead. She hoped that once the truth came out, she wasn't the reason that Black was dead, because she wasn't sure that she could live with that guilt. She sat quiet for a few moments, pondering the question that the detective had just asked. She wanted to make sure whatever she said was right.

"Okay, but you have to give me some space. I can't have you on my back."

"We can do that but, again, we need to place a wire on you when you meet them. We can't charge them if we don't have any evidence."

"I understand, now can I go home please?"

"Yes, my partner here will walk you out and here is my card. It has both my office and cell on it. Call me the moment you hear from them, okay?" she said, passing Diamond her business card.

Diamond took the card and placed it inside of her back pocket. She stood up and shook the detective's hand before following her partner out of the room and down the hall toward the elevators. She nodded as the detective waved at her. She understood that they had a job to do but she had one to do as well. Smelling the fresh air she immediately retrieved her cell phone from her purse and dialed the one person she knew would be there for her through thick and thin: Tommy.

"Diamond, what the fuck happened? That shit is all over the news. Where are you?" he yelled through the receiver.

"I'm just leaving the police station. They took me down for questioning. I really need your help, Tommy. Could you come pick me up please? I'm at the Roundhouse."

"All right. I'll be there in fifteen minutes," he replied.

"Okay, see you when you get here," she said before hanging up. She put on her sunglasses and took a seat on the steps to wait for Tommy to arrive. She watched her surroundings, making sure that there wasn't anyone watching her. Her cell phone began to ring, startling her. Looking at the caller ID, it was her mother, Pam.

"Diamond, baby, are you okay? What's going on?" she yelled immediately.

"Mom, I'm okay. I'm just leaving the police station and I'd rather not talk about it out here, so I promise I will call you as soon as I get in a better area."

"Okay, promise me you'll call. I've been worried sick about you. Your father is losing his mind," she yelled.

"Okay, I promise. I will call you back."

"Okay, I love you baby," she replied before ending the call.

Diamond ended the call and placed the phone back inside her purse. She sat patiently waiting for Tommy to arrive, and as promised he was pulling up in front of the building fifteen minutes after they'd hung up. He immediately got out of the car and walked toward her. She removed her sunglasses to allow him to see the damage to her face. Without saying a word he wrapped his arms around her and hugged her. Tears began to fall from her eyes and soak into his shirt.

He held her tightly and whispered in her ear. "I got you now; everything will be okay."

She wanted to believe him, and from previous attempts on her life, he'd been there to save her. Though he'd never spoken the actual words she knew that he loved her, and, deep down, she loved him too.

"Come on, let's get out of here," he said, releasing her from his grip, and he began to guide her toward his car. After closing her door behind her, he walked around to the driver's side and got in. He looked over at her beautiful face, which was covered with cuts and bruises. Her lip was swollen and her hair, which was normally perfectly styled, was matted in spots where blood from her wounds had seeped out and dried up. She continued to cry as she began to try to explain the events that took place.

"They shot him right in front of me, Tommy. I will never get that vision out of my head. They took my baby girl, Tommy." She turned to him with devastation written all across her face.

"What do they want? Was there anything that stood out to you to maybe see who they were?" he asked while merging on to I-76 West.

"They want five hundred thousand dollars by Friday."

"All right, that's not a big deal. I can handle that. But why did the cops keep you so long? Did they think that you had something to do with it?"

"Because I wouldn't stay at the house for questioning. I was focused on figuring out how to get my hands on the money I needed to get my daughter. But when I got there of course she brings up the shit about Kemp, saying that I must be either guilty or really unlucky to have two of my husbands end up murdered."

"Well, they don't have no proof of that, that's why they let you go. That's just formalities and shit, but I think I should take you home so you can get cleaned up and try to get some sleep. Let me deal with getting the money that you need."

"I can't do that, Tommy. I'm afraid that they will think I don't care, like I'm not trying to do all that I can do to get her back."

"Do you think they are watching you? Did they say that?"

"I don't know. They didn't say that but it's very possible, Tommy. After the shit that I went through with Money, hell, anything's possible. You know it's hard to trust anybody. I've been through this shit before," she said, shaking her head. She still couldn't figure out how she'd ended up in this situation. For the past couple of years she'd made it her priority to walk as straight of a line as possible. She wanted to be there for her daughter and not risk this, but Black had other plans, which could have caused him his life.

"So what do you want to do, Diamond? I really think you should try to lie down. I know your body has to be in pain."

"Not in as much pain as I will be in if they hurt my daughter. I don't need to rest, Tommy, but I will go home just to make some calls and change. But I need you to keep in touch with me throughout the day to update me on what's going on. I will do the same."

"Okay, I'll take that," he replied, knowing how stubborn Diamond truly was.

For the remainder of the ride they didn't speak, both of them thinking about the things that needed to be done. Diamond trusted Tommy with her life, but after pulling up in front of her house she instantly felt a rush of emotions. She knew once inside she'd have to look at the bloodstained walls and floors and the spot where Black's body drained of life. She wasn't looking forward to it but she knew that she couldn't avoid it forever. She took a deep breath, hugged Tommy, and exited the car. Tommy watched her enter the house before pulling out of the parking spot.

Chapter Seventy

Sudden Impact

"You wild as hell, Romeo. Straight fool, nigga, you need to be down The Laff House doing stand-up." Reed laughed at Romeo's joke.

"I'm dead serious though, these wretched hoes are so thirsty, and they'll do anything to get wit' a nigga." He continued, "This is real-life shit, no games."

Reed continued to laugh. Laughing and joking with his small group of friends was just what he needed to clear his mind from the events of the past evening. He was hoping that they would update him on his nemesis, Brook, but he was actually glad that the conversation was starting out on a much lighter note.

"I'm surprised we got you out today since you're all in love and shit. Damn, you ain't even run through a few chicks first."

Reed shook his head. "Well I'm sorry I couldn't meet your standards but I'm good." He paused when his cell phone began to ring. "Speak of the devil, here's my baby right here." He smiled before pressing accept. "Hey I was just thinking about you," he spoke, showing almost every tooth in his mouth.

"Hello, who am I speaking with?" a professional male voice responded.

Reed looked at the cell phone to verify that it was Lucky's number and then put the receiver back to his ear. "Who is this? You called me," Reed replied.

"Sir, this is the Philadelphia Police. We found your telephone number as one of the last numbers dialed on this cell phone. Can we ask how you know Olivia Brandon?"

"Olivia is my girl. What is this about, Officer?"

"And what is your name, sir?" the officer asked.

"Reed, Chancellor Reed. Now what is this about?"

"She was involved in a shooting, sir, and she was taken to Temple University Hospital. We weren't able to reach any of her family members so we began to call names of her call list."

"What do you mean? She was shot?" he screamed. He was now on his feet with fear written all across his face.

"Yes, sir, she was shot while driving. You should go to the hospital as soon as you can. An officer will meet you there to ask you a few questions."

Reed let the phone drop to the floor, immediately causing the battery and cover to pop off and fly in different directions.

"What happened?" Romeo asked, walking over to where Reed was standing frozen.

"I gotta get to Temple. She was shot in my car. I swear if this muthafucker Brook is behind this shit I will murder his whole fucking family," he yelled, and bent down to pick up the pieces of his phone.

Romeo quickly grabbed his keys and followed Reed as he stormed out of the door and began making his way to Romeo's car. Romeo got in the car and quickly started the ignition, trying to get him to the hospital as fast as he could. He didn't even know what to say but he knew that he needed to find out what the hell happened. He hoped that Brook wasn't truly behind it because somehow Reed would most likely blame it on him for not taking care of things faster. He decided to keep quiet until Reed sparked a conversation.

He dropped Reed off in front of the emergency room and took his car around the corner to park. After going to the ER, he wasn't allowed in to see Lucky, so he stood patiently in the waiting room until Reed returned. Reed nodded into the direction of the door and Romeo followed.

"She's in a fuckin' coma, Romeo. Those muthafuckers shot into my car ten times, man. Ten fucking times! I know that nigga Brook is behind this shit! Probably thought it was me driving the car, *fuck!*" he screamed. "This shit is all my fault, man, all my fucking fault." He shook his head.

"Damn, man, I'm sorry. Is she going to be okay?"

"She critical right now, man, so I don't know. I left the nurses my number. Let's get outta here. I need some air," he said before walking out of the waiting room doors.

Romeo quickly followed him toward the street. As long as Romeo had known Reed he could only remember seeing him this distraught after the death of his mother. He'd actually said good-bye to his mother ten years earlier in the very same hospital. Reed's mother, Jane, had a husband who abused her on a daily basis. For most of Reed's life he'd have to sit and hear her, or watch her try to cover up bruises with makeup. Once Reed reached his teenage years he would hit the gym faithfully, vowing to get big and strong enough to take on his father's strength. When Reed was eighteen he moved out of his mother's house, and that decision would be one he regretted to this day, because his father, in a fit of rage, had murdered his mother and then turned the gun on himself. He could remember, as if it were yesterday, when Reed spoke of how he wished he could bring his father back to life just for the satisfaction of killing him. He hadn't even attended his father's funeral. It almost frightened Romeo to see Reed so upset because of past experiences.

After entering the car, Reed sat quiet for a few seconds before breaking the silence. Looking over to his left at Romeo he spoke in a low tone, "Do you have that .45 on you?"

Romeo turned to look at Reed, knowing exactly what he planned to do. Deep down he tried to quickly figure out what he could say to change his mind. "Yeah, I have it."

"You know where he lives at right?" he asked.

"Yeah, I know the spot but—" He was immediately cut off by Reed.

"I need you to take me there right now. I don't need you to try to talk me out of it either. If you don't want to be involved you can drive me there and sit in the car but I'm going to kill this muthafucker. Not tomorrow, a week from now, but today," he said with a serious tone and facial expression.

Romeo had never been one to back out on a friend, especially not one who had always been there for him. He understood Reed's anger and hurt but he didn't want him to end up back in prison or, even worse, dead. So instead of talking him out of it, he made a suggestion. "I'm not going to try to talk you out of anything, but I'm not sure it would be a good idea for us to go there alone, especially not with one gun. Let's ride by and pick up some backup and a few guns."

Reed looked at Romeo and, as angry as he was, Romeo was being more than logical. "Okay, let's do that," he replied.

Romeo exhaled, feeling a lot better about his response, and began the drive to gather up the things they needed to execute the man who, in such a short time, had caused so much havoc.

"Hey, baby, I'm going to head out with the girls. I need to do some shopping," Raquel said as she walked over to where Brook was sitting in the living room with Tone, one of his best friends.

"You always shopping. Ain't shit new, just text me periodically so I know you're okay. I haven't gotten word back yet about that nigga Reed's condition."

"Okay, I will," she said before walking toward the front door. She blew Brook a kiss before opening and closing the door.

Almost instantly there was a loud boom, followed by shattering glass, and Raquel's body was now lying on the floor inside the foyer with a huge hole in her chest. Both Brook and Tone jumped up and reached into their waistbands to retrieve their guns. Raquel lay on the floor, gasping for air before choking up blood and grabbing at her chest.

Within seconds, Reed entered the house, stepping through the broken glass door, holding a Ruger semi-automatic assault rifle in his hands, shooting directly into the living room where Tone and Brook hid behind the sofa for cover. Romeo followed with two other men, George and K-Mack, accompanied by their own heavy artillery. As if his entire body was covered with bulletproof materials, Reed continued shooting without thinking about being shot. Romeo followed closely behind.

George and K-Mack made their way around to the side of the chair where Tone was cowering and both men pumped bullets into his body, killing him. Feathers from the inside of the sofa were flying in the air as if it were snowing inside of the large living room. Brook would every so often reach over the sofa and shoot blindly into the air until realizing that he'd used his last bullet.

"Come on, muthafucker, just get it over with," Brook yelled from the floor.

Reed walked around the sofa and faced him as Romeo, George, and K-Mack stood behind him with their guns raised.

"You tried to kill me, you bitch-ass nigga. Should have made sure it was me behind the wheel and you wouldn't be standing here facing the barrel of a gun."

"Fuck you, nigga, it's no need to—"

Reed shot Brook in the leg, cutting off his statement.

Brook gritted his teeth and moaned in agony. Reed stood in front of him, unmoved. He thought about Lucky and how she didn't have anything to do with the situation that had led them to this moment. Reed allowed him to suffer for a few more seconds before shooting him in his head, taking off part of his face.

The four men immediately left the house, got into their vehicles, and sped off. Once they crossed the Benjamin Franklin Bridge they drove to an old warehouse, where their vehicles were waiting. The men exited the cars they'd driven to the scene and covered them with gasoline before sticking a cloth into the gas tank and lighting them both on fire. They entered the cars and went their separate ways, with Reed and Romeo together in one car.

"Are you good, man?" Romeo asked, concerned about Reed's mental state.

"Yeah, I'm good. Could you run me to the crib to change and then back to the hospital?"

"No problem," Romeo replied.

Chapter Seventy-one

On a Mission

Before giving birth to Dior, Diamond never thought that she could love someone as much as she loved her. There was never a moment that she could imagine living without her.

Diamond was determined to do whatever she had to do to get her baby back. She had already lost Black. She would never forgive herself if she lost Dior too. She grabbed her phone and dialed the number she'd been told to call.

"I have the money," Diamond spoke to the caller on the other end of the receiver.

"Good girl. Meet me at the Hustle Chop Shop down South Philly, you know where it is?" Justice spoke in a direct tone.

"Yes, I know where that is. Will you have my daughter—"

Click.

"Okay, now you have to make sure that you keep cool. If you act out of the normal, they will probably get suspicious and that could turn bad. So just be cool; hand them the bag only when you see your daughter. We will be close enough to get to you if something goes wrong," Detective Jones, the female detective who'd been on the case from the start, said to Diamond.

"I hope that you're right with this. I really do," Diamond replied, afraid that things wouldn't go as planned. "Here we go," she said, grabbing the oversized duffle bag that was filled with marked bills.

Diamond left the hotel room located near the Philadelphia Airport. Going to the parking lot she got into her car and began the drive toward the chop shop as instructed. When she arrived her stomach was steadily doing flips. She was afraid to enter for fear of what was waiting for her, but she knew she didn't have a choice if she wanted her daughter. She entered the building, which was empty.

"Hello," she said aloud. Her voice echoed throughout the building.

"Stop right there," a voice called out from the back.

Diamond stopped in her tracks.

Justice appeared from the back of the building, wearing a bandanna covering his nose and mouth, holding a large gun in his hand. "Slide the bag over," he ordered.

"I'm not sliding anything over without seeing my daughter," she yelled.

He began to laugh. "I see you still haven't learned shit. You aren't running shit over here, bitch. I will murder you and your fucking daughter."

"How will I know if she's alive?"

"Because I told you so, that's how."

"Why should I trust you? You have completely wrecked my life in a matter of days!" she yelled in anger. She knew that it probably was her best bet to follow their commands, but there was something in her that wouldn't allow her to go down without a fight.

"Listen, you have two options: live or die. It's totally up to you."

Diamond took a deep breath before speaking, "Well, then I guess you'll have to shoot me in the back because I'm going to walk out of here." She was scared shitless but kept a straight face. She slowly began to turn around.

"Bring the fucking baby out," he yelled toward the rear of the building. Another male all in black revealed himself, carrying her daughter in his arms, and she immediately cried when she spotted Diamond.

Diamond turned around and began to cry. She'd missed her so much and at this point she wanted to hurry up and give him the money and leave with her. Wiping the tears from her cheeks she spoke, "Okay, I have all of the money."

"Slide it over," he ordered again.

Diamond dropped the duffle bag on the floor and kicked it across the floor. Justice bent down to unzip the bag. He looked up at the man holding Dior and nodded. The masked man passed Dior to Justice and picked up the bag from the floor before disappearing into the rear of the building. Diamond began to walk toward Justice.

"Not so fast," he said, raising the gun.

"I did what you asked me to do. I don't understand." She stopped in her tracks.

"I have a message for you."

"A message?" she asked, confused.

"Yeah, a message from Johnny. You remember him, don't you?"

"From Johnny? What the hell does he have to do with this?"

"Everything. He wanted you to feel the pain that he felt when his sister was murdered. His sister, my cousin, my blood." He removed the bandanna that covered his face.

Diamond looked at him and suddenly his face became familiar. She remembered him and now everything that had happened all made sense. His name was Justice, the younger brother of Deidra, Mica and Johnny's cousin. "I'm sorry about that. I never meant for Mica to be hurt," she cried, trying to plead her case, hoping that he'd spare her daughter's life.

"The tears are pointless. You took someone very dear to me and because of that you deserve to suffer. I could kill you but I'd rather you live with the pain of all the shit you caused. I hope it was worth it. Remember that line? The shit you said before you shot my cousin."

"Please don't hurt her, she's all that I have," she cried.

"It wasn't my fault," she continue to cry.

Justice displayed a devilish smirk on his face before pointing his gun at Dior's and shooting her.

Dior instantly went limp in his arms.

Diamond began to run toward him, screaming, hoping that what she saw wasn't reality.

Before Diamond could reach him he let Dior's body slip from his hands.

Diamond reached her just as the SWAT team burst into the building and pumped bullets into Justice, causing his body to jerk before hitting the ground.

"Oh God, not my baby, please don't take my baby," she cried, cradling Dior in her arms.

The medics who were on site within two minutes quickly took Dior away in the ambulance while fighting to save her life. Diamond was as quiet as a mouse as the detectives drove her to the hospital. Upon arriving in the family waiting room she was told that Dior was pronounced dead on arrival. She immediately fell to the floor and blacked out.

When she woke up she was staring in the face of Detective Jones.

"I'm so sorry, Diamond, I truly am. If there is anything that—"

"It's all your fault. I could have saved her had you let me do things my way," Diamond yelled.

"Diamond, no one could have predicted what would happen and we did everything by the book."

"By the book? Is that what you call it? In three days I've lost my husband and my child. How can you call anything that happened 'by the book'? I refuse to do this with you right now."

"I will let you rest, however, we still need to talk. I understand what you're going through, Diamond. I will speak with you tomorrow," she replied before turning to leave through the curtain.

Diamond turned her back and closed her eyes, trying to remember the life that she'd just lost. Sadly all she could see was pain and misery.

Chapter Seventy-two

Lost

Diamond sat peering out of her bedroom window, remembering how she'd brought Dior into the world. What started out as a plan to hold on to Black ended up making her the happiest woman on earth.

Diamond couldn't imagine how her life would have been had she never had the joy of being a mother. She would have never thought that she'd only have such a short time to shower her with all of the love that she had for her.

"Oh my God, Diamond, I'm so sorry. Why didn't you call me sooner?" Kiki said, coming through Diamond's front door, pulling her out of her trance. The two embraced before Diamond closed the door. "I can't believe it," she said, shaking her head.

"I can't even close my eyes without seeing it. I have to bury both my husband and my daughter." She fought to hold back tears. She'd been crying so much that she felt dehydrated.

"Well, I'm here for you, girl. Anything that you need me to do I will have your back. Did you make the arrangements yet?"

"No. I actually have to go this evening. My mom and dad are meeting me down there."

"I know how you feel, girl," she said, sitting down on the sofa.

Diamond sat there, looking at Kiki, wondering how she could know how she felt. She'd never lost any of her loved ones, let alone a husband and child. She also wondered why it had taken her so long to come over and show her condolences. It almost made her think back to all of the time that they spent not speaking. She wondered how she could truly call herself a friend and not be there in her times of need. As Kiki sat and talked about how she felt sorry for Diamond and how she could feel her pain, she began to see her lips moving but could no longer hear the words that were coming out of her mouth. She wasn't in the fighting mood, so she decided to sit tight to see what would come out of her mouth.

"I'm just trying to figure out my life and where I'm going. I feel like I'm in a never-ending nightmare," Diamond said with her hands on both sides of her face. She shook her head as quick flashes of the murders crossed her mind.

"Are you okay?" Kiki asked, noticing the sudden change in Diamond's facial expression.

"No, I'm really not okay, but I don't want to keep reliving everything so let's just stop talking about it. What's been up with you? Anything new in Kiki's world?" Diamond asked, changing the subject.

Kiki's face clearly said that something was wrong, but Diamond could never know how what she was about to hear would eventually cause more devastation in life. "He's not around anymore and it's breaking my heart," she replied with a pout.

"What happened?" Diamond asked, concerned.

"Girl, I don't even want to talk about it. It makes me sad. The crazy thing is I've been feeling so sick lately and I think that I might be pregnant, but the way things have played out I'm almost afraid to take a pregnancy test."

Diamond sat, trying to fight back tears. She'd just lost her only child and here Kiki could be carrying a baby. Deep down she felt nothing but jealousy and envy, and at that moment she wanted to run out of the room and tuck her head under a pillow. "Really? Pregnant? I never thought I'd see the day," she said, forcing a laugh.

"Me either. I never thought I'd fall in love either but, hey, life has a way of surprising you."

"You can say that again." She forced a smile. At this point she wanted to get the conversation over with and politely escort her out of the house, but she held it together. Her stomach felt nauseated and her body was numb as she hoped this was all a part of a dream, or better yet a sick joke.

"I don't know. I will probably take a test eventually, but right now I just can't bring myself to do it." She shook her head.

"Well, if you are, you will find out soon enough."

"Yeah. Well, girl, I just wanted to check on you. I have to get down to the club, but if you need me for anything make sure that you call me," Kiki said before getting up out of her seat to go hug Diamond.

Diamond reluctantly hugged her. There was something about Kiki that had changed, something that she just couldn't put her finger on. The warm feeling that she once got from her had turned completely cold.

Chapter Seventy-three

Chance Meeting

Diamond sat at the bar, sipping an apple martini alone. Lately, she'd been trying to find a way to clear her mind without having to hear other people's opinions, thoughts, or concerns about her or the events that had taken place. She'd buried her family and now she stood alone, trying to figure out what it was she wanted to do with her life. She looked at her watch, noticing that she had just a few more hours before she met with Tommy to square all of their business stuff away. Knowing that she should probably have a clear mental status, she couldn't bring herself to deal with anything sober. Somehow, the alcohol would help block out some of the bad things that clouded her brain.

"Is this seat taken?" a deep male voice said in her ear.

"No," she said without turning around to face him.

"I'm sorry to be forward, but I'm wondering why a beautiful woman like you is sitting here all alone? And looking so sad."

"I just like spending time alone without anyone talking to me."

"Oh, I'm sorry. I don't mean to bother you. I just wanted to see if there was anything that I could do to brighten up your mood, that's all."

"I doubt very seriously if you could help me but thanks anyway."

"Well, Diamond . . . That is your name, right?"

"How did you know my name?" she asked, immediately paranoid.

"The earrings." He laughed. "I'm not a stalker or anything."

Diamond laughed, feeling silly.

"Look, my name is Chance. If you would let me buy you a drink, I will leave you to your drinks if you'd like me to. I just wouldn't feel right walking away without at least trying to give you something to smile about."

"Well, I guess one drink won't kill me," she replied, finally taking a look at the handsome stranger.

"Cool. Bartender, can you bring her another round please?" he yelled to the bartender.

"Thank you," she said.

"So, Ms. Diamond. Are you in a relationship? Married?" he asked.

"I was married but I lost my husband."

"Sorry to hear that, I really am. I wish that I could take that pain away because I can see in your eyes that it's still hurting you." Chance smiled.

"I'd rather not talk too much about it but I can appreciate your concern."

"I understand. I won't push the issue. Let's change the subject. I really think that you are a beautiful woman and I would like to take you out to dinner sometime if that's okay with you."

"Uh I'm not sure if—"

"I'm not asking you to marry me. I'm asking for one harmless dinner."

"Umm, I don't know." She shook her head.

"Please just one dinner. If I'm the biggest asshole on the planet then by all means, walk away."

Diamond sat silent for a second, pondering the question that he posed. He was trying to convince her that he was her Prince Charming but she wasn't biting as fast as he thought that she would. Diamond looked down at her watch, knowing that Tommy would be there any minute to scoop her up for their meeting. She didn't want him to walk in and catch her talking to another man so soon after Black's death. Not that she owed anyone an explanation, but she still wasn't in the mood for anyone's opinion.

"Okay, one date; that's all that I will promise," she blurted, trying to hurry up and get rid of her uninvited guest.

"Cool. Well, here's my card. I will let you go so you can get on with your day. I really hope that I didn't bother you too much or take up too much of your time," he said before grabbing her hand and kissing it on the back of it.

She allowed him to kiss her hand before quickly pulling it away.

"Give me a call, Ms. Diamond, so we can set something up." He began to walk away.

"Will do," she replied. She didn't have any intention of calling but she entertained it long enough to get him to walk away. He was cute though, there was just so many things going on that she found it hard think about being with a man. It wasn't that he wasn't attractive or that she didn't see his politeness as something that she could get used to, she just wasn't ready for a relationship as she was still trying to cope with her losses. She turned around to finish her drink when Tommy walked into the bar and headed in her direction. He immediately hugged her once he got near her.

"We need to go somewhere else and talk," he said with seriousness written across his face.

"Why? What's wrong? I don't like the way this sounds," she replied, immediately nervous.

"Come on. I will tell you in the car," he said, gently grabbing her by the arm. He pulled out a one hundred dollar bill from his pocket and threw in on the bar to cover Diamond's bill.

She could barely wait to get in the car before questioning him again. He entered the car and his ass was barely planted in the seat before she began to speak. "What is it, Tommy? What's going on?" she asked.

"I don't know how to tell you this." He paused.

"Just tell me, Tommy, whatever you have to tell me."

"I promised Black that I would be here to take care of you in the event that anything ever went wrong and he wasn't here." He sat quietly, thinking back to his promise to Black.

"What is it, Tommy. I can't take it anymore," Diamond yelled, breaking his moment of silence.

"I got word that Johnny is behind the murders of Black and Dior. I—" He was cut off by Diamond.

"What? Johnny? I can't believe that, Tommy. Why would he do that, Tommy? He loves me."

"Correction, Diamond, he loved you. That's some little puppy-love shit that went out the window the moment you shot his sister."

"He wasn't a street dude, Tommy. Who does he even know who would do that?" she asked, still trying not to believe that her first love had ruined her life.

"You meet a lot of people on the inside, Diamond. I got this info from a reputable source and they told me that he planned all of this shit with some nigga named Reed who was paroled. I haven't located Reed yet but I have people out trying to find out who the hell he is."

"I can't believe this, Tommy. This shit is all my fault." She began to cry. "What am I going to do? Does this mean that he wants me dead too?"

"I don't know, Diamond, but you don't have to worry about that. I have your back and I'm going to make sure that no one can hurt you." Tommy reached out to hug Diamond in an attempt to console her.

"Am I even safe in my home?" she cried.

"I'm not taking you home. I'm going to take you to my house and I will have someone watching you anytime that I have to leave. I'm taking you there now. I really don't want you to worry about this. If you know one thing about me it's that I keep my word and I promise you I will get everything under control. Do you trust me?" he asked, staring her in the eye.

"Yes, I trust you," she said, wiping the tears from her cheeks.

"Okay, let's go." Tommy turned on the car and pulled out of the parking spot, heading toward his house. He had a lot of things to take care of and planned on keeping her safe by any means necessary.

Chapter Seventy-four

Expect the Unexpected

"Where are you going?" Tommy asked as Diamond emerged from the bedroom wearing a short black dress that hugged all of her curves.

"Uh last time I checked I was grown, Tommy," she replied with a twisted lip.

"Diamond, I can't protect you if you're going to just run around the street unsupervised. Looks like you have a date or something to me with that tight-ass dress on," he replied with a bit of force in his voice.

"As a matter of fact, I do have a date, Tommy, and I really appreciate you keeping watch over me and all, but you're not my father or my man, okay?" she said, heading toward the bedroom door. Since meeting Chance, Diamond had decided to give him a try even if just to keep her mind off the drama for a little while.

"I'm not your man yet," he replied, stopping her in her tracks.

"Yet? What the hell does that mean?" She turned around to face him.

"It means exactly that, Diamond. Come on, you know how I feel about you, and there is no way that I'm going to sit back and watch you ride off into the sunset with the next nigga when I've been down for you since day one."

"I can't do this with you right now, Tommy, I'm already late."

"Well, I will be here when you come back, believe that. This conversation isn't over, and your little date, he may have won you for the night, but I'm sure to win you for the rest of your life."

She stood there with chills running through her body. She'd tried for years to hide her own feelings because of Black, and now that Black was gone there wasn't anything keeping them apart besides her. Tommy made it loud and clear that he wanted her but she fought with herself to give in, and decided to go on with her date, thinking that maybe she'd be able to deal with it better when she returned or, better yet, maybe he'd forget all about it. Instead of responding she turned and walked out of the room.

Tommy didn't bother to follow her, confidant that things would work out in his favor. He grabbed his cell phone from the pocket of his jeans and dialed Tip, one of the men he'd hired to keep an eye on Diamond.

"Yo," Tip yelled into the receiver.

"She's on her way out. I need you to follow her," he instructed.

"Got it," he replied before ending the call.

Diamond exited the house and looked over at Tip's car before she hit the alarm on her own car. She was certain that Tommy had already instructed him to follow her but she didn't plan on letting any of that ruin her evening. She was on her way to meet the mystery man who went by the name of Chance. Since the night that she'd met him almost a week prior they'd kept in contact via phone. She was excited to finally get out and have that companionship that she'd missed since Black's murder. Unaffected by Tip's trailing vehicle she blasted her Beyoncé CD and sang every word.

She arrived at the restaurant twenty minutes later, only five minutes later than she was supposed to. She walked into the dining room to find Chance already seated. He stood from the chair when the hostess escorted Diamond over to the table. He was dressed all in black with Gucci sneakers and a Gucci belt to match. His watch almost blinded her as she approached. He immediately reached out to give her a hug and gently inhaled, smelling the fragrance that she had generously applied before leaving the house.

"You look beautiful," he said, looking her up and down.

"Aww thanks, you look very handsome tonight." She smiled.

After they were both seated he didn't waste any time sparking up a conversation. "I couldn't wait to see you tonight. I couldn't stop thinking about you ever since we met."

"If you're trying to make me blush, it's working. I can appreciate a man who knows how to make me smile." She giggled.

"Oh, I'm a professional at that. Shit, that's listed on my business card." He laughed. "But naw, really, I think that you are one of the sexiest women I've seen in a long time. I'm really glad that you decided to come out with me."

"Well, you were practically stalking me." She laughed.

"Oh, you gonna play me like that, huh?" He laughed.

"I'm just being honest," she joked. "But tell me more about yourself, Mr. Chance, because right now there's a bit of mystery and I'm not sure if I'm one hundred percent comfortable with that."

"Mystery?"

"Yeah," she replied with a smile.

"Well, Ms. Diamond, there isn't much to know about me. I'm a hustler by nature, a fighter by necessity, a gentleman by experience, and a provider by mentality. Does that explain it all?" He paused.

Diamond sat there without a word. She wondered if dancing around the question was a bad sign. She hadn't been able to get many clear answers out of him since she'd met him. Most of their phone conversations had been about her and most of the time he'd find a way to turn the attention back on her whenever she tried to give him a survey. The more that he avoided her questions the more she'd ask. She wasn't giving up that easily.

"No, that doesn't explain it all; that's all superficial if you ask me. I'm trying to find out about the man inside, the things that you can't see from the outside. All of that is skin deep."

He began to laugh before speaking. "Diamond, you're funny as hell, but real, and I can appreciate that. We'll have plenty of time to talk about me. I'm just merely trying to enjoy this date. I mean you only promised me one date so why not enjoy it?"

Diamond shook her head, realizing that he was obviously more stubborn than she thought. She glanced over to the bar and noticed Tip sitting there with a glass, watching her. She immediately became annoyed but because she didn't want Chance to realize his presence she tried to play it off as if she'd never seen him.

"What's wrong?" he asked, noticing the quick change in her facial expression.

"Oh, nothing, I thought I saw someone I knew that's all."

"Don't worry. I know your guard dog is over there keeping watch. Don't fret, it doesn't bother me. I know all about your husband's murder so I expected some extra company on this date."

Shocked she replied, "Huh? How did you?"

"I know more than you think I know, Ms. Diamond, and soon you'll know more about me. But let's continue this date and make the best of it. If he wants to watch, let's give him a show." He leaned across the table and grabbed Diamond by the chin before softly kissing her on the lips.

She didn't resist, as his lips were as soft as butter and as sweet as honey. Tip stopped drinking his drink and picked up his cell to make a call to Tommy to update him on the scenery.

"Yo," Tommy yelled into the receiver.

"I'm sitting here watching her, and this nigga just kissed her. I think he knows that I'm watching."

"Who is this muthafucker anyway?" Tommy yelled, immediately annoyed.

"I don't know. I'm gonna snap a picture and send it to you. In the meantime I'll keep a close watch and I will hit you back if I see anything else."

"Make sure she doesn't go home with this nigga either. I need to find out who the fuck he is."

"Okay," Tip agreed before hanging up the phone.

Diamond and Chance continued their conversation unaffected by Tip's presence. As promised, he calmly snapped a photo of Chance from his cell phone and sent it to Tommy. Diamond was beginning to enjoy the conversation. The two sat and talked in between bites. Neither of them was really interested in their meals as their exchanges were enticing. The waitress has since dropped of the check as the two continued their conversation.

"So what made you want to talk to me?" Diamond asked.

"I thought I already told you. You caught my eye when I first walked in. You were the most beautiful woman in the building and I just had to have you."

"Have me? Is that right?" she said, placing her hand on her hip.

"Yeah, that's what I said. Look, I'm a cocky nigga and I know it. My conversation got you here with me tonight so I know that it will get you to my house eventually."

"Oh, really?" she said with attitude, though she was impressed by his confidence.

"Really. I don't go at anything without the intention of coming out a winner. I plan on taking home the trophy and that trophy is you."

"Trophy, huh? Is that all you see me as? I've been a trophy wife before, not really trying to go that route again."

"Not at all. I'm just saying I'm going to win you over, you'll see."

"And what about tonight? What are your plans for this evening?" she asked with a smile.

"This evening, I've already done what I wanted to. I just wanted to entertain you. I'm not trying to get you in the bed tonight, but that's damn sure my plan eventually."

She laughed, but deep down she was hoping that he would have taken her home. She could definitely use a bit of sexual healing. "I'll accept that," she replied.

"Cool. Well, let me walk you to your car then so your watchdog can sit." He began to laugh. Chance placed two crisp one hundred dollar bills on the table to take care of the bill and tip.

"Okay," she agreed.

Chance walked her to the car and gave her a long hug before backing away and kissing her once more. She got in the car with a huge smile on her face. For the first time since Black's and Dior's deaths she finally had something to look forward to.

She headed back to Tommy's house, though she wanted to go home. She knew that it would be a night filled with argument if she went anywhere else besides his house, and she wasn't really in the mood for fighting after such a great night.

After pulling up in front of Tommy's house she waved at Tip, who pulled up just behind her. She wanted him to know that she knew he was trailing her. She entered the house and took her shoes off at the door, hoping that Tommy was asleep.

"So you had a nice time?" Tommy said, appearing from the dark living room.

"Damn, Tommy, you scared me. Why are you hiding in the dark and shit?" she asked, walking over to turn on the light.

"I'm not hiding. You see me don't you?"

"Yes, I see you, Tommy. Thanks for almost ruining my date having Tip practically sitting at the damn table."

"I do that because I care about you, Diamond. I don't know why the hell you needed a date anyway when I'm right here," he said, moving close to her.

"Please, Tommy, I'm really tired," she said as she backed away, trying to avoid letting the feelings she had for him rise to the surface.

"Diamond, stop fighting me. I know that you want me just as much as I want you." He moved in closer, backing her up against the wall.

"Tommy, please." She resisted as he grabbed her by the waist and leaned his body on hers, forcing her to stand still.

Without warning his lips touched hers. He moved them from side to side, rubbing them against his, savoring the moment before gently forcing his tongue in between her lips. Once his tongue met hers she obliged, no longer fighting him. She could feel his dick rising in his lounge pants, bumping up against her pussy. She felt her panties getting moist as the kiss began to get more passionate. He used both of his hands to lift her dress above her waist and grabbed both sides of her lace thong and pulled them down. He quickly turned her around to face the wall and dropped his pants in one swift motion. He backed up toward the chair that sat against the wall in the hallway and sat down, pulling her on top of him. Her pussy was soaking wet as his dick slid deep inside of her. He lifted up off of the seat slightly as she moved up and down on his dick.

"Oh shit, Diamond. Damn this pussy is so wet," he said aloud.

Besides a few moans she silently rode his dick like a rollercoaster, trying to avoid screaming as the girth of his dick was much bigger than she was used to. She used the handles of the chair as leverage, afraid to let him fill her completely.

"Don't run from this dick, take it all," he said, trying to lift his body to go deeper inside of her. He moved his body in a circular motion until she let out a load moan, followed by the trembling of both of her legs. "Are you cumming, baby?" he asked.

"Oh shit, oh shit," she moaned, feeling her cum running out of her body and down the shaft of his dick. Her walls were contracting around his dick as he quickly stood her up and bent her over the chair with his dick still buried inside of her. With his hands forcing her back into a deep arch he pumped his dick in and out of her with force causing his body to slap loudly against her ass. He drilled her like a machine, causing her to cum three more times before he exploded inside of her.

"Boy, I don't know what you are trying to do to me," she said as he stood her up and embraced her from behind with his dick still inside of her.

"I'm trying to make you love me, that's all," he replied. "I'm not done yet though. I just want to get you up to the bed so I can really get inside of you."

"Well, come on and finish what you started," she said before forcing him to release his grip. She walked toward the stairs and used her finger to motion for him to follow.

He laughed looked up to the ceiling and said, "Thank you," before following her up to the bedroom. Though the night didn't begin as he planned, it couldn't have ended any more perfectly than it had.

Chapter Seventy-five

The Unimaginable

"I hope she's here," Jasmine said to Octavia as they stood on Diamond's step. They'd been looking for her for the past three weeks, trying to give her the word on the street. They finally saw her car parked in the driveway and took a chance at knocking. A few seconds later Diamond opened the door, dressed in a long maxi dress and a pair of jeweled flats.

"Girl, we've been looking everywhere for you," Jasmine said, giving Diamond a hug. Octavia followed her, making her way into the foyer of Diamond's house.

"What's so important, ladies? You know I've been trying to get shit settled over here. What's up?" she asked.

"Have you heard from Kiki?" Jasmine asked, sitting down on the sofa.

"No, I haven't heard from her. Why?"

"So you haven't heard either?" Jasmine asked with a look of fear in her eyes.

"I think you should sit down," Octavia chimed in.

"Sit down for what? Just tell me. What is it?"

"Well, word on the street is your girl Kiki, your sup-posed-to-be sister, supposed-to-be best friend in the world—"

"Just spill it, Jaz," Diamond cut her off.

"That baby she's pregnant with, she's been going around telling everybody that Black is the father, and they were having an affair for over two years before he died."

"What?" Diamond raised her voice.

"Yup, she's telling everybody how he was going to leave you and everything," Octavia said.

"Where did you hear this? That can't be true. Black would never do that to me, he loved me too much," Diamond said as she sat down in the chair and placed her hand on her chest in disbelief. Now she had to face the truth. It was one thing to suspect and another to know but now everyone knew and Diamond refused to look like a fool. She couldn't have her image tarnished any further.

"Diamond, I wish that I didn't have to be the one to bring you the bad news but it's true. She's been freely telling everybody, Diamond. I told you that bitch was bad news," Jasmine replied.

Diamond sat silently, trying to take it all in. She didn't know whether to cry, scream, or yell. The pain that shot through her body was unlike any that she'd felt before. How could she move forward if everyone was behind her back laughing at her? How could she look Kiki's baby in the face and not remember her own? Her head was spinning and as Jasmine continued to talk, she could no longer hear her. After a few seconds she interrupted her. "Do you know where she is right now?"

"No, but I can certainly find out," Jasmine replied, retrieving her cell phone from her purse.

"Okay, well I need you both to go with me to see her. If I go alone I may end up in prison tonight."

"No problem," both of the ladies said before they all got up and headed toward the door.

As usual, Tip was sitting outside in his car. He noticed the three ladies walking toward Diamond's car and turned on his ignition to begin to follow her. The women drove to Kiki's house and parked. Diamond jumped out of the car and walked to the door, banging on it as if she were the police.

"Hold on, damn," Kiki yelled from the opposite side of the door. She walked to the door and opened it without asking who was on the opposite side. As soon as she opened the door Diamond punched her in the nose, causing her to fall to the floor. Diamond quickly got down on top of her and punched her in the face repeatedly.

"You trifling-ass bitch! All of the men in the world and you had to fuck mine. I should kill you, you fucking bitch," she yelled, banging her head into the floor. Blood was pouring from Kiki's nose and lips. Kiki tried to push Diamond off of her but fueled with hurt and anger she overpowered her. Jasmine and Octavia sat and watched, allowing Diamond to take all of her frustration out on Kiki's face.

Outside, Tip heard the commotion and ran over to the house, pulling Diamond off of Kiki. Diamond kicked her as she was being pulled off of her. "Let me go, Tip," she screamed. "If I ever see your fucking face again, bitch, I'll kill you," she screamed. "The only man I ever loved, you just had to have him."

Kiki got up from the floor, silent, trying to recover from the beating that she'd just taken.

"Let me go," Diamond continued to scream.

"Get her out of my house before I have her arrested." Kiki finally spoke, holding her stomach with one hand and the side of her face with the other.

"Diamond, let's go," Tip yelled, pulling her toward the door.

"I'll go for now but this isn't over," she said calmly, pointing in Kiki's direction. She turned to the door as if she was going to walk out, but the second that Tip released his grip she ran past him, Jasmine, and Octavia and punched Kiki in the face again, knocking her back to the floor. "Now we can go," she said, walking out of the door.

Tip shook his head and walked behind her to her car. "You're crazy as hell, Diamond," he said with a laugh.

The three women got in Diamond's car and drove back to Diamond's house, where Chance was sitting on her steps. Jasmine and Octavia looked at each other and then back at Diamond. "Who is that?" Jasmine asked.

"That's Chance, he's a friend of mine," she replied with a smile, as she was happy to see him. She'd been spending a lot of time with him but she always had Tip lurking at Tommy's command, making it hard for them to get close.

"Chance? I heard that name before. Where do you know him from?" Octavia asked.

"I met him at the hotel bar downtown."

"I can't remember where I heard that name but have fun. Hope he can make you smile after the shit that we just told you," Octavia said before exiting the car.

"Well, thanks for telling me. I'm glad I didn't hear it from the streets."

Jasmine and Octavia hugged her before walking to Jasmine's car and leaving. Diamond waved and walked up the driveway to her steps to hug Chance, who stood when she got near him.

"I thought we were meeting at five," he said, kissing her on the forehead.

"I know. I had to go handle something. Sorry I'm late."

"Is everything okay?"

"Now that I see you, everything is just fine."

"Cool. So are we going now?" he asked.

"Yes. I just need to run in the house and grab something really quick. Come in," she said while waving her hand, directing him to the door.

"Are you sure? I'm finally invited into your castle?" he asked, holding both of his hands in the air.

"Yes, you are invited." She laughed before walking to the door and opening it.

He laughed and followed her inside. "Very nice," he said, looking around as if he'd never seen the inside of her home before. He immediately looked into the dining room and flashbacks of Black's body came across his eyes. He knew that he had to deal with Diamond just until he found out where she kept the money. Since their plan hadn't gone as they'd hoped, he ended up coming out of the deal empty-handed. He was furious when he got word that the exchange hadn't gone off as planned. He waited patiently by the phone only to see it all play out on the news. Sure, Johnny got exactly what he wanted. She would always have to suffer with the thought of knowing that she was the reason her family was gone, but he didn't get the money that was promised and he planned to get it by any means necessary.

"What's wrong?" she asked, noticing him staring into the dining room.

"Oh nothing, just admiring the décor." He laughed. "Everything here is just as beautiful as the owner." He smiled.

"You just love to compliment me." She laughed. "I'll be right back. I'm just going to run upstairs really quick."

"Okay, I'll be here."

She ran up the stairs and heard her cell phone ringing as soon as she reached the top of the stairs.

"Hello," she yelled, out of breath.

"Are you fucking him?" Tommy yelled.

"No, Tommy, I'm not fucking him. Why are you so loud?"

"Well, what is he doing in the house, Diamond? That wasn't part of the plan."

"I had to get something, Tommy, calm down," she whispered as she walked into her room and closed the door.

"I don't want you in a closed place with him, you hear me? I need you to get back outside to a public area where Tip can see you."

"Okay, I'm going, Tommy."

"All right, come to my house when you're done."

"Okay," she replied.

"I love you, Diamond," he said before hanging up.

She put the phone into her bra and walked back out of the room to find Chance standing in the hallway.

"Are you okay?" she asked, shocked.

"Just looking for your bathroom."

"Oh, it's right there on the left," she said, pointing to the open door.

"Cool," he said, walking to the bathroom and closing the door.

Her heart was beating a mile a minute. Just a week prior Tommy had told her about his true identity and what he was there to get. She had to continue to act as if she was falling for him to avoid getting hurt. Tommy wanted to be sure that there weren't any other assailants before taking him out. To stare at the man who had a part in her husband's and daughter's murders made her sick to her stomach. She wanted to just murder him herself but she decided to allow Tommy to lead this time. Things hadn't always gone good for her when she tried to handle things on her own. She was nervous that he'd realize she was on to him and lose her own life, but she kept it as cool as she could when he exited the bathroom with a smile on his face.

"Are you ready?" he asked.

"Yup," she replied.

The two left the house without incident and got into his car to head out for dinner. He looked over at Diamond and noticed that she was uneasy. He couldn't figure out what was on her mind but he was determined to find out one way or another.

"Are you sure you're okay? You haven't been acting like yourself."

"I'm fine really. I just had an eventful day that's all."

"Anything you want to talk about? You know I'm here if you need to let off some steam."

Realizing that he wouldn't let up easily she decided to tell him about the Kiki incident to deter him from the real reason she was so jittery. "Well, I just learned today that my one-time best friend is pregnant with my deceased husband's child."

"Wow, that's heavy. Damn, Diamond, I'm sorry you have to deal with that shit. Did you talk to her?"

"No, I didn't talk to her, but I beat the shit out of her. That's why I was late meeting you."

"Damn, I'm sorry about that, baby girl. That's real fucked up but that's why you can't trust people. They'll always backstab you for their own gain."

She looked over at him and shook her head. Hell, she couldn't trust him either. It was almost as if everyone in her life was out to get her. She didn't know what to believe, or whom she could depend on. The only person who had been there for her from the beginning was Tommy, and she couldn't wait until this was all over with so she could let him know just how much she appreciated him.

"But I'm fine. I don't want that to ruin our evening."

"Well, I'm glad that you're okay," he replied.

After dinner Chance drove Diamond home with every intention of getting back inside of her house. He wasn't concerned about the watchdog or anyone he would bring with him. He needed to make her as comfortable as possible to find out all that he needed to know.

Once they were in front of the house she had to figure out how she would end the night.

"So am I invited in again?" he asked, standing in front of her on the steps.

"Uhhhh, that depends on what you plan to do once you're in there," she said in a sexy tone.

"Well, that's for me to know and you to find out, but, trust me, you will enjoy it." He smiled and moved closer to her.

She looked over at Tip and gave him the signal that she was letting him inside.

Tip grabbed his phone and called Tommy to let him know that tonight was the night.

She knew that she couldn't hold him off much longer without him knowing that something was up. With a smile she whispered, "Come inside."

"My pleasure." He smiled and followed her inside.

Both smiling but both hiding a secret agenda, they entered the house, not knowing what the night would bring.

Chapter Seventy-six

Game Time

"Let's go merk this nigga," Tommy said to Tip outside of Diamond's house. He'd been waiting for this day and couldn't wait to get it over with. He wanted to get on with his life with Diamond and not have guards constantly following her around. Chance was a constant reminder of a night that he wanted her to forget.

"Let's do it," Tip said, retrieving his gun from his waist.

Using the key that Diamond gave him, they quietly entered the house and made sure that the door closed behind them without making a sound. Tommy gave directions with hand motions. They moved through the house like snipers, checking around every corner before entering the next room.

Diamond and Chance had retreated to her bedroom, where she was in the bathroom and he was patiently waiting on the bed. Tommy and Tip crept up the steps and made their way down the hall toward the room. They stopped just short of the door, which was left open. They could hear Diamond talking to Chance through the door. Tommy nodded, giving Tip the cue. Both men walked into the room and began pumping bullets into an unsuspecting Chance. His body jerked as each bullet pierced his body in different spots. Blood splattered all over the walls, bed, floor, and other exposed surfaces.

Diamond sat on the floor in the bathroom with her hands covering both ears, trying to block out the noise.

Tip stopped shooting once Tommy stopped and put his hand in the air.

"Diamond," he yelled as he made his way to the bathroom.

She was still crouched in the corner with her eyes closed and her ears covered.

He bent down in front of her and touched her leg, startling her. "It's okay, babe, everything is okay."

She reached out and hugged him.

"Come on, let me get you out of here," he said.

"I can't go out there, Tommy. I can't. I will see Black and Dior. I just can't." She shook her head and cried.

"Just keep your eyes closed. I promise you won't see a thing," he said, holding her close. He walked her out of the bathroom and out of the room. "Go get in your car and go to my house, okay? I will be there soon, I already have someone outside waiting to follow you there."

"Okay," she said as tears began to fall from her eyes.

"Baby, it's over, okay? It's all over," he said, grabbing the sides of her face and kissing her tears away. "Just go get in the car. I will be there soon."

She did as she was told and made her way to her car to leave.

Tommy returned to the room where Tip was already wrapping Chance's body up in the bed linens. "Did you call them to come clean this shit up?" he asked.

"Yeah, this will be all cleared away in the next two hours," Tip replied.

"All right, I'm gonna go home and get her together. Call me when this shit is done."

"All right."

Tommy left the house and made his way home to meet Diamond. Once he arrived he found her balled up on the sofa in the dark. He knew that it would take some time before she was comfortable again, but he would work as hard as he could to make sure that happened. He set his gun down on the table and walked over to her. Without saying a word, he hugged her and cradled her face as she cried.

"I got you now, and I'm keeping my promise to Black. I will handle you with care," he whispered in her ear before leaning his head back onto the back of the chair and closing his eyes. He truly believed that Black would be looking down on them, satisfied with the way that he handled things. If there was anything that he could have done differently, he'd want Black here by his side, but he knew with Black here,

Diamond could never be his. He'd worked hard to keep her unharmed and now that he had her he didn't plan on letting her go. "I love you, Diamond," he whispered.

"I love you too," she replied, finally letting him know that the feelings were mutual.

Chapter Seventy-seven

The Culprit

Alisha sat, looking out of the hospital room's window with many thoughts running through her mind. She was saddened thinking about the events that led them to the place where they currently were. Just a few weeks earlier she and Lucky were out shopping and shooting the breeze; now she lay clinging on to life. She was frustrated because she'd tried her best to steer her away from a life with a criminal, fearing that she'd end up exactly where she had. Thinking back, Lucky was always drawn to the rough, street type and every relationship led to a horrible ending. Every so often she'd look over at Lucky and then back out of the window when she hadn't noticed a change. Though the prognosis wasn't good she was optimistic. One thing that rang true about her best friend was the fight in her, and she'd always managed to pull herself through any circumstance. After standing and peering out of the window for ten minutes, she walked over to the bedside and grabbed a hold of Lucky's hand before saying a silent prayer with her eyes closed. As usual she held her friend's hand tightly, but unlike any other time before then she felt a twitch in her hand. She immediately opened her eyes and looked at Lucky.

"Lucky?" she called out.

Lucky's eyes began to flutter as she fought to see the face behind the voice that was so familiar to her.

Alisha was now standing and calling her name over and over, hoping that it would bring her around. "Nurse," she called frantically from Lucky's bedside. She was afraid to move from the room for fear that Lucky'd fall back into the deep sleep where she'd been since being shot. "Nurse! I need a nurse in here," she yelled and pressed the red call bell located on the wall. She continued to yell for what seemed like forever until a nurse entered the room.

"She's waking up," she yelled at the nurse who came over to the side of the bed, checked the monitor which displayed Lucky's vital signs, and walked out into the hallway to call a doctor.

Alisha backed into the corner of the room while the doctor entered the room to see if she could be removed from the ventilator, which had kept her alive the past few weeks.

"Ma'am, we're going to have to ask you to sit out in the waiting area while they evaluate her," the female nurse said, gently pushing Alisha out of the room.

Alisha looked on but obeyed the nurse's command, as she didn't want to interfere with anything that could bring her best friend back. She grabbed her bag and walked out of the room, looking back one last time at the crowd of medical staff, which now surrounded Lucky's bedside. She walked out in the hallway with her stomach full of butterflies. She could barely stay still as she attempted to sit in the waiting room. She paced the floor for what seemed like an hour before the nurse came out to the waiting area to get her.

"What happened? Is she okay?" Alisha said, rushing over to the nurse.

"Yes, she's fine. She is asking for you. She's also asking for someone by the name of Chance. Do you know how to reach him or her?"

Alisha stood silent for a few moments, not sure what to say. She dreaded the moment that she'd have to tell Lucky that Chance had been murdered. She let out a sigh before responding to the nurse, who now stood with a look of confusion on her face.

"Actually, he was killed and I really don't know how I'm going to break the news to her."

"Well, maybe you should wait you know. It probably isn't the best time to share that sort of news with her. I'd say let her get out the woods before dropping the bomb."

"Okay, can I see her now?"

"Sure, I'll walk you back."

Alisha walked into the room with a huge smile on her face. She was excited to see her but she was also nervous because she knew Lucky wouldn't rest until she saw Chance. She knew it would be even more difficult once she learned that she was carrying his child. Luckily the trauma hadn't terminated the pregnancy and with the help of medication and life support the baby was actually doing well.

"There's my best friend." Lucky's face lit up when she saw Alisha enter the doorway.

"Girl, I am so damn happy to see your eyes. You just don't know," she said, walking over to the bed right into Lucky's opened arms.

"Girl, what the hell happened?" Lucky asked, still unsure about the events that led her to the hospital.

"You were shot, girl. I thought I lost you. I couldn't have that. What the hell would my life be without you?" She laughed and sat down on the stool next to the bed.

"Boring as all hell." She laughed. "Have you seen Chance? I really need to talk to him. I know he's probably out working like the workaholic he is." She smiled.

"No, actually I haven't seen him, but I can try to contact him for you."

"Great, girl, because they just told me that I'm pregnant! I know he'll be so happy. I wasn't ready for kids just yet but, hey, God has His own plan." She smiled and rubbed her hands across her belly.

"I know, they told me when they brought you in. I'm happy for you, I really am. I'm just glad that you are awake." She struggled to hold back tears, as she wanted to tell her that her unborn child's father would never hear the good news. She decided that she'd leave and allow her to rest. This way she could figure out how and when she'd break the news to her.

"Well, I'm going to let you get some rest, girl. The nurses have my number if anything goes down, but I will be back first thing in the morning to see you, okay?"

"Promise?"

"I promise, girl." She leaned in to hug her before turning her back and leaving the room.

Lucky sat there, wondering where Chance was and why he hadn't been by her bedside when she opened her eyes. She decided not to worry herself with it that evening and soon she drifted off to sleep.

The following morning she was allowed to use the phone and she dialed his phone only to find that the number was no longer in service. An hour later Alisha walked through the door with flowers and a huge teddy bear.

"Hey, girl, here as promised with a little friend," she said, setting the flowers down on the counter.

"I called Chance and his number is disconnected. What's going on with him, Alisha? He's not breaking up with me is he?" she said with her face full of sadness. Dry tears were on both sides of her face. It would break her heart if he'd walked out on her, especially when she needed him the most.

Alisha sat down on the stool and looked down at the floor. She knew that it was inevitable and she was going to have to tell her regardless of the nurse's advice. She couldn't leave her out in the dark any longer.

"What is it, Alisha? Please be honest with me," she pleaded.

"Look, you know I love you and I never want to see you hurting."

"Just spill it already, Alisha." She raised her voice. She wanted to know what it was regardless of how it would feel.

"He's dead," she said after a short sigh.

"What?" She sat up in bed. "That's a joke, right? No way he's really dead, Alisha."

"I'm sorry, Lucky, but it's not a joke. He was murdered. Shot over ten times."

"Noooooooooooooooooooooo," she screamed in agony. She had prepared herself for something else. She thought for sure he'd left her for another woman, but never dead. It had never crossed her mind as one of the reasons why she didn't see him when she opened her eyes. Her body was aching and tears began to pour from her eyes.

Alisha hugged Lucky and let her tears fill her shoulder. She felt her pain and she knew that the news would be devastating. She wished that it was really a cruel joke and Chance would come walking through the door, but she was there at his funeral so she knew for certain that it would never happen.

"Who killed him? Do they even know?" she asked, pulling herself away from Alisha.

"They do know but they haven't told me. I told Romeo you were awake and he said he would come talk to you."

"I can't believe this. Why him? He was everything that I needed in a man. Now I'm going to have to raise this baby alone." She continued to cry.

"You're a fighter, Lucky, and I know you'll get through this. I'm here for you. Anything that you need."

"I don't know what to do. I can't understand this, I just can't."

Alisha reached in to hug her again. The two hugged until they heard a knock at the door. Lucky sat up and quickly tried to wipe the remnants of sorrow from her face.

"Hey, I came as soon as I heard," Romeo said with a letter and flowers. He set the flowers down and handed Lucky the envelope.

"Aww thanks, Romeo. What's this?" she asked, waving the envelope in the air.

"It's from Chance. He told me to give it to you if anything ever happened to him. Sorry that I had to deliver it. I'd rather it be him to speak to you instead."

"Do you know what happened? I mean how did this happen to him?"

"Yeah, I know what happened and believe me, we're going to take care of it. I don't want you to worry about that though. I just want you to get well and worry about that baby you're carrying. He wouldn't want it any other way."

"I just . . . I just . . ." she stuttered.

"I know, believe me. He was my best friend. Killed me to bury him. I wanted to go kill everybody, literally."

"I just don't know what I'm going to do. I have nothing. I left everything to be with him."

"Don't worry about that. You'll be taken care of. His house, I'll have it signed over to you, and also the money that he had put up for something like this. I don't want you to stress about anything. You're family to me because he was like my brother and he loved you to pieces."

"I know he did. I just can't believe that I won't see his face again. I miss him so much already."

"Well again, I don't want you to worry. I'm gonna roll out to handle some business but I wanted to make sure you got that letter. Here's the key to his house. Call me when they are discharging you so I can come by to make sure everything is good at the crib." He passed her a small key chain with two keys on it.

"Thanks a lot, Romeo. I appreciate you coming."

"No problem. Get well soon, all right?" he said before leaving the room.

"I'm almost afraid to read this letter," she said, looking down at the white envelope.

"Well, I can give you some privacy if you want me to," Alisha said, placing her hand on top of Lucky's hand.

"No, you don't have to leave. Really, I want you to stay. Who knows what the hell is in this letter. I want you here as a shoulder to cry on if I need one." She laughed.

"Well, let's do it," Alisha replied with a smile.

Lucky took a deep breath before flipping the envelope over to the back and tearing it open. She was anxious but nervous at the same time. She pulled out a single sheet of paper with a handwritten note that read:

Dear Lucky,

If you're reading this, it's most likely because I am no longer here to tell you how I feel. When I came home from prison I looked forward to returning to my life the way that it was. My home, my business, my child, and my wife were all that kept me going while I was away. When I came home and realized that nothing was the same it was a hard pill to swallow. I didn't know how to handle it. All I could think about was getting back on top, getting my life back, minus the conniving woman I married. I had no intention of jumping into a relation-ship but then I met you. You were truly a breath of fresh air and I can honestly admit for the first time in my life, I was head over heels for a woman. When I met you, I vowed to take you away from the life that you lived. I wanted to see you blossom into the woman you were meant to be. I know how much you care for me and I know that it's breaking your heart right now to be without me. I want you to know that I'm sorry. I'm sorry for any pain that this will cause you because one thing that I never planned to do is hurt you.

I'm sitting here now writing this letter knowing that what I am about to do could lead to my death in the end but I need to gather the things that belong to me. I want to get the things that I need to give you the life that I want to provide. One thing that I want you to know, which, if you're reading this, you probably already know, is that you never have to worry about money or a place to live because everything that I have is yours. I know that none of what I am saying will ever take the place of me being there with you but I want you to know that I am sorry. I never wanted to cause you any pain and regardless of how things may seem I love you. I want you to make sure that you finish school and use the money that Romeo provides wisely. I know you're a smart girl so I trust that you will.

Well, I'm going to end this letter with this. If things had turned out different, I'd be asking you to marry me and become the mother of my child. I love you, Lucky, with all of my heart.

Reed

Tears flowed out of her eyes as she took the letter and neatly placed it back inside of the envelope.

"How could you?" she said aloud. "If you loved me why would you leave me here alone? Why would you leave us alone?" she said, rubbing her stomach. She had a lot to figure out and there wasn't any amount of money that could take the place of a father. She hated the fact that she was going to have to raise their child alone. Her child would never know the amazing man she fell in love with.

The more she thought about it, the angrier she got. She wanted to know who the culprit was. She needed to know just like she needed air to breath. She wanted them to pay for what they'd done and taking Romeo's word wasn't going to be enough. Their heads on a platter would be the only things that could suffice for the pain that she felt.

Alisha sat next to Lucky, silent. She knew that her friend would never be the same. She didn't know anything that she could say at that moment that could make her feel any better.

Finally, after a few minutes more of crying, Lucky wiped her face and looked at Alisha. "I need you to get Romeo on the phone," she said with a sharp, even tone.

"Okay," Alisha replied, knowing that she meant business. Alisha pulled her cell phone out of her bag and dialed the number that Romeo gave her. The phone rang twice before a deep male voice boomed through the receiver.

"What's wrong?" he said, wondering if things with Lucky had suddenly turned bad.

"Lucky wants to speak to you," she replied before passing Lucky the phone.

"I read the letter and I just want you to know that I appreciate all that you have done and will do for me, however, it doesn't change the fact that my child will now be born without a father. I need them to pay, Romeo. Do you hear me? I need their family to feel the pain that I'm feeling at this very moment."

"I got you, Lucky. I have everything under control, okay? If you know anything about Chance you know that he wouldn't trust me with his assets if he didn't think that I would do the right thing. Trust me, okay? He was like my brother, I told you this. Just worry about you and that baby getting well and I will see you when you get home."

She paused before responding, hoping that he was as trustworthy as he appeared. "Okay, I will see you soon," she replied.

"What did he say?" Alisha asked anxiously.

"He says that he has it all under control."

"Do you believe him?"

"What other choice do I have, Alisha?"

"Well, I guess you're right. Well, I'm going to go and let you rest. I will see you first thing in the morning okay?"

"Okay. Thanks for coming, girl," Lucky replied before reaching out to hug Alisha.

"No problem," she said before leaving the room.

Lucky leaned back on the bed and turned her head toward the window. With the letter still in her hand she placed it close to her chest and hugged it tightly. The scent of his cologne could still be smelled on the outside of the envelope and the scent was just enough to soothe her until she could fall asleep, confident that his soul was with her and that everything would truly be okay.

"I love you too," she whispered before drifting off to sleep.

Chapter Seventy-eight

Finale

"I have a gift for you," Romeo said, walking into the living room as Lucky sat on the sofa, watching TV.

Six months had passed since she was released from the hospital and her due date was approaching quickly. She hadn't been outside much as she didn't feel comfortable with her present shape and situation. Luckily, Romeo had stepped up and been there for her just as promised.

"A gift for me? Why do you keep spoiling me, Romeo?" She smiled.

"I'm trying to cheer you up. I don't want you sitting around here all miserable and shit. It's a lot out there that you can be doing you know. I told you I took care of everything so you don't have to ever worry about those niggas in the street. I'll be damned if I'd let any muthafucker hurt someone I care about," he said, holding a small box behind his back.

"You care about? You care about me?" she asked, surprised by the last comment.

"Come on now, you know I care about you. Why else would I be here every day?"

"Because you promised Chance," she replied.

"No, I promised him that I'd see to it that you were taken care of. I didn't promise to be here with you every day." He laughed.

"Well, I guess that I care about you too, Romeo."

"You guess? Well shit, I might as well walk back out with my gift then, shit." He began to back away toward the door.

"I'm just joking." She laughed. Up until this point she never knew how he felt about her so she hadn't really thought about revealing her own feelings for him. Naturally, when you spend time with someone you gain feelings, especially when they bend over backward to make sure that you're happy. She could see why he and Chance had been such good friends, because he resembled him. He reminded her of the things in Chance that she fell in love with. "Now can I have my gift already?" She laughed while holding her hand out.

"You still haven't said that you care about me, Lucky." He stood still.

"Yes, Romeo, I care about you and I mean that from the bottom of my heart."

He smiled, showing all of his pearly whites before walking over to the sofa and sitting down. "All right, here," he said, putting the small box into her open hand.

The small white box was decorated with a teal-blue bow. She gently untied the bow and lifted the top off of it to find a small ring box inside. She looked up at him, confused.

"What?" he asked.

"What is this, Romeo?"

"Just open it and see," he replied with a smile.

She pulled the ring box out of the box and slowly opened it, revealing a platinum ring with a huge five-karat pink diamond in the center.

"Before you say anything let me tell you what it's for. Before Reed died, around the same time that he gave me that letter for you, he gave me this ring to hold. He told me that if anything happened to him to wait until this day and give it to you. He was going to ask you to marry him with this ring, on this day, his mother's birthday. Now, he truly believed that on this day, I would care about you and he also told me that he wouldn't want or trust any man to be with you except me. At first, I was confused, believe me. I looked at him like he'd lost his mind. At the time, I thought for sure he was talking crazy and he would be here to give it to you himself. I also thought in the event that he wasn't here, I'd never be comfortable loving the same woman he did, even with his blessing. However, regardless of the way I felt that day, I do care about you and I do love you, Lucky. This ring is his blessing. It's his way of letting you know that it's okay to care about me, and it's okay to love me. I'm not asking you to marry me, Lucky, but what I am asking is that you let your guard down and let me in. I promise that I will be here for you and the baby. The baby will never want for a father because I will be all the father he needs." He paused to wipe the tears from her face. "Can you do that for me?"

She sat there stunned and relieved at the same time. She never wanted to do anything that would disrespect his memory. Knowing that he wanted her to move on and be happy relaxed her mind and made her heart smile. She looked down at the ring and looked back at Romeo, who was sitting silent, waiting for her to respond. She wasn't going to fight any longer. She wanted to be happy and she truly believed that Romeo was more than capable of keeping her that way.

"Can you help me put it on?" she asked, breaking the silence.

He smiled and grabbed the ring box before pulling the ring off the holder and placing it on her finger. As he slid the ring on, she grabbed his hands and moved in and kissed him. He gently grabbed both sides of her face and took control of the kiss, doing what he'd wanted to do for so long. After a few seconds they separated and stared at each other.

"So what does this mean?" he asked.

"I guess this is your lucky day because I'm going to give you the chance that you're asking for." She smiled and looked down at the ring that glistened on her finger.

"You've just made me a very happy man," he replied before leaning in to kiss her again.

The two got comfortable on the sofa as she lay in his arms and continued watching television. This evening, both of them had a lot to look forward to, with the blessing of Chance. Finally, she could look forward to her future and a happily-ever-after. Even if that wasn't possible she was going to look forward to it.

Chapter Seventy-nine

Life After Black

"Do you, Thomas, take Diamond to have and to hold from this day forward, for better or for worse, for richer, for poorer, in sickness and in health, to love and to cherish, from this day forward until death do you part?" Reverend Brooks asked, holding his Bible in his hand.

"I do." Tommy smiled.

"And do you, Diamond, take Thomas to have and to hold from this day forward, for better or for worse, for richer, for poorer, in sickness and in health, to love and to cherish, from this day forward until death do you part?"

"I do," Diamond spoke loudly.

"By the powers vested in me, I now pronounce you husband and wife. You may now kiss your bride."

Tommy moved close and planted a kiss on Diamond's lips.

"Ladies and gentlemen, I present to you Mr. and Mrs. Thomas Jones."

The guests in attendance all stood up from their seats and began to clap. Diamond and Tommy smiled as they began their walk up the aisle and out of the church. At that moment Diamond couldn't imagine her life being any different. Looking back, she wondered why things had turned out the way that they had but at this moment, she was the happiest woman in the world. She had a loving husband and a bun in the oven. Her baby Dior would never be replaced, nor would the love that she had for Black; however, her new family was making life worth living. She'd wanted to give up more times than she could count, but she realized that things happened for a reason and if it were meant for her to die she'd be dead by this point.

"Can you believe it? We're married. Wow. I never thought I'd be standing here," Tommy said with a huge smile on his face as he held Diamond close.

"I never would've imagined this would be my life but I'm glad that it is. I love you, Tommy, more than you'll ever know."

"Well, you'll have the rest of our lives to show me," he replied.

The two made their way over to the reception hall after taking photos with their wedding party. Things couldn't be more perfect. The evening went off without a hitch and Diamond was smiling from ear to ear. Once the evening was over they retreated to their house to gather their things and prepare for their honeymoon.

"Where did this come from?" Diamond asked, noticing a small envelope on their coffee table.

"I don't know, maybe one of the guests. Open it and see," he said as he walked out of the living room, into the kitchen.

Diamond grabbed the envelope and sat down on the sofa before flipping it over and ripping it open. Inside was a card, which read "Congrats to the bride and groom" on the front. Once opened, she closed her eyes and hoped that what she read was somehow totally different than what was really written. Tears flowed from her eyes as she tried to figure out what she'd done to be in this position yet again.

Tommy entered the room after hearing her sobbing. "What's wrong, babe? What is it?" he asked, sitting down on the side of her.

"It says, 'you took everything from me. Don't think you'll live happily ever after.'"

Tommy snatched the card from her and read it again. Anger filled his veins as he'd covered all ends to make sure that this night would be perfect. Now, instead of ending the night on a high note he had to figure out who the hell sent the card and what the hell they had planned. He grabbed his wife and cradled her in his arms. He wanted to make her feel safe just like she had in the past.

"Don't worry about anything. Whoever sent this is going to be taken care of. You hear me?" he asked.

"Yes, Tommy, I hear you," she replied. She wasn't sure if she believed him but she didn't have any other choice but to depend on his protection. She looked down at her round belly and began to rub it. Since Tommy had gone to great lengths in the past to save her she hoped that he'd go even further to protect his seed. She closed her eyes and rested in his arms while saying a silent prayer that things would be okay.